Ghost Assets

A Trinity Operations Novel

By
Shane K Twede

This book is dedicated to the courageous souls who challenge themselves into epic adventure

"And many false prophets will arise and lead many astray. And because lawlessness will be increased, the love of many will grow cold, But the one who endures to the end will be saved."

Matthew 24: 11-13

CONTENTS

Central Mexico.. 1

Three Weeks Later 7

Flight to Mexico.. 13

Texas 21

Tamales 29

Repainted 33

Norfolk, Virginia... 35

New York City 39

Bogota, Colombia 45

The Museum 49

Bogota Police Department 55

Historical Archives 59

He's Your Son.. 65

Coffee Shop 67

Cerveza 73

Sidney, Australia... 79

North Tolu Beach, Colombia 81

Bad News 83

Mexican Clinic 91

Art Center Museum of Los Angeles 95

Verrugosa 103

North of Town.. 109

Mad Dragon 115

Field Trip 119

Cabana on the Hill... 125

The Curves Are Deadly.. 135

South Colombia 141

Just a Hunch 145

Captured 149

Cold Shoulder 157

Criminal Moguls 163

The Recital 167

Another Flight 171

The Painting 173

Loverboy 177

Warehouse in Cartagena 183

Another Warehouse 191

Abducted 197

Export A 203

The Clue 207

The Wiretap 211

Famous Piece of Work 213

No Tricks this Time 217

We got Something 221

Interrogation 223

Mitu, Colombia 227

Knight in Shining Armor 235

Playing for the Wrong Team 245

Sold 251

The More You Cooperate, the Nicer You're Treated 263

We're Here for the Girls 265

Rescued 269

Little Boy 279

Get Rich Quick 285

Plastic Badge Detective 291

Cora Liberal 295

Preparation 301

Plane Ride 305

Let the Men Finish 311

The Final Campaign 315

Beyond Tired 325

Goodbye 327

The Edge 333

Get Him 339

Don't Be So Hard on Yourself 347

Stories 353

Last Kiss 357

We Came on a Little Strong 363

Homeward Bound 367

Thomson's Air Museum 369

PI Office, Washington State 373

The Barbecue 377

Central Mexico

"Ted, are you sure you're up to flying home?" John helped Ted stand to his feet.

"Considering what I just went through, John, I think I'm doing pretty good. You know I dedicated this flight to the memory of my father."

"I know, Ted."

"Well…I plan to complete it." Ted ran his hand around one of the large airplane tires. He continued his check of the Douglas C-47 fuselage before lifting his eyes towards the runway. A bird took several hops, then lifting off the ground, a small coyote, partially hidden behind the brush, stirred just off the end of the dirt and turf strip. "This trip would have made him proud."

"I'm sure it would have," John replied. He stepped up into the beautifully restored military plane and walked up the narrow-sloped aisle to the cockpit. Ted followed and took his place next to John, buckling himself into the green padded captain's seat.

"This place is eerily quiet today isn't it?" John said. "Let's see, what did I do with the checklist?" John fumbled around his seat, glancing sporadically out the windshield. Derelict planes adorned the rutted taxiway. A crashed Cessna 180 marked the far end of the runway, and to the side, a terminal hut with a broken porch light and cracked windows sat uninhabited.

"I'm with you, John. This side of Mexico is not much for vacationers, that's for sure. Read off the checklist, will you? Let's get out of here." John, finding the checklist began reading down the list out loud. Ted, now in his 60s, still possessed the body and tenacity of a young fighter pilot. Other than lines on his face, a slight droop to his cheeks, and hair usurped by silver, he didn't look much different than his wartime photos from Vietnam. John was half Ted's age; cocky and a know-it-all, believing he knew more than pilots with twice his experience. Ted hired him to help out around his aircraft museum in Texas. So far John proved to be a good employee, and a respectable pilot, although not quite to the caliber he believed himself to be.

John continued reading off the checklist. "Mixture idle cut-off?" John's eyes darted from the checklist to Ted, then out the window and back to the checklist.

"Are you sure that's the next item on the checklist?" Ted asked.

John glanced at the checklist. "Sorry, cowl flaps open? I would've caught that."

"If you wouldn't mind, John, please read the items as they appear on the sheet."

"Left hand fuel-select?"

"Fullest tank, check." Ted and John stopped talking. They heard a truck coming up behind them.

"Ted!"

"I see it." The truck drove up to the left side of the airplane.

"They're trying to get your attention."

"What do you think they want?"

"I'm not sure, but I think we should get out of here."

"John—look!" Ted said, pointing out the front windshield. A different truck skidded to a stop. Two men wearing drab green uniforms jumped out holding automatic weapons, aimed at the cockpit. Ted and John's worried eyes met.

"Open the door!" One of the men shouted, as he pounded on the side of the fuselage with his open hand.

"Are they going to kill us?" John shrieked.

"Open the door and come out or we'll begin shooting!"

"I don't know, John," Ted replied, studying the faces of the men outside the windshield. "Let's see what they want."

Ted and John unbuckled themselves and walked to the back of the airplane. John opened the door and yelled, "What's this all about?"

A dark stocky man in his 30s, built like a heavyweight boxer reached up and yanked John's shirt, pulling him from the plane. John fell head-first to the dusty ground.

"Hands up!" the man shouted to Ted. Ted raised his hands and jumped down from the C-47. Two other men rushed over, and another ambled their way to the back of the plane. Ted noticed the last to appear was a young woman dressed in a drab green uniform like the other three. She was young, perhaps attractive, but instead, her face was contorted with an expression of hate and lack of respect.

"What are you gawking at old man?" the woman asserted, eyeballing Ted.

John, now back on his feet, asked, "We don't want any trouble, please. What is it you want?" John gazed about, seemingly looking for someone.

The three dressed in drab green and aiming their guns at Ted and John glanced over to a fourth man in uniform. He was the youngest of the bunch. The sides of his head were shaved to the skin, the top, a 1-inch mohawk, and in the back, a 6-inch braided tail. Quietly and slowly he walked around inspecting the outside of the plane. "I am Javier, I like your airplane."

Ted observed with concern as Javier stretched his head through the doorway and peered inside. "Yes, I like your airplane very much. This is very good, just what we need." Javier glanced to his three partners. "I want this plane."

"This airplane is not for sale!" John blurted out, eyeing Ted.

Javier chortled. The other three laughed with him. Brigitte, the young woman, adjusted her gun to her shoulders and walked slowly up to Ted. Her dusky eyes moved slowly from his feet to his head, and her fingers slid across his cheek down to his chin. Then she snapped her head around and faced John, letting her brown shoulder length hair whip Ted in the face as she did.

"Now this one is trouble. I can sense it." Brigitte winked at John as she circled him, her hand gliding across his chest and back as she walked. John stood erect, not saying anything. "It looks like you got a scratch on your face when you fell—poor baby." She reached up as if to touch John's face, but instead slapped it. The sound reverberated through the morning air. John's cheek reddened.

"Please, we don't want any trouble," Ted said. "My co-pilot and I will cooperate. I do need to call in shortly though. We are on a scheduled flight plan and they will be wondering why we haven't contacted them yet."

Javier pushed Brigitte back and faced Ted. "I am the pilot of this airplane now. You no longer own this airplane. Here?" Javier lifted his hands to the sky. "They don't see you or care about your stupid flight plan. Strap them in," Javier commanded.

Two men, Miguel the boxer and Fabio, Javier's older brother along with Brigitte, loaded Ted and John into the back of the C-47, lashing them to the pull-down seats running lengthwise inside of the fuselage. Javier and Miguel took the pilot and co-pilot seats and started the engines while Fabio closed the door. Minutes later, the plane kicked up dirt and dust from the unimproved runway. Javier pulled back on the yoke, familiarizing himself with the feel of the airplane.

The plane ride was long, and Ted and John jostled in their seats, becoming more and more worried. After several hours, the plane landed, and the tanks were topped off with fuel. Ted and John were kept fastened in their seats. John pleaded to use the bathroom, but his request was denied.

The plane flew for several more hours before landing again. This time, John and Ted were untied and led outside the plane.

"Where are we?" John shouted.

Miguel laughed. "Your final destination, my friend."

Ted looked behind him and saw the plane had landed on an isolated dirt patch, high up on a bluff, at the sea's edge. Miguel pushed John and Ted closer to the cliff. Brigitte and Fabio followed close behind with their guns.

"Please don't kill me," John pleaded. "Don't you know who I am?"

"Of course, you are the first man we're going to kill," Miguel asserted.

"But you can't!" John's eyes rapidly scanned between his captors.

"Turn around and shut up," Miguel said.

John and Ted turned slowly around. The gun barrels were now aimed straight at their backs, with the cliff's edge only a few yards away. Realizing this was the end, Ted's only thought was of his daughter. Fabio spoke up. "We're gonna give you 60 seconds to run. Kind of a game, okay?" Fabio laughed, grinning his yellowed imperfect teeth. Like his younger brother Javier, his head was shaved, but without the tail. Unlike his brother, Fabio had a body built like a bar-bouncer. "Ready? One, two—"

John shot Ted a remorseful and terrified glance before running as fast as he could away from the plane. "Three." Ted heard the guns open up on John and immediately turned and jumped off the cliff. He felt bullets wiz through the air next to him. Miguel, Brigitte, and Fabio ran to the cliff, staring intently to the sea below.

"He's dead," Fabio pronounced. "I shot him before he jumped."

"Nobody could live after falling from that height anyway," Miguel replied.

Fabio and Miguel threw John's dead body off the cliff. They watched as his body smashed into the sea. "Ewww, that looked painful." They both chuckled. Javier had his hand out the pilot's window, waving them back to the airplane.

Fabio closed the door while yelling up to the cockpit. "They're both dead, Javier. Let's get out of here."

"I know, Fabio. I have eyes—I can see for myself, thank you very much." Javier shook his head and turned to Miguel. "Wait till the boss sees how nice this one actually is. I think we might even get a bonus for this beauty. It's a shame we have to repaint it."

Three Weeks Later

"Good morning, Mary," I said. "Beautiful day isn't it?"

"Why yes, it is Cougar, and good morning to you. I see you're in a cheerful mood as usual."

"Only way I know how, Mary. Any calls this morning?"

"Still no calls, but there is a young lady here who insists on seeing you this morning."

"Oh, yeah?"

"I made her a cup of tea and had her wait in your office."

"Thank you, hold my calls will you please?" Mary returned a sarcastic grin while handing me four windowed envelopes. Mary is the first and only employee I've hired in my private investigation practice. An office manager in her 40s, and with no immediate family, she didn't mind working the strange hours that came with the position. I pulled open my office door. Standing against the bookcase was a beautiful young lady, thumbing through one of my books.

"Good Morning, Miss...?"

"Amelia." She turned sharply. "It's Amelia. I'm sorry, I wasn't snooping, I just find your library of aviation books very fascinating."

Amelia shelved the book and hurried over and shook my hand. She wore a worried look and a sense of urgency. She was beautiful, shapely, with hair as white as coconut that hung just beyond her shoulders.

"Won't you please sit down?" I pointed to one of two worn brown leather winged chairs that lined up perfectly with the grout lines on the tile floor.

"Thank you, Cougar. May I call you Cougar?"

"Of course." Amelia stepped confidently over to the chair and sat down. I couldn't help but notice her youthful appearance—and her snug faded jeans. The dichotomy screamed loudly. She had to be in her mid-20s, but her poise articulated a much older person, and her hair color, although stunningly beautiful, added to the contradiction.

"Is that your Aero Commander?" She asked, pointing to a wooden model of an airplane behind my desk.

"Yes, the model is mine," I responded with a grin.

"No, I mean is that a model of your airplane? I thought I saw a picture of it on your website."

"I'm teasing. Yes, that's a model of my Aero Commander. You must be an aviation enthusiast yourself, especially with a name like Amelia."

"I am, and that's why I'm here today." Her eyes narrowed as she leaned forward in her chair. "You see, my father is a pilot...and well...he made a special trip to Mexico for a life-saving cancer treatment in his restored Douglas C-47." Amelia's eyes glistened as she talked. "He never made it home."

"I'm very sorry, Amelia." She rubbed her eyes and stared at her shoes. "Was it the cancer?"

"No."

"Did he crash?"

"I don't believe so," Amelia stated emphatically. "That's what the NTSB and the Directorate General of Civil Aeronautics from Mexico concluded; but they never found any evidence to verify that. My dad's a great pilot...ex-fighter jet and aerobatic pilot...the best I've ever flown with. And the airplane they were flying was meticulously restored and in amazing condition."

"Did this occur about a month ago?"

"Yes! How did you know?"

"I remember reading about it. A C-47 tends to attract one's attention. When was the last time you heard from your dad?"

"I received a message from him the morning he was to depart for home. We live in Texas. He was flying with another pilot named John Burrow. John helps out in our air shows, museum, and with aircraft restorations. He's a good pilot and knows C-47s well enough. In case my dad was not 100 percent after being released from the medical center, he would be able to help him fly home."

"What is it I can help you with?"

"I did a thorough search on the internet…and well, I want to hire you to find my dad and his plane—and John. I want to know what really happened. I don't believe he crashed in the sea—not my dad."

"So, you think he's still alive?"

"I don't know." Amelia glanced to the ceiling. "Sometimes I get this feeling he is. A friend told me it's just my mind playing tricks on me because I'm not dealing with the loss appropriately. Regardless, I want to know the truth. I need to know the truth. My dad deserves a better investigation than what he got out of the Mexican government." Amelia's eyes drifted to the only window in my office. "I lost my mother a year ago, my dad is all I have left. Will you please help me?"

Her eyes penetrated into mine. I reckoned only one answer was acceptable to her; besides, we needed the business. "Okay, I'll take the case."

"Thank you so much." She soared out of her chair and over to my side of the desk and hugged me. Her body trembled as tears soaked through to my skin. When she looked up, the little make-up she wore now streaked her cheeks. "I'm sorry, but you're the only person who has said yes to helping me."

"Well I will do all I can. Maybe a good place to start is for you to give me all the details about your father's trip. By the way, have you eaten anything this morning?"

"No, I came here right from the airport. I wanted to be here when you opened."

"Well this is going to take some time. Why don't I have Mary order in some breakfast before we start. Then you can share all the details with me while Mary, my personal assistant, records the information." I handed Amelia a box of tissues and stepped out of my office.

Mary asked if everything was all right. I shook my head and asked her to order in breakfast, then stepped back into my office, shutting the door. Amelia stared at the well-manicured landscape below. "So, were you and your father close?"

"Yes. My family runs an airplane museum in San Angelo, Texas. I'm an only child, and after my mom passed away, my dad and I had to really pull together to cover all the administrative tasks my mom used to do, as well as keep the museum operational and the flight shows on schedule. My dad and I have always been close. We both share a love of aviation, but after my mom died, we've been inseparable."

"And the C-47 was part of your family's collection?"

"It was more than that. My grandpa, Conrad Thomson, was a Pan Am pilot before World War II. He entered the war and flew the hump between India and China. The C-47 my dad flew to Mexico was to be kind of a commemorative flight. It was his way of honoring his dad's service in the war. You see, my dad's medical certificate was in jeopardy due to his ongoing battle with cancer, and he didn't know how much longer he would be able to fly. So, he poured his time into restoring the C-47, the actual C-47 my Grandpa, his dad, flew during WWII. He wanted to fly it on some big flight. That was really important to him."

"The actual plane your Grandpa flew?"

"Yes."

"That's amazing. I think I'm beginning to understand. Did you say you're also a pilot?"

"I feel we're a lot alike, Cougar, once I read your bio online." Her eyes lit up. "Yes, I'm a pilot. I can fly almost all of the airplanes we have at the museum. We are one of only a few museums where all of our airplanes are airworthy."

Amelia talked about the many airplanes at their museum, and about a Phantom F4, similar to one her dad flew in Vietnam. She also discussed her dad's cancer journey in more detail. How the doctors in the US just wanted to cut him open or radiate him until he died. That's when she and her father decided they would take matters into their own hands. They researched everything they could get their hands on, trying to understand cancer better and possible cures. She told me her dad and her were not patch-it-up type people, but restorers. They heard about a place in Mexico that uses an oxygen treatment to kill only the cancer cells inside the body, leaving the healthy cells alone. They couple that with immunotherapy to strengthen one's immune system to fight off any remaining cancer cells. That sounded better to her dad and her, so they contacted the medical center in Mexico.

"Did you ever fly with your grandpa?"

"I never met my grandpa, that's part of the reason the C-47 airplane is so special to me—and my dad. Don't get me wrong, my dad is my number one priority, and I hope and pray he is alive, and you find him. But my grandpa died shortly after my dad was born. My dad never knew his dad, and all I know about my grandpa is what I read in old newspaper clippings, scrapbooks, and what my grandma shared before she died."

The office door opened. Mary entered carrying two large bags and a cup holder with drinks. "Excuse me," she said, "is this a good time?"

"Perfect timing, Mary. Let's take a short breakfast break. After breakfast, Mary has a few forms she'll need you to fill out, and then I'll ask you a series of questions while Mary documents your answers, is that okay?" Amelia nodded. "I will also need your dad's contact information, his daily schedules and routines, the Mexican contacts, flight plan information, aircraft information, medical information, and anything else you can think of that might help in the investigation."

Flight to Mexico

One hour to go before I land at the same airport Ted and John did when they flew into Mexico for Ted's cancer treatment. Central Mexico was Ted's last confirmed location, so I concluded that was as good a place as any to begin the investigation.

The flight's been uneventful, although landing in Mexico for a standard customs check was another episode in bureaucracy and delays. It seems no matter how much time I plan for a customs check, the officials there make it their quest to take even longer. Inside my twin engine Aero Commander, I have two hidden compartments, one under the pilot seat and another behind the rear bulkhead. In these compartments, I'm able to store weapons and ammunition undetectable even to the most discerning customs agent. In Mexico, away from civilization, it can be very dangerous.

I reached under the seat and removed my Smith & Wesson pistol from the hidden compartment and slid it into my chest holster. I pulled back on the throttles, lowering the manifold pressure on both engines. Below me, lush vegetation produced thermals in the air that buffeted the wings. An occasional farm dotted the clearings between dwarfed trees and green fields. Dust clouds were kicked up by ranch hands in trucks and on horses. A tractor toiled in a field. It was like watching an old-time western movie at 5,000 feet.

I paid a visit to the local FAA branch before setting off for Mexico. I also read through the NTSB's report and the details of Ted's supposed last flight and crash into the Gulf of Mexico. The NTSB did not think Ted made it past the Tropic of Cancer, which made for a peculiar irony. Because they believed the crash occurred in Mexican waters, the NTSB relied primarily on the Directorate General of Civil Aeronautics of Mexico for the accident investigation and findings.

According to my GPS, the small town and home to the clinic where Ted had his treatment should be visible by now. I examined the fields. A few scattered buildings, some houses, and livestock were all I saw. Then suddenly a dirt runway littered with plane parts and rusted junk materialized beneath me. I retarded the throttles, ran through the pre-landing checklist, turned, and lined up with the runway for a short approach. Familiar clunks emanated from the landing gear as they hit their stops; panel lights glowed green, confirming all three gears were down and locked. I pulled at the throttles while bouncing in my seat from the turbulence that sat off the approach end of the runway.

The landing gear compressed with the weight of the Aero Commander. Dust devils swiveled up around the plane. I tapped the tops of the rudder pedals, the airplane slowed. Derelict airplanes and airplane parts edged the runway. Not a single plane had tires that weren't flat. I taxied the Commander to an open area next to a shack with a rusted corrugated tin roof and waited for the propellers to stop spinning.

A tranquil stillness draped the airfield. An elderly man off in the distance hoed a moderately sized field. I grabbed my gear, secured the airplane and headed for the small shack. On the wall, nailed to the siding, was a sign that read, *office*. It wasn't just derelict planes that sat deteriorating into the grounds along the runway, old rusted trucks and dented cars without windows were also a part of the tapestry. I unbuttoned my shirt and wiped my forehead. A turquoise, white and rust 56 two-door Chevy sat on its axles. This classic would never see a car show, or another road for that matter.

The office door swung open without effort. Pictures of airplanes hung crooked on water stained paneled walls. Each picture showed signs of humidity damage. None of the airplanes pictured were newer than 1960. A desk against a windowed wall sat empty except for a green glass and tarnished brass bankers' lamp. A phone attached to the wall was in arms reach of the desk and tacked next to it, a sheet of paper with phone numbers. I picked up the receiver and listened for a dial tone. *At least the phone works.* In the back office, stench from a washroom hit me before stepping into the room. The sink and toilet were porcelain and rust. Cracked brown tile led to a sink pedestal. I washed up as best I could from the dribble of water that flowed out the squeaky faucet.

I dialed one of the numbers posted on the wall next to the word *taxi*. After a brief conversation, I left the office and trekked through a narrow dirt and rock path. The farmer, a weathered-skinned man under a large sombrero hat, turned as I approached. "Excuse me señor. ¿Hablas inglés?"

"Sí. You fly eso aero plane in?"

"Eso?"

"That." He pointed to the airport.

"Yes. May I ask you a few questions?"

"I am very busy, señor."

"This will only take a couple minutes."

"Very busy," he repeated.

I reached in my pocket and pulled out a few bills. "How about I pay for your lunch." I handed him ten American dollars.

"Gracias, señor. I have uno momento?"

"If I asked you about an airplane that was here about a month ago, would you remember it?"

"Sí maybe, not too many aero planes."

"This was a big plane, 2 engines, tail dragger, painted in military colors."

He nodded his head as I spoke. "I remember that one. Nice aero plane. It sat at the airport almost a month. Sí, very nice."

"Did you see it leave?"

"Sí, I saw and heard it fly away."

"Did you see who was flying the plane or watch it take off?"

"Sorry, señor, I was on horse in my field."

"Did you notice anyone else around the airplane during the month it was here?"

"Sorry, señor, I did not notice. I get back to my gardening now."

"You saw nothing unusual?"

"Sorry, amigo, nothing unusual." He turned briskly and picked up his hoe.

"Muchas Gracias, señor." I headed back to the airport. A trail of dirt followed a rusty Volkswagen beetle headed for the office. By the time I made it back, the driver was reclined on a wooden bench in front of the office, shaded from the sun by a small roof overhang.

"Did you call for a ride, senior?" The man asked in plain English.

"Yes, that was me. Can you give me a few minutes, por favor?"

"Take all the time you need Senior; we are in no hurry here."

I figured that was true. After all, most of the world is not in a panicked rush to get places like we are in the States. I do envy a slower culture at times. I sat at the Aero Commander's table in the back and flipped a couple switches. LEDs from the communication equipment lit up the panel. My Aero Commander is old but has been significantly remodeled and modified. I use it primarily in my PI business to locate and recover missing assets. It possesses state of the art navigation and communication equipment as well as having some unique military style defensive features. The Aero Commander is a good size twin, built by Rockwell back in the 50s, 60s, and 70s. Mine was built in 1975, a 500-S model. In its original configuration, the plane seated 7. Today it seats five, with a communication station, a flip up table that I use as a desk, and seats that fold into a bed.

I slipped the headphones over my ears and tapped a couple buttons on the communication screen. When Mary picked up, I gave her status and my location before turning off the equipment. The ride to the doctor's office was a mix of me asking the taxi driver questions about Ted and John, the clinic where Ted had his treatment, and the taxi driver sharing about his family and how the US government is bullying Mexico.

He remembered Ted and John and said they both were quite friendly and tipped very well. We turned from a dilapidated narrow tar road onto fresh cement, leading to a newer building. The architecture was simplistic: stucco columns, large windows, and two large dark stained doors at the entrance. The medical center was an enigma compared to other structures along the way, which were not many, being at least 20 years newer. The driver handed me a card with his number on it.

"Call me when you're finished, I come pick you up. There's a phone on the wall in waiting room." I thanked him and shut the door. The bug's engine squealed as he accelerated to the exit of the small, mostly vacant parking lot. I turned, opened the large stained wood door, and stepped inside.

The receptionist was polite and asked me to take a seat and wait—and waiting is what I did—for an extended period of time. Finally, the doctor called my name.

"Doctor Flores, thank you for seeing me."

"You're very welcome, but I'm not sure how much help I can be. We have a privacy policy here."

"I understand. As I mentioned over the phone earlier, I'm representing Ted Thomson's daughter, Amelia. Ted has been missing about a month now. In as much detail as you're able to provide, could you tell me the condition Ted was in when he left here?"

"Come back to my office, will you?" I followed Dr. Flores into a small well-appointed office with mahogany walls. "Ted was here for cancer treatment. I'm sorry I can't share the treatments we administered, but I can share how we typically treat patients with recurring cancer similar to his."

"Thank you, that would be very helpful." Dr. Flores described the standard treatment plan. "And how was Ted when he left?"

"Again, I am unable to give you specifics, but I can tell you this. He shared with me that he and a friend flew down here in an airplane, and once finished here, planned to fly it back. The treatments he had in the last week would not have affected his ability to fly an airplane. In fact, I can tell you he was in better condition to fly home then when he got here. Now, I've said too much, and I need to get back to my patients."

"Thank you very much, Doctor." Dr. Flores let me out of his office. A man shuffled past us, towing an IV bottle-stand.

After a swing through the small town and a stop at the local cantina, I was back at the airport. No one at the cantina remembered seeing Ted or John. The Aero Commander sat proud as I approached it, although amongst the mostly deteriorating parts and wrecks that wasn't too difficult. Heated air wafted out the open door. I jotted down a few notes the doctor had shared then stepped back out of the airplane's stifling interior. On the far side of the runway, across from where I parked the Aero Commander was a large opening. An opening large enough to park a Douglas DC-3 or a C-47, the military version of a DC-3 like what Ted owned. The DC-3 was large for its day. They were tail-wheeled airplane, having one small tire in the back and two larger tires in the front attached under the wings, causing the cockpit to sit high up in the air when parked. Powered by two large reciprocating radial engines, and in a passenger configuration, they were able to carry 32 people.

As I approached the opening, the dirt still held imprints from large tires; the size that would be used on a C-47. *This must be where Ted and John parked the airplane.* The arcing track dug in the dirt and weeds was most likely created by the tail wheel as the airplane swung around to face the runway.

A dirt road bordered the far end of the runway. Skid marks stopped just shy of the C-47 tire marks. In the dirt was an object—too perfectly shaped to be a stone. I reached down, picked it up and rolled it between my fingers. It was a small piece of plastic: a button. A button about where the door of the C-47 would have been. I dropped the button in my pocket and took a number of pictures of the area, including the tire marks of multiple vehicles. Something wasn't right. Call it a hunch, intuition, or experience, but something happened here, and I don't think it was good.

The divots in the runway were more pronounced as I taxied to the end of the dirt strip. The farmer was back in his field. Whether he knew more than he shared, I didn't know. After a quick prayer, I advanced the throttles. The Commander's engines roared loudly, thundering the plane down the runway, and leaving a cloud of brown dust behind it as it picked up speed. It was hot and humid. The trees at the far end of the runway drew close rapidly. With five hundred feet remaining, I pulled hard on the yoke. The Commander staggered into the air, clearing the cluster of trees by less than twenty feet. The farmer's field shrunk out my left window as I banked and headed northeast. I entered the same flight path Ted and John filed in the system after Ted's treatment and sojourn here, based on the data I assembled from the FAA files. The winds were calm. Translucent brush-stroked clouds floated high in the sky, filtering the sun and its offensive glare into the cockpit ever so slightly.

Chapter 4

Texas

"**G**ood morning, Amelia," Cougar said. Amelia sat on a swivel work stool underneath the belly of a pristine yellow North American T-6 Texan WW II airplane. She wore a tattered green flight suit mottled with grease. Her platinum hair was tucked under a baseball cap with only a ponytail jutting through the hole in the back.

"Cougar! You startled me…hi…I didn't expect you so soon, how was your flight?"

"The flight was good, although sitting for that long cramps my right leg." Cougar shook his leg like Elvis. "An occupational hazard I'm more than willing to accept. I'm sorry about startling you, I tried shuffling loudly as I walked into the hangar. A man near where I parked told me you were in here."

"I didn't even hear it, sorry," Amelia replied.

"Don't be. I'm sure your mind has been on other things." Cougar stepped back. "This is really a beautiful T-6…G is it? One of the best I have seen."

"Wow, you know your planes, thank you. This one's my favorite in the whole collection. This was the first airplane my dad and I bought together for the museum. He taught me to fly it. I have so many good memories in it…with my dad…memories I'll never forget…" Her words drifted in the air, becoming soft and thin. "Did you find out anything?"

"I did."

She rolled out from under the airplane and stood next to it. She had grease on her cheeks. Moisture from a tear created a small rivulet around one of the grease spots. Cougar shifted closer, reaching his arm to comfort her. Amelia wrapped her arms around him. Cougar held her tight, letting her grief materialize as her body shook. A minute passed before she leaned back. "I miss him so much. I can't stop thinking about him and what could have happened." Cougar pulled her in close.

She wiped her face with the back of her hand, spreading grease and tears across her nose and hair.

"I'm sure I look wonderful now," she said, wiping her nose on her sleeve. "You didn't come to see me fall apart. I'm sorry." Her cheeks lifted; a forced smile spread across her face.

"It's okay, really. You are being too hard on yourself. Your father is missing, you lost your mother a year ago, and you have this museum to run, which I'm sure takes a lot of time and is a huge responsibility."

"Is that supposed to make me feel better?" Amelia quipped.

"All I'm trying to say is that you have a lot to deal with right now. It's not so unusual for your body to feel this stress. It's okay to listen to what it's telling you. My heart is breaking for you. I can see how much you love your dad, and this place you and your parents built." Cougar scanned the walls of the cavernous hangar. "It's extraordinary."

"Thank you, you're very sweet. If you wouldn't mind, Cougar, can you give me a few minutes to clean up?" She wiped at her nose again. "Besides, I'd like a little time to prepare myself before you share what you have learned." She unzipped her green overalls and stepped out of them.

"Of course."

"Thank you. I'll show you around the museum when I get back." She bit her lower lip and drew a long breath through her nose. "I'm eager to hear what you found out in Mexico, I am. I guess I'm just a little anxious. Okay anxious is stating it mildly, more like petrified. Does that make sense?" Amelia's lower lip protruded, her eyebrows lowered, furrowing closer together.

"It does. You can show me around the museum first. Then, if you're okay with it, we can find a quiet table at a local restaurant where we can talk. I doubt I'm the only one who hasn't eaten today, am I right?"

"That sounds perfect."

"If it's all right with you, I'll wait out by my Aero Commander. I need to make a few calls."

Amelia smiled, then leaned over and gave Cougar a greasy peck on his cheek before ambling over to a staircase leading up to her residence on the second floor.

Cougar sat in a soft leather chair next to a beautifully crafted curly-maple wooden table he had flipped up, making a desk in the back of the Aero Commander. Flipping switches brought the communication system to life. Cougar called his neighbor, Sarah Jozel. Sarah graciously watched Cougar's dog, Derby, when he was out of town on missions. Derby was the only family Cougar had. An only child, Cougar's parents had died when he was away at college. Derby helped fill the emptiness left by his parents as well as providing him with an emotional element for returning home safely from each mission. "Good afternoon, Sarah."

"Well, hello, if it isn't 007 himself," Sarah jested. "How are you doing, Cougar?" Sarah knew of Cougar's profession as a PI, but not about being a top-secret government agent. Sarah was married to Frank Jozel, a laid-back man in his 50s who shuffled around like men 20 years his senior. Sarah, at 47, was the complete opposite, having the energy of a small atomic bomb. When she dog-sat Derby, she walked him around the neighborhood three times a day, once in the early morning and twice in the evening. This was in addition to working a full-time job and leading the neighborhood watch group.

"Well it's a beautiful day in Texas, that's currently where I am. How is Derby?"

"He is… staring at me and wagging his long whippet tail. I think he knows you're on the other end of the phone."

"Please tell him hi and that I'll see him soon…and Sarah, thank you as always for taking such great care of him."

"You're welcome, Cougar; but actually, I think he's the one taking great care of me. Be careful, and Frank, Derby and I will talk with you later."

Cougar tapped in Mary's number. One ring sounded before going to voice mail. "Hi Mary, Cougar here. I'm in San Angelo, Texas, and will be meeting with Amelia in a bit to give her status. Would you upload the background checks for Ted Thomson and John Burrow to my folder? Thank you." Cougar removed his headset. An older business jet, a Falcon-10, touched its main wheels on the runway. A puff of white smoke lingered at the touchdown zone. Its nose wheel tire settled to the pavement, followed by the noise of spooling engines. The plane slowed, then made a left turn onto a taxiway.

Amelia washed up, then slipped on a pair of jeans and a black tee-shirt with the silhouette of an F-14 Tomcat fighter jet on it, from the movie *Top Gun*. She struggled applying her make-up, her mind kept reverting to her parents. Painstakingly she added eye liner and rose lip-stick. She missed her father tremendously, and the pain from her mother's death came back like it was yesterday.

As she descended the stairs of her loft, confusion and loneliness stabbed at her heart, but by the time she reached the bottom stair, strength and determination returned. In the past, whatever she sought after she accomplished. It may not have come easy; but she succeeded. This too is just another test, she said to herself. A test of her metal, to define what she's truly made of. She must win over her emotions of sadness, grief, and fear, for there's too much to do to pause now. She must find out what really happened to her father no matter what it takes. And one way or another, she would keep hers and her parents' dreams alive by keeping the museum open.

She walked up to Cougar's black, gray, and yellow Aero Commander. The aft door was ajar. Inside, Cougar was typing at a keyboard.

"Are you ready for the tour?" Amelia asked.

"I'm all yours, just…one…second."

"Wow, this is really nice. Can I look inside?"

"Sure, come on in."

"Okay…this is really cool; I'm very impressed." Inside the Aero Commander was a modern glass flight deck with instruments she had never seen before. "Why all the electronics?"

"In my line of business, I need all the help I can get," Cougar replied, hoping she wouldn't ask too many questions, especially about the equipment he used during Trinity missions.

"I'm very impressed," she said, repeating herself. She sat in the captain's seat moving the yoke and simulating flipping buttons like a school kid.

"Okay, now I will show you our airplanes. Of course, they won't have all this stuff in them." Cougar closed the Commander's door after Amelia exited. "We have three hangars." Amelia extended her arms like a flight attendant when reviewing emergency procedures. "Two are open to the public, where we store and display most of the airplanes, and a third hangar, the one you found me in and where I live, is mainly used for maintenance and restorations. We also have a couple airplanes tied down outside. Are you ready?"

"Looking forward to it, lead on."

Amelia adjusted her shoulders back and headed toward the first hangar. They passed several small planes tied up on the ramp. A Cessna 172, a couple older Pipers, and a newer Piper Meridian.

"That's our visitor's parking area," she said. "We get visitors flying in from all over the world to view our collection and watch our air shows."

Cougar stopped to consider those who flew in from around the world. Amelia hadn't stopped. Her shapely body kept moving, her hair gently tapped the back of her shoulders as the air twirled it into soft knots.

She toured Cougar around each vintage aircraft inside the hangars and a few outside on display. Cougar's cell rang. He grabbed it out of his pocket. "Excuse me, Amelia. I hate to be impolite, but I really need to take this call."

"Don't be silly, I'll wait for you over here," She pointed toward the third hangar.

"Hello, can you hear me?" Cougar said, speaking quietly into the phone.

"Good afternoon, Cougar, this is Riley, yes…I hear you loud and clear. Do you have a few minutes to talk?"

"Of course, sir, just one minute." Cougar found a private spot to talk. "Okay, I'm ready."

"Where are you?" Riley asked.

"In San Angelo, Texas, investigating two missing pilots and their airplane."

"And how is that going?"

"It's still very early in the investigation. The NTSB and Mexican authorities believe it crashed in the Gulf of Mexico; however, I've un-covered a few clues that might point to something more sinister. What's up, sir? I know you didn't call to ask about my PI case."

"No, I didn't, but I really should call more often. My day seems to improve whenever I do." Riley cleared his throat. "We have a situation brewing between the United States and Colombia. I'm sure you already know how delicate the relationship is between our two countries. Well this situation is adding additional strain. The president of Colombia has asked our government for help."

"What do they want?"

"It appears priceless art was stolen out of a museum here in the US. This art was on loan to the US from Colombia for an upcoming special art exhibit."

"The Treasures of Colombia exhibit?" Cougar asked. "I read about an upcoming show, is that the one you are referring to?"

"Yes," Riley stated. "The art that is missing is considered a national treasure in Colombia and is priceless. The Colombian government regards this historic art collection as being a piece of Colombia itself. That is why our governments are involved and why Trinity is being asked to investigate."

"Wouldn't the police and bureaus be investigating this? It seems they should be able to solve this one."

"Yes, and Trinity has been activated for this mission as well. The president wants the art recovered as quickly as possible. Art collections have a way of dissipating rather quickly, and in a very short timeframe this collection may never be recoverable in its entirety again. The Colombian government is holding the USA fully accountable for its cherished missing national treasure."

"I think I understand," Cougar remarked.

"I hate to insist Cougar, but I need you to report immediately for this mission. Gerry and Kathy are standing by and will be teamed up with you on this one." Kathy Lacey and Gerry Graham joined Trinity the same time Cougar did. They all were just out of college and recruited for a new special operations project, code named Trinity. The name reflected the small three-person team, comprising of different skills and abilities. Kathy filled the communications role, Gerry the technology position, and Cougar, the team leader, pilot, and field agent.

"Yes, sir. I'll report as soon as possible."

"Thank you."

"Sir…I have some information to share with my client. Would it be okay if I met with her first before reporting?"

"Of course," Riley responded. "Check in at headquarters in the morning. If your plane is in Texas, I would advise leaving it there. You'll be flying commercial on this one."

"Affirmative! I will see you in the morning, sir…and thank you."

"Good luck with your client, Cougar. Again, I'm sorry you must put your investigation on hold, but we need you on this one. You know the contract," Riley stated almost apologetically.

When Cougar first wanted to start a private investigation business specializing in asset recovery, the leaders of Trinity were not very understanding. They had invested a lot of time and money training him and he was by far their best field agent and pilot. But Cougar had fulfilled his mandatory mission commitment with the Government, and with a clause in the contract giving him an opportunity of reducing his fulltime obligation to part-time, and feeling led to provide a similar type service for those whose situations would never garner the attention of a government special operations team, he appealed to the leaders of Trinity.

Finally, they reached an agreement. Cougar could open a PI business, as long as he gave Trinity top priority when called upon.

Tamales

The stairs clanked behind me. Amelia's high heels worked their way down from the second floor of the hangar. Above her heels she wore designer jeans and a soft turquoise blouse that draped over her hips and tied at the waist. Her platinum hair bowed over her shoulders, before falling haphazardly behind her. Her darkened eyes lowered to my feet. Unhurriedly she raised her head, her lips widened in a tender smile. "Well, you clean up nice," she said.

"And you are stunning!" The words flew out of my mouth unabated. "I apologize, that observation probably should have stayed in my head. Let me try that again. Amelia…oh what the heck…you look amazing."

She chuckled, I chuckled. "You mean now that the grease is out of my hair?"

"Exactly." We laughed, the kind of laugh that removes embarrassing awkwardness. "Are you ready for dinner?"

"I sure am, and I'm prepared to hear what you found out about my father."

Amelia drove us into town to a restaurant located within a small strip mall. "I love this place," she said. "It's not the fanciest; but they have unbelievable tamales made from scratch, and they make them fresh daily. I also picked this place because they have an area upstairs that is secluded where we can talk. You do like tamales, right? I'm sorry, I guess I should have asked you first."

"Anyone who doesn't like tamales shows bad taste," I replied. Amelia's face brightened for a second before turning somber again. I thought about Amelia and her father, patronizing this restaurant together, laughing and enjoying good times.

"Two please," I said to the hostess.

"Right this way," the waitress replied, turning, and grabbing two menus. "How are you doing, Amelia? We are so sorry to hear about your father."

"Thank you, Robin. I'm doing okay and thank you for asking. Can we get the upstairs table please?"

"I believe it's open. Follow me, please."

"Thank you." We both replied in unison.

Chips and salsa were set on the table. Amelia said, "Okay, I'm ready to hear what you've found out about my father. I'm sorry I wasn't prepared to hear earlier. I know I hired you to find him, or at least find out what actually happened to him, but that desire comes from the strong woman inside of me. There's also another side to me, the fragile little girl side. That side is petrified to know the real truth."

I squeezed Amelia's hand. "It's still early in the investigation, and I don't have a lot of information to share, but what I do have, I felt you'd want to know. I also have another matter I need to talk to you about. I'll get to that in a few minutes." Amelia's eyebrows furrowed. She gently pulled her hand from mine, grabbed a chip, and dipped it into the salsa. I shared what I learned from the doctor, the gardener, and what I saw at the airport.

"So, my dad did leave Mexico?"

"That I'm not sure."

"What do you mean?"

"I only know your father's plane took off from the airport the day of his planned departure." I shared my theory about a possible hijacking.

Amelia pulled her arm back, removing a chip from her mouth. "What? What makes you think that?" She slowly slid the chip back in while tilting her head, grasping to understand the meaning of what I just shared.

"There were tire marks behind and in front where I believe the C-47 was parked—skid marks. I also found this." I pulled the button out of my pocket and held it up.

"A button?" Amelia asked, trying not to talk with her mouth full.

"The button was where the C-47 door would have been located." I stopped talking as the waitress set two plates of tamales down.

"Careful, these plates are really hot," she said, turning and walking back to the stairs.

Amelia stabbed apathetically at the plate of tamales. "So, you really think my dad was hijacked?" she blurted out.

"It's a possibility is all I'm saying. Skid marks and a button are not conclusive. It's just as plausible that the plane was lost at sea as the NTSB concluded. I wish I could continue the investigation to be sure."

"What do you mean, you wish you could continue? I want you to continue, that's why I hired you, so you would investigate until I learned the truth about what happened to my father!" Her voice ended several decibels higher than when it started.

"Amelia, unfortunately I have been called away on an urgent matter and I won't be able to finish your investigation at this time. I'm very sorry. I know your heart is broken…I will refund your retainer."

"What do you mean, another matter? Am I not paying you enough?" Diners on the first floor glanced up.

"Amelia, it's not like that, and I apologize, because I can't even explain the situation to you. I understand your being upset with me."

"I am upset…and mad! I'm upset about my dad, the museum revenues, and now you…and this tamale?" She shoved the tamale away from her after only having a couple bites.

I felt awful. Amelia deserved real answers, not a couple hypothetical details from some PI that walks off into the sunset, leaving her with even more angst.

"Amelia, I can't promise you much, but I will do as much investigating as I can until I can get back to your case full time. That's the best I can do for now, and all the expenses are on me."

Amelia's head hung low; her white hair brushed the table. "I will continue the investigation on my own," she said, drying her eyes.

"Amelia, if what I suggested about your dad's plane actually occurred, then it will be much too dangerous for you."

"So, if my dad is still alive, do you want me to just wait around until he's dead? And why don't you think I can handle it? Am I too young or not experienced enough? Or is it because I'm a woman?" Amelia lowered her voice as she spoke.

"Amelia, I don't want you to get hurt, period! And from everything I have seen, you are a very capable person…and being female has no bearing on that fact. I have seen a world you most likely haven't. I've seen how people are when fighting for their next meal. I've seen greed at its worst, horrid individuals working for the ultimate big payoff. Human life can be very expendable at times. I don't know what happened to your dad or John. In fact, one of the reasons I flew in here was to learn more about them and the museum. Unfortunately, I won't be able to complete that part of the investigation at this time. They may still be alive, or they may be dead as supposed by the Feds. But going out and getting yourself killed will not bring them back or make any of this better."

"That phone call…it was that phone call wasn't it?"

"Yes," I replied. Amelia breathed deep. I wanted to share more with her; but would it really make any difference? She needed concrete answers to what happened to her father, and I needed to be in Virginia by tomorrow morning.

"I'll drive you back to the airport," she said. "I am not angry with you, I'm just confused…and hurting…really, really hurting."

Chapter 6

Repainted

Gustano ran his hand along the fuselage of the newly painted C-47. "She looks pretty, huh boss?" Fabio stated. Gustano didn't answer, instead pulled in a lung full of smoke with his lips tightly pinched around an Export A brand cigarette. He pushed Fabio out of his way. Slowly, smoke coursed through his nostrils, spiraling up, hiding his face.

Javier stepped down from the large C-47 transport. "Well boss? What do you think?" Javier asked.

"You did good," Gustano remarked. "Hard to tell it's even the same airplane." Gustano crushed the remains of his cigarette under foot.

Miguel jumped down and patted Javier on the back. "That was quite a landing," he remarked.

"She's a fun one to fly," Javier said. "Do you want to take her up boss?"

"Not now. I have work to do." He turned to Fabio. "Did you get all the crates packed?" Gustano lit another Export A, the tip of the cigarette glowed orange as he pursed his lips around it.

"Almost, I could use a little help now that Miguel and Javier are back."

"I could use a little help?" Gustano mimicked. "Why is it, you can never manage anything on your own? Here's your help." Gustano swung his foot into Fabio's butt. He turned to Javier. "How in God's green earth could this man come from the same mother that had you? I swear if he weren't your brother, I'd have shot him months ago."

Fabio produced a half-calked grin. "I'll give him a hand," Miguel said, quickly grabbing Fabio by the arm and leading him into a cavernous former ex-military barracks. Gustano walked back to a house that was only in slightly better condition than the barracks building. Javier parked and secured the C-47 next to a couple of airplanes and a dilapidated outbuilding. He zipped up a pair of overalls, filled containers of oil from a barrel, and topped off the C-47 reservoirs.

Miguel yelled at Fabio, "What are you trying to do, get yourself killed?"

"Oh, Miguel, the boss likes me too much."

Miguel shook his head. "You're a bigger idiot than I thought you were if you think the boss likes you. The boss likes perfection, and people to do their job—period! You give the boss a grin like that again and he'll knock your frick'n teeth out. That's if he doesn't kill you first. Come on, let's get this finished before he comes in here. I don't want to have to bury another body tonight."

Chapter 7

Norfolk, Virginia

"Cougar, I'm glad to see you made it." Riley said, rising from his chair and extending his hand. Cougar gripped it, shaking it respectfully. "How did it go with your client…please have a seat."

"Not so good, sir." Cougar shared the details of his conversation with Amelia.

Well, again, I am sorry I had to pull you over for this one, but it does require the best team we have. I was also specifically requested to make sure you were part of the team…and don't ask me by who," Riley stated.

"Yes, sir, thank you. Tell me about the art that was stolen." Cougar asked, breaking Riley's trance. Cougar got up and poured himself water from an upside-down bottle set into a water dispenser. "A little parched," Cougar said scratching at his throat as he sat back down.

"That sounds good, will you fill this up for me too?" Riley handed Cougar a coffee mug with pictures of buffalos on the side. The mug was a souvenir he picked up last year when he and his wife took a two-week vacation to Yellowstone National Park, the first real vacation Riley had taken in a decade. "Let me state again how sensitive this situation is between our two countries." Riley pulled out two large folders from a drawer to his right and set them on his desk.

"With tensions already high between our two countries, displaying Colombia's historic art was to be a fresh start in respecting their culture and highlighting our rich pasts together. The Colombian art is now missing. The art consisted of paintings from all eras, pre- and post-Colombia, and ancient ceramic pots and statues. Many of the statues had anthropomorphic and zoomorphic forms to them and were heavy, many being made from stone. The most priceless artifact missing is the Poporo Quimbaya, a gold relic used during devotions that looks like, well, here's a picture of it."

Cougar grabbed the picture. "Looks like a frog."

"It does, but I can't stress to you how valuable that frog looking piece is to Colombia…in fact, all of the art. Not only does art capture a county's history and culture, it represents something much greater, it represents beliefs and values. It preserves ancestry, victories and defeats, highs, and lows. It also provides a glimpse into the beginnings and derivations for all who come after to see how one's county learned, reformed, and evolved. You see, in a way this art is Colombia. The Colombian government said losing this art is like taking away their dynasty, removing the very foundation they built their country upon and weakening who they are as people." Riley paused, the buffalo on the cup turned upside down, as he swigged the last of his water. "You will have to forgive me for my monologue, Cougar. I have a little passion in this field." Riley's office was filled with art he had collected over the years.

"I agree with your sentiment," Cougar stated, "and I can also understand the government of Colombia's point of view. It seems like only yesterday, sitting in a college classroom and studying South America. And I do recall Colombia's rich art history."

"Good, because you'll need to meet with the police in Bogota, Colombia, and the curator from the museum where the art originated." Riley shuffled through a few pages in the folder. "Before you leave for Colombia, you'll want to talk with the New York City Museum curator. That's the museum the art was stolen from. His name is…there it is,

Jim Montoya. Gerry and Kathy will meet you in Colombia after you're done here in New York."

"Yes, sir. I am a little curious though why you're sending Gerry and Kathy to Colombia if the art was stolen here in New York?"

Riley rubbed his chin and narrowed his jaw. "The police and our CIA are investigating the theft here in New York. I want you guys to start at the beginning, investigate this like any of our other missions…a complete understanding of all the players, the missing artwork, shipping details, the works. When you are convinced you have uncovered all the information from Colombia, then you and the team can make your way back to New York."

Riley paused. "I have a hunch on this one, Cougar, and I think it might turn out to be more involved than it appears. It's not that I mistrust the Colombian government, but I don't want to miss the tiniest of details. We have been burnt by them in the past. If we are truly going to mend some fences between our governments, we need all the facts. Also, sending you guys to Colombia will give the police and CIA time to finish their investigation here before we ascend on their jurisdiction. I don't need to remind you how territorial they can be. I also don't need to remind you how unwelcomed the FBI or CIA would be in Colombia after the last embarrassing situation."

"Copy that. I'll go through these folders while heading to New York City," Cougar said, rapidly thumbing through the pages.

"One more thing—your cover," Riley interjected. "Your name is Arlan Jensen, an insurance investigator from the FAIB, the Fine Arts Insurance Board."

"I was just about to ask you who insured the art." Cougar pulled out a page from the top folder.

"It's all in the paperwork I handed you, and yes, there was a fine arts insurance policy taken out and the art is covered under a temporary loan and traveling exhibition policy. But that won't placate the Republic of Colombia, it's not about the monetary value."

"That being so, my cover as an insurance investigator for the FAIB will be to scrutinize the policy and claim before approving the specific insurance company to settle, correct?"

"Yes, the Fine Arts Insurance Board was contacted by Delrow Insurance Agency Inc., the holder of the policy. It's standard practice for losses of this magnitude to go through the board first," Riley stated. "Your cover should also serve you well in New York when meeting with the curator there. The New York police and CIA shouldn't hassle you too bad if they believe you are just doing your job."

Cougar tucked the folders into his briefcase, shook Riley's hand and headed for his hotel. Traffic was heavy as usual in Norfolk, Virginia, Trinity's headquarters. The headquarters were not located on government property but in a generic red brick building in the downtown area, only a short distance from the Navy base. The headquarters occupied the top several floors of the building, with a bookstore and coffee shop below.

The cab driver entered the freeway, veering the hybrid into a slot no bigger than a toaster. Cougar thought about reading the files but nixed the idea, choosing rather to keep an eye on the traffic and willing the hotel to materialize.

As Cougar sat in the hotel room digesting the information, he found it unusual for such a large quantity of art to go missing in just one night. From the details in the report, twelve large wooden crates, measuring approximately 4 feet by 4 feet wide by 30 inches high had all disappeared. The alarm vibrated on Cougar's wrist. He packed and headed to the airport.

New York City

The wheels of the mostly empty Boeing 737 touched down later than scheduled, due to a last-minute delay in Virginia. The halls of La Guardia International Airport echoed my steps, as I made my way to baggage claim. The hotel lobby was equally as empty, and it didn't take long to get checked in. The room reeked of stale smoke. For a non-smoking hotel, this room had been smoked in, and not that long ago. I pulled out my cell, one battery bar left. I pressed in my office assistant's number and let it ring.

"Good evening, Mary, Cougar here, I hope I didn't wake you?"

"Cougar, I am glad you called, are you in New York?"

"I am…in my hotel room now."

"It must be late there, it's 10pm here."

"There was a slight delay in Virginia."

"Well, I'm glad you made it safe. Amelia called earlier and left you a message."

"She did? What did she say?"

"She wanted me to tell you that she was sorry for how she reacted, and that she had no right blaming you for putting her investigation on hold for a higher priority."

"Well…she has nothing to apologize about. If it were me, I would have felt the same way. I wish I could help her, but as you know, I do have a higher priority."

"That's not all, Cougar. She wanted me to tell you that she is going ahead with the investigation on her own, and that she understands the risk. I asked if she had talked to you about that, and she told me you had urged her quite emphatically not to. She also added that if it were her missing, her dad would stop at nothing to find her, and at the very least, find out what actually happened."

"I was afraid of that…actually quite certain of that." I mumbled to myself while leaning back on a stained wooden chair back.

"Cougar?"

"Did she say where she was going and when?"

"No, she didn't." Mary's voice sounded despondent. "She's a lovely girl, Cougar. Is she going to be all right?"

"I don't know. I have a pretty good idea where she'll go first though, and unfortunately, I won't be able to help her. She should have listened to me. Mary, if you hear anything more, please let me know. I'll try contacting her later this morning."

"You got it. Good luck in New York."

"Thank you." I clicked off. Poor Amelia. She really doesn't know the risks or what she could encounter. I plugged the phone into the charger, turned down the sheets, and fell asleep.

After several hours, I woke to my alarm watch, dressed, and took a creaky elevator down to the lobby floor, searching for something healthy to eat. A small continental breakfast was the only offering. A carousel full of pastries seemed the most popular, with two ceramic bowls containing fruit, neglected and off to the side. I grabbed a banana and an apple, along with a bowl of oatmeal and sat down with the newspaper that had been left in front of my hotel room door. I glanced at my watch. One hour before my meeting with Jim Montoya.

I laid the paper down. Not a single "good-news" story. I tried Amelia's number again, still no answer. I left another message, stashed my phone, and stepped out of the hotel to a waiting taxi. "Good morning, Metropolitan Art Museum please."

"Oh, you will like it there," the driver responded cheerfully as I stuffed myself and my bag into the small hybrid. "You from here?" the driver asked. "My name is Danny."

"Good morning, Danny, my name is Arlan. No, I'm just visiting. I'm from Washington State."

"Washington? I have a niece that lives out that way…city of Moses Lake. Do you know where that is?"

"I sure do, eastern part of the state. My buddies and I used to go there quite a bit during college. Nice place."

"I haven't seen her for a very long time," the cabbie said. His words were more of a statement to himself. "Sweet girl ya know…the kind that makes a family proud. Went to college, good girl…smart. Where do you want to be dropped off? Main entrance?" The driver pulled onto Fifth Avenue.

"The main entrance is fine." A beautiful edifice emerged in the midst of conventional glass and steel surroundings. On the back side of the museum lay Central Park. Perfectly manicured grass stretched for acres. Fountains jetted streams of water that curled in synchronization to ponds below. Massive steps extended outward from the museum, like a dragon's tongue, leading to the entrance. "Thank you, Danny." I handed him an extra twenty-dollar bill.

"Thank you! Have a nice visit, Arlan."

At the information counter, I asked where I could find Jim Montoya's office. I followed a hall until coming to an impressive office with an open door and a man sitting at a desk. His back was hunched over with his right hand steering a pen over a sheet of paper.

"Jim Montoya?" I said, as I knocked quietly on the open door.

"Yes, you must be Arlan Jenson."

"I am, may I come in?"

"Please."

Jim swiveled his chair around and stood to his feet. He stepped with a slight limp around a couple frail statues displayed on small tables and shook my hand. Jim was middle-aged, short, and balding, with thin light-brown hair combed over the crown of his head. When he smiled, his face grew wrinkles and his weak eyes darkened.

"How best can I help you? A very disastrous situation it is," he said.

"Indeed, it is," I replied. "To begin with, I'd like to see where the art was held before it went missing…then I'd like to see your books, inventorying the loaned art."

"Yes, of course. Excuse me if I'm out of line for pointing this out, but you used the words 'went missing' like it will show back up. I think stolen is a better term, don't you? Right this way please. It's a bit of a walk I'm afraid."

"You're probably right. Please, lead the way, I'll try not to fall behind." Jim limped out of his office and led me through narrow and wide halls. Magnificent Greek statues and busts inhabited one of the halls. As we continued, Jim's limp became less noticeable, an indication that maybe he had been sitting too long on tired hips. An elevator took us down a few floors. When the doors opened, cold cement greeted us, a stark contrast to the floors above with their world class architecture and materials.

"This way," he prodded. "A detective from the New York Police Department is also here investigating."

Wood pallets leaned against a scarred wall. To the side, paper, and plastic packaging material along with broken-down wooden boxes were tossed in and around several large dumpsters. A truck beeped as it backed into one of the loading docks. The police detective had a notebook out and was talking with a man in the corner using a tape measure on a crate. "What was the art in when it arrived?" I shouted.

"Wood crates, like the ones over there," Jim said, pointing to wooden boxes being dismantled next to the detective.

"And how many crates?"

Jim scratched at his face. "Twelve, I think. Yes, twelve," he said assuredly the second time.

"And how much did each these crates weigh?"

"I have the exact figures in my office, but around 1000 to 5000 pounds each. Some contained very heavy ceramics."

"May I look around for a bit?"

"Please, go right ahead. If you don't mind, I should get back to my office. When you're finished here if you would be so kind as to meet me there? I'll show you the inventory details you asked about." Jim paused. "Do you think you can find your way back okay?"

"Pretty sure, thank you," I said. Jim turned to leave. "Oh, one more thing before you go, please."

Jim rotated completely around. "Yes?"

"How was the art left—you know the night it went missing, and who inventoried the art?"

"The art was left in the crates—and a man from Bogota's museum and one of their security guards were present the night we inventoried the art as well as an insurance agent from Delrow Insurance Agency, the company that insured the art. They were here as we opened the crates, verifying the inventory every step of the way. I was also here taking inventory as we opened each crate and box."

"Were your security guards here overseeing the process as well, and was this area guarded that night?"

"Of course, this museum has state of the art security," he said indignantly.

"One more thing, were all the crates the same size?"

"More or less, I guess a few were slightly larger and some a little smaller, why?"

"I'm just collecting the facts, that's my job."

"Right-right, okay. If nothing else, I'll see you back at my office."

Jim didn't wait for another question. He limped off toward a waiting elevator with just a wave of his arm as he turned. The room was swept clean. A man picked up scrap wood and metal bands off the loading dock floor. Museum workers pushed a large dumpster in front of a recycling truck.

"Excuse me," the detective barked. "Who are you?"

"Arlan Jensen with the Fine Arts Insurance Board."

"I see, and what are you doing here?"

Riley was right about the New York City Police being territorial. I had experienced it several times in the past, and it wasn't just reserved for New York City's Police Department either.

"I'm investigating the missing art on behalf of the insurance company. I'm sure you're aware of this procedure."

"Don't get cute with me. Do you see this badge—Arlan?" The officer flipped open a wallet, displaying his badge. "This means I'm in charge. You can look, but don't touch and no pictures. I don't need some amateur messing in my investigation." The man with him, also from the NYPD, snickered.

"I understand, Detective—Ramous. I'll just be a few more minutes and then I'll be out of your way." I interviewed three loading dock workers, but gained negligible information, only confirmation on what Jim had just shared.

After I finished examining the area, I returned to Jim's office. The documents he handed me listed all the contents and weight for each crate. Twelve crates carried a significant amount of art, according to the inventory sheets, and most of it priceless. I wrote down the names of all who were present the night the art disappeared and spent another hour gathering as much information as I could.

In my hotel room, I sketched a layout of the museum storage room, elevator, hall, and loading dock. Once I finished writing down the rest of my thoughts, I closed my notebook, and packed for Bogota, Colombia.

Chapter 9

Bogota, Colombia

The early afternoon was humid and warm, white bulbous clouds partially obscured the mountain tops that bordered the unique city of Bogota.

"Good afternoon."

"Good afternoon to you," the hotel clerk replied in perfect English. "Are you checking in?"

"Yes, I am," Cougar said. "Your English, it's very good. My name is Arlan Jensen."

"Thank you, Arlan. I use English every chance I get—trying to keep my skills up."

"Well, thank you, I feel right at home."

"I learned English while in the United States during a student exchange program too many years ago I am afraid to say." The elderly lady shot off a friendly smirk and a wink. She played the computer keyboard like a piano, her fingers danced over the keys in musical cadence. "On the same card you reserved with, Mr. Jensen?"

"Yes, please."

"There you are." She laid down two plastic door keys. "I hope you enjoy your stay here in Bogota."

"Thank you, Angie." Cougar replied, reading off her nametag.

Cougar pushed open the hotel room door and stepped inside. The room was clean and traditional, with a view of the city out its only window. He grabbed his cell and placed a call to the Bogota Museum. On the third ring, a lady answered in Spanish. "Bogota Museum of Art and History."

"Good afternoon, may I speak with Mauricio Lopez, please," Cougar asked in Spanish.

"Un momento."

The museum's curator answered. "Mauricio Lopez, speaking."

"Hello Mauricio, this is Arlan Jensen. We spoke yesterday on the phone?"

"Yes, I remember, The Fine Arts Insurance Board investigator from the United States of America."

"Yes, well I'm now in Bogota; will this afternoon still work for us getting together?"

"Can we make it early evening, say around four? Something came up needing my attention this afternoon."

"I'll see you at the museum at 4pm, thank you." Cougar clicked off, then pressed another two buttons and waited.

"Yankee Stadium." A voice said on the other end.

Cougar replied using the codeword. "Peanuts and hotdogs."

"Cougar," Kathy Lacey said. "How was your trip? We've been waiting for you. Just a minute, let me put Gerry on too."

"Hi Cougar."

"Good afternoon, Kathy and Gerry, when did you two get in?"

"Yesterday, Riley wanted to make sure we were set up before you arrived," Gerry stated.

"Anything new I should know about? I'm meeting the curator at four to go over the specifics of the agreement that was in place for the loaned art. While we are here, we need to find out as much as we can about the art and who might be interested in possessing it."

"Cougar, there's a detective here in Bogota named Andrea Dias. She has been assigned the case from the Bogota police force. She was in New York a day prior to you and met with the local police there. That's really the only new information we have," said Kathy.

"You might want to question her, Cougar," Gerry added, "see if she's found out anything."

"I'll do that. After learning all we can here, we'll return to the States and continue our investigation there, most likely out of New York. Riley had a hunch on this one and that's why he sent us here first. Whoever took the art probably won't keep it in the States. That was another assumption of Riley's. Since there's usually only a short window of opportunity for finding stolen art collections, and with NYPD and the CIA investigating in New York, Riley wanted us here. If we don't find the art soon, we may never locate it in its entirety again—ever."

"We understand, Cougar. What do you want us to do?" Kathy asked.

"Gerry, I'll need to record my meeting with Mauricio, so we don't miss anything."

"I got the gear with me; we're in adjoining rooms 207 and 209."

"Great, I'm just one floor above you two. I took a separate room for now until we know what we're dealing with. Kathy, we'll need details and history on every artifact missing. I have the inventory list from Jim Montoya, New York City museum's curator. I will get you the matching inventory list from the Bogota museum tonight. Do you have the Delrow list?"

"Yes."

"Let's hope they're all an exact match. Also, if you would research art robberies and missing art over the last ten years—where they took place and by whom—if known. Let's see if we can compile a list of probable suspects. That should be a good starting point anyway. Have you guys had lunch?"

"Not yet, we were waiting for your call first," said Gerry, "and by the way, I have the bigger room when you're ready to bunk with me."

"And hear you snore?" Cougar quipped.

"I can order up some food while we continue planning," Kathy suggested.

"That sounds good, Kathy. Gerry, I'll need to keep this room registered under my name until we understand more. Don't take it personally."

"You're hurting my feelings, Cougar."

"Oh brother," Kathy commented. "Bromance."

"I'll be down in about 10."

Cougar tried Amelia's number again. It rang several times before she answered.

"Why do you keep calling me?"

"Amelia, are you okay?"

"Of course, I am. Like I told you, I'm a lot tougher than I look."

"Where are you?"

"I'm still in Texas; but leaving today."

"For Mexico?"

"Yes."

"Who's going with you?"

There was a long silence. "Cougar, what do you want? I told you I would be okay. I'm flattered that you're concerned about me, I am, but I'm going to see this through with or without you."

"Would you do me a favor—please?"

"Maybe, what is it?" she asked.

"Will you keep your phone with you, and when I call, if you're able to, answer it?"

"I'll do my best, now you need to concentrate on your other more important priority, and I need to go. Goodbye Cougar—and stop worrying about me."

Amelia ended the call. Cougar held the silent phone in his hand. He did worry.

The Museum

I checked my watch. "I better get going. Thank you for the lunch, Kathy."

"One more—second," Gerry said. "Okay, try speaking again."

"Testing-testing, one-two-three."

"Got it, it's working now. I'm not sure why it was cutting out," Gerry said, while twisting a couple knobs on his recording equipment.

"Cougar, can you hear me?" Kathy whispered into her microphone.

"You're coming in loud and clear."

"Perfect—and you're welcome for lunch. That was pretty good food for room service."

Gerry rigged me with a standard transmitter and an inner ear speaker for recording my conversation with Mauricio Lopez. It also allows Kathy to verify and investigate information as it comes in. If Kathy needs clarification on something that's said, she can easily prompt me.

The museum was only a short distance from the hotel; however, the streets were congested, and by the time the taxi pulled up in front of the museum, twenty minutes had gone by. The museum entrance, very similar to the museum entrance in New York City, had grand stairs leading up to a majestic buttery-colored brick building. Inside the foyer, a male statue stood perched on a bronze base. It rose high into the air, almost touching the arched ceiling. Just standing there in that magnificent entrance gave me a sense of antiquity. At the information booth, I conveyed that I had an appointment to see Mauricio Lopez. The lady hung up the phone and told me he would be right out. I thanked her and kindly stepped to the side.

Next to me, hanging from the wall, was a unique painted animal sculpture. A banner adverted an exhibit on display from Australia. After waiting several minutes, an attractive young lady walked past me to the information booth. The lady in the booth pointed her in my direction, and the young lady retraced her steps over to me.

"Mr. Jensen?"

"Yes, that's me. Please, call me Arlan," I replied.

"My name is Daniela Perez. I'm the educator here at the museum and also Mauricio's assistant. Mauricio is tied up in a meeting but will join us as soon as he is finished. He asked me to help you with any questions you have about our—missing art." Daniela's face saddened.

Daniela bore the resemblance of a model or an actress with her long brown hair, vibrant brown eyes, and bronze complexion, although almost immediately I sensed her obliviousness to the beauty she possessed. She wore a frumpy black business suit with a white pearl necklace that dangled from her neck and plunged into her modest cleavage. Her black shoes were nearly flat with only a slight heel, leaving her height around 5 foot 8 inches. "I'm very sorry about your art being stolen. I can see in your eyes how much this art meant to you."

"What it meant to Colombia," she retorted abruptly. "Art is vital to a country, and in Colombia, we treasure our art greatly. It is our past, present, and future, the life-blood that makes our country function."

"I couldn't agree more," I remarked. "That's a lot of the reason I got into the art business myself. If I might ask, your English is impeccable, have you always lived in Colombia?"

"No, I lived and studied in Europe and then the United States for a few years, but I knew English from as young as I can remember. My father's a businessman, and he travelled often to the United States. He spoke English fluently and made sure I did too. He thought it would be important as I got older."

"Thank you for sharing that with me." The sounds of children shouting and laughing filled the silence as they ran excitedly about the lobby. Daniela's passion about art and the way she spoke of Colombia could lead one to believe she was older than the late twenties she appeared. "I would like to learn more about the art that was loaned for the show in New York. Would you be able to describe each of the pieces in full detail for me? I know this will take some time, but as a member of the Fine Arts Insurance Board, I will need to have a thorough understanding before the board and I can give the insurance company approval for the settlement."

"I would be happy to share that with you, and I'm relieved you're interested in more than just the monetary value of the artwork. Please, follow me." Daniela led me into the museum. "You can understand why this is such a tragedy for us here at the museum and for Colombia. The art we sent to New York City was our finest collection of Colombian art ever allowed outside our country. It spanned hundreds of years."

Daniela took me through several grand halls showing me where the art had been permanently displayed before being shipped off to the US. As we walked, murals decorated the high ceilings and statues greeted me as if trying to tell me about their history and the abduction of their loved ones who were no longer on display with them. As Daniela expounded on the history of the Poporo Quimbaya, a gentleman materialized from an inconspicuous door on the side of one of the exhibit halls and extended his hand.

"I'm truly sorry for the delay. Mauricio Lopez, and you are Arlan Jensen?"

"Yes, and don't apologize, your assistant, Daniela, has been more than helpful in providing me with details, including the history of the artwork that's gone missing."

"Yes—Daniela," he said warmly, like a father. Daniela is one of our most prized possessions here. She is what Colombia aspires to be, rooted in the past and advancing toward the future."

Mauricio's hair was back and well groomed. He stood just under six feet tall, and his face, darker than Daniela's, wore gold rimmed glasses on top of a middle-aged nose. "Mauricio, can you think of any person or group that might want this art for means other than just monetarily?"

"I have spent many nights, my friend, trying to figure out why someone would take our beloved national treasure. Each time I come up empty."

"Who all knew of the shipping details and when the art would show up in New York City?"

"Many people. This display was not a secret, but well publicized."

"Can I get a copy of the shipping details?"

"Of course, Daniela can get that for you." Daniela stepped back over when she heard her name, slipping her cell phone back into a small pocket at the front of her skirt. "We have already given the detective in charge of the investigator here in Bogota all of the information. I encourage you to talk with her, I'm sure she can be of some help to the board as well. The detective's name is?" Mauricio turned to Daniela to complete his sentence.

"Andrea Dias," Daniela inserted.

"Thank you, I will schedule a meeting with her once we're done. May I look at the area where the art was packaged and the loading dock where it was shipped out from?"

"Daniela can show you those. Is there anything else I can answer for…you…Mr. Jensen?" Mauricio's attention diverted to his cell phone.

"Do you know the curator from New York City's museum very well?"

"The curators from most of the prominent museums get together on occasion and learn from each other—kind of a benchmark of each other's best practices. Yes, I know Jim Montoya. May I ask why you are asking?"

"No reason I guess, just curious. Thank you for seeing me today."

"You're welcome. Daniela will see to any other question you might have. If I can be of any more help, please don't hesitate to ask." He paused before leaving. "We want our history back, Mr. Jensen." Then he escaped using the same door he entered from.

Daniela and I stood facing each other in silence. "Right this way, Arlan," she said, blushing almost imperceptibly. "I will show you our loading dock now."

"Thank you, Daniela. How long has Mr. Lopez been the curator here?"

"Almost two years."

"Did he work here before becoming the curator?"

"No, before coming here, he was the curator for an Australian museum. We are fortunate he wanted to come back to his home country. He's a Colombian citizen but has studied and worked all over the world."

As I followed her down the hall, I contemplated the missing art, Colombia's history, Mauricio Lopez, Jim Montoya, and Daniela, before my mind turned to Amelia, and my disappointment for having to discontinue her father's investigation. Daniela's skirt turned. "Are you coming?"

"Yes, sorry. I got lost in thought, trying to make sense of all the information I have so far."

"Is that what the FAIB does—tries to make sense out of stolen art before granting insurance agency's consent to settle? Honestly, I'm not real clear on what the Fine Art Insurance Board's role actually is."

I wasn't completely sure myself. "Well that's one of the things we look into besides ensuring policies are standard, appropriate, and binding. Fraud and abuse can become prolific if not held in check to standards. In the insurance world, you would not believe what some people will risk doing for money."

"I can only imagine," she replied. "I don't particularly care about money. The treasure that was stolen is priceless. There is no insurance settlement that could ever compensate Colombia for what we have lost. Right through here, Arlan." She pointed to a door.

A huge loading dock, twice the size of the one in New York unfolded before me. Eight truck bays, three dumpsters, and pallets of wood and other packing materials were neatly positioned against the far wall. I walked from one end to the other, thinking to myself. *The art was packaged into crates here, trucked to the airport, flown out by a cargo plane to New York, shipped to the loading dock of the New York Museum, and inspected there. Then the art disappeared before staging it for the show.*

Daniela interrupted my thoughts. "I can go with you when you talk to the detective if you would like. I'd like to know myself if they've uncovered anything new. I know they're working hand-in-hand with the New York City police department.

"I see no harm in that," I replied. Daniela parted her lips, showing perfect teeth. "Would you be able to send a copy of the inventory to this email address?" I handed her my card. "I think I'm done here for today. I'd like to come back and see the art pictures and historical records you said you have on the missing art, if that's not too much trouble."

"No trouble at all. I'd be more than happy to show you our historical archives and make copies of any of the material you need. I'll send you the inventory list as soon as I get back to my desk."

"Thank you. I'll get in touch with Detective Dias, schedule an appointment, and call you once I have the day and time."

Daniela reached into her skirt pocket to pull out her cell phone. She flipped open the cover and pulled out her business card. "Here's my number." Her long fingers pointed to the number on the card.

"Thank you—and also thank you for your undivided attention today. I very much appreciate your assistance."

"You're very welcome, Arlan." Her eyes stayed on me like I was a book needing to be studied and understood. Background noises became muted and indistinguishable as time decelerated. Seconds elapsed before we exchanged pleasantries and I left.

Chapter 11

Bogota Police Department

Detective Andrea Dias was in Captain Eduardo Moreno's office as Cougar and Daniela entered the police station. Captain Moreno, a hardnosed decorated military veteran with 16 years on the police force stood over his desk, pointing at Andrea. A police officer at the front desk led them back to Captain Moreno's office and tapped on the glass door. "Come on in," Eduardo barked.

"Thank you for seeing us so soon," Cougar said. "I'm Arlan Jensen from the Fine Arts Insurance Board, and I believe you already know Miss Daniela Perez from the Bogota Museum."

"Pleased to meet you, Arlan, and nice to see you again, Daniela," Detective Andrea Dias replied. Andrea was middle-aged, short with black frizzy hair shaped in an afro the size of a hefty pumpkin, and according to Captain Moreno, an average detective. In Eduardo's view, one was never good enough. Many times, he watched Andrea snacking as she worked, from his glass-paned office. He wanted to tell her that if she quit snacking so much, she wouldn't have to carry around those extra 40 pounds on her hips she endlessly complained about; but he knew better.

"Insurance investigator, huh?" Captain Moreno said, eyeing Cougar. "Not crazy about insurance-anything, especially insurance investigators—they get in the way."

"I'll try not to, although we both have jobs to do, right?" Cougar stated eyeing Captain Moreno guardedly. "I'm hoping you can share with me any information you have concerning the case of the missing Colombian art. I know you are working closely with the detectives in New York City on this."

"*I am* working closely with the police there, Arlan," Detective Dias replied in staccato, emphasizing "I AM".

"Working closely with them?" Captain Moreno spit out. "If it weren't for us driving this investigation, New York would let the insurance companies deal with the mess and move on. Oh no, not this time. This isn't some insignificant artwork that has been stolen, Mr. Jensen. New York City let a piece of our country disappear, and Miss Perez will attest to that."

Daniela nodded in agreement. Captain Moreno backed up and sat on his desktop, closed his hands together for an instant, then lifted his arms wide. "Our president has asked your government for help as well; but we have not seen any response." Captain Moreno stood up and moved around his desk to his chair and sat down. "Detective Dias can fill you in on any pertinent information that may be of assistance to you and the insurance board. I better not see you interfering in our investigation though. I plan to find out what happened in New York, and to locate our art and bring it back to Colombia. I have two detectives in New York working with the police there. And Detective Dias?" pointing to her, "she is leading the investigation. Now if you'll excuse me, I have other matters to address."

"Thank you for your time, Captain Moreno," Cougar said.

Detective Dias spoke up, "I can answer your questions now, there's a room down the hall where we can talk."

"Thank you," Daniela replied.

The detective answered every question Cougar and Daniela asked, unfortunately most of the answers were, "we don't know." And "we don't have that information yet".

As Cougar and Daniela left the police station and were descending the stairs, Daniela turned to Cougar, "I don't think they're going to find our art," she said disappointedly. Her cheeks raised slightly; her mouth widened in a pained frown. "They haven't uncovered anything, have they?"

"Are you willing to help me?" Cougar asked.

"Help you?" she asked. "With what?"

"Help me recover your national treasure."

"What can you and I do that the police in New York and Bogota aren't already doing?"

"You want the art back, right? And the FAIB wants your country to have the art back as well—very much in fact. And despite what Captain Moreno said in there, both our governments want the art to be found and returned."

"I know the Colombian government wants it back," she retorted.

"Then help me. I have some experience finding missing art."

"Like I stated earlier, I'm really not sure what the Fine Art Insurance Board's roll is. So, are you a detective?" Daniela questioned.

"Investigator."

"Well—I guess it couldn't hurt. We absolutely must get our artifacts back."

"Thank you, I appreciate your trust." As the cab drove them back to the museum, Cougar asked. "Can I stop by tomorrow and look through your archives? I will need as much information as you're able to give me on each missing piece. I have a team, through the insurance board, that can run this information through a system, verifying if there's been any recent activity related to any of the pieces."

"Yes, certainly, that would be wonderful. I can meet you anytime tomorrow, just let me know."

"Is 9am too early?"

"No, that should work fine, and thank you Arlan for wanting to help. I do feel a little better knowing someone else is here to help." Daniela rested her hand on Cougar's, then opened the taxi door. She dug in her purse.

"I got it—I'll see you tomorrow." The door shut, and the cab pulled away from the museum. Cougar pushed a number on his cell. The ringing stopped as the voice mail picked up. Cougar clicked off, then pressed another number. "Hi Mary, this is Cougar."

"Hello, I've been expecting your call, and no, I haven't been able to get ahold of her, it just goes to her voicemail. How are you doing in Colombia?"

"Good—making a little progress. It looks like I'll be staying in Bogota longer than I initially shared with you. Amelia probably doesn't have cell reception; but please keep trying."

"I will, you be careful."

Cougar opened the hotel room door, Kathy and Gerry were combing over some printed papers.

"Cougar, glad you're back, we have some information to share with you," Kathy said.

"What do you have?"

"We researched missing and stolen art over the last several years and came up with some very interesting information you'll want to see."

Kathy, Cougar, and Gerry combed through the information carefully. Cougar responded, "That is interesting, and very helpful to have before my meeting with him."

Historical Archives

Breakfast patrons occupied tables. Plates clattered behind me. A hurried busboy stacked plates into a tub, while a couple standing next to him, waited to be seated. I sat alone at a table next to a window, contemplating the splattering of information we had obtained so far and finishing my second cup of tea. I checked the time, less than an hour until my meeting with Daniela Perez at the museum.

"Excuse me, are you alone?" I glanced up; Detective Dias stood next to the table. "May I sit down?"

Not waiting for an answer, Detective Dias squeezed in opposite me. I pulled the table closer to me, giving her room. "Is this a coincidence Detective Dias, or are you following me?" I prodded.

"Pure coincidence, I promise," she said. "This is my morning routine, so you see, I could ask the same thing of you." The detective's cheeks scrunched as she smiled, exposing two prominent dimples I hadn't noticed yesterday. "And please call me Andrea, that detective Dias stuff is just for the office." She winked and displayed her dimples again.

"Coffee, Andrea?" the waitress said, turning over a bone china cup.

"Yes, thank you, Angie."

"More tea, sir?"

"No, thank you, and I'm done with this." I pushed my plate toward the waitress.

"You don't want these?" Andrea asked, stopping the waitress from grabbing the plate.

"No, I'm quite full," I replied. Andrea grabbed the two half pieces of whole wheat toast off my plate and handed the now empty plate to the waitress.

Andrea's eyes caught mine as she whispered. "I don't like wasting food." After rubbing jam on them, she made the two half-pieces disappear, then chased them down with hot coffee. "So, what have you found out so far?" she asked, dabbing her lips on a napkin.

"Not much, is there anything else you know that might be of help to the insurance board?"

"Ah, I see, this is just a one-way information flow thing, huh?" she said, emptying another sugar bag into her coffee cup.

"That's not what I'm saying. I really don't have any information that would help the police department—yet; but if I do, I will let you know."

"Good, because Captain Moreno can be a bit of a pain if he thinks insurance investigators are doing a better job than his police force. He gave me strict orders to keep an eye on you, and I plan to watch your every move."

The waitress sat down a plate of hash browns, sausage, two eggs—sunny-side-up, and a muffin in front of her.

"Can I expect the same courtesy if you uncover any new information?" I asked.

Andrea answered with her mouth full. "You have my word."

I waved the waitress over. "Can I get my check please?" After five long minutes the check arrived, with Andrea's meal on it as well.

Andrea looked up. "Thank you for breakfast."

"You're welcome." I paid, leaving Andrea sitting there, and walked the rest of the way to the museum.

"Nine o'clock on the nose," Daniela remarked. "You are a man of your word, aren't you?"

"Integrity is the highest honor bestowed a man. It either fits him like a well-tailored suit or hangs on him like a cheap garment," I replied.

"Hmm, quite eloquent, Arlan; you are an enigma." Daniela studied my face, this time like one of her museum artifacts. "Shall we go to the historical archives now?"

"Lead the way, Miss Perez." Daniela turned on her heels and started off down a hall I hadn't been in before. She glanced back a couple times, ensuring I was following. Her honey-colored legs climbed up to a business skirt which matched her vest. Daniela was slim and shapely. I also thought Daniela an enigma—or was it that I thought Mauricio the enigma? Daniela appeared genuinely interested in art, whereas Mauricio seemed more the business type than someone deeply moved by artistic expression. We descended a flight of stairs and entered a room through a large steel door.

"Here we are," she said. "I'm glad I didn't lose you along the way."

"Well, the good news is, when I get back to the hotel, I can reduce my treadmill work-out by 10 minutes." Daniela chuckled.

She rolled a ladder to a shelf and climbed four rungs up, grabbed a couple large books off the shelf, handed them down to me, and descended. She took the books, set them on a viewing table and opened one of them. Her index finger traced over the page. She shuffled through a few more pages, then stopped. "Here," she said. "This page describes the statues from the Ruins of San Agustin. Three of these were part of the traveling art show."

I thumbed through the pages and read about the historical ruins. "Wow, I had no idea there were so many statues. All made of rock?"

"Yes. Much of the area is still unexcavated. I think you would enjoy going to the sites and seeing some of the larger statues in person."

"It's a grave site, right?"

"Some of the area is, yes." Daniela returned with another book. She opened to a page about ceramic artifacts. A ceramic style vase was pictured on top of a display stand. She flipped to another section in the book where several gold artifacts were pictured.

"Now this looks like it could appeal to thieves. How much of this information is available online?" I asked.

"Maybe 10 percent. That is something I'd like to change some day; but all that takes time and I'm afraid that has been in scarce supply lately. I sit in for Mr. Lopez when he is not here."

"Is he gone a lot?"

"Yes, his job takes him all over the world. He has meetings with other museum curators on a regular basis."

"Do you travel much?"

"Some, I like being here mostly." Her eyes sparkled as she scanned the large room. Daniela and I spent another 45 minutes opening up books and reading through material.

"There is a lot of information here. I realize I'm asking you for a huge favor, but earlier you said something about copying this material for me. Is that too much to ask?

"Not at all."

"I'd like to take you to lunch as a way of thanking you, if that's okay with you of course." Daniela blushed. Suddenly we noticed Mauricio standing in the doorway.

"What's he doing in here?" Mauricio barked.

I quickly interrupted. "Daniela was good enough to help me with the detailed information I need on the artifacts that are missing. This information will help the FAIB, should any of the artifacts resurface."

"Mr. Jensen, what museums need are insurance companies that pay claims when there are losses, and in a timely manner. We want our art back, that's why the police are involved. Let them do the job of investigating. Captain Moreno said you've been busying yourself around there too. Donny Tallman is ready to move forward with the settlement, but he says Delrow must have the approval from the FAIB for a settlement of this size. Please, I don't mean to be curt with you; but the treasure is gone, and we have a business to run. The museum director is not the only one taking heat on this."

"I understand and I apologize if it seems I'm not working with the museum's best interest in mind. I have a meeting with Mr. Tallman tonight. I can't make you any promises about a speedy settlement; but I will see what I can do. The board insists on a thorough investigation, I'm sure you can understand that." I glanced over; Daniela shrunk in her chair.

"Daniela!" Mauricio called. "I need you in my office at noon please."

"Yes, Mr. Lopez."

Mauricio spun toward the open door; the sound of his footsteps faded down the hall.

"I'm afraid I'll have to take a raincheck on lunch, Arlan." Daniela said despondently.

"I understand. You believe I'm here to help, right?"

"I know you mean well, Arlan. I didn't know you had a meeting scheduled with Mr. Tallman tonight. I think once the claim is paid, our art will be lost forever."

"I'm trying to ensure that doesn't happen. Please, you need to trust me."

"Okay, but I could get in trouble and possibly lose my job if I don't do exactly what Mr. Lopez asks of me." Her eyes darted to the wall clock. "I have until noon, let's get this information copied for you and your assistant."

Chapter 13

He's Your Son

Miguel stepped into Gustano's office. "Gustano, we're ready to go—"

Gustano held up his hand. Miguel immediately stopped talking and stood at attention. Gustano slammed the phone down.

"That condescending, arrogant—"

"Honey, are you sure you don't want me to go with you?" Brigitte asked after stepping around Miguel and entering Gustano's office.

Gustano lifted his eyes to Brigitte. "You know I don't like being interrupted…and no…you stay here and watch over things until we get back…and how many times have I told you not to call me honey?" Brigitte didn't answer. "How many, Brigitte?"

"I'm sorry, Gustano, it's just that—"

He turned his glare from Brigitte. "Miguel, I will be there in a minute, tell Javier to get the engines started."

"Gustano," Brigitte said quietly. "I love you, and I know deep down you still care for me. I get the fact that you must be tough in front of the others, but sometimes your words really hurt me." Before Gustano responded, a young boy yelled and entered Gustano's office. He wore a holster and a cowboy vest, waving a toy gun around, shooting at imaginary bad guys.

"Keep him out of my office!" Gustano yelled, pounding on an old steel and laminate desk.

"Gustano! He's your son for crying out loud. He needs your attention." Brigitte demanded angerly.

"Keep him out of here. I got to go." Brigitte corralled their son and left Gustano's office.

"Javier, let's get this thing in the air." Miguel and Fabio closed the door of the freshly painted C-47. The plane taxied down the dirt runway. Javier stood on the left rudder pedal turning the large tail-wheeled plane 180-degrees. Miguel tightened his seatbelt and turned a couple knobs while slipping a headset over his ears and pointing out a gauge to Javier. Fabio and Gustano were seated behind them, just behind the bulkhead. The engines rumbled clamorously, the synchronization of the propellers made a "eyow-eyow" sound, and dust flew up around the plane as it bounced down the narrow dirt runway.

Javier pushed the control wheel forward, raising the tail. A moment later, the big blue airplane was airborne. "It's going to be a little bumpy," Javier yelled back. "I'll keep it low and stay in the clouds as much as possible."

"That's the plan, let me know the instant you see any planes on the radar," Gustano ordered, yelling up thought the aisle as he rechecked his pistol. Fabio had his head tilted forward, earphones on, and a cord dangling into an iPhone. His thumbs dropped bombs on towns and enemies, scoring points in the game he was playing.

An hour later, Gustano yelled up through the aisle way. "Miguel, how far out are we from Villavicencio?"

"About 50 miles."

Gustano turned to Fabio and yanked his earphones off. "Get ready, and remember we need to be quick; I don't want to stay any longer than necessary."

Coffee Shop

"Cougar, ten more minutes," said Kathy.

"Finishing up now, thank you." I tapped in a few more keys on the laptop. Then I tapped softly on my collar. "How do you hear me, Gerry?"

"Coming in loud and clear."

"Okay, let's see what kind of man Donald Tallman is." Donald Tallman was the agent from Delrow Insurance Agency Incorporated that wrote the policy, insuring the travelling Bogota artifacts.

"Good luck Cougar, I mean Arlan," Kathy said quietly.

"And you two as well. If you uncover anything that can't wait, let me know—and thank you guys."

"You're welcome—Mr. Polite," Kathy bantered as I shut the door.

I set off towards the coffee shop Donald Tallman had picked for our meeting place. As I walked, I thought about Kathy's comment about my manners. Her persistent ribbing about my manners is all in fun, and I don't mind. I can certainly think of worse ways to be teased. My parents taught me about character and politeness from as early as I can remember. Being polite is like breathing for me, and I thank God for the upbringing I had. If my parents were alive today, I would call them once more, just to thank them again for how they raised me. I miss them tremendously. Both my parents were killed in a horrific car accident while I attended college. The accident and losing both my parents instantaneously shook my world. Thankfully, the foundation they planted inside me provided the guidance that eventually helped me find my way back, becoming an even more optimistic and grateful person. Still, the pain of their loss continually stabs at my heart, and I know it has weakened my emotional stability.

I rounded the corner, spotting the Bogota Coffee Roaster. Stepping through the open door, the aroma of coffee impaled my nostrils. Warm colored wood transformed the stony world I just stepped from. A man in his 40s, stocky with bushy red hair and mustache, was seated at one of the tables, setting a china coffee cup onto its saucer. Another taller coffee cup sat next to an empty chair to the left of him. He glanced my direction. I stepped over and asked. "Are you Donald Tallman?"

"Call me Donny." He stood and shook my hand. At 6 foot 2, his eyes were just above mine. "You must be Arlan Jensen. I've been looking forward to meeting you, Arlan. I hope you don't mind…" As Donny spoke, Mauricio Lopez walked out of a door with the name Baño on it. "…I invited Mauricio to our meeting."

"Arlan, good to see you again," Mauricio said, sounding sincere as he finished drying his hands with a table napkin.

"Nice to see you as well," I replied.

"Now Arlan," Mauricio continued, "tell us what we need to do to get this process moving forward. Donny here is ready to proceed once he has the board's blessing."

"May I ask you a few questions, Donny?"

"Why of course." Donny's weak eyes darted back and forth between Mauricio and me.

"In the traveling art policy, did you write in an exclusion for mysterious disappearance?"

"No Arlan, the art is too valuable to Colombia for that, and Mauricio and the board insisted that the New York City Museum pay a premium to ensure there were no exclusions," Donny stated categorically.

"You see Mr. Jensen, it's all covered," Mauricio said abruptly. "Please don't misinterpret the museum's intent for a speedy settlement.

We want our treasure back, but our treasure is stolen, and without any leads…well," Mauricio lifted his hands in the air, "even Captain Moreno said the investigation has grown cold. Without those displays in our museum, clientele and donations will be down. I'm sure you understand what that means, the museum director certainly does."

"But the exhibit was to be on loan for quite a period. Wouldn't you have the same financial concern if it were on loan?"

"You see, Arlan, when art is loaned out, contributions materialize, like gifts, grants, donations, and endowments. When art goes missing, there are only bills."

"I see," I turned back to Donny. "Donny, how was the valuation of the assets determined?"

Mauricio interrupted again, "Donny and I, along with other museum members including Miss Perez used standard work-up sheets to determine each artifact's value."

"That's correct," Donny stated. "It was quite a laborious process. Jim Montoya fully concurred with our valuation and thus signed the policy in New York."

A teapot and a cup were set down in front of me. I poured the tea slowly into the cup while considering Donny and Mauricio's responses to the questions and their eagerness to get the board's approval. "Am I to understand Donny that you live here in Colombia? How is it you live in Colombia, yet represent Delrow Insurance Agency in the US?"

Donny jiggled his just-filled cup of coffee back onto its saucer without taking a sip. "My place here in Bogota is for vacations, kind of my summer home. My main residence is still in the States. After doing some work down here, I just had to buy a place. It is much too beautiful not to, am I not right?" Donny's eyes flickered as they moved to Mauricio who was draining another creamer into his cup.

"I see, and how long have you and Mauricio known each other?"

Mauricio cut in. "Mr. Jensen." Droplets of coffee and biscotti crumbs fell from his lower lip. "Enough of this questioning—you are not the *Policía*. Your job is to approve the settlement. Now if you'll excuse me, I have other business to attend to."

Mauricio drained his full cup of coffee in one fluid motion, then grabbed two unwrapped biscottis, laid down a few *dólares* and left.

Donny spoke first. "Sorry, Mauricio is just very upset about the theft. He didn't want to lend the art in the first place to New York; but the Bogota museum, as with most museums, are always looking for ways to bring in extra money. Some months don't attract enough visitors if you know what I mean."

"I can understand. One more question if I may. Did the policy include a buy-back clause?"

"I figured you had already studied the policy?" Donny asked.

I had studied the policy, but I wanted to hear Donny's answers. "Only parts, the full policy was sent to the board's office, and only recently emailed to me. Due to my flight and meeting schedules, I haven't been able to analyze in detail the entire policy; but I will. The board must ensure it meets both legal and procedural requirements."

"To answer your question, yes, it had a buy-back clause as well."

Kathy chimed in my ear, "Ask Donny what he thinks of Mauricio."

"What are thoughts of Mauricio, is he a good curator?"

"Mauricio? He's a giant in the museum business—knowledgeable, and very passionate about art and history. I respect him very much."

"And Jim Montoya?"

"Jim is a good curator, although he doesn't have the vision like Mauricio does."

"What vision?"

"Most curators are so consumed with art and history that they forget it's also a business. They leave too much on the director's shoulders and that's not right. Mauricio has big plans to make the Bogota museum a success at an international level, one of the top museums in the world. It takes money to find and bring in really great exhibits."

"And success being?"

"Revenue of course," Donny stated.

"Is that all Mauricio is after, revenue?"

"Certainly not! Like I stated, Mauricio is passionate about art and history, but one needs a stage in order to share it with the world."

I thanked Donny for the meeting and left. A large group of men spilled out onto the sidewalk from a neighboring bar. I pulled open the hotel room door. "Did you get all that, Gerry?"

Both Gerry and Kathy nodded. "Those are two odd characters if you ask me," Gerry stated.

"If you ask me, there's something strange about the way those two collaborate. I'm no expert on Colombia's social customs, but it seemed a little too congenial for an insurance agent-client relationship."

"My thoughts exactly," said Kathy.

"Kathy, can you try to verify Donny's comment about Mauricio not wanting to loan the art to New York? Either he did or didn't. Donny made it seem he had no choice. Let's pull up the museum's financial records and find out for ourselves just how healthy or unhealthy the museum is."

Chapter 15

Cerveza

Amelia sat at a table in a small bar in the middle of nowhere Mexico. The visit to the doctor's office where her dad, Ted Thomson had been treated for cancer a month earlier, provided no new information to help her understand what happened to her dad. She sat contemplating her next steps as a tear rolled down her cheek. In all her years, she never saw her dad make a mistake when flying. But now she was questioning everything—even her own beliefs. Maybe he did make a mistake, maybe he did crash and die as was reported by the Mexican and NTSB authorities.

"Excuse me," the heavyset waitress said, disrupting her thoughts. "The man at the bar sent this over for you." The waitress set a bottle of cerveza down, her large fingers leaving imprints on the bottle otherwise dotted with condensation. Amelia swept her vision from the beer to the bar. A lone middle-aged man gave a wink as Amelia asked the waitress to thank the man; but she wasn't drinking today. The waitress scratched at her hairline, shaking her head. She picked up the bottle of cerveza and returned to the bar, leaned over, and whispered to the man who had sent Amelia the drink.

Amelia breathed deep, purging the negative thoughts that were clouding her mind, recommitting herself to find out the truth about what happened to her dad. "Excusa me señora." The man from the bar had slithered over to her table. "¿No te gusta la cerveza, o simplemente no te gusto?"

"I don't understand, I'm sorry. I only speak English—no hablo in español."

"He wants to know if you don't like his beer… or if you just don't like him," a younger man asserted loudly, two tables behind her.

"Please, I just want to be left alone," said Amelia.

"Well, we can't let a pretty little senorita be left all alone in a small town like this. Bad things can happen. She needs an amigo to protect her." The younger man stood as he talked, inching himself over to her table and sitting down next to her. Stroking her platinum white hair, he said. "You must be some kinda angel." He sniffed at her hair. "Don't you think that's what she is Rodrigo, an angel?"

The middle-aged man who had been standing, pulled out the chair opposite Amelia and sat down. Amelia caught the waitress's attention. The waitress shook her head again and disappeared through a food-stained swinging door to the back kitchen. The bartender's eyes were fixed on wiping down glasses and neatly stacking them behind the bar.

"Where're you from? I say heaven, don't you agree, Rodrigo? ¿No es del cielo?"

"Ella es mía, la vi primero," Rodrigo replied.

"Simmer down. I think she might like us both." The young man slid his arm over Amelia's shoulder.

The waitress returned from the kitchen, standing next to the bartender. Amelia emptied her water glass on the young man's lap.

"You little—"

The tavern door opened with a jingle from the bell hanging above it. The town sheriff entered; his gaze skimmed 180-degrees before it returned to Amelia's table. He walked noisily over to the table, tilting his hat.

"Everything okay, señorita?"

Lucas, the younger man sitting next to Amelia said, "I need to get back to work, Angel." He edged his chair back, shaking the water off his pants, then tilted his head toward the sheriff.

"Rodrigo, don't you have some place you need to be?" The sheriff asked.

"Sí sheriff." Rodrigo ogled at Amelia, leaned over the table, and said, "Nos vemos más tarde" He raised his money in the air, then set it down on the bar and left.

"It can be dangerous here, señorita, are you by yourself?"

"Yes, sheriff. I appreciate what you did; but really, I can take care of myself."

"You are not the only señora who has told me such a thing. Such a pity. Well, if you find I can be of some help, don't hesitate to ask. I'm only a couple doors down." The sheriff tilted his hat at the waitress and left. Amelia signaled for the waitress.

"Thank you," Amelia said to her.

"For what?" The waitress gave Amelia a wink. "You would do well to go back from where you came, and the sooner the better."

"I'm leaving today; can I have the bill?"

The waitress shifted a couple plates onto her left arm, reached into her yellow apron pulling out a slip of paper, and placed it on the table in front of her. "Are you sure you don't want that cerveza now?" the waitress asked.

"I'm sure but thank you."

Amelia closed the taxi door. "To the airport, por favor."

The driver backed up, then sped off in the direction of the airport and her awaiting Yellow T-6 Texan WWII aircraft.

Twenty minutes later, the taxi dropped Amelia off in front of the derelict pilot office. "Muchas gracias," she said, turning toward the runway and the host of dilapidated planes, cars, and rusted appliances that littered it on every side. She stopped to use the bathroom before heading to her plane. Suddenly, while washing her hands under the trickling rusty water, the restroom door banged loudly against its feeble sliding lock. It startled her. She hadn't seen anyone else around.

"Just a minute, please," she said. Amelia opened the door. Lucas stood there blocking her way out. "Excuse me, please," she insisted.

"Like I tried to tell you—you need an amigo to protect you."

"If you don't move away from the door, it will be you who needs protection," Amelia said with as much intensity as she could.

"Well, aren't you tough. The sheriff isn't here to protect you this time."

Amelia kicked her leg as hard as she could into Lucas's groin. He bent over, grimacing in excruciating pain. Amelia stepped quickly to the side of him. He lifted up, caught her leg, and strained to pull her to the ground. His eyes met the barrel of Amelia's pistol.

"Are you sure you want to continue?" Amelia asked calmly.

Lucas dragged himself outside, leaned over the railing and retched several times. Amelia followed him, standing in the doorway with her gun pointed at him. He waved to an old pick-up truck. A metallic crunch sounded as Lucas opened the dented passenger door and jumped in. The truck kicked up dirt and rocks as it zigzagged down the dirt road.

Amelia walked toward her T-6—shaking uncontrollably. As she got closer, something wasn't right. The canopy wasn't closed all the way. She ran to her plane. Her flight gear duffle and clothes were gone, including her headset and iPad. She sat in the cockpit hunched over. Fingers held her head as tears trickled down her cheeks. She sat weeping and pounding at her thigh.

After letting her emotions run their course, her eyes swept up from the cockpit to the runway, and to the fields around the airport. She noticed a man plowing in the field with an ox, not far from the airport. She waved her hands at him, but he didn't return the wave. *Maybe he didn't see me.*

She jumped out of the airplane and ran toward the man. The vegetation was thick, and she lost sight of him. She slowed, pushing small limbs out of the way in front of her. She felt a bite on her leg. A large grotesque bug was latched onto her leg. She slapped at it twice, before finally killing it. A trail of blood ran down her leg, soaking into her sock and shoe. When she broke through the heavy underbrush, the farmer and ox were only thirty feet away.

"Excuse me? Excuse me?" Amelia yelled, carefully stepping over the rows of farmed green vegetation.

"Señorita, you shouldn't be out here in pantalones cortos. Venenosos bugs will make you sick."

"Señor, por favor. Someone has taken stuff from my yellow plane over there." Amelia gestured toward her plane. "Did you see anything?"

The man's eyes darted from her bleeding leg to an area behind the office building. Amelia followed his eyes while he nodded his head and pointed a finger.

"Gracias, señor," Amelia replied.

"Señorita, there is a trail." He pointed to a clearing.

"Gracias." She turned and headed off in the location the farmer revealed to her. Amelia's stomach rolled inside her. She wiped the sudden perspiration off her feverish head. Ignoring feelings of nausea, she searched the shrubs for her belongings. Something glittered to the right of her gaze. She pushed away the branches and found her duffle bag ensnared in the limbs. Below it, strewn about, were most of her flight gear. Her clothes were a little further down, tangled in thorn bushes.

It took Amelia close to an hour to gather up everything. Her iPad and handheld radio were the only two items not accounted for. She carried her stuff back to the plane, climbed up on weak and shaky legs, threw her gear in the pilot seat, then dropped to the ground and vomited. She made several trips to the office bathroom before lying under the wing and falling into a deep sleep.

Chapter 16

Sidney, Australia

Shirley Jones observed each piece of art on display with the precision of a gemologist. She was one of the top art historians in the world, and curator for the Art Center Museum of Los Angeles. The Australian auction drew in plenty of local and international buyers of fine art. One particular piece caught Shirley's attention while previewing the art before the auction. Not because she wanted to display it in her museum, but rather something about it looked familiar.

"Beautiful, isn't it?" said Susie. "I'm sure that one has a profound history." Susie worked for the auctioneering company and set up the preauction display.

"Do you have information on this piece?"

"I'm sorry, we don't have the pedigree on this one, it was a late entry."

"Do you know the name of who entered this piece?"

"Not off the top of my head—no. I should be able to get that information for you though." Susie put her hand on Shirley's. "Because there's no paperwork for this piece, I'm sure it will go for a very fair price."

"I'm sure you're right," Shirley replied as she continued down the row of art to be auctioned. Thirty minutes later as she sat in her seat, ready for the auction to begin, she suddenly realized where she had seen a picture of the rare pot on display.

North Tolu Beach, Colombia

The uniformed police officer stepped from his car. "Probably just another partier, skinny dipping at night after the park closed," he said to his partner as they headed for the beach.

"It's dreadful!" A young woman squealed at the officers, after waving them over.

"Where is the body, ma'am?"

She pointed to a gathering crowd. "My boyfriend's over there. We found it during our morning walk."

"You stay put, ma'am. What is your name?"

"Carine."

"Well Carine, you stay here, and we will get to the bottom of this. You're okay now."

The officers backed up the onlookers. "Looks like a shark attack."

"Or chopped up by a boat propeller," the second officer replied.

"My girlfriend and I found it while walking. It looks like a shark attack or something." The head, legs, and shoulders were intact, but the torso was mostly torn away.

"Please stay back. What time did you say you found the body?"

"It was shortly after the park opened, about 9:30."

"Thank you. If you wouldn't mind, I'd like you to stick around for a bit."

"Of course. My girlfriend's not doing so good though."

"We'll get her some help, too." The officer pressed a button on his radio. "…here at North Tolu Park and have what looks to be a male body…badly torn up…with most of the torso missing. Can you send a medical examiner and a backup unit…no, I'm not sure we're at that point yet…no…once the report's back from the M.E., the captain can make that call."

"Beach closure?"

"Yeah, but I think it's a little premature."

"Not much left for the medical examiner."

"Dental records—should be able to find out who it is at least."

Bad News

"**G**ood morning, Cougar," said Gerry, pouring a packet of coffee into a hotel coffee maker. "You're up early, did my snoring wake you?"

"No…I couldn't shut my brain off, so I went for a walk. Then I spent some time in the room upstairs trying to pull the limited information we have into something tangible—something we can move forward on. By the way, I don't think we'll be needing the upstairs room any longer."

"Well, what did you come up with?"

"Unfortunately, not much. We all agree that there's something fishy about the way Mauricio and Donny interacted and their close ties with each other, right?"

"Right."

"Maybe it has nothing to do with the art's disappearance, but I'm pretty sure there's something there, I just can't put my finger on what it is." My cell chirped. "It's Kathy. Good morning."

"Good morning, Cougar. Riley just sent me a text. He wants to meet with us in ten minutes. Can you two pop over?"

"I can, but Gerry will need to put a pair of pants on first. Sleepy head just woke up."

Gerry shouted from the bathroom. "I've been up for fifteen minutes, don't listen to him."

"We will be over in five." I clicked off, then tapped in Mary's number.

"Asset investigation and recovery service, Mary speaking."

"Mary, Cougar here."

"I figured it was you. I just wanted you to hear my new professional introduction."

"It sounds top-notch, Mary. Any new clients clamoring for our service?"

"The phone has been silent since we talked last."

"I was afraid of that."

"I know what you're thinking…I'm sorry. You're worried about Amelia; I am, too. Is there anything I can do to help?"

"I wish there were. The timing of this investigation isn't the best."

"Which one, Amelia's or the Trinity mission?"

"Either. I can only be at one place at a time, which reminds me, can you call Sarah Jozel and see how Derby's doing? Please tell him his dad misses him."

"Well, I'm not fluent in speaking canine, but I'll do my best."

"Thank you, Mary. I'll give you a call later, I need to hop off for a meeting."

"Be careful, Cougar." Mary clicked off.

"Gerry, are you—"

"Let's go, we don't want to be late." Gerry emerged from the bathroom with his hair slicked back. A waft of after-shave assaulted my olfactory system as he stepped past me.

"Looking good, Gerry." A couple minutes later Kathy's computer rang. She sat down, typed in a few staccato strokes, and up popped Riley on the screen.

"Good morning, Riley," we all said in unison.

"Good morning, team, thank you for gathering so quickly. I have a few pieces of information for you. Cougar, we received some information over our surveillance system based on the details you gave Kathy about the missing art. A lady by the name of Shirley Jones, and no, not that one, was at an auction in Australia yesterday. She became suspicious about an artifact she believes might be part of the Colombian art collection that was to be displayed in New York City."

"Has the piece been verified?" I asked.

"Not yet, but Shirley Jones is a top curator and historian from the US. She knows her stuff. She's out of the Art Center Museum in Los Angeles."

"What piece did she find at the auction?" Kathy asked curiously.

"I'm having David send you that information now." David Subbarao is Trinity's lead computing genius. Young and intelligent, David knows his way around the cyber world. Scuffling sounds came over the speaker.

"Kathy, you should see it about—now," said David.

Kathy's computer dinged, showing an incoming encrypted email.

"Well, if that's true," I added, "that means the collection is already being broken up and peddled through the black market."

"I'm afraid so," Riley admitted rather despondently. "Cougar, I have more bad news for you. Your client Amelia?"

"Yes?"

"The body of her fathers' co-pilot was found washed up on a Colombian beach. Some objects believed to be from the airplane were also found not far from the body."

My heart sank. "Wait, did you say a Colombian beach?"

"Yes."

"That makes no sense. That's a long way for a body to travel if it crashed flying from Mexico to Texas."

"I can look up the currents for you Cougar—for that time period," said David Subbarao.

"Thank you, David. I appreciate that. I'll eventually need that information."

"Anything else?" Kathy asked.

"That's it for now. Cougar, I suggest you pay Shirley a visit. She'll be back in Los Angeles tomorrow."

"Thank you, sir, that sounds like a good plan. That will also give me a chance to ask a few museum questions to someone other than Mauricio, Donny, or Jim Montoya." Riley clicked off. Kathy, Gerry, and I, spun our chairs around, facing each other. "Something's been gnawing at me."

"Out with it, Cougar. Is it me?" Gerry jested.

I patted Gerry on the back. "It would never be you, brother. No, it's about the shipping arrangements of the art. Mauricio and Jim Montoya both said the crates containing the art were anywhere from 500 to 5000 pounds each."

"Yes?" Kathy said.

"You said the art was shipped on a Boeing 737-300 freight airliner, right? If my memory serves me correctly, the maximum payload for one of those is around 60 thousand pounds. If the crates were all at 5 thousand pounds, that would total 60 thousand pounds."

"Yes, but not all of them weighed 5 thousand pounds, according to the documentation you gave us from the New York museum," said Gerry.

"True; but the payload of 60 thousand pounds includes fuel. A 737 flying from Bogota to the US would need at least half their payload in fuel—even with stops."

"So, you're thinking some of the art never left Bogota?" Kathy asked.

"That's what I've been pondering about all morning long."

"Remember what you said about Riley's hunch? If some of the art never shipped to New York, it could still be here?"

"You know the term *Ghost Assets*, right?" Cougar added.

"Vaguely," Gerry said.

"Ghost asset is a term used in business when assets show up on accounting ledgers, but for one reason or another, the asset isn't physically there. It might be lost, scrapped, stolen, or sometimes, was never there to begin with."

"Of course," Gerry and Kathy both replied in unison.

"But wait," Kathy said. "The art was verified in New York.

"Yes, but I believe it was verified by Donny, Mauricio, and Jim Montoya…and maybe a few others that could be working for them. I still need to confirm who was actually there."

"I think you may have hit your head during your morning walk. You're implying they're all art smugglers? The curators from two of the top museums in the world—art smugglers? That's an interesting theory, Cougar. Maybe you need another cup of that green tea you incessantly drink," Gerry quipped.

"I know it sounds a little farfetched. Kathy, would you do me a favor and check the airline manifest for the weight of the crates that were flown to New York City? See if you can get a copy of the official weight and balance from the airline. Also see if you can get the freight forwarder's weight invoice. I need to get in touch with Amelia, and then see if Daniela is willing to make a trip to Los Angeles with me to verify the alleged Colombian artifact."

"I'm truly sorry about Amelia's dad, Cougar," said Gerry.

"They haven't found her dad yet. There's still hope, Cougar," Kathy stated.

"I hope you're right, Kathy, but it's not looking good. I'm pretty sure Amelia's father's plane was hijacked in Mexico. Most likely Ted and his co-pilot were killed, and their bodies dumped into the sea." My phone chirped. "It's David Subbarao. Yes David…uh huh…all month long? Okay, thank you very much…No, I appreciate the information…I know, thank you."

"Well?"

"If the plane crashed between the Mexican airport and Texas, the body would never have made it to Colombia that fast. David thinks the body must have entered the sea closer to where they found the body in Colombia."

"I guess your theory is sounding more plausible. Either way, it doesn't sound like it will bring Amelia any more comfort," said Gerry. Kathy walked over and reached her arm around me.

"We're here if you need us on this one, too," said Kathy.

"Thank you, guys." I walked out of Kathy's hotel room. This part of the job was never easy. I paced the hall for a few minutes before opening up the door to Gerry's and my room. As I sat down on the bed, I stared out the window and watched subtle movements from people in buildings across the street, going about their normal lives; vehicles, bikes, and pedestrians, weaving a tapestry below me.

I keyed in Amelia's number. After a few seconds, the phone rang. It rang six times before her voicemail picked up. I delivered the message about the co-pilot's body, then added a sympathetic ending which I felt came off sounding trite and meaningless. I should've been there to deliver the message personally. I still remember the phone call I received like it was yesterday, telling me of my parent's tragic car crash. I had been summoned out of class by a college counselor. I was then handed the phone. On the other end—the State Patrol. In a very matter-of-fact manner, I heard both my parents were killed. No, 'I'm sorry sir'—no preparation—just the facts, laid out until I understood.

I breathed in slowly several times, then let the air out just as slow, and with it the tension I was carrying in my neck and shoulders. I raised my phone, the face of it lit up as I dialed in the number Daniela gave me.

"Hello?"

"Good morning, Daniela, this is Arlan Jensen."

"What a nice surprise. How did your meeting go with the insurance agent last night?"

"You mean the insurance agent and your boss."

"Mr. Lopez?"

"Yes, it seems he invited himself or Donny, the insurance agent invited him. I wasn't exactly clear on who invited who. At any rate, the meeting went fine, and I didn't give Donny the approval from the board."

"Thank you, Arlan."

"I have some other news for you, if you haven't already heard."

"Heard what?"

"We think a piece of your museum's collection was auctioned off in Australia."

"Oh, no! I hadn't heard that. Why haven't the police contacted us?"

"Well, we aren't sure of its authenticity. It was bought by a museum in Los Angeles. I'm calling to see if you would like to accompany me to Los Angeles to verify its authenticity?"

"I would like that very much, but I would need Mr. Lopez's approval first."

"Have you seen him today?"

"No, but I've only been here for thirty minutes. When I walked past his office, the door was closed, and the lights were off."

"Daniela, I have a hunch, will you play along?"

"Of course, Arlan, I already told you I'll do whatever it takes to get the art back."

"Thank you. When Mauricio shows up to his office, can you inquire about how the investigation is going concerning the missing art? If he doesn't mention the artifact that was at the auction, ether he doesn't know about it yet, or he doesn't want you to know. If he doesn't say anything about it, just go about your business. If he does, ask him if you can go verify that it is indeed from your collection. Once you have that conversation, please call me back."

"Okay, I can do that."

"If he doesn't say anything about it, which I don't think he will, after lunch, tell him you're feeling ill and go home."

"Okay, I think I got it. I'm a little nervous, this is way out of my comfort zone."

"You'll do fine, I'll be here waiting for your call."

Chapter 19

Mexican Clinic

Amelia woke up confused. Memories crashed at her like ocean waves hitting a beach, the bug bite, the sickness, the attack by the men from the bar, and her lost equipment. She crawled out from under the wing of the T-6 and scanned the airport. The missing pieces of equipment will make navigating and communicating more difficult, but not impossible. She was just glad to have found most everything else.

Steadying herself against the wing, she got to her feet and brushed herself off. Her stomach turned inside. Step-by-step she found her way to the airport office, dialed the number for the taxi, then made her way back to the airplane and collected her stuff. This time, she would take it all with her.

The taxi showed up thirty minutes later. "Hi, can you…take me…to the…d-o-c-t-o-r."

"Médico?"

"Sí, gracias."

The taxi sped down the dirt road to the airport exit and onto a paved road. Amelia sat back, holding her stomach. The bite on her leg was black and puffy. Bouts of nausea and light-headedness broke over her in waves. Her consciousness ebbed and flowed. She heard the driver talking to her; but couldn't understand what he was saying. When she awoke, she was in a hospital bed. A fading sunset illuminated the rooms curtains.

A nurse, walking in to check Amelia's vitals, noticed she was awake. "How are you feeling, dear?"

Groggily, Amelia replied. "You speak English?"

"Yes, dear, now how are you feeling?"

"Better." Amelia took a few seconds and looked over her body. "Yes, much better."

"You were lucky you got here when you did, you know. You have a nasty bite on your leg. A few more hours and…well, we may not have been able to save it."

The nurse's words sluggishly wedged themselves into Amelia's consciousness. She had no idea the bug bite was that lethal. Amelia pulled herself upright using the bars on the hospital bed and flung the blanket off her leg. Wrappings covered the area where the bug had bitten, but there was a leg—her leg.

"When will I be able to leave?" she asked.

"When the swelling goes down, maybe as early as tomorrow," the nurse replied.

Amelia's right leg was visibly larger than her left one. She moved her toes, then her foot from side to side.

"You get some rest, dear," the nurse said.

"Excuse me, I had a bag with me."

"Right in here." The nurse patted a veneer covered cabinet door.

"May I have my phone, please?"

"Of course; but don't stay up too long—get some rest." The nurse handed Amelia her phone.

Amelia turned the phone on and waited. After a minute, the reception bars showed good levels of reception. Her phone buzzed, showing there was a voice mail from Cougar. After listening to the message, she dropped the phone to her side. A wave of nausea flooded back over her as she heard John Burrow's body had washed up on a shore in Colombia, and still no signs of her father. Her hopes of finding her dad alive were vanishing like a contrail in the sky. Maybe it was time to stop searching and return home; but how? How would she manage to keep the aircraft museum open without her dad? There were no answers to her question, all she knew was somehow she had too.

She held up her phone and pushed redial. The phone rang, then clicked. "Cougar?"

"Amelia, are you okay? I have been worried about you."

"You have?"

"Of course, where are you?"

"I'm in a clinic in Mexico. I got bit by a really nasty bug. Note to self, don't wear shorts if you walk through the underbrush here."

"Are you okay? What did the doctor say?"

"I'll be okay, although my leg resembles a ripe plum more than the leg of a drill team captain."

"Huh?"

"Long story—bottom line is I'll be wearing long pants to any dances I get invited to around here."

"Well, I'm glad nothing worse happened. Did you get my message?"

"I'm afraid I did. I felt my dad's loss all over again, and I feel terrible about John."

"Amelia, remember what I told you about my suspicion, and the clues I shared with you?"

"Yes, what are you saying? Doesn't John's body washing up mean the plane went down as they alleged?"

"I don't think so. I believe it supports my conjecture. You see, if your dad's plane crashed between the Mexican clinic and Texas, John's body would never have washed up in Colombia. The currents couldn't have carried his body there, and certainly not that fast. No, I believe your dad's plane was hijacked."

"And my dad?"

"Unfortunately," Cougar paused, "he is most likely dead, too. If the plane was captured for drug running, that is normally the way it plays out. I'm very sorry Amelia."

"What if my dad is being held hostage in Colombia? Maybe they're using him as a pilot?"

"It's possible, but not likely. If that were the case, they probably would have kept the co-pilot alive, too."

"I need to be sure, Cougar. Are you able to help me yet?"

"I'm afraid not. I'm still involved with my other priority."

"Then I will fly to Colombia myself."

"Amelia, where would you look, it makes no sense. You are lucky nothing worse happened to you, please don't push your luck. Go back to Texas, and as soon as I'm done with this current activity, I'll help you—I promise. Or you could find another private investigator to help."

"I need you, Cougar, but I can do it alone if I have to. I will go to every airport and search for my dad's plane."

Cougar desperately wanted to tell her that he was already in Colombia; but he couldn't jeopardize his current mission. "Amelia, if you insist on going to Colombia, I'll find a way to meet you there; but I can only meet you for a few hours. I can't search for your dad or his plane right now; but I can help. I will put together a search and rescue grid-pattern for you to use. Let's meet in Bogota, they have a good airport there."

"Thank you. I'll take whatever help and time you can spare for me. I should be able to leave here tomorrow. I will make my way down there and call you once I'm in Bogota."

"Okay, be careful. It will take me a couple days to get there myself, so don't push yourself." Cougar ended the call. *Amelia is a stubborn and determined person*, he said to himself, *just like me*. Deep down he admired her for that. His phone rang again. "Hello?"

"Arlan, this is Daniela, can you talk?"

"Yes."

Art Center Museum of Los Angeles

As our plane touched down in Los Angeles, California, I glanced over at Daniela. She sat quietly staring out the window. Her countenance provided a calming effect, and her extreme beauty wasn't lost in my rather quick glance either.

"I think it's our turn," she said, pointing to the opening in the jet's aisleway.

I grabbed our carry-ons and thanked the man holding back the pressing passengers until Daniela and I made it into the aisle. I watched her calves rhythmically advance up the gateway and into the terminal. A sign pointed to hotel shuttles and taxis.

"Good evening." I placed my ID on the hotel's front desk counter.

"Checking in…Mr. and Mrs. Jensen?"

Daniela stepped to the desk, "No, we aren't married, I have my own room reserved." Daniela's cheeks reddened as she backed away slightly.

"And your name is?" Daniela placed her ID on the counter. "Miss Perez…there you are." The agent stared at the computer screen and worked her keyboard. "Okay, Mr. Jensen, you are in room 424 and you Miss Perez are on the same floor, room 408."

"Thank you." I picked up the bags and headed to the elevator.

"I'm sorry, I didn't mean for it to come off sounding like being married to you was a bad thing," she said. The elevator jerked us skyward.

"I understand—no worries. I hold pretty traditional values as well, in fact, some might even call me old-fashioned and backwards."

"I call it a breath of fresh air. I wish more men treated women with the respect and dignity you have shown me." Daniela covered a yawn with her hand. I glanced at my watch.

"Let's meet in the morning at the elevator. We can go for breakfast and then I can show you around town. Our meeting with Shirley is not until 6pm. Can you be ready by nine?"

"Nine sounds great. Daniela gabbed my hand and gave it a squeeze. "Thank you again, I'm not sure what to expect tomorrow night, but being with you gives me hope."

"There's always hope," I countered. Once again, my words seemed shallow and empty to me, like an automaton. Daniela slid the card key in her door as I walked further down the hall.

My room was indistinguishable from 50 others I've stayed in. I set the suitcase down, pulled out my phone and pushed call. The phone rang twice before Kathy picked up.

"Cougar, I see you made it there okay."

"Watching my card transactions again?"

"A girl needs to stay informed you know."

"So I'm to understand." I heard Kathy snicker through the line. "Were you able to find out anything more on the manifest and weights?"

"Yes, we did," Gerry yelled from a distance. The voice grew louder. "As a matter of fact, I just got back a few hours ago…talked with the airline and the freight forwarder."

"And?"

"Well, there's a mismatch, but not by much."

"How much?"

"A hundred pounds is all. Sorry, Cougar, I know you thought you were on to something there."

"Thanks, Gerry—a hundred pounds could just be tare weight or scale error. What was the total weight?"

"Thirty-eight thousand pounds."

"Hmm, also in line. That would place each crate at just over 3000 pounds; some being heavier, some being lighter."

"Anything else you want us to check on?" Kathy asked.

"Keep a look out for any more stolen art. And Gerry, can you track Mauricio and Donny's movement?"

"I'll try to tie into Bogota's street camera system, internet and cell transmissions."

"I've linked into the museum server; but nothing unusual has shown up," Kathy replied.

"Thank you both, I'll let you know how it goes here. We should be back on the plane tomorrow night."

"Good luck, Cougar."

"Thank you."

Daniela stood next to the elevator, reading a brochure. "First time I've seen you in pants," I said.

She laughed. "I wear pants a lot, just not when I'm working." Her face blushed as she followed my eyes.

Thankfully, before embarrassing myself any further, the elevator door opened. After breakfast, sightseeing and lunch, we returned to our hotel rooms for a short rest before meeting back at the elevators.

Daniela was already standing there, gazing through a window at the steel, glass, and concrete landscape below. She wore midnight-blue jeans and a camel colored knitted top. The jeans confirmed her gentle curves and slim waist. She turned as I stepped to the elevators, her eyes scrutinizing my attire. "Well, you clean up nice," she said.

"And you look stunning." I raised my arm, "After you, Daniela."

We caught a taxi outside the hotel and pointed the driver to the Art Center Museum. The inside of the taxi was narrow, and Daniela edged closer. The smell of her perfume, hypnotic.

"Don't you find it strange that Mr. Lopez doesn't know about the Colombian artifact auctioned off in Australia?" she asked.

"Doesn't know or didn't tell you he knows? Besides, we don't know for sure if this piece is actually part the stolen collection."

"We should be able to confirm that very soon," she replied.

We stepped out of the cab and watched it pull away. I grabbed Daniela's hand, walked into the museum and up to the information counter. As we waited for Shirley, we pointed and commented on the architecture and features along the ceiling. An elderly lady with short hair stepped over to us.

"Arlan Jensen?"

"Yes, and you must be Shirley Jones. This is Daniela Perez from the museum in Bogota."

"I didn't think anyone was coming from Bogota's museum," she retorted.

Shirley wore bleach-blond hair with spiked tuffs in all directions. Her outfit was much hipper than her age revealed, despite attempts at youth-giving surgeries. "Yes, I was fortunate enough to talk Miss Perez into accompanying me so we could verify the artifact's authenticity."

"I see, well, Mr. Jensen, I did some background checks on you, and you have quite a resume of art history." Thank goodness David Subbarao uploaded enough relevant information to substantiate my cover as a Fine Arts Insurance Board member.

"Why thank you Mrs. Jones."

"Call me Shirley."

"Thank you, Shirley. And I did a little research on you as well, and may I say, very impressive. It appears you are one of an elite group of curators that have traveled the world and worked on nearly every continent."

"You have done your research, that information is not easily unearthed." Shirley lifted her eyebrows, raising her Botoxed forehead, allowing her eyes to study me carefully. "Follow me, if you will, I'll show you the piece from the auction. I'm sure, Miss Perez, that you will find it to be genuine."

"Please, call me Daniela."

Shirley led us through a large ornate gallery with thirty or more pictures hanging on the wall. Additional artifacts were under glass and in display cases, peppering the floors, making a straight path nearly impossible. This particular gallery held conceptual paintings much too enlightening for my taste. Art enthusiasts, staring at the work, seemed much more appreciative. We passed through the gallery and several others similar to it, before Shirley opened a door using a magnetic card, leading to a large room resembling a small warehouse.

"I have it over here," she said as her hips brushed bubble wrap off a table and onto the floor. Daniela picked up the bubble wrap, set it back on the table and looked over at me with animated eyes. The room was cool, about sixty degrees. Every ten feet, cold air blew at me from the ceiling. Shirley stopped at a table. There were a few things on the table, but none of them looked like a ceramic pot. Her head swept back and forth.

"Is there something wrong?" I asked.

"I'm not sure. Just a minute." Shirley stepped over to the wall, tapped in a number and held the phone to her ear. Daniela's forehead scowled.

"I'm sure it's nothing," she said. I wasn't so sure. Shirley holstered the phone and stepped back over to us.

"I don't understand. The pot was sitting right here less than an hour ago. Nobody's been in here."

"Are these surveillance cameras operating?"

"Yes, but security never saw anyone in here."

"And it didn't get moved or placed somewhere else?" Daniela asked.

"No, dear, I'm afraid not. Like I stated, I was in here not more than an hour ago."

"May I see the security tape?"

"Of course. I can show you up to security."

"Thank you." We followed Shirley up several staircases to a landing with an elevator door. After a short ride, Shirley punched in a number and the door opened to a room of monitors and two security guards.

"Burdock, this is Arlan Jensen from the Fine Arts Insurance Board. Can you show him the footage from storage room B?" Burdock took me over to a terminal, tapped in numbers and pointed to a screen. Shirley and Daniela stepped to the side to discuss features of the ceramic pot purchased at the auction.

The video showed the room with a pot visible at the same table Shirley led us to. One minute the pot was there, the next frame, it wasn't. "Daniela," I said. She excused herself and stepped over to the screen with Shirley following close behind. "Does this look like the ceramic pot from Colombia?"

Daniela studied the screen. "It's hard to tell from this video, but with everything Shirley has shared, I believe it is authentic. Of course, I can't know for sure without seeing it and holding it—look?" Daniela exclaimed. "The pot just disappeared?"

"Yes, it appears someone tampered with the security system, allowing the removal of the pot without being noticed."

"I will call the police," Shirley said.

"Yes, that's a good idea, although I'm not sure they'll find much. Evidently someone didn't want this pot to resurface."

"I don't understand," Shirley said.

"I'm not sure I do either," said Daniela.

"Is there some place we can talk?"

"There is. Are you two hungry?" Daniela and I shared a look. "I want you to know I feel just awful. You two have travelled all this way and I don't have the Colombian artifact."

"It's not your fault, Shirley. It could have been worse. Nobody's hurt, right?"

"I guess you're right, come. Burdock will call the police and file the report. I'll talk to them after we're done. There's a table in our beautiful restaurant where we can talk. I'm sure you two are hungry. It's the least I can do after having traveled all this way."

"Thank you," Daniela replied.

"Yes, thank you, Shirley."

In the elevator, Daniela asked. "Was the ceramic pot the only piece at the auction you think could have been from the missing Colombian art display?"

"Yes, but I can't be sure. I'm not as familiar with the collection as you are." Shirley shifted her weight, her eyes glistened as she watched Daniela's. "You know, you remind me a lot of myself when I was first starting out in my career. I can see your love for art—and concern in your expression. It's not unusual for art to show up soon after a burglary, you know."

"How do you mean?" I asked.

"Unfortunately, in this business and for as many years as I have been doing this, I've run into this sort of thing more often than I care to admit."

I listened carefully, still not understanding what Shirley was driving at.

"Art has a way of turning up in different locations, periods of time, and in different hands. It's been that way since the dawn of time. Wars befell to acquire art. A king or a country's art was plundered after a victory. Taking one's art was not only enormously lucrative, it removed the very sole from the party who lost it."

Daniela said, "That's exactly how I feel. Is that why you think the art was stolen?"

Shirley shook her head, "I really don't know, dear. It seems these days are not much different from those of old, greed. Since this piece, which I think you would agree probably was authentic," Daniela nodded her head, "made it to market so soon, I would guess it falls more into the greed category. Many times, after a heist, we don't see art resurface for years and sometimes decades. Some art is never seen again. The fact that this particular piece has been stolen twice in only a month is quite unusual."

The elevator chimed, and the doors opened to a posh restaurant with a view overlooking the museum grounds.

"They have the most amazing food here, I promise you. Chef Sato is extraordinary, and I must say, he's an artist in his culinary field." Daniela walked toward the hostess table.

Shirley turned to me. "I really am sorry about this."

"Please, don't be. I am sorry, too. Daniela really had her hopes up."

"If you don't mind me asking," Shirley said, "what is your relationship with Miss Perez?"

"Daniela? Just business," I replied.

Shirley kept her eyes on me. "Are you sure? In a few areas I'm a bit of an expert—art being only one of them. In the short time since you two have been here, I can tell Daniela is very fond of you. I don't see a ring on your hand. If you're single, you may want to think outside the proverbial business box. She seems to be a very sweet, intelligent, and attractive young lady, wouldn't you agree?"

I felt my face reddening as I replied, wondering why I continually ignore and dismiss such signals. Shirley and I caught up to Daniela as the hostess led us to a table overlooking beautifully landscaped grounds, with flowers of every shade, and the greenest grass I can remember. Daniela shared more about the missing Colombian treasure with Shirley and I gathered more information about the Australian auction, LA's security personnel and security system, and other art and museum information.

Chapter 21

Verrugosa

Daniela closed the taxi door and headed for the elevator to her apartment. Although being extremely tired, she wanted to shower before heading to bed. The hot water felt good running down her fatigued body. She thought about Arlan. Even if the trip to LA didn't turn out the way she had hoped, she was grateful he included her. She couldn't explain her feelings, but something inside her wanted to know him more. *Maybe he's the right man for me*, she thought, then quickly reminded herself that he doesn't live in Colombia, and long distant relationships never work.

She wrapped the towel around her hair. Through the open door, something caught her eye, near the foot of her bed. She took another towel and wrapped it around her body and stepped out of the bathroom into her bedroom. She didn't see anything unusual. She looked under her bed; nothing was there. She stood, then immediately froze. Sweat erupted on her forehead. A large snake coiled behind her. Without thinking, she threw her towel towards the snake and leaped onto the bed. The snake uncoiled as she did, pushing the towel towards her like a ghost. The first strike missed her only by inches.

She screamed for help, while watching the snake slither out of the towel and around to the foot of the bed. Moments later there was a knock on her door. She yelled. "Hay una serpiente en mi habitación, ayuda" There was no answer. She heard footsteps fade down the hall, then a door close. Her gaze shifted to her cell phone on the charger. The snake lifted its head, searching for her. It slithered up the side of the bed.

Daniela threw the second towel from her hair towards the snake, jumped off the bed and ran to her phone. Grabbing it, she slid into the bathroom and closed the door behind her. While her chest hammered and grappled for air, she stuffed hand towels in the opening at the bottom, and dialed Arlan's number.

"Daniela, I thought you'd be asleep by now?"

"Arlan, help! There's a snake in my apartment."

"A what?"

"A snake! A really big snake. I've locked myself in the bathroom—it's in the bedroom."

"What's your apartment number…got it. You're not that far from my hotel, I'll be right over—and Daniela?"

"Ye-ssss?"

"Don't move, I'll be there in ten minutes." Cougar quickly changed back into his clothes. From the adjacent bed, Gerry lifted his head off the pillow.

"Everything okay?"

"There's a snake in Daniela's apartment."

"Do you need me to go with you?"

"No, but I may need you to run some information once I see what kind it is."

"You think it was planted there?" Gerry asked.

"Not sure—I'll call you in a few minutes." Cougar ran out the door, down the stairwell and out onto the sidewalk. The streets were starting to come to life. Cougar yelled for the attention of a taxi too late. He watched it drive past him then down the road. He turned back, noticing another one parked a block up. Waving his hands and running toward it, the taxi moved from its spot toward him.

"Calle 66 por favor," he said getting in. Más rápido, por favor." The driver accelerated down the road.

"Hey!" Cougar pointed to the approaching apartment building. The driver stopped at the curb. Cougar ran in and found a staircase up to Daniela's floor. Her door was locked. Using a magnetic translator, he unlocked her door, pulled out his M&P pistol, and inched the door open.

"Daniela, I'm here. Stay put."

From the bathroom he heard Daniela yell, "I have to."

With his head on a swivel, searching for the snake, he stepped carefully into the apartment and over to the bedroom door. As he pushed open the door, a large reptile was positioned halfway up the wall, in the corner of the room.

"Stay there," Cougar said, searching for a suitable object. On the floor was a yoga mat and a set of dumbbells. He grabbed the dumbbells. The large snake had spotted him and was now slithering over to him. Cougar jumped at it, quickly backing off. The snake instantly recoiled. Cougar teased it once more, the snake snapped at him, uncoiling. Cougar threw one of the dumbbells.

The weight missed, making a loud thud on the floor. Cougar grabbed the cover off the bed and threw it over the snake. Where the head was, he threw the other weight. He picked up the weight and threw it down several more times until there was no more movement under the blanket. Carefully, he slid the blanket back. The snake's head was crushed, its lower jaw skewed to one side, and its tail—still moving but harmless. Cougar snapped a picture of it with his phone, all eight feet of it, and sent it off to Gerry.

Cougar stepped over to the bathroom door and grabbed the handle. "You can come out now, it's safe."

"No, I can't!" Daniela pleaded.

"The snake's dead." There was a long silence.

"I don't have any clothes on, and my robe and remaining towels are in the laundry basket out there. I had just finished taking a shower when I saw the snake. Would you please grab me something to wear? In my dresser, the second drawer down, I have sweatpants and tops."

Cougar found a matching set and knocked on the door. An arm extended, snatching the clothes, and pulling them inside. A minute later, she appeared from behind the door. Her hair, mostly dry, was frizzed and wavy. She carefully stepped over toward Cougar, grabbing him, and examining the dead snake. "Is it really dead?" she asked.

"Yes, sorry about your blanket, it's a little bloody."

"Blankets can be replaced," she said. "Why is it still moving?" Still holding onto Cougar, her eyes tracked from the snake, then up Cougar's shirt until they rested on his blue eyes.

Cougar's phone buzzed. "Excuse me for just a second. Yes Gerry…uh huh…yes…thought as much. Can you also ask David to find out what area it comes from? That might help us narrow down the guilty party."

"Guilty party?" Daniela asked, confused.

"I'll talk to you later, Gerry." Cougar stashed his phone.

Daniela's body trembled. Tears moistened Cougar's shirt as he pulled her in close. "That's the biggest snake I've ever seen. If I were sleeping it would have killed me, huh?"

Cougar held her tight. Her convulsing eased. "Yes, that's a very dangerous snake." He said, noticing that its thrashing had stopped.

"Wha…What kind is it?"

"That was the phone call. I sent a picture of it to a friend. It's a South American Bushmaster. I guess the proper name is Lachesis Muta, known in Colombia as a Verrugosa."

"I've heard of Verrugosa," she said. "Very poisonous."

"Not this one, not anymore anyway." Cougar stated.

"I heard you say, 'guilty party'. You think somebody planted this snake in my apartment—why?"

"Did you tell anyone about the auctioned artifact or that you were going with me to Los Angeles?"

"No one—just that I was not feeling well like you asked me to."

Cougar placed the large reptile into a bag. "Someone, I'm afraid, might be trying to scare you or worse. Can you think of any other reason someone might want to scare or hurt you, other than helping in the museum's art investigation?"

"No."

Daniela and Cougar searched the apartment for anything else out of place. "I'll take this with me," Cougar said, picking up the bag with the dead snake in it. As Cougar stepped toward the door, Daniela stopped him, wrapping her arms around him, and thanking him. She let her eyes close while leaning forward until their lips touched. Halfway through the kiss, she recognized it was more than just a thank you kiss.

When their lips parted, Daniela regained her composure. "Thank you, Arlan, you're always there for me. How is it that you are so—"?

"Good at killing snakes?" Cougar interrupted.

"Yes," Daniela said, a smile widening on her face. "That's exactly what I was trying to say, good night or rather good morning, Arlan." Daniela backed into her apartment and closed the door.

Cougar sat in the cab, staring out the window.

"¿Adónde, señor?"

"What?"

"Where to?"

"Oh—yes, yes, sorry…"

North of Town

I rubbed my eyes and reached for the ringing cell. "Hello…Amelia…you are? That's great, any troubles…? Yes, I'm here…okay, how does," I glanced at my wrist, "2pm local time sound? Great…I will find it, see you then."

Gerry's bed sat empty. I dressed, then knocked on the adjoining hotel room door. Gerry opened it. "Good afternoon, Cougar, I tried being quiet this morning. Did I wake you?"

"Never heard a sound."

"Good afternoon, Cougar," said Kathy. "We found something you'll want to see."

"Oh?" I followed Gerry to Kathy's screen. "What did you find?"

"Two things," Gerry interjected.

"First, the snake at Daniela's place?" Kathy said. "David was able to pinpoint its natural habitation area in Colombia—about here." Kathy stabbed at a map displayed on her screen.

"That's quite a distance from Bogota." I said.

"It sure is. Now the bigger news." Kathy thumped on her keyboard, and up popped college graduation pictures. "Do you recognize anyone in these?"

I stared at them, while reading the names. "Donald Tallman and Mauricio Lopez? So, they went to the same school?"

"Yes," said Kathy.

"I'm not getting the 'bigger news' —must have been the late-night flight and early morning reptile hunt. What you're saying is Donny and Mauricio went to the same college, right? I wouldn't think in their field of study that would be so unusual. There are not that many highly-rated art colleges from what you shared a few days ago."

"That's true, but that is a link that helps support your hypothesis the other day. Oh, and we also found out Mauricio's family is ultra-rich. However, about the time Mauricio went to college there was a family squabble, and Mauricio was cut out of his family's money and inheritance."

I scratched at the back of my head. "What are you thinking?" Gerry asked.

"Oh, just some things Shirley Jones shared about art and country. How all through history art has been the motivation for kings and nations to war with others to lay claim to their treasures. Whoever holds one's art, she said, holds the power and heart of that nation. But most of the time, as she put it, art burglaries are nothing but good old fashion greed. People want either to possess a piece of art they otherwise can't afford, or steal something valuable, sell it, and make a fortune."

"So, where do you think Donny and Mauricio fit in all this? Do you think there's a chance they are behind the missing art?" Gerry asked.

"Not sure, that's a huge leap in assumption; but not far off from where my thoughts have been lately. I've already decided I need to pay Donny Tallman another visit, and with this information, it makes it even more imperative."

Kathy said. "I would like to see his expression when you ask him about going to school with Mauricio."

"I'll have Gerry wire me up again so you can at least hear the timbre in his voice, how's that? Oh, and by the way, Amelia is here in Bogota. She flew her T-6 into a small airport outside the city limits. I'm meeting her a two at a restaurant called…Hierbas, north of town."

"I'm glad she's safe," Kathy commented, "aren't you, Cougar?"

I scanned their faces. Their grins hid nothing.

"So, Cougar, Amelia? Daniela? Any of your time given to thinking about these two beautiful women other than just business?" Gerry ribbed.

"Their beauty and intelligence have not escaped me, Gerry, if that's what you're poking at. They both, however, need me to keep my attention focused on helping them, and that's what I intend to do—all I intend to do."

"Then why are you blushing, Cougar," Kathy prodded again.

"Come on you guys, it's just really warm in here. And you guys know…I'm still not ready," I said, wiping my brow. "I need to get something to eat, have you guys eaten already?"

"Breakfast, but I can order up lunch if you want."

"I just need something to tide me over until two."

"I'll order up something," said Kathy.

"Thank you…Kathy and Gerry." I shook my head as they grinned irrepressibly.

The décor was unconventional for Bogota; but I found it refreshing. Elvis pictures adorned the walls, and the wait staff dressed like famous entertainers; most I didn't recognize. Amelia waved her arm from a table near the bar. As I approached, she slid off the stool, gazed into my eyes, and hugged me tightly. I wrapped my arms around her, too. It felt good.

"Are you all right?" I asked.

"I am now. I'm really glad to see you," she blurted.

"So, what happened in Mexico?"

"It's a long story."

"I'm all ears, please." Amelia shared the events, including the men at the bar, the attack at the airport, and getting sick from the bug bite. She asked me for the information concerning John Burrow's body, and where it had washed up.

"I'm going to fly to that location and check it out. Maybe my dad's body is somewhere around there." Amelia's eyes disclosed more acceptance to the reality of her father's death.

"Possibly, but currents can do unusual things. That could be like trying to find a needle in a haystack."

"I know, but I have to try. I think your assumption is probably right, that my dad was hijacked. I want to find the people who did this to him, and I want to find his airplane."

"There's quite a number of old DC-3s and C-47s around this country. If it's here somewhere, it could be repainted and hard to find. It also may not be at an airport, assuming it is still flyable."

"I know; but it's a place to start." Amelia breathed in slowly.

"If it is being used illegally," I said, "it's really not a great idea to go chasing after it."

"I have to try Cougar; you should know that by now. I didn't fly all this way to just give up."

I already knew what her reply would be. We ordered and ate lunch while discussing airplanes, Bogota, and her childhood. I gave her a quick lesson on search and rescue techniques and how to spot airplanes from the air and about grid patterns.

We stood outside the restaurant, facing each other; behind us, a backdrop of small puffy white clouds, speckling the sky. Heat radiated off the restaurant wall, and a gentle breeze stirred Amelia's perfume. "Please be careful, Amelia. I truly wish I could help you at this time. I promise, as soon as I'm able, I will."

"I believe you, Cougar, although, I sense there's something you're not sharing with me. You're too vague." Amelia's eyes traveled from my head to my feet, then back to my head. "I can't place my finger on it yet, but I will. I'm good at solving mysteries. My dad and I used to watch old-time mystery movies and I would solve them using very few clues. It used to frustrate him. He would say, 'quiet, let's just watch the movie'."

"I can see that" I said, shaking my head. "Please, focus on staying safe, not my vagueness." Amelia stepped closer, reaching her arms out. We embraced. The smell of her freshly washed hair stabbed at my senses. Time stood still as we froze in embrace. I felt my rigid posture softening, ever so slightly. She released her arms and took a step back when a group of five walked past us along the sidewalk. When they were gone, she grabbed my hands, pulling herself back in close. This time she kissed me on the cheek.

"Relax, Cougar." She turned and departed, not looking back. She just kept walking down the sporadically occupied sidewalk.

Chapter 23

Mad Dragon

"Is all the treasure accounted for and secured?" asked Gustano not looking up. He lifted a lit *Export A* from the ash tray to his mouth.

"Yes," answered Miguel, matter-of-factly. He tilted his head and watched Gustano scratch out some numbers on a piece of paper. "Boss, are we going to take any more of the artwork for ourselves?"

Gustano inhaled deeply, then released a rapid cloud of smoke from his nostrils like a mad dragon. "When it can be done without going straight to auction. We screwed up. We get paid very well for carrying out our part—let's stay focused on what we're paid to do. There will be opportunities for cashing in soon enough. Is Fabio back yet?"

"Yes, I was just with him."

"Have him come see me."

"Yes, Boss." Miguel turned abruptly and left Gustano's cluttered office.

Gustano grabbed his cell. "Tell me good news."

The man on the other end said, "The job is done, when can we meet."

"Do you have all the art?"

Gustano took another pull from his cigarette. "Yes, all of it."

"No, you don't! Don't ever try a stunt like that again or you'll be back to your old job peddling drugs."

"One piece! It was only one piece," Gustano replied, sweat beading up on his forehead. Fabio stepped into Gustano's office. Gustano directed him into a chair, pointing with his cigarette.

"One piece? Only one piece? What makes you think you had rights to any of it? You could have jeopardized my whole operation."

"Your operation?" Gustano yelled into the phone. "If it weren't for me and my team, you would have nothing! Don't you forget that."

"Don't talk to me like I'm your partner. You're hired help, that's all. Groups like yours are a dime a dozen."

"You know that's not true. If it were, you'd have asked someone else long ago. I deliver on my promises. That's why I have the reputation I do, and that's why I'm the man people call when needing a job done right. Now, when can we meet?"

"You'll get your money soon enough. By the way, your boy Fabio missed his mark."

"What do you mean?" Gustano covered the phone with his hand. "Fabio, you put the snake in her apartment, right?" Fabio nodded.

"I mean, Daniela, she's still alive."

"My guys can't program the snake. We placed it where you asked us too."

"Well, I'll get to the bottom of what happened. At any rate, I need another favor from your team. I'll meet you at noon on Wednesday, the same spot as before."

Gustano clicked off, dropped the phone on his desk and stood up. His face flushed with anger. He squished what was left of his Export A into the ash tray. "One of these days, I'll have enough of that pompous idiot." Gustano swung his leg, sending a trashcan into the wall.

"Boss, I don't know how she got away. That species has never failed us."

Gustano scratched at his chin. A day's growth shadowed his face. He wiped his bald head using the sleeve of his satin shirt. "We have another job. I'll get the details on Wednesday."

"Is that all, Boss?"

Gustano nodded as he sat down at his desk and lit another cigarette. His stomach soured, contemplating his irritation.

"Gustano, may I have a word with you?" Brigitte asked. She stepped into his office as Fabio filed out.

"What do you want?"

"You." Brigitte stepped behind Gustano's chair and began rubbing his shoulders. "You're really tight. Is everything all right?"

"Not really, that man makes my blood boil—even if he is paying us a ridiculous sum of money"

"Gustano—sweetheart."

"I told you—"

"Sheesh! I know what you told me, but right now you need me. And the guys need you, too."

"What are you talking about?" Gustano swung his chair around, facing her. Brigitte's hard attractive face softened. Gustano's stare rested motionless on hers.

Brigitte cupped her hands around his face and kissed him. "Let's have a celebration tonight. Right here," she said. "We've all been working so hard, and we deserve to celebrate our success."

Gustano scratched some more at his chin hair. "Alright, you've talked me into it. Maybe that will keep me from going and killing that pious twit." Brigitte kissed him again, then strolled out of his office, exaggerating her hip movement as she did. Gustano watched until she was out of sight.

Field Trip

The museum steps were crowded with kids. The entrance and gift shop were also heavily occupied. I spotted Daniela before she saw me. Her hair was up, and her pace condensed, as she made her way to the lobby in a fitted business suit with a narrow slit up the side.

"Miss Perez," I said, catching her attention. Her head turned; a genuine smile broadened across her face.

"Field trip day for most of the schools," she said. "This is one of my favorite days of the year. The look in their eyes when they see art for the first time is so precious. Some are not that interested you know—it's just a break from class; but there are those who get it, even at this young age." Daniela observed the group of children, the smile still on her face.

"Is there some place we can talk for a few minutes? I don't want to keep you long."

"Yes, of course, let's go to my office."

Daniela and I weaved through the kids, teachers, and chaperones into a deserted hallway that ran between the museum offices.

"Mr. Jensen," Mauricio commanded. I turned as Mauricio stepped through a door facing the hall. "Any news on the insurance settlement? Donny said you wanted to talk to him. I hope that means an approval from the insurance board is forthcoming."

"The board is working expeditiously for a recommendation to the Delrow Insurance Agency. International traveling arts shows have always been a bit troublesome for the insurance board, but we are making headway. In fact, I'm here to have some paperwork signed by the museum's director, confirming the loss and insured value. I only need a few more details, and Daniela has graciously offered to fill in those blanks for me."

"I see...how are we doing with school day, Daniela?"

"Very well, Mr. Lopez. Attendance is up even from last year. The children are looking forward to your speech."

Mauricio glanced at his watch. "You're meeting Donny at the party, right?"

"Yes, unfortunately that is the soonest he could see me."

"Don't be so disappointed, Arlan. I sponsor the event, and it's quite the proper affair. The complex where Donny lives has the most beautiful cabana the size of a ballroom, and the view of the city will literally take your breath away. It will be a party to remember—you'll see. Daniela will be there as well." Daniela's expression changed to confusion as she eyed Mauricio inquisitively.

"I will?"

Mauricio flicked his eyes to Daniela. "Oh, the guest invitations are just going out today; you should have yours in your inbox shortly."

"Thank you, Mr. Lopez."

"You're both welcome." Mauricio gestured with his outstretched hands.

"Thank you, I'm honored."

"I'll see you in the theater, Daniela...Mr. Jensen." Mauricio tipped his head and disappeared into his office.

Daniela and I were silent until the door of her office was closed. "I didn't know anything about this party," she replied.

"I did, that's what I came here to tell you, and invite you as my guest."

"Well, since I'm going anyway—it appears." Daniela batted her dark long eyelashes at me.

"Then it's a date," I responded.

"Well, I'm sorry; but I must get back to the children now. After Mr. Lopez's speech, I give the children an overview of Colombia's history. Did you really need me to look over some paperwork?"

"That can wait," I said, patting my briefcase. "I'm in no hurry to deliver the paperwork to the insurance board anyway." I lifted myself from an old-fashioned chair—one that could easily fit the décor in one of the museum galleries. Daniela made her way around the desk, grabbed my hand, squeezed it softly, and said. "Thank you for coming to see me—and for the invitation."

"You're welcome. I look forward to tomorrow night." I leaned and kissed her cheek, then walked out of the museum, down the stairs, and caught a cab back to the hotel room.

"How did it go, Cougar?" Gerry asked.

"Amelia's off to where John's body was found, and Daniela and I have been invited to a party, hosted by none other than Mauricio and Donny. Gerry, tomorrow will be a good time to set up the wiretaps in Mauricio's office while he's away at this party."

"I'll take care of that, Cougar, while you're off enjoying yourself at some party with your lovely 'lady-friend'. I'm not complaining though. I could use an excuse to get out of this hotel room. I don't mind helping Kathy with the research, but my unique skillset is starting to get rusty."

"I have a hunch the rust will be coming off soon."

"Hmm, Mauricio and Donny continue to be awfully chummy," Kathy stated.

"You guys can make your own conclusion as to their relationship. I'll have Gerry wire me up tomorrow night. I, for one, find it odd that an insurance agent and his insured client are throwing a party together." Gerry and Kathy both nodded their heads. "I'm going to hit the gym really quick, any of you want to tag along?"

"Wow," Kathy said. "If that doesn't sound like fun." She rolled her eyes and opened her mouth sticking her tongue out.

"I'm up for it," Gerry replied.

"I guess I am, too." Kathy lifter her fingers off the keyboard. "My wrists could use the break."

"We'll meet you in fifteen minutes down in the gym," I said.

"Meet you there," Kathy replied, while shutting down the equipment and locking it up.

I opened the adjoining door to our room. A maid ran out the door and into the hallway. I tore off after her, pulling open the outer hotel room door, and scanning the hallway. The back of a maid's outfit sped down the hall with no cart. "Excuse me? Disculpa?" The maid turned a corner and vanished. After a couple minutes of searching, I gave up and reentered Gerry's and my room. Gerry already had his meter out, checking the room. A minute later, he held two listening devices in his hand. He looked at them carefully, noting how they were made. Then he deactivated them.

"English made," he said.

"Donny's originally from England."

"These aren't too difficult to acquire. I think most anyone can order these."

"These devices could have been planted by the Bogota Police Department. I figure Captain Eduardo Moreno and Detective Andrea Dias are probably getting a little curious about me; either that or they're just bored."

"Should we be concerned?" Gerry asked.

"Can't say for sure; but whether it's the police or Donny, we better stick to our script." I knocked on the adjoining door. No one answered. I knocked again. I glanced back at Gerry; he had a concerned look on his face. I started for the hall door just as the adjoining door opened.

"What's so urgent, can't a girl get dressed?" Kathy stood there in a psychedelic yoga outfit.

Gerry and I glanced at each other, chuckling. Gerry held up the wiretaps in his hand. Kathy waved Gerry into her room. After a few minutes, he pronounced the room clear.

Chapter 25

Cabana on the Hill

The evening air was noticeably cooler than it had been the last few nights. The sun slid down from the sky, leaving a soft glow over the city. Cougar knocked on Daniela's door. When the door opened, Daniela was standing there in a shapely light green evening gown. White pearls hung from her earlobes and around her neck. Her dark brown hair, just curled, touched her shoulders before falling gracefully down her back.

"You look…amazing. Are you ready?" Cougar asked. He felt like a high schooler, picking up his prom date. Daniela detected the gleam in his eyes.

"Thank you, Arlan. Please, lead the way." She closed the door behind her and they both walked quietly to the elevator.

The traffic became lighter as they reached the outskirts of town. The four-lane road narrowed to a two-lane road as it wound its way around hills made of rock. As they drove the rental car up the mountain, only occasionally did they break out of canopies of darkness to see Bogota's city lights off in the distance. Cougar and Daniela discussed Bogota, art, and international cuisine before Daniela turned the conversation to snakes and why someone would do such a thing, still questioning if they were trying to scare her or actually kill her. After another thirty minutes of climbing and winding, the road finally leveled off near the plateau, high up in the mountain. To the left was a large housing complex. Cougar turned into the drive, stopping at the guard gate.

"Good evening," Cougar said loudly. "We are guests of Donald Tallman for the Bogota museum party." The guard exited his shack and walked closer to the vehicle, peering in. He snatched the invite and turned without saying a word, snagged a clipboard from the shack, and returned.

"Nombre?"

"Arlan Jensen and Daniela Perez."

"Cualquier arma en usted o en el coche?"

"No weapons, sir." The guard handed the invitation back, turned to his shack and pushed a button, lifting the gate. Cougar pulled through, lightly touching his chest where his holster was.

Extravagant homes bordered a sizable building with large glass windows. Huge exotic trees and various colored plants and flowers freckled the grounds. Expertly cut grass bordered walkways leading from each large house, giving the development more of a resort-like atmosphere. The entire grounds were flooded in soft light by tall decorative lamp posts made to resemble gas lit lanterns. Path lighting, every five feet, transformed sidewalks into a pedestrian thoroughfare that connected the houses with the enormous cabana and other amenities. A man wearing a formal suit guided Cougar to a parking space using a flashlight that glowed red at the end.

"Wow," said Daniela. "Insurance agents must make pretty good money." Music thumped through the car windows, rattling something in the trunk.

"Good thing I opted for my black suit instead of my jean jacket," Cougar replied.

"Oh, you're funny, Arlan. I think we will both fit in just fine. Do you think you'll be able to ask Donny about attending school with Mr. Lopez?" Cougar had shared the information he found out on Donny and Mauricio during the ride up.

"I'll see how well he keeps his word about our meeting."

Daniela flipped the visor down, and glided lipstick over her lips. "How do I look?"

"Like a model."

She blushed from the inside out. She hadn't given her growing feelings about Arlan much more thought; but now, and all of a sudden, she was overwhelmed by them. Here was a man she hardly knew, a man who treated her with dignity, respect, and care; a man, she quickly reminded herself again, that lived in a different part of the world. Still, something inside made her want to push aside those fears and let go of her heart.

Cougar and Daniela approached the entrance to the huge cabana. Large cement columns marked the entrance. After the guest check-in, they entered a formal ballroom. White silk curtains billowed from the ceiling. Gas lit style sconces bordered each column. The music had changed; now the band gave dancers a waltzing beat. The inside of the building was segregated into four areas. One held an indoor pool, with the other three consisting of a ballroom, lounge, and kitchen and dining area.

"Arlan and Daniela." They turned to see Donny standing there. "I'm so glad you two made it. Please, make your way to the bar and have a drink—everything's on the house."

"This place is magnificent—and the view," Cougar said.

"The way I see it, Arlan, if you're going to have vacation property somewhere in the world, you go all out. My home back in States is very modest."

"How much of the year do you reside here in Bogota?" Cougar asked.

"Not nearly enough, Arlan. You two get yourselves a drink. Relax and mingle. This is a party!" Donny waved his arm in the air as he spun in a half circle, stumbling slightly.

"Don't forget I want to have a few words with you regarding the insurance policy."

"Plenty of time for that later…" Donny walked off in mid-sentence to welcome more guests. Cougar scanned around for Mauricio but didn't see him. With Daniela's arm in his, they sauntered to the bar. The bartender poured Daniela a glass of cabernet, and Cougar, a glass of Perrier with lemon.

"No wine for you?" Daniela asked.

"Not tonight." Cougar swiveled his head.

"What is it?"

"Nothing, let's try some appetizers."

"Arlan, please share with me what's wrong."

Cougar's face eased. "It's nothing except an overly sensitized imagination. I'm just keeping my eyes open for snakes."

"In that case, I'll help you." Daniela squeezed closer to him.

Cougar and Daniela mingled as they took in the large auditorium and adjoining areas. When they got to the indoor pool, the water rippled as ladies dressed in matching scant bathing suits performed a water-dance routine for the guests lining the edge. Inebriated men watched with sleazy eyes.

"I've seen enough of this," Cougar said, towing Daniela behind him.

"You really are a good man, aren't you?"

"I try. I love the fact we're made male and female, and all the amazing and challenging dynamics that go along with that. But I don't appreciate men denigrating women or the other way around. I think it does our society harm."

Daniela fixed her eyes on Cougar's. "You're a strange breed—in a good way, I mean."

"Come, let's get something to eat, and then if you are up for it, a waltz?"

"Now you're speaking my language."

Mauricio's driver pulled up next to the building's entrance. Mauricio let the Town Car's door shut with a firm thud. "Good evening, Mr. Lopez."

Mauricio nodded as he walked past the check-in podium, only slightly parting his lips. Donny noticed Mauricio as he walked in and excused himself from his conversation to meet up with him. "Good evening, Mauricio."

"It's always beautiful up here; but that drive."

"Price one must pay," Donny replied.

"How are our guests doing?" Mauricio asked.

"Most are here and seem to be enjoying themselves immensely. Some are already feeling no pain."

"Well, let's just hope that translates into bigger donations. What about our annoying insurance board investigator?"

"He came with Daniela. I saw them at the table having something to eat."

"Any sign of—" Smoke grabbed Mauricio's attention before hearing the familiar voice.

"Mauricio—Donny." Gustano walked up behind them, freshly shaved, and sporting a black suit with a white satin shirt and a bolo tie.

Cougar and Daniela had plates crowded with stuffed avocado, artichoke hearts, stuffed mushroom caps, and petite crab cakes. "Daniela, do you recognize the man standing next to Mauricio and Donny?"

"Oh, my gosh, these are good," Daniela said, turning toward the entrance. She patted her lips with a napkin. "I have never seen him before. Maybe he's one of our donors. I haven't met very many of them."

The three men stood talking before dispersing into the crowd.

"Are you ready to waltz?"

Daniela set her napkin down, lifting herself from the table. "A slow waltz please, I may have overindulged with the appetizers."

The music played in time as they twirled slowly around the dance floor, pausing momentarily with the beat, as they gazed into each other's eyes. Daniela once again felt butterflies. There was no doubt she was falling for him.

Cougar tried resisting his feelings; but as much as he tried, and as ridiculous as it seemed to fall for a girl who lived so far away, he also couldn't prevent his feelings from intensifying.

As the party shifted into high gear, the band turned to rock 'n' roll. Most of the party goers were on their fourth, fifth, or sixth drink. As the music's volume increased, so did the voices as Cougar and Daniela tried talking amidst the fringes of the ballroom and dining room. Cougar saw Donny finishing up his meal. "Will you excuse me Daniela, I think it's time to have that talk with Donny." Cougar got up and slid his chair in. Daniela rose to follow him. "Daniela, I think it is best if I talk with Donny myself."

Daniela watched as Cougar tapped Donny's shoulder.

"Donny."

"Arlan, I hope you and Miss Perez are enjoying yourselves tonight?"

"Very much, thank you. Could we have that talk now?"

Donny glanced at the wall clock. "Meet me at my house in ten minutes. It's at the corner of the development, past the third lamppost." He pointed toward the corner of the cabana. "It's the one bordered by rose bushes—can't miss it."

"I'll see you in ten."

"Well? What did he say?" Daniela asked. Cougar filled her in on their brief conversation.

"How long will you be?"

"Not long. Afterwards, if you want, we can leave."

"I'm ready whenever you are, Arlan. I've already had a very nice evening."

"I feel the same way, Daniela." Cougar reached for her hand. He held it, squeezing it affectionately. "I'll be back shortly."

He stepped into the cool night air. Stars shined bright over the city of Bogota. Off in the distance, dark clouds hovered over the mountains. The wind had picked up slightly, rustling leaves on the plants bordering the huge cabana. Cougar's steps sounded on the cement walkway. Thumping from the music reverberated off the houses. After the third lamppost, Cougar turned, threading himself between rose bushes, and up several steps to the door.

"Well Arlan, what's so important that you spent your entire evening waiting to meet with me?"

"I have a few questions that still need answers. For instance, how long have you known Mauricio?"

"Come on, Arlan. That's not how two men start a conversation here in Colombia. Tell me honestly, have you and Daniela enjoyed our little party? She is a looker. I must say, going to the museum has more than ancient artifacts to look at, right?"

Cougar's face remained stoic.

"I'm just bantering with you. Actually, I'm glad for the break. Don't get me wrong, I enjoy entertaining; but I get tired of rubbing elbows with Mauricio's financial backers. There's really nothing in it for me. I just own a residence with a cabana hall big enough to host these parties. Also, Mauricio likes this location. He says it helps the museum donors open their pockets."

"Why doesn't he use the museum?"

"These parties get pretty wild. Besides, some of the donors are not what you would call museum enthusiasts. Come, let's have a drink." Donny didn't wait for an answer. He turned, leading Cougar to a study at the far end of the house.

Daniela glanced at the wall clock for the third time, it had been forty-five minutes since Cougar left for Donny's house. She set her drink down, asked for her coat, and walked out of the party. Only a few partiers were outside. The wind had picked up some more, and the dark clouds that were once far off in the distance were now closer and more menacing. At the rose bushes, Daniela turned and stepped quietly up the stairs. She put her ear to the door but didn't hear anything. Her knuckles echoed off the door, startling herself at the intensity. After another minute, she put her ears back against the door. Her heart skipped a beat as she twisted the doorknob, letting herself in.

Faint voices were heard from a room down the hall. One of the voices belonged to Arlan, the other to Donny. She was about to turn and walk back to the cabana when a picture caught her attention. Through a partially open door, she recognized the painting hanging on the wall, although in that instant, she couldn't place where she had seen it. Stepping quietly to the partially open door, she widened it just enough for her to enter and get a better look.

Books filled shelves across the back wall. A worn leather chair, a small table, and dusty lamp were the only furniture occupying the floor space. She studied the painting. It was an original for sure. Noise came from the back room. A door creaked open; footsteps moved toward the room she was in. She quickly stepped behind the door and held her breath. Her heart pounded loudly in her chest.

"I'm glad I was able to set your mind at ease, Arlan. We always want to be in good standings with protocol you know."

"Well, like I said, Donny, fraud is always a concern."

"Shall we return to the party? I'm sure your girlfriend's wondering where you ran off to." Donny stopped for a minute in the living room. A smell of perfume lingered in the air.

"Well, I'm not sure I would call us boyfriend and girlfriend, Donny."

"I noticed how she looks at you…and vice versa."

"She is sweet, isn't she?" Cougar waited for Donny to answer, but instead Donny grabbed a light jacket out of his closet and walked to the door, looking back one last time while sticking his nose in the air.

The door shut. Daniela waited a minute before moving. Droplets of sweat moistened her dress, under her armpits. She gasped for air. Moving carefully out of the room, she peered out the front window and watched Donny and Arlan walk back to the party. Quickly, she exited the house and ran to the other side of the building. Light rain began falling. She ducked under the entrance, gave her coat back to the attendant, and grabbed two drinks from the first server that walked by.

"There you are," Cougar said, with Donny next to him.

"Looks like the forecast about rain was correct," said Donny. "Wouldn't you agree, Daniela?" Donny brushed raindrops off his hair using his hand. Daniela felt water soaking into the back of her dress.

"Yes," she said, handing Cougar the second glass of port wine she was holding. She interlocked arms with him and moved away from Donny, toward the dessert table.

"Were you outside?"

"Yes," she whispered. "I went to find you."

"Sorry, I didn't plan on being there that long. Donny was in a talkative mood, so I just let him talk."

"Did you find out anything?"

"More than he thinks. I'll share once we're in the car. Are you ready to leave or did you really want another dessert?"

"Yes, and yes—but I better pass on the second dessert."

They gathered their coats. Seeing Mauricio near the entrance, they stopped and thanked him for the party invitation. Mauricio turned from Gustano and graciously accepted their praise. "You two be careful driving back," cautioned Mauricio.

"Thank you," Cougar replied, "we will, and it was nice to meet you, too…?"

"Gustano," the man said, his eyes traveling back and forth between Cougar and Daniela. "Yes, do be careful," he said. "I hope you haven't had too much to drink. A little inebriation and those curves will kill you."

"I'll keep that in mind," Cougar replied. He and Daniela walked out into the blowing rain as Gustano gave Mauricio a quick wink.

The Curves Are Deadly

I ran to the car, shut the door behind me and tossed my rain-soaked suit jack to the back seat. Daniela stood by the entrance of the cabana, under a canopy. I pulled the car up and pushed open the door. She ducked in headfirst; her face, inches from mine as she re-adjusted herself and slid into her seat. She leaned back for a split second, then thrust herself back up and kissed me.

Rainwater dripped off her hair, her eyelashes fluttered under the dome light. Cinnamon gum scented the air as she spoke. I leaned over to her and we kissed again more passionately. She twisted, wrapping her arms around me. Our lips parted. She smiled and whispered in my ear. Warm cinnamon touched my face. I put the car in drive and drove past the guard shack. A flickering light emanated from inside the shack's fogged-up windows. The streets were void of cars. The only noticeable lights were from streetlamps, and they were only marginally helpful in the pouring rain. Daniela shivered. I turned the wipers to high and set the defroster to full. "One thing for sure," I said. "Donny idolizes your Mauricio."

"He does?"

"Yes, it seems they've worked together for a quite some time, although Donny wouldn't elaborate on how long or in what capacity, only sharing about his role as a museum insurance agent."

"What did he say about knowing Mr. Lopez in college?"

"Only that he ran into him a few times and had him in a few classes; however—"

"What?"

"Well, first off, he couldn't stop talking about how brilliant Mauricio is. He went on and on about all Mauricio has done for the art industry. I kept wondering what all the infatuation was about. After three drained tumblers of scotch, Donny, not me, referred to Mauricio two times as his boss, correcting himself each time, blaming the liquor."

"Wouldn't that be a normal appellation for a curator and an insurance agent?"

"Not in my world." I slowed down for the next turn. Lights glared at us from the oncoming lane. As the truck drove past, our car buffeted from the relative wind. "As Donny poured himself another drink, I glanced at a picture on his wall, behind his desk. It was a class picture from college. In a separate photo, Donny and Mauricio were standing next to each other, wearing the same outfits with their arms around each other. It appeared they were more than just casual classmates."

"Do you really think they could be involved with stealing the art?"

"I'm not sure. And unfortunately, I don't have enough information to stop the board from approving the settlement, or for Delrow to distribute the funds to the museum." I slowed for the next turn. "What do you think about Gustano? Did he strike you as a museum benefactor?"

"He looked a little scary, actually."

Lights crept up behind us as I negotiated a winding curve. As the car drew closer, they flashed their headlights several times. I glanced in the rear-view mirror. As I straightened the wheel, I pulled to the edge of the lane to let the car pass. The car pulled up next to us, paced us for a few seconds before hurrying on by.

"That was odd," Daniela said.

"I was just driving careful like Mauricio recommended."

A few minutes later, the car that had passed us was pulled over with their flashers on. A man stood outside the car in the pouring rain, waving his hands. I slowed down, locked the doors, and pulled to the side of the road. Daniela pushed the button for the passenger side window. I called over. "What's seems to be the trouble?"

"Car trouble."

"Where's the other person that was in your car?" I asked.

A knock on the driver side window startled me. I turned. A gun barrel pointed straight at me through the window. The man on the passenger side reached for something as he tried the door handle. Daniela screamed. I didn't wait to see what he was reaching for. I smashed the accelerator down, spraying loose gravel from the right rear tire. The rear end of the car jerked to the right, forcing both men to the ground. Our left tire whined, searching for better traction. Steam billowed off the pavement as the tire finally gripped the road, swinging the rear of the car back around. A bullet ricocheted off the car.

"Down!" I yelled.

The back window shattered. Metal sounded on the car's trunk as both tires, now on the pavement, pushed us into our seats. I turned fast through the first two corners, fishtailing as distant lights trailed behind us.

"Arlan!" Daniela screamed.

"Hang on." The car gained on us. I pressed down harder on the accelerator, increasing our speed even more through the corners. The right rear tire left the roadway, spraying dirt, and gravel in the air. I heard Daniela praying in Spanish.

The car skidded back and forth as I tried to keep it in the center of the road. There was no way to outrun them in this rental, the German vehicle they were driving was far more powerful. I spun the wheel, the car slid sideways through the next curve. "Arlan!" Daniela screamed again.

The car pulled up fast, ramming us. *Bang!* The hit shoved us against our seatbelts. I kept the car pointing straight and in the center of the road. At the next turn, our car slid hard into a guardrail. The rail held, preventing us from plummeting into the darkness. The car's passenger side and bumper scraped loudly as we exited the turn. At the end of the guardrail, the post securing it caught our bumper, ripping it off completely, and spinning the back end of the car around. In an instant, the pursuing car caught up to us. Daniela's screams filled the air. I spun the steering wheel; the back end of our car came around, contacting the pursuer's car. All I saw through their open window were a set of teeth. Miraculously, we made it through two more curves without being shot at.

The tachometer stayed pegged in the red zone. I had the rental moving as fast as it would go. The wiper blades were tapping out a staccato beat as my eyes strained for the next turn. I needed to think of something fast. The straightaway ahead provided the gap I needed. By the time the other car made it to the straight section of the road, we were one hundred feet in front of them. Ahead, the straight section ended with a turn to the right, back out toward the cliff. I remembered this turn while driving to the party. Once out of the curve, the road straightened for about three hundred feet back toward the mountainside.

I slowed our car down. The pursuing car gained on us, covering the one-hundred-foot separation in seconds. The car smashed into the back of us. Without a bumper our trunk lid buckled badly, although now it provided a small shield form the onslaught of bullets. I floored the accelerator, making the right turn, the short straightaway, and then the left turn at the cliff. I over-steered once I was through the corner, skidding the car around so I would be facing the pursuing vehicle as they made it through the turn. I reached into my shirt, wrapping my hand around the M&P handle. Daniela screamed when she saw the gun.

As the approaching car made it through the turn, I aimed, squeezing off four shots into their front tire. The car swerved violently back and forth. I stepped on the accelerator and spun the steering wheel to the right. Our car used up the entire lane as we skidded into the next turn away from the hill. The chasing car swerved one last time before running up onto the embankment and rolling over onto its top. I spun the wheel again as the rental met up with another hairpin turn to the left, banging against the railing. My heart pounded beneath my holster. I slowed down to a manageable speed for the treacherous road conditions and glanced over to Daniela's seat. Her mouth hung open, staring at me. "Are you okay?" I asked.

"Who are you?" she shrieked. "People don't just…just…know how to drive like that."

"I told you who I am." As we twisted around the last big bend in the road, the city lights brightened. The rain slowed and I was able to turn the wipers to intermittent. My heart rate settled back to normal. Just another exciting day on the job for me; but not for Daniela. She was scared and now confused. I wrestled with telling her the truth."

Daniela's face was pale. I wasn't sure telling her the truth was the right move, but I still needed her help—and besides, my feelings for her had progressed too far not to. "What I'm about to tell you, you can't share with anyone."

I could sense Daniela studying my face. "Go on," she said.

"My real name is Cougar. I'm a special agent, currently working to help both our countries. My job, along with a couple associates that are staying here in Bogota, is to find and retrieve Colombia's historic treasure."

Daniela stared out the window, then responded. "I cared for you. I trusted you. Am I just a part of your assignment?" Tears brought black streaks down her face.

"It's not like that, Daniela."

"How is it like then, Arlan, or am I now supposed to call you Cougar?"

I turned off the wipers. The rain had quit, but the winds were still blowing hard. "What you felt, I felt, too.

Daniela was quiet the rest of the drive back to her place. I pulled up to her apartment. She gathered her things and turned to me but said nothing. She spun around to leave, then turned back. "I'm confused, angry, and scared. Let me process this in my own way." Daniela shut the door, stepped up onto the sidewalk, and not looking back, went through the entrance to her apartment.

Chapter 27

South Colombia

Amelia brought the T-6 Texan engine to life. Black smoke streamed from the exhaust pipe, a glow of orange burning fuel-air mixture illuminated the side of the fuselage. The morning dawn brought birds from their nests, and an older brown dog limped the perimeter of the airport, searching for anything abnormal.

Thoughts of her dad, demonstrating how to handle the dated World War II plane, spilled into her consciousness. "Work with the plane, not against it," he would say. "You are a team, get to know her intricacies and respect her vulnerabilities and you two can do anything and go anywhere."

Amelia taxied to the runway, checking off the preflight items and readying the plane as she did. She stepped on the rudder pedal, aligning the big single engine airplane to the runway centerline. There were no signs of people in the parking lot or by the two dilapidated terminal buildings. With a thrust of power, and in less than a hundred feet, the tail lifted from the ground. Amelia gently massaged the rudder pedals, keeping the plane heading straight down the centerline.

As the T-6 lifted into the air, Amelia turned southeast, watching the distant city of Bogota pass beneath her. Today she would search for her dad's airplane. Yesterday's search to the north for her dad, where John Burrows' body had been discovered, proved impossible, like trying to find a screw or nut when working on an airplane once it had fallen to the ground. Over the last two days she hadn't seen any signs of her father, wreckage, or his airplane. The two-day search proved even more difficult due to low clouds and choppy air. Today's weather was much improved, although to the south the forecast still showed signs of low ceilings and moderate turbulence.

She wasn't entirely sure what to look for. At first, spotting an airplane from the air seemed easy, but not around these parts. Flying over mountainous terrain and thick vegetation meant scanning for anything shiny or man-made. She marked up Cougar's grid pattern to help her but realized she could never cover that much area. She wished Cougar could have broken away from his obligations to show her how to properly search from the air. Nevertheless, she wouldn't be denied the responsibility in performing this critical obligation. If her father's plane were hi-jacked, as Cougar inferred, and still in one piece, she would do all she could to locate it. She recognized it may be the only way of really knowing for sure what happened to her father.

The T-6 rolled out of a shallow turn, heading directly south. The western coast of Colombia lay hundreds of miles somewhere off her right wing. Tall mountain peaks challenged her flight path. She sat back in her seat, listening to the drone of the big radial engine, wondering if someday she would get to teach her children to fly like her dad had taught her.

"You're lucky to be alive," Brigitte said, as Fabio walked into the kitchen. "Did you put ice on that last night?"

"Lucky to be alive?" Fabio shouted. "You should've seen the look on Gustano's face. The entire flight home I could tell I'm as good as dead."

"Good morning Brigitte—Fabio," Gustano said shuffling into the kitchen and pouring a cup of coffee. "You're not dead—yet. Fail me again and you will be.

"I know, Boss, I'm sorry, but you should have seen this guy drive—and he had a gun."

"He's an insurance company employee. You ought to be ashamed, letting him out drive you like that." Gustano's eyes moved to the stove where Brigitte was standing. "What's for breakfast?"

"Eggs, sausage, and potatoes, it will be ready in ten minutes."

Gustano grumbled, turned, and walked out of the kitchen.

"That guy is no insurance employee," Fabio stated under his breath.

"What?" Brigitte asked.

"Nothing."

Just a Hunch

"Good morning, Cougar," Kathy said, pushing her chair back from the computer.

"Any luck?"

"I think so. David and I worked into the night and early morning."

"How is David?"

"I think I heard him open three cans of Red Bull. His words kept coming faster and faster, and with more animation."

Gerry walked in as Kathy and I were talking. "Hey, you two, what's up?" Gerry wiped at his eyes.

"Kathy and I were going through what she and 'Red Bull' David uncovered last night while you were setting the wiretaps in Mauricio's office."

"By the way, what time did you get in last night, lover boy?" Kathy asked.

"Not quite 'lover boy' anymore," I said, explaining the details of the chase down the mountain, Daniela questioning me, and disclosing my real name and purpose to her.

"Why didn't you say something last night about the car chase?" Gerry asked.

"I wasn't exactly in the talking mood last night, sorry."

"I understand,"

"I'll bet she'll come around," Kathy stated. "Just give her some time."

"I'm sure you're right." Gerry put his hand on my shoulder. "What did you and David uncover?"

"Well," Kathy began. "At first it was like searching for the proverbial needle in a haystack. We traced all the places Mauricio worked since he left college."

"And?"

"Well, trying to put Donny at those same places turned out to be much more difficult."

"Okay, the punch line now?"

"Donny and Mauricio worked together at five other museums."

"Five?"

"That's not all. At those five museums, three of them had insurance claims. And get this, Donny worked for multiple insurance companies under various names."

"From yesterday's meeting, I can tell you conclusively, Donny is not the brains behind a major heist. If they're guilty, Mauricio must be the leader. Donny couldn't say enough about him last night."

Gerry interrupted. "Well his office is bugged, so if Mr. Genius is involved in Bogota's art heist, we should hear something."

"We still have no clue what happened to the art." I stepped over to Kathy, drawing Gerry with me. "We have to find the art and get it back to Colombia."

"We couldn't agree more," said Gerry, "but we're still not positive it was these two."

"True," said Kathy, "but it's looking more and more likely."

We all three turned, hearing a knock on the hotel room door. "I got it."

There was a cart loaded with breakfast food, plates, and juice. The lady standing next to it asked. "Su desayuno, señor."

"Puedo tomarlo desde aquí, gracias." I tipped her and watched as she made her way toward the elevator. Gerry and Kathy swarmed the cart. I pulled my cell out. "It's Daniela, save some for me please." I exited through the connecting doors into Gerry's and my hotel room.

"Hi Daniela, I'm glad you called. I want you to know—"

"Save it, Arlan or Cougar. I'm only interested in getting our art back. I will continue to help until the art is found and put back where it belongs."

"Thank you, Daniela. I have some new information and could really use your help today." I waited for a response.

"Okay. Meet me in the museum's historical archives at three."

"I'll be there, and thank you, Daniela." I clicked off and went back into Kathy's room for breakfast.

"Everything okay?" Kathy and Gerry asked in unison.

"It will be. By the way, lately I've had this image stuck in my head, and with it, an ever-pressing gut feeling."

"About what?"

"When I was at the New York City Museum. I noticed some large thick plastic bags next to five-gallon water bottles near the dumpsters."

"Water bottles?"

"And thick bags like bladders, the kind liquid can be stored in."

"Wait, you're thinking they shipped water instead of art?"

"It's a hunch. Kathy, can you get me on a flight to New York after six?

"I'll get right on it."

"Thank you, Kathy. Gerry, anything out of Mauricio's office yet?"

"Nothing. He must be sleeping off his party hangover, I'll let you know when he arrives and if he shares anything incriminating."

"Also, can one of you check water container and packaging companies around town and see if a large order of bags and/or bottles were purchased recently? You might also check suppliers of other liquids too, just to be sure."

"Will do, Cougar."

"Oh, one more thing, Kathy. You will need another rental car."

Kathy smiled as she turned toward her computer. "Another one? I can only imagine what this one looks like. Thank goodness it was just the car. Be careful out there."

Captured

B rigitte yelled, "lunch is ready," through the opening of the slid-ing metal door. The huge military barracks building, once in immaculate condition, now sat colored in rust. The tattered cor-rugated tin roof seemed to spring a new leak with each passing storm. "Where's Javier?"

"Working on the DC-3," Fabio yelled from the back of the building.

"It's a C-47 you idiot," Miguel yelled, correcting him.

"Whatever it is, it's old and ugly just the same."

"It isn't half as ugly as you, Fabio," Miguel retorted.

"Can't you two work together for even an hour without agitating each other?" Gustano bellowed, from behind one of the crates. The two men wisely didn't answer. "Come on, let's grab lunch."

"Brigitte, this stuff tastes like socks!" Fabio commented, expecting a laugh from his brother Javier.

Gustano asked Fabio. "Pass the tomatoes, will you?"

Fabio picked up the plate and handed it to Gustano. Gustano drove his fork into Fabio's forearm. The plate dropped, shattering against an-other bowl as Fabio instantly pulled his arm back. Tomato slices landed on the table, Fabio's lap, and the floor. "Why did you do that?" Fabio cried, straining to be respectful. Fabio pulled at the fork. A steady flow of blood erupted as he did.

"You can be excused from the table," Gustano said, "and if I hear anymore from you today, that fork will end up in your throat. Maybe you would like to cook for all of us, do our laundry, clean the house, and babysit that kid? That would be fine with me. If she were Miguel's partner the other night, that insurance idiot and his date would be dead by now."

"I was just trying to be funny."

"You're not. Now quit bleeding all over the floor and get some peroxide on that arm. Then get back to the storage building, you're not hurt."

"Yes, Boss." Fabio walked out of the dining room holding a paper towel on his arm.

"Still on edge?" Brigitte asked Gustano while comforting her child sitting next to her.

"I'm right where I need to be." Gustano pushed his chair back. "This stuff does taste like socks." He threw his napkin on the table.

The sound of a plane's engine caught their attention.

"What's that?" Miguel said.

"Airplane, radial engine." Javier pushed back from the table and ran outside. Gustano and Miguel followed.

Amelia spotted what looked like a dirt runway, a couple miles ahead. As she drew closer, she spotted a DC-3 or C-47. She couldn't tell at three-thousand feet up if it was like the one she and her dad owned. It certainly was not painted the same. She slowed the airplane down and descended to one-thousand feet to get a better look.

"They're coming back," Javier yelled.

"Miguel, get on the machine gun and shoot it down. Javier, grab the missile launcher." Both men ran off as the airplane approached.

Amelia saw men running from a house towards a large hangar-like building. She studied the C-47 as best she could as she flew over.

"What's going on?" Fabio yelled.

"Now!" Gustano yelled, moving his arm down violently.

A yellowish orange glow marked the tip of a camouflaged machine gun. A second later, smoke billowed from the yellow T-6. The plane pitched up and down violently. A moment later, the plane disappeared out of sight. In the distance, black smoke marked the spot where the plane went down.

"Yes!" Miguel screamed.

Javier stumbled from another building, carrying a rocket launcher. "Already got it," Miguel shouted, an elated grin spreading across his face.

"Grab the Jeep!" Gustano yelled.

Amelia pulled at her leg, but she couldn't free it. Blood ran into her left eye. She wiped at it, streaking the back of her hand with blood. The airplane had landed in thick vegetation. The engine smoldered, and the propeller tip was disfigured, with one end buried deep into the ground. The flames died down seconds after they started, as the wet vegetation cooled the plane's underbelly. She had to free herself before those that shot her down located her, and with smoke still rising from the engine, it wouldn't take them long. She immediately grasped the dire situation she was in. If they were drug runners, they would most likely kill her—or worse.

She struggled at her leg. Her boot was pinned between the rudder pedal and the frame of the caved in fuselage where it came to rest against a large rock. She stretched, locating her shoelace, and pulled at them. Her foot moved. She heard a vehicle off in the distance.

Javier jumped from the Jeep, grabbing a rifle out of the back as he did. Gustano and Miguel stepped out right behind him. Miguel grabbed a rifle, Gustano lifted his pistol. They ran into the overgrown vegetation, making their way to the smoke, using machetes to cut through the thick vines and plants.

Javier stepped onto the wing, peering into the cockpit. Then as best as he could, checked around the fuselage and under the wing tips. "They're gone," he yelled. Gustano and Miguel arrived at the crash site. Gustano jumped onto the wing and looked inside.

"Blood!" He pointed to the pilot's seat.

Javier removed a fire extinguisher from the airplane and put the last of the fire out.

"Split up, let's find them," barked Gustano.

Amelia's heart raced. She struggled at the thick plants and soft ground. Her only shoe kept sticking in thick, foul-smelling mud. After what seemed like an hour, but actuality only thirty minutes, she finally made it to a clearing. There was no one around. She tried running; but her head hammered relentlessly, and her foot felt like it was either broken or badly sprained.

"See anything?" Gustano asked as he and Miguel stumbled into the same spot.

"Nothing."

"Where's Javier?"

"Not sure."

"Let's get back to the Jeep."

"Javier? Javier?" There was no answer.

Gustano jumped in the driver's seat as Miguel slid in beside him. Dirt sprayed from the tires as they headed back to get Sting, the rottweiler.

Amelia made it to an old dirt road. She leaned over, holding her head.

"Hold it right there," Fabio yelled. Amelia thought about running, but she knew it was pointless. Fabio grabbed her from behind and jerked her head back. "What's your name? How many of you are there?" Amelia didn't answer. "Answer me or I'll kill you. Answer me!" Amelia kept silent. "Get on your knees. I'm not going to ask you again, get on your knees." Fabio swung his hand into her face. "Stupid girl!"

Gustano and Miguel sped along the overgrown access road. Fabio was standing in the middle, with a gun pointing at a person on their knees. Gustano skidded to a stop.

"See, Boss, I'm not totally useless," Fabio shouted.

"I see…and who do we have here?" Gustano moved in closer. "A girl?"

"Yeah, and she's a stubborn one, too."

Amelia spit blood at the ground. "Where's the pilot?" Gustano asked.

Amelia, hesitating for a second, realized their assumption. "He's gone for help."

"He has, has he?" Gustano measured her delayed response. "No worries, if there is another pilot, they won't escape here alive."

Javier walked up to the Jeep, out of breath. "Well, she's a pretty one. I get her first."

"Who are you and why are you spying on us?" Miguel asked.

Amelia didn't answer.

"Little lady, if you don't answer the question, I may grant my impetuous young companion here his desire," said Gustano.

"I'm not spying on you. I don't even know who you are. I'm looking for my father who's missing."

"Missing? Oh, you can do better than that, little girl."

Amelia's stomach twisted. She felt hot and dizzy. She leaned over, throwing up on the ground. Miguel rotated out of the way. "Poor girl probably has a concussion," Miguel said.

"What's with her white hair? Is she some sort of angel?" Javier asserted, trying to get a better look at her face. Amelia's green flight suit was ripped down the left leg. Blood, dirt, and vegetation stained her chest and arms.

"Pick her up and put her in the Jeep. Then tie her up in the barracks. Have Brigitte care for her head. Miguel, come with me."

"Fabio," Miguel said as he was turning, "better let Javier let the dog out. One smell of blood from your fork wound and he might bite your arm off." Miguel chuckled as he caught up to Gustano. They both walked along the road, and then back into the thick vegetation where the airplane sat. Miguel pulled out the emergency locating transmitter while Gustano searched the plane.

Javier and Fabio drove Amelia back to the base camp, held at gunpoint. Javier turned to his brother. "Fabio, you're going to get us both killed if you keep doing stupid stuff."

"I didn't do anything."

"That's the problem, you don't do anything."

"Oh yeah? Well, that's easy for you to say. You just sit at the controls of airplanes all day, pushing buttons, while Miguel and I do all the real work."

Amelia sat quietly listening to them argue. She felt sick, scared, and realized she was in serious trouble. As the Jeep pulled to a stop, she eyed the C-47. The two brothers pulled her out of the Jeep and walked her over to a large rusted building that had looked like a hangar from the air.

Amelia's heart nearly beat out of her chest, as they walked past the C-47. There was army green painted on the inside the wheel wells. *Could it be? Could this be my dad's C-47?*

"Get in here," said Fabio. "I tell you what, this is one messed up girl."

"She's hot, what are you talking about," said Javier. "Look at those green eyes, white hair, and that shape." Javier patted her on the butt. Amelia twisted, kicking her foot into Javier's leg.

"Ow, you stupid—"

Fabio burst out laughing. "You still think she's all that? She's a feisty one, that's for sure. Maybe she's military?"

"Maybe." Javier rubbed his shin and pursed his lips. "I kinda like 'em spirited."

"I do think you might be right about this one, brother," said Fabio, ogling as he walked around her chair. "She may be an angel. I think I could like this one, too." Amelia slipped her arm free and slapped Fabio in the face.

Javier chuckled. "You could like anything with two legs and a pulse."

"This one likes to play rough," said Fabio, pulling her hand back tightly behind her.

Cold Shoulder

Heat from the sun radiated my shoulders as I made my way up the museum cement steps. The sapphire sky bleached white where the sun hung, just past its apex. The museum was un-crowded, and I found my way to the archive room without trouble. Daniela unlocked the door. Her hair, situated in a bun, had a wooden darning needle spiked through it to hold it in place. Her green business suit turned abruptly and headed to a table. She glanced back, ensuring I followed. "You said on the phone you had some new information."

"Yes—and thank you again for still wanting to help me."

"What help do you need?" She turned and shelved three books.

"How familiar are you with Mauricio's past?"

"I already told you what I know."

"Did you know Donny and Mauricio worked at five museums to-gether?"

She stopped. "Five—together?"

"Not counting this one, and that's not all. Three of the five they worked at had insurance claims."

Daniela sat back in a chair. She took in a deep breath. "What does that prove?" she said sharply. Daniela had held a student-teacher rever-ence for Mauricio, but in her expression, I could see that image melting away.

"Maybe nothing; on the other hand, the circumstantial evidence is mounting."

Daniela blurted out. "So, all your personal attention and kindness toward me, that was all just part of your job? Your duty? How many women do you string along like that in your line of work, huh?"

"Daniela." She turned away from me as tears flowed down her cheeks. "Nothing about my feelings toward you was part of the job. I truly care for you." Daniela pulled out a tissue and wiped her cheeks. She raised her head; her eyes softened. She let me put my arm around her. I finished sharing the information I had on Donny and Mauricio. Her eyes dried and darted about the room. I told her I was leaving for New York in a few hours. Even though I didn't ask, she made it clear she didn't want to go. After the hour-long visit, I returned to the hotel room.

"Where's Gerry?" I asked.

"Out picking up a package," Kathy replied.

"Any leads from the liquid packaging companies?"

"Nothing from the ones I contacted. Gerry's stopping by one of the companies that didn't want to talk."

"And from the surveillance?"

"Nothing about stolen art. Your flight is in three hours." Kathy swiveled her chair around. "Here's the information you need." She handed me a sheet of paper with the flight details.

"Detective Andrea Dias is insistent on meeting with me."

"Do you think she's found out anything?"

"I'll find out shortly." I reached for the doorknob between the two rooms as Kathy's door flew open.

"Cougar, how did it go?" Gerry questioned, nearly out of breath.

"Daniela's still upset with me, but I did verify they don't use bottled water in their museum."

"Hmm." Gerry said, turning and facing Kathy. "That company you had me check out?"

"Yes?" Kathy prodded.

"Well, they weren't very helpful towards me either. I did snap a few pictures of some of their products when they weren't looking. I'll forward those to your phone, Cougar."

"Thank you, Gerry, I'll glance through them on the airplane." My phone alarm chirped. "I better get going."

"A little early isn't it?" Gerry asked.

"I'm stopping at the police station first."

"Have they uncovered anything?"

"I think it's the other way around."

"Cougar."

"Yes, Gerry?"

"I…um…wanted you to know that I installed a bug in Daniela's office too. I hope that's okay."

"Of course, Gerry. One can never be too sure—good thinking."

I grabbed my overnight bag and headed to the police station. Andrea Dias was talking with Eduardo Moreno as I approached the counter. Through the glass wall I saw Eduardo's hands flailing as he talked. The clerk at the counter ushered me to a chair next to Andrea's desk. Then he walked to Captain Moreno's office and knocked on the glass door, pointing in my direction. The door opened, and Eduardo waved me to his office.

"Arlan, please, we've been expecting you. Won't you sit down?" Eduardo gestured to a familiar chair.

"Detective Andrea—Captain Moreno, nice to see you both again," I said politely.

Andrea spoke first, "Well? It seems you've been nosing about quite a bit?"

"Just doing my job. Have you uncovered any information that could help the board? I'm going to release my report to the Fine Arts Insurance Board in a few days. I'll be stating that we have found no further reason to delay Delrow Insurance Agency from processing the claim to the museum." I eyed both of them with an inquisitive stare.

"We have information placing you at a party the other night at Don Tallman's residence."

"Guilty as charged," I said.

"By any chance did you happen to see a car chase or hear gun fire after the party?"

"I'm afraid I didn't notice anything. The party was still in full swing when I left."

"Were you alone?" Andrea asked, adjusting her shirt, smoothing out the pooching at her belly.

"No, I wasn't. Miss Perez was with me."

"I see." Eduardo scratched at his chin, like he had at our first meeting—probably a tactic he learned in Interrogation Training 101. "Seems you two are spending a bit of time together lately," Eduardo suggested.

"Is that an issue?"

"There's no law against it," Eduardo added in disappointment. "And you didn't notice anything unusual at the party?"

"If you're referring to gunfire, car chases, or hailstorm…then no, funny little sandwiches…yes. Now if I may," I turned to Andrea. "How long have you known Mr. Mauricio?"

Before Andrea could answer, Eduardo interrupted. "We ask the questions around here, *Arlan*." He spit my name out like it was bad cheese.

Andrea's eyebrows relaxed, "Long enough. Mr. Lopez is a model citizen here in Bogota. It's you we're having trouble figuring out. You seem almost too…" Andrea held the word in her mouth like a jaw breaker, "polite, and that has us…distrustful."

"Because I'm polite?"

"Something about you is off," Captain Eduardo added. "I'm good at judging character. I haven't made it to this glass-walled office by taking people at face value, you know."

"Well, if you come up with anything that might be of help to the board, please let me know. Meanwhile, I'll try not to be so polite. Now if you'll please excuse me, I have another commitment."

"See," Eduardo said, "there's that polite subterfuge again. I, on the other hand, gravitate toward toughness. Now stay out of our investigation and be a good little insurance agent and go home!"

"It's been my pleasure, Captain." I nodded, then turned to Andrea, "Detective." I exited the police station and caught a taxi to the airport.

On the airplane I pulled out my phone and scanned through the pictures Gerry had sent me. They were of large plastic water and chemical bags and liners. One picture in particular caught my eye. I had seen similar bags, crumpled on the ground, next to empty water bottles by the dumpsters at the New York City Museum.

A middle-aged lady with streaks in her hair and wearing a blue uniform asked, "disculpe señor, ¿le gustaría algo de beber?"

"Perrier with lemon, por favor," I replied, while passing two plastic cups of soda to the travelers sitting next to me. "Muchas gracias."

I leaned back in my chair and thought about Daniela. I knew she liked me—I liked her too, despite the recent bitterness she showed. For a moment, I felt at peace. The thought of a relationship with her felt right, almost human. But she lives in Colombia and I in the United States—the northern border of the United States none-the-less. Why am I thinking about a relationship with her when I know she loves Colombia and would never want to leave? Art and history are her life; that's what she lives for.

Amelia also entered my thoughts. I hadn't heard from her in a couple days, not that she owed me a call. Still, from time to time she had been checking in, keeping me up-to-date on her search efforts. I worried about her. I found I cared for her in a different way. Not in a romantic way, although I did find her very attractive. Amelia came to me through my private practice, and I have a cardinal rule in place. *Don't get involved with clients.*

"Excuse me, can I trouble you?" the man sitting next to me asked. "I need to stretch my legs and use the restroom." *I could use a little stretch myself.* I stood up and walked down the aisle to the front of the plane then walked back. I did this a few more times until the man re-seated himself.

As I sat back in the seat, my mind shifted again, this time to Trinity and my early training. Gerry, Kathy, and I were younger and had no idea what we had signed up for. For me, Trinity was a chance to fly cool airplanes and make good money. For Kathy and Gerry, they had their own reasons. Through Trinity, I learned to fly some of the most sophisticated airplanes and jets in existence. I also had the privilege of flying some relics, older planes, right out of World War II. As a civilian, flying alongside seasoned military pilots was a dream come true. Learning hand-to-hand combat and training with special guns and ammunition also proved exciting. Early on, I studied every waking minute, so I'd be prepared when my first actual mission came.

Mission flying for Trinity has a special appeal. What is less appealing is seeing people at their worst. Criminals of all types, year after year. Most of our missions are successful; some not. Our record for successfully recovering assets is better than any other civilian or military agency, according to the statistics Riley has shared. Leaving Trinity full time to start my own asset recovery business was not heralded as a wise move, but so far, working for Trinity part-time and my PI business part-time (sometimes more) seems to be working out just about right.

Chapter 31

Criminal Moguls

K athy's phone rang. "It's Riley; Good morning, sir."

"Good morning, Kathy, is Gerry there with you?"

"Yes," Kathy pressed a key on her computer. "We're both on now." Shuffling noises were heard in the background.

"David's got some information on Gustano, the man Cougar was introduced to at the party. It seems Cougar's instincts were correct. Loading the picture from Cougar's button camera into the database, we were able to get a pretty good portrayal of him." Rustling sounds. "I'll let David tell you himself."

"Good morning, Kathy and Gerry, how's Bogota this morning?"

"Very mild," said Kathy.

"Well, Gustano is one bad dude from everything I've been able to uncover, although he stays largely in the background. His dirty business dealings get noticed from time to time, but no one does anything about it. Colombia harbors several of these criminal moguls. The police know about them, too; but don't do much to dissuade them or their illegal activities. Many of them are powerful and influential. In a way I guess they help keep order, although certainly not law and order. Gustano doesn't appear to be a top mogul, but he does have some power and influence. A few years back, he led an uprising, discrediting a popular candidate during one of the elections. The candidate was initially pro-jected to win by a landslide. Instead, he withdrew from the race."

"Anything more recent?"

"Like I mentioned, he stays pretty much in the background and off the grid. It appears he only surfaces when he needs money or when there's a cause worth fighting against. We did find links between him and several killings, including the assassination of a notorious drug lord. There were also several robberies tied to him."

"I see…were you able to find out how big his posse is?"

"Not really. It appears with his power and connections, he either attracts or hires his gangs as circumstances warrant. They fluctuate from just a few to an army—enough to create a massive disturbance anyway."

Riley broke in. "Make sure Cougar has this information."

"Of course, sir."

"David?" Gerry asked.

"Here, Gerry."

"Did you find out where Gustano lives?"

"Not exactly. We think he's somewhere south of Bogota, but that's as much as we could find, and even that may be old information. There are several of these entrepreneurial moguls living amongst the hills in the south."

"How is Cougar's friend Amelia doing? You know I feel bad about trumping his personal client this time; but as you guys may not know, there's a lot of pressure from the White House on us finding the historic art. More strained relations with Colombia we don't need right now."

"We're not sure. Amelia is flying around Colombia trying to locate either her dad's body or his airplane. After the co-pilot's body was discovered in Colombia and based on Cougar's conjecture about her dad's plane being hijacked and used for drug smuggling, she committed herself to search here until she found something."

"That doesn't sound like a very good idea, flying around trying to identify a drug runners' airplane?"

"We didn't think so either. Cougar tried to talk her out of it, but she was insistent on finding out the truth," said Kathy.

"Well, let's hope you guys can quickly uncover some evidence that moves this mission forward. The sooner that happens, the sooner Cougar can get back to helping this lady. I wish I could prioritize things different; but I'm unable to this time."

"We understand, sir. We're doing all we can to bring this mission to a close. This one has been especially difficult; but with a guy like Gustano being at Mauricio's party, well…that may be the break we need. Mauricio told Cougar that Gustano was an important museum donor. That doesn't line up with what David just shared."

"No, it doesn't," Riley said. "Remember, the police are probably not going to create waves with the illegal underground establishment. Some in the police force may even be associated with them, so be extra vigilant."

"We will, sir, and thank you."

The Recital

"Mr. Montoya—"

"Please, call me Jim."

"Jim, when I was here before, I noticed some large flexible bags, like for holding liquid, down by your loading dock next to a dumpster. I also saw a large number of empty five-gallon water bottles too. Does your museum use bottled drinking water?"

"I'm not sure I can help you with your first observation. What you saw may have been packing material. As far as bottled water..." Jim pointed to a small alcove in his office. Slightly obscured from view, was a refrigeration dispenser with an inverted five-gallon bottle of water resting on top.

"Do you mind?" I asked.

"Please."

I poured myself a cup and tilted it back. "Thank you, I'm a little dehydrated from the flight." I scanned the books lining the shelves and the back of his office. "You had shared earlier that you inspected the crates alongside an insurance agent from Delrow and several others, is that correct?"

"That's correct."

"Was it Donald Tallman?"

"Yes, he's the agent we've been dealing with."

"And you personally inspected all twelve crates?" Jim pulled at a drawer, removed a tissue from a box and wiped his forehead.

"I did say that" he confessed slowly, his eyes scanning the ceiling.

"Jim…did you inspect every crate and every artifact?" He pulled at another tissue.

After a long obstinate silence, he replied. "It was the night of my niece's recital. I promised my sister I would be there. When I went to our holding area, the lids were already off the crates. I saw several Colombian artifacts as I walked along. Mr. Tallman was next to me and inspected the contents. Two men representing Mauricio Lopez were also there, inspecting right along with our museum security guard."

"How much of the crates did you personally see?"

Jim smacked his lips apart. "I had shared earlier with Mr. Tallman my meeting conflict for that evening. He told me it wouldn't be a problem and for me not to be concerned. Along with the two gentlemen from Colombia, he said he would confirm that all the art was accounted for and note it on the manifest. I had no reason to doubt him, besides our museum guard would be there to verify the contents and secure the area before leaving."

"How did she do?"

"Who?"

"Your niece."

"Oh, right-right. It was…memorable. That's why I have forgotten it already."

"Do you recall what was under the artifacts you did see?"

"Protective wrap, some straw. That would be standard packaging from a place in South America."

"I would like to see the storage room and loading dock again. I can find my way there."

"Please go right ahead. I'll be here when you're finished. I have a bum hip that continues to play havoc when walking long distances."

I turned, and before leaving his office, asked. "The guard that was here the night the crates were inspected, is he working today, and can I talk with him?"

Jim mumbled something to his desk. "Excuse me, Jim, I didn't catch that." I moved back near his desk.

"Our guard was so distraught over the disappearance of the Colombian art that he quit after hearing of the burglary."

"Do you have an address?"

"I was told he left the country to go back to his homeland."

"Which is?"

"I believe he was from Brazil."

"I see." I couldn't tell if Jim was slow or just plain naïve. He didn't seem the type to be involved in a major theft ring.

I left Jim in his office and made my way to the loading dock. The place was clean, no workers, no trash around the dumpsters, and no flexible liquid containers. Even the dumpsters were empty. It seemed I learned all I was going to from Jim Montoya. He had not inspected the crates, at least not all the way. Artifacts could have easily been placed on top of packaging material with liners filled with water just beneath them—enough water to satisfy the necessary weights for the freight forwarders' manifest. I still couldn't prove this theory, but one thing is for certain. Donny appears to be in the middle of whatever took place. And if Donny Tallman is involved, his college buddy, Mauricio, is most likely involved too.

Another Flight

Cougar stepped to the side of the passageway, set his bag down and grabbed his phone. "Hi Daniela, is everything okay?"

"Yes. Could you come to the museum today?"

"I'm still at the airport." Cougar glanced at his watch. "Is three hours too long?"

"No, that's fine. I'll see you in three." Daniela clicked off. Cougar caught a taxi back to the hotel.

"We have some information on Gustano," Kathy said.

"Oh, Yeah? What did you find out?" Cougar surveyed the food tray. "You don't mind if I finish off this bread, do you?"

"Really? I didn't think you were much of a bread eater."

"This looks like a vegetable compared to what they tried to pass off as food on the airplane. Please continue."

"Gustano is about what you thought, only somewhat worse. He's a two-bit trafficking thug with bouts of prominence in the underground establishment."

"Drugs?"

"It seems most anything that pays."

"Art burglaries?" Cougar asked.

"Could be. Riley didn't have anything recent on him or his location, but from what David dug up, it's possible he could be the muscle behind the plan. There's some sketchy information indicating he's done similar type activities," said Kathy.

"Did those pictures help that I sent you?" Gerry asked.

"Well, they might have. Whatever I saw the last time was gone. Since the NYPD detective wouldn't allow me to take pictures on my first visit, I contacted them and asked if I could see theirs."

"Let me guess," Gerry said.

"You'd be right. I did get a confession from Jim Montoya. He only superficially inspected the crates. Donny Tallman, a couple men from Bogota—not Mauricio, and a New York City museum security guard were the only ones that inventoried the art. Oh, and the New York City Museum guard? He quit shortly after the art went missing and returned to his homeland, supposedly in Brazil. I have his name; but I don't think we'll get any matches."

"It's worth a try," Kathy stated.

"His name is—get this—John Smith." Kathy rolled her eyes.

"Gerry, anything from Mauricio?"

Gerry shook his head. "You would think he's an outstanding civic leader from all we have heard. I don't get it."

"Daniela asked me to meet her at the museum today. I think she may have found something."

Kathy tapped on her keyboard. "I have another lead you may want to check out." Kathy showed a warehouse on her screen. "The Bogota museum pays its utilities."

"Recently?"

"Last month."

"Good work, I think we're getting warm. See how soon you can get me on a flight, I'd like to check it out. I'll go see what Daniela wants."

Chapter 34

The Painting

"A rlan?" Mauricio called, as Cougar passed by his office door. "Can you step in here for a minute?"

"Sure, what can I do for you?"

"Captain Moreno says the FAIB is giving Delrow Insurance Agency their approval letter to commence settlement. I just want to say thank you and I'm sorry you had to trouble yourself and come all the way to Bogota. I guess you'll be going back soon?"

"I guess information shared with the police is not so confidential here."

"Oh, Arlan, you must know by now that in Colombia we're a close-knit bunch. We're not like you Americans. In America, you can walk side by side with someone—right next to them in fact, and never say a word. Now that's strange. In Colombia, and most parts of the world, it's much different. You must get out more."

"I agree. In fact, I like it so much here in Colombia, I'm planning to stay a couple more weeks. I sent word back to the FAIB that I'm delaying my report until then."

The edges of Mauricio's eyes creased behind his gold-rimmed glasses; his cheerfulness dimmed. "I'm sorry to hear that." His eyes sank back to his desk. "You let me know if there's anything I can help with."

Cougar walked past two more offices. Not seeing Daniela in her office, he backtracked to the historical archive room, and knocked on the door. A moment later, Daniela stood in the opening. Her hair was gathered eloquently over her shoulders like it had the night of the party. The nostalgic moment passed quickly as Danila turned abruptly.

"Come in and close the door please." Daniela's high heeled shoes rocked slightly with each step until they stopped at a computer station. "I want to show you something." She tapped on the computer keyboard until a picture displayed. "This is the painting I saw in Donny's house."

"Donny liking fine art doesn't surprise me, with his background and education."

"That's not it. After seeing the picture in his room that day, I couldn't get it out of my head." She tapped on the computer, shifted the computer mouse back and forth, and clicked until a new page displayed. Daniela pointed to a story on the screen about a theft at an art museum in the UK. She clicked through a few pages, stopping at one that showed the same painting that was in Donny's house.

Cougar stared in silence. "Are you sure it was the original?"

"Ninety-five percent."

"Do you think Donny could have bought it at an auction? Maybe he had nothing to do with the burglary."

"It's possible, I guess." Daniela stood up, facing Cougar and grabbed his hands. "Arlan, is it okay if I still call you that?"

"Of course."

"I'm scared."

Cougar gently squeezed her hands. "Daniela, I'm going to Cartagena tonight."

"What for?"

"We think your museum has a warehouse there."

"We do? I never knew that. Would you like me to come?"

"I would like that, but I don't think it's such a good idea. Besides, I'll only be there for the—"

"Mr. Lopez," Daniela interrupted. "I didn't see you come in." She dropped her arms.

"Well, did you two lovebirds find a hideaway? And all this time I thought you were researching information to satisfy the FAIB's requirements."

"I am, we are. I'm sorry Mr. Lopez, it's just that it's been a hard week," said Daniela.

"Arlan, I entrust you have the necessary information now. I don't think the museum's director or Board of Trustees would look as favorably towards this…conflict of interest as I would. I'm still young enough to appreciate the desires of the heart; but they…well, they're businessmen. Daniela."

"Yes, Mr. Lopez."

"I need you to stay late tonight and check in the new exhibit from Brazil. It should be here around 9pm. I hate to ask, but I have another engagement I must keep tonight."

"Of course, I would be happy to, Mr. Lopez."

"Thank you, Daniela—Arlan." Mauricio walked out the door, closing it behind him.

Daniela spoke first. "How long do you think he was standing there?"

"I'm—really—not—sure." Cougar replied, his forehead creasing slightly. "Are you going to be okay tonight?"

"Yes, Arlan, I'll be fine." Daniela raised up on the front of her shoes and kissed Cougar on the lips.

Mauricio reached for his phone as he ascended the stairs leading back to his office. "Gustano…make that two jobs tonight."

Chapter 35

Loverboy

Amelia woke from her slumber, hearing the squeal of rusty wheels on a metal track as the large sliding door opened. She recoiled, thinking about the two men who had tied her up and had made several advances towards her throughout the day. Light from the doorway revealed it was the same woman who had brought her breakfast. In the morning, the woman had set the food down, untied her hands, and let her eat. Afterwards, and at gunpoint, she let her use the nearly inhabitable bathroom in the corner of the old military barracks. She had spoken only a few words, and those she did were staccato commands.

Brigitte carried a lunch tray over and sat it on Amelia's lap and untied her hands. Speaking in another staccato command, she said, "eat".

Amelia rubbed at her wrists. Her legs were zip tied to the base of the chair. As Amelia ate, she observed the woman hovering over her. She was not much older than she was, and her exposed body parts were covered in tattoos. Her shoulder length brown hair frizzed like it hadn't been brushed in days. Amelia thought, if her hair and face were cleaned up, she could be quite pretty. Instead she looked hard, old, and mean.

"What are you gawking at?" Brigitte demanded.

"I wasn't gawking," Amelia replied.

Brigette's eyes travelled up and down Amelia's body. She adjusted the pistol on her hip.

"Why are you keeping me here?" Amelia blurted out.

"You poor thing," Brigitte said, using her fingers to stroke Amelia's face. She let her other hand glide through Amelia's platinum white hair. "You know it feels like normal hair." Amelia's head snapped backward. The tray of food fell to the ground. "Oh—no!" Brigitte chuckled. "Well you probably didn't want to eat too much anyway—spoil that slim body of yours, huh?" Brigitte kicked the tray away.

"Why are you doing this? I've done nothing to you."

"I know your type—rich girls. Born with a silver spoon in their mouth. Flying around in expensive airplane like you're better than all of us. I see how you look at me—judging me."

"I need to use the bathroom."

"Who are you working for and what do you want?"

"I want to use the bathroom."

"A girl like you is probably working for the government, or maybe Canelé. Are you working for Canelé?"

"I really need to use the bathroom, and I'm on vacation, just flying around Colombia."

"Nobody just flies around Colombia, especially not around these parts, not if they have half a brain." Brigitte cut the zip-ties and pushed her towards the bathroom. Amelia fell, only reaching out at the last minute to protect her head from the cement floor.

Amelia studied the bathroom more carefully for a way to escape before Brigitte followed her in and stood watch until she was finished. "Don't get any ideas, A-meel-i-a. I have killed people with these hands, and recently, I might add. Brigitte's tanned and tattooed cleavage shook as she pushed Amelia out of the bathroom. "Back in your chair!"

"Can I please get some fresh air? Just for a minute?"

"Chair!" Brigitte shrieked, forcing her to sit down. After Amelia's legs were zip-tied to the chair and wrists tied, Brigitte closed the rolling door. Darkness enveloped the room. Once her eyes adjusted to the dim light, Amelia could once again see to the corners of the building, aided with the help of tiny pinholes in the roof.

Less than an hour transpired, or so it seemed, before Fabio entered the barracks. Amelia flinched as he stepped over to her. "Did you miss me, Angel?"

"Please, don't hurt me."

"I'm not going to hurt you; Fabio likes you." He sniffed Amelia's hair.

"If you like me then please let me get some fresh air. I'm feeling claustrophobic in here, and the smell is awful."

Fabio strutted around Amelia's chair, eyeing her like a prized possession. "If I do you a favor, will you be nice to me?"

"I'm not sure what you mean," Amelia voiced cautiously.

"I'm still mad at you for slapping me."

"I won't slap you," she blurted.

"Well, I guess I can do that, but only for a couple minutes." He put his finger to his lips. "We need to be very quiet though so Brigette doesn't find out. She gets angry easy." Fabio untied Amelia's hands. Then cut the zip-ties off her legs. "I'm warning you, don't try anything."

"I'm not going to try anything." Fabio re-tied her wrists behind her back and walked her out through the rolling door. The brightness momentarily blinded her. After blinking several times, she opened her eyes, seeing the C-47 still parked there. The smaller twin, a Piper Seneca was gone. "Wasn't there a Piper Seneca here before?" she asked.

"No questions!"

"I love airplanes. Are you a pilot?"

"I said no questions." Fabio puffed up his shoulders. "My brother's the pilot—and the boss, he's also a pilot. I have other skills."

"What kind of plane is that?" Amelia asked, staring at the C-47.

"Not sure, a C-something. I think it's a military version of a DC-3…I think."

"Can I get a closer look? It's really cool."

Fabio looked around to make sure Brigitte wasn't anywhere in sight. "I guess it wouldn't hurt." Amelia ducked and walked under the C-47 over to the rear door to look in.

She stood there in silence, her lungs ineffective, her heart unable to pump. Time stopped. Then her heart slammed back in service. Blood coursed through her body, only now her heart was palpitating so fast she thought her ribs would break. Each flip down seat she remembered fastening in with her dad. And the decals. Each one had taken so long to reproduce, and then came the placement. Each one painstakingly placed per spec, just like it was when her grandpa flew this airplane so many decades earlier.

With all the strength she could muster, she asked in a calm tone, "How long have you had this one?"

Fabio grabbed Amelia and turned her toward the barracks. "Time for you to go back, you've had your fresh air."

"That's a nice airplane," Amelia prodded again. Fabio straightened up, throwing his shoulders back. "We got it a month ago. I killed a couple guys to get it. That's my job, I do most the killing." Amelia once again couldn't breathe. Her throat dried up, making her gag; but nothing came out. "Water please," she finally uttered. She fought back her tears. In seconds, her sadness turned to anger and hatred.

"Your daylight vacation is over." Fabio pushed her down into the chair. Amelia fell backwards, immediately kicking her leg into his groin. Fabio buckled over. She quickly stood up and swung her leg at Fabio's knee. He went down to the ground.

"You little tramp!" Fabio threw Amelia back in the chair and zip-tied her. "Now let's see who's the tough one." Fabio moved in to force himself on Amelia. He heard a click. Standing behind him, Brigitte had her pistol out, aimed at Fabio's head.

"Let her go," Brigitte said.

"She likes me." Fabio stroked her white hair. Brigitte hit him with the stock of her pistol.

"Ouch, what did you do that for. You women are all the same—insecure." Fabio rubbed the back of his head and backed off of Amelia.

Brigitte swung the butt of her pistol, this time hitting Amelia's right cheek. Amelia grimaced.

"That's for encouraging him." Blood oozed from Amelia's cheek and lip. "Come on lover boy. You have work to do."

The door squealed closed; Amelia wept uncontrollably.

Warehouse in Cartagena

"Excuse me," I asked, "is there an open table?" The waitress stopped in mid-stride and gestured me to the bar. "Gracias." I ordered a variant of a cobb salad paired with a sparkling water and lemon. I was left alone, other than an occasional bump from the butt of a pool que.

The location of the warehouse was still a few blocks down the road. The sun sunk low as I ambled my way toward the docks. Within a few minutes, a vibrant glow of orangish-purple brightened the sky behind the warehouses and manufacturing buildings as the sunset bloomed.

"Buenas noches," I bestowed to a couple men passing by in a hurry. The uneven sidewalk ended as I reached the docks. Quietness enveloped, although my ears were still ringing from the commotion in the bar. In the time it took to locate the warehouse, the glow of the sun had extinguished, and the sky had blackened, revealing dock lights every twenty-five feet.

The warehouse walls were cement with doors made of steel, facing the road. I worked my way quietly to the dock. A chain link fence blocked me from proceeding any further. There was a pitch-black window on this side of the building and no sign of activity. An old rusty package freighter squeaked against rubber tires as it nodded gently in the oily water. It was not a huge ship, barely two-hundred feet in length.

The chain link fence stopped at the dock's edge, with razor wire protecting the last few inches.

I backtracked, walking down the street in front of the warehouse, searching for an easier egress. The front gate had a chain around the posts with a locked padlock. All the steel loading dock doors were closed. In the upper left, another window, only this one held a faint red glow. A truck disturbed the silence, shifting gears and increasing speed. As it drew closer, still picking up speed, I jumped against the fence. The truck's mirror missed my head by only a foot or so. I doubt the driver even saw me. Wearing black has its advantages—and disadvantages. As the truck turned the corner, I pulled out a tool, picked the lock and ducked into the warehouse parking lot.

There were a few cars in the lot. Two of them had flat tires and dirt caked on the windows. I unzipped my jacket, touching my holster. The knob on the pedestrian door wouldn't turn. The red glow in the upper window meant the building alarm was probably set. I grabbed my cell, tapped in Gerry, and held it to my ear. "Gerry, can you hear me?"

"Cougar, are you there?"

"Yes, I need your help on the alarm system."

"Okay, do you have the sensor turned on?"

"Standby." I pulled Gerry's device from another pocket and slid the 'ON' button up. "Affirmative."

"Okay, now click the yellow read button and scan the building."

I pressed the yellow button and moved the sensor the full length of the building in both directions and for both floors. "Done."

"Okay, standby."

"Gerry…you still there?"

"Yes, sorry. Best I can tell, just the top floor alarm is set."

"Are you sure?"

"As sure as I can be without being there to check it out myself."

"How accurate is your gadget?"

"Seventy-five…no eighty percent"

"Seventy-five percent from one of your gadgets is good enough for me."

"Be careful, Cougar."

I stashed my phone and Gerry's miracle gadget and tried each of the rolling doors. None of them budged. Staying close to the walls, I proceeded to the far side of the warehouse and around to the dock. The dock lights lit up the back side of the building like sunrise. I stayed low and away from the light as much as possible. Three doors in, I noticed a four-inch space beneath it. I crouched, approaching slowly. A pallet was stuck under the door, preventing it from closing all the way. That's probably why the first-floor alarm had not been activated. After attempting to set it a few times, they probably gave up, figuring further delays would make them late for happy hour.

I bent down and looked through the door opening. A few empty pallets and some larger crates were all I could see. I reached my arm underneath the door until I heard a chain clank. One clink at a time, I pulled the chain, slowly raising the door. When I could fit under it, I slid through.

I clicked the light attached to my forehead and stepped over to the crates. The stenciling showed the crates were from Brazil—both empty. I followed the light beam while panning across the floor and walls of the large warehouse. No art, no treasure. Nothing screamed asylum for stolen goods.

Suddenly, the warehouse lit up like a runway. I dove behind the crates.

"Get him," I heard. "He's behind the crates."

I couldn't tell how many of them there were; two, maybe three? How did they know I was here? Footsteps clambered down a steel circular staircase from the second floor. With only a spilt second to make my move, I pulled out my gun, ran toward the opening under the door, and slid through it like a baseball player sliding into second base. As I got to my feet, footsteps from two different directions came at me. The first guy grabbed me from behind around my chest, causing my pistol to drop to the ground. As the second man approached, I reared back against the first man and kicked the approaching man in his chest, sending him to the ground. His head contacted the cement like a ripe gourd. The metal doors were now being hurriedly opened.

The man with his arms around me ended up on the ground after my kick, with me landing hard on top of him. In the process, he released his hold on me. We both got to our feet and he reached for his gun. Before he could pull it out, I spun around, delivering a roundhouse kick into his jaw. The sound of his jaw cracking was followed by his legs wobbling and collapsing. I glanced at their uniforms; they were warehouse guards. A bullet ricocheted off a metal dock strap, not far from my foot. Two men ran out from the warehouse. They were not dressed like the first two, and both were carrying military rifles.

"Get him!"

I picked up my gun, let off a couple shots and ran to the edge of the dock, diving in next to the rusty freighter. I hit the hull of the ship, scraping my arm and body on the way in. Pings peppered the side of the ship as they hunted me down like cheating men at a fishing derby. The chilly saltwater created instant pain from the scrapes. The gunmen kept up their doggedness, sending bullets ricocheting off the ship's hull and into the water. I kicked for the dock, until I was swimming beneath them.

"There he is," I heard.

A bullet found its way between the dock boards, grazing my arm. I kicked to the nearest pylon. Barnacles, mussels, and other sea life clung tight to the underwater pylon. I had to get to the other side of the freighter. Their shadows cast reflections through the board gaps as they walked. An eyeball squinted between the boards. I pulled off a cluster of mussels from a pylon, thrust myself up and flung them toward the underside of the dock, shattering them on impact.

"My eyes! My eyes!" I heard. A man jumped around screaming for help. I dove under, kicking hard back towards the ship. I held my breath for two minutes until I was sure I was on the other side of the ship's stern. I surfaced when I could hold my breath no longer and gulped for air. Peering around the aft end of the hull, I saw a man stooped down low, with his hand over his eye. No sign of the second man. The two guards I hit earlier were now standing up, one rubbing his head.

"Do you see him?" one of the guards called out in my direction. I looked up; but only saw the hull of the ship.

"Shut up, you idiot, before I shoot you," a person on the ship replied.

Careful, as to not generate ripples, I edged my way to the bow of the ship. Across the canal were more ships and more docks. The lights were closer together and all of them lit up bright. A crane held a load in its grasp. I searched until I found what I was looking for; a ladder attached to a pylon leading up to one of the docks. I took three deep breaths and slipped under the water, kicking toward the other side of the canal.

Halfway there, a humming grew in my ears. I surfaced and spun around, searching for the source of the noise. A tender with its outboard at full throttle headed straight at me. I frantically dove under; the spinning propeller missed my foot only by inches. Somehow, they had managed to locate me in the dark. When I couldn't stay under any longer, I surfaced. A flash of light crossed over my head, followed by a bullet, tracing through the water. I ducked back under, swimming down as far as I could and held my breath. My ears pounded, my shoulder hurt, and the side of my body throbbed from hitting the ship's hull.

I waited until the humming stopped. I swam under and away from where I saw the boat last. My lungs craved air. I slowly surfaced my eyes and mouth, just enough to fill my lungs and dissipate the light-headedness. The boat sat thirty feet away, bobbing in the water. The silhouettes of two men and their guns framed the picture. The spotlight danced across ripples in the water heading my direction. They throttled the outboard and in seconds were on top of me again. This time they didn't fire their guns. Instead, they zigzagged back and forth, attempting to shred me to pieces.

I stayed under for what seemed an eternity; my autonomic system compelled me to inhale. When I couldn't hold out any longer, I surfaced. The outboard had stopped. I spun my head, searching for the boat. A muffled shot skimmed the water next to me. I heard two men laughing. Evidently, this was big fun for them. I swam down and away as fast as I could. My ears pounded and my chest grew tight again.

Another humming joined the sonata in the water, only this one had a lower throbbing beat. I ascended again before my lungs involuntarily gasped for air. The lights of a trawler slowly approached. I descended, kicking with every ounce of energy I had left to where I figured the boat would pass. The tender was now circling, searching, and waiting for me to surface again. As the boat passed, I soared up out of the water and grabbed onto a bumper that hung from the trawler's starboard side, opposite where the tender was circling. I held on tight, letting the boat drag me through the water and away from the gunmen. Ten minutes of banging against the hull and shivering uncontrollably, I let go after seeing a ladder similar to the one I'd seen earlier.

Grabbing the last rung, I pulled myself onto the dock and collapsed. My mind raced, trying to make sense of what just happened. Was I set up? If so, how? And by who? It seemed the men in the warehouse were waiting for me. But who knew I was coming here? Only Daniela—and possibly Mauricio if he had overheard me.

I laid my waterproof cell on the dock and hit redial. "Gerry!"

"Are you okay? You sound out of breath."

"I'm fine—now. I'll give you the debrief when I'm back. Have you heard anything out of Mauricio's wiretap?"

"Nothing unusual. He left work about six. It appears the engagement he had shared with Daniela was accurate. One of the city cameras caught him entering a gallery on the other side of town. What did you find at the warehouse?"

"A setup. Someone knew I was coming. Besides that, nothing, the building was completely empty. Is Mauricio still at the gallery?"

"We haven't seen him leave. Kathy's been monitoring the situation."

"Do me a favor. Track him when he leaves the gallery. I want to see what he's up to and who he's with. I'll catch you guys later."

I took a quick inventory of my body. Blood seeped from several areas. Nothing life threatening. Luckily, the bullet had only grazed me.

Another Warehouse

"What time are you getting up today?" Gerry asked, standing over Cougar's bed.

Cougar rolled over and moaned. "Ahhhh!"

"What's wrong?"

"A minor scrape…and…a lot of bruising evidently. I miscalculated a jump."

"Well, if you're ready to get up, Kathy found some information about another warehouse that the museum used several years ago."

"Oh, yeah?" Cougar sat up. "Where's this one located?"

"Local, edge of town, east side."

"How did she find this one?"

"You know Kathy, she keeps peeling back the onion one layer at a time. If something's there, she'll eventually find it."

Cougar called from the bathroom while shaving. "You guys eat already?"

"Only breakfast."

Cougar glanced at the time while fastening his watch around his wrist. "Eleven o'clock?"

"It's lunch time. I think Kathy already put in an order for us." Gerry stepped through the double door into Kathy's room. Cougar rubbed his leg where the ship had left a gouge. *Only a flesh wound,* he said to himself. He twisted his arm around. The bullet that grazed him didn't require stitches. He started at it in the mirror. *Luckily, just another flesh wound. Thank you, God.*

"Good morning, Kathy."

"Morning, Cougar, I'm glad you made it back safely."

"Thank you—me, too. Gerry said you located another place where the artifacts could be hidden?"

"I hate to send you on another wild goose chase, especially after last night; but I think this one's worth a look, and you don't have to take a flight to get there. It's on the outskirts of town."

"What makes this one more promising?"

"Well, I'd like to take all the credit; but actually, David helped find this one. A few years ago, Bogota held a huge festival." Cougar wore a puzzled stare.

"What?"

"Nothing, please continue."

"I know what you're thinking, Bogota has huge festivals all the time; but this one evidently was the granddaddy of festivals; music, art, theater, history, and everything else you can imagine, all at one-time. Anyway, art, costumes, and artifacts were shipped in from all over Colombia to Bogota for this onetime special celebration. David was able to determine the address of a warehouse these objects were stored in before the celebration."

"I'm sure there's a link but I'm still not following, what does that have to do with the museum?" Cougar picked up his cup of tea and drained the last of it.

"The Bogota museum oversaw all the pictures and artifacts, and a year ago, the museum had several shipping invoices to that same address, all signed by Mauricio. Take a look." Cougar edged over to Kathy's screen.

"Now you've got me curious."

"By the way, Cougar," Kathy said in a softer tone. "Have you heard from Amelia?"

"Still nothing. If I don't hear anything today, I'll ask Riley to check her Emergency Locating Transmitter."

"I hope she's okay. I don't even know her; but I would hate for anything to happen to her. It's sad enough that her father died."

"I couldn't agree more." Cougar straightened up, turning toward Gerry's direction. Let's use standard operating protocol on this one. Whoever is tracking me, I want to know who they are and who they work for…that, and I was a little outnumbered yesterday."

"I couldn't agree more. Time for Trinity's SOPs, Standard Operating Procedures." Gerry stood with his arms forward like superman. "And by the looks of that arm, you could definitely use my help."

"Thank you. Right now, I need to touch base with Captain Moreno and Detective Dias. The two of them are driving me crazy. Detective Dias sent a message last night asking if I knew anything about a rental car that was involved in the car chase and shooting the other night. I thought I had put that to rest, but evidently not. It appears she's been doing her homework. She matched the tire tread pattern of a rental car recently involved in an accident with the tire and skid marks at the location of the shooting."

"There's no way to trace that car back to us," Kathy stated.

"I'm not too worried, but we don't need them interfering with our investigation or getting suspicious, so I'll pay them another visit. If she does pay the gate guard at Donny Tallman's place a visit, he could match our car with Daniela's and my picture. I'll try to give her some information that will keep her busy for a while."

"Are you going to tell them you ran into a little trouble last night?" Kathy asked sarcastically.

"Not a chance." Cougar winked at her, then patted Gerry on the back." When's lunch getting here?"

"Should be about—" A knock resonated from the door. "Now." Cougar and Gerry eyed Kathy with astonishment.

She reached for the door. "Women's intuition." The hotel staff, a gentleman in his mid-thirties, wheeled in a cart of food. Gerry stepped over to tip the man. As Gerry counted out the money, the man scanned the room, stabilizing his stare on Kathy's computing equipment on the desk.

"Excuse me?" Gerry said, bringing the man's focus back to his hand. "Gracias."

Once the door shut, Cougar said. "I didn't like the way he was looking around."

"I noticed that, too," said Kathy.

"I think it's time for a new hotel."

"I think you're right," Kathy agreed, "I'll get right on that. I'll pick one where the food is just as good."

"Actually," Gerry said, "I don't think the bar is set too high."

Cougar grinned at Gerry and shook his head. "Did I ever tell you about the time I was on a Trinity mission in the Amazon? I think you two were working with James at the time. I had a new com and tech partner."

"I don't remember this story," Gerry said as he grabbed at a roast beef and cheese sandwich.

"I was floating down the river with one of these guides. We were supposed to find our way to a specific tributary where a person of interest was hiding out. Instead, we turned into the wrong tributary and ended up miles away. We only knew we were lost when we hit a motionless part of the river where a tribe of indigenous people lived. About the same time, we developed a problem with the engine on this raft the guide referred to as a boat."

Kathy laughed. "I'm sorry; but I can picture the image clearly in my head."

"Oh, no, that was the enjoyable part of the story. We were there five days. These indigenous people were some of the nicest people you'd ever want to meet—seriously, although neither the guide nor I could communicate very well with them. Dinner time came and they treated us to worms, large centipedes, and tubers grown in a unique way near the water. On the second day, I understood we were going to be treated to fish. Have you ever eaten piranha? It is the fishiest tasting, foulest smelling fish I've ever eaten. I can still taste it." Cougar smacked his lips together.

Gerry and Kathy busted up. "So, Gerry, count yourself lucky the hotel food doesn't taste like dead fish that has been laying in the sun for weeks."

"I'm starting to lose my appetite," Kathy said.

"Not me." Gerry took another bite from his sandwich.

"Do we have all the equipment we'll need for tonight?"

"Yes," Gerry said with his mouth full. "That package I was waiting on showed up yesterday evening."

Abducted

"Wait till the boss gets back, he's not going to be happy you failed!" said Fabio.

"We didn't fail," Javier countered. "We shot him, and he drowned."

"You know Gustano, he wants pictures of the bodies."

"Well, we're not dredging the canal to find his body—just to take a picture of it, stupid," his brother insisted.

"Where's Miguel?" Brigitte asked.

"Dropped him off in Bogota." He turned back to Fabio. "Gustano already knows we killed him. I don't screw up like you," Javier said, taunting his brother. Fabio swung at Javier but missed. Javier rushed at him, pushing him to the ground.

"Stop it you two barbarians. Can't you behave like adults for five minutes? Or is that juvenile behavior bred in both of you?"

Fabio pushed Javier off him. "Doesn't matter, I have that white-haired little angel out in the barracks, and she likes me."

"You really are brain damaged," said Brigitte. "That girl would no more like an idiot like you then I would."

"So, you're saying you like me?" Fabio puckered his lips.

"I'm saying you're brain damaged—too many drugs and maybe a bad fall."

"What did you do to her?" Javier asked, brushing off his denim jeans.

"I don't kiss and tell."

"Fabio, you sound like a dumb schoolboy. Anyway, lover-boy here—tried, but I stopped him. That girl will get what's coming to her soon enough; but not from an idiot like you." Brigitte turned Fabio around and pushed him out of the kitchen.

Amelia heard a twin-engine plane flying overhead. She listened intently, finally hearing the tires touch down on the turf. Moments later, the engines stopped just down from her dad's C-47 and a single engine airplane that landed earlier. She heard a commotion, then a lady's voice. The door to the barracks squealed open. Light flooded in.

"Let go of me…you disgusting animal."

Amelia's eyes followed the shadow of a woman. After her eyes adjusted to the brightness, a woman her age and very pretty, wearing a business suit, stood next to the one they called boss. The girl's eyes met Amelia's. She screamed and kicked, struggling to get away. Javier ran up and grabbed her around the waste while Fabio wrestled with her legs. The girl's skirt came up, and she screamed and squirmed even more.

"You can have that white-haired witch," Javier said. "This one's mine."

"Tie her up next to the other one. You can have them both once we're done with them." He gazed unsympathetically at the two ladies, then left the barracks, leaving Javier and Fabio to finish tying her up.

"What are you looking at?" yelled the woman. "Ouch!"

"It'll get tighter if you keep resisting." Javier glanced at Fabio, giving him a lewd expression. They both chuckled like teenagers. "See you two real soon."

"I know you'll be dreaming of me, Angel." The two left, sliding the door shut. The barracks grew dark. Light gradually worked its way in through the cracks in the walls and pinholes in the roof. Amelia sat in silence as the woman sobbed.

When she found her strength, she asked. "How long have you been here?"

"A few days—I think. My name is Amelia, what's yours?"

"Daniela." She pulled at her wrists, then asked. "Why are you here?"

"Not sure. They think I work for some drug enforcement unit; either that or one of their rivals, I guess."

"How have you been treated?" Daniela asked, searching for Amelia's expression.

Amelia shook her head. "Not good, but it'll be even worse if those two delinquent brothers have their way. Why are you here?"

Tears ran down her cheeks; black mascara mingled with them, streaking her face. "I don't really know. A friend of mine and I were working on solving the disappearance of some very valuable Colombian art. I think Gustano, the guy that abducted me, is the one who stole it from the museum I work at. You said they're drug lords?"

"I think so. I'm pretty sure they killed my father to get his airplane. That big blue airplane outside belongs to my father."

"Are they going to kill us?"

"Once those two men are finished using us first." Amelia tilted her head back and inhaled deeply. "But I won't let that happen. I'll die fighting before letting those sick perverts touch me." Amelia rubbed her head on her shoulder, drying off a wet cheek. "Why are you so dressed up?"

Daniela glanced at her once perfect business suit. She remembered the day she had picked it out. The skirt was a little snug, the top a little loose, but it made her feel professional and beautiful. Now her skirt was twisted and ripped, her blouse dirty and the blazer was snagged and spotted in grease. "I work at a museum in Bogota. I was asked to stay late and receive in a new exhibit. That's when I was abducted by Gustano and that other guy."

Daniela's gaze moved from the sliding door to the holes in the ceiling. "They didn't say much, they just pushed me up against a wall and zip-tied my wrists. One guy held a knife to my throat and said if I made any noise, he would kill me. I recognized Gustano from a party my friend, Arlan, and I were at a few days ago. It was my boss's party." Daniela's gaze rested on Amelia. "Are you a pilot?"

"Yes," Amelia followed Daniela's scrutiny of her flight suit. Like Daniela's outfit, hers was ripped and dirty.

"Which one is your airplane?"

"None of those out there. They shot my airplane down as I flew over." Amelia took in a deep breath and then slowly exhaled. "I crashed a couple miles away."

"Do you think anyone is out looking for you? Don't airplanes have some kind of signaling device in them?"

"It had an emergency locating device, but they destroyed it. I was working with a private investigator; but he's on another case and most likely won't know to search for me until it's too late. What about you, will anyone be looking for you?"

"Maybe. My friend, Arlan, the one I mentioned earlier, he is some sort of special agent." Daniela's eyes turned glassy. "I am—was—falling for him before he told me the truth about himself." Daniela rubbed her eyes on her shoulder. "Doesn't matter. We're as good as dead now."

"We got to think." Amelia said. "It's up to us if we're going to make it out of this alive."

Daniela scanned the barracks. Amelia twisted in her seat. "I got an idea."

"What—?"

Squealing halted their conversation. Brigitte stepped through, holding a box in one hand.

"Are you two lovelies hungry?" Brigitte sat the box down and pulled out two plastic plates with chopped potatoes and dark meat on them. I'm sorry to say that I can't undo your hands." She sniggered to herself. "If you're hungry enough, you'll find a way. She sat the trays on their laps, backed up a few steps, and watched.

Amelia bent over, pushing her face in the food. After Daniela observed for a moment, she did likewise.

Brigitte reached in her pocket and pulled out a pair of scissors. She grabbed Daniela's hair, snapping her head back and cut a slice through it. "Now you, princess." Brigitte yanked hard on Amelia's white hair, then cut a section around her ear. She put it up to her head and danced around. "Look at me, aren't I pretty?"

Amelia slid the plate of food down her legs using her chin, letting it fall to the ground. "Wow, is that supposed to intimidate me?" Brigitte responded. "And by the way, I'm not cleaning it up." Brigitte grabbed Daniela's plate, scooped up potatoes and meat, and threw it at the women. "Now Gustano won't find either of you attractive." She turned on her heels, and with exaggerated hips, walked through the sliding door, slamming it closed behind her. A padlock fell against the metal, then silence. The barracks darkened.

"Tell me your idea, Amelia," Daniela asked.

As dusk fell, the stars from the night's sky provided little light through the pinholes in the roof. Amelia and Daniela sat tensely.

Export A

Kathy found us a different hotel at the edge of the city. We met there and prepared for the night's mission.

"What do you think of the new hotel?" Kathy asked.

"It's off the beaten path, that's for sure. Good work finding this one."

"Food's not bad either." Gerry said, rubbing his stomach.

"Let's synchronize and check the gear one last time."

"You're both showing up on my screen now," said Kathy. "Cougar, do you think Daniela's okay?"

"I'm not sure. She still might be upset with me or just extremely busy. Let's go, Gerry."

"That makes Amelia and Daniela unresponsive, Cougar," Kathy stated.

"They're just not returning my messages."

"I was going to say something witty, but I decided against it. I'm actually a little concerned, too," Gerry added.

I was worried, too—not so much for Daniela, it had only been a short while since hearing from her, but for Amelia. Gerry and I made our way out of town. We spotted the older warehouse building next to a good-sized grassy field. The warehouse sat inside a perimeter wall made of gray cinderblocks with chain link fence attached to the top. A sole light cast a dull ring onto an empty asphalt parking lot. Faded daylight draped the sky.

"Looks like this should be an easy in and out," said Gerry.

"Maybe," I said as I scanned the area. We parked the car a half-mile from the warehouse fence. I reached in the trunk and grabbed my gear. Gerry pulled out one of his specially designed surveillance drones, referred to as a SAM or Specialized Aerial Machine, and powered it up. He leaned back in the passenger seat, flipping switches on the console. The SAM's LEDs flashed twice before it lifted high into the air.

I stashed the equipment from my bag into my pockets. "Don't forget to lock the door."

"Good luck."

Gerry shut and locked the car door. I headed in the direction of the large field and warehouse, taking my time. I walked past a few weathered houses. Several had graffiti on the walls and broken windows; no lights emanating from any of them. Streetlights were sparse, the one above me had fragmented glass. I walked past a small factory. Rusted sheet metal, angle iron and I-beams lay near the road's edge. Cement molds, rusty tools, and a half-broken yellow wheelbarrow littered the ground next to three large sliding metal doors.

A wooden plank fence surrounded the large field, the type used for cattle. "Com-check?"

"All good," Gerry replied. A pigeon took flight near a fence post. Two more joined in, their flapping wings the only sounds I heard.

"Sorry guys, I was talking to Riley," Kathy said.

"Anything we need to know?"

"The Colombian government is insisting the US government compensate them for damages in regard to the stolen art. This is beyond the insurance settlement."

"I'm not saying that Captain Moreno, Lieutenant Andrea Dias, and the two detectives they sent to New York are not respectable; but if this art is that important to their country, why wouldn't they have put a higher caliber investigative organization on this?"

"From what Riley shared, the Colombian government is placing full responsibility on the US. That's why they asked our president to act. They also insisted on government oversight, reminding the president of the last secret service debacle in Cartagena."

"That was a major embarrassment to our country," Gerry replied.

"Let's continue this discussion later. I'm at the warehouse now." I stood in the center of the large field. There were no cows or horses, nothing except long ruts in the grass. I bent over and inspected the grooves. "Are you seeing this?" I asked Gerry.

"Probably not as good as you are, let me fly in a little closer." Gerry's drone swooped in low, hovering about six feet off the ground. "I got it." The SAM flew down the field and out of site. A few minutes later I heard it fly past me.

"What are you seeing?"

"Looks like this is used as a runway. There are two distinctly different tire ruts in the grass, meaning at least two different size airplanes have landed here."

"The larger tracks look pretty fresh," I said. "I have a feeling we're getting warm." Gerry put the SAM in stealth mode. The warehouse walls held little paint, and what was left showed multiple peeling layers. A mostly yellow pallet jack sat pushed up against a door, it, too, had several faded colors along with the yellow. Gerry scanned the building's alarm system.

"Wow!"

"What do we have, Gerry?"

"State-of-the-art system."

"In this old building? Out here in ghost town? Only one reason I can think of to have a state-of-the-art system in a dump like this. Can you disable it?"

"I'll need your help on this one."

Gerry began jamming the alarm system using the SAM. I breached the door and looked in. No lights. Nothing moved. I found the electrical panel, opened it, and jumped several circuits. After I had the last jumper in place, I disconnected a white banded wire. "Complete."

"It's showing disabled now," Gerry said.

"Good work," Kathy reverberated.

The warehouse floor showed green through my night goggles. I flipped on the infra-red, no signal detected. I used hand signals for the SAM that was hovering next to me to circle the inside of the warehouse. A gentle breeze from the drone's propulsion blew at my short hair as it moved past.

Four minutes later, Gerry gave me the all-clear signal. After another minute or so, my eyes adjusted fully to the LED beam on my forehead. The SAM took a position high inside the warehouse as I combed through stacks of pallets and empty crates. Two adjoining rooms also turned up empty of artifacts. A computer relic sat on a steel desk in the corner of one of the rooms. I fingered through papers on the desk, none of them having any links to the museum or artifacts.

I emptied the trash on the floor and rifled through wadded up papers. "Looks like we're coming up empty, guys." As I stepped out of the office, something stuck to my left boot tread. I reached down and removed a cigarette butt. "Hang on."

"What is it?"

I carefully unfolded the butt and read three letters 'Exp'. The rest was missing. "How common are Export cigarettes in Bogota?"

"Probably not too common—not too common anywhere except Canada I think, why?"

I instantly recalled meeting Gustano at the party. In his hand was a burning cigarette, and in his shirt pocket a box of Export A cigarettes. "Gotcha!"

"What is it?"

"Gustano was here!"

The Clue

"Cougar, you don't look so well," Kathy said.

"I had some troubling thoughts—couldn't sleep. I tried both Amelia and Daniela this morning and neither of them answered."

"Anything we can help with?"

"Yes, will you get Riley on speaker."

"Calling now," Kathy replied.

"Good morning, Kathy."

"Good morning, sir. Cougar and Gerry are here with me."

"Good morning. Good work last night. I doubt running a DNA match on the cigarette butt will do much good, but we can try once it gets to us."

"Sir. I need to ask a favor, please."

"What do you need, Cougar?"

"It's Amelia. I haven't heard from her for a few days. Her case is not active, but she's been checking in with me. She left to search for her father's plane a few days ago and that was the last time I heard from her."

"Sorry, Cougar, you know the answer is no."

"That's not what I'm asking, sir. I just need someone to run an ELT check, to see if she crashed."

"We can do that. In the meantime, you guys stay focused on this mission."

"Yes, sir. Message received loud and clear."

"Again, I'm sorry, Cougar. but this must be your priority. There's too much heat from on high on this one."

"You don't need to apologize, sir. I understand."

"Have you made contact with Daniela Perez?"

"Negative."

"Please send me a sitrep at noon." Sitrep is short for a situation report.

"Will do, "Kathy replied.

"Sir," I added.

"Yes, Cougar?"

"One more request, sir."

"Go ahead."

"It's a long shot but it might pay off." Riley agreed to perform a satellite search for any C-47 or DC-3s in Colombia. I left Kathy and Gerry in the hotel and caught a taxi to the museum. A cold front had stalled over Bogota, but that didn't stop an enthusiast crowd waiting for the museum doors to open. I waited in the long line. If Daniela wasn't returning my messages, she wouldn't be at the entrance to let me in.

I walked towards her office. Mauricio's eyes were focused on his monitor screen. I snuck past without being noticed. Daniela's office sat empty. I returned to Mauricio's office and tapped on the door. "Excuse me, Mauricio?"

Mauricio peered over his monitor. As soon as he recognized me, blood emptied from his face. "Arlan! How is it you are here? I mean how come you're here?" I watched the blood slowly return to his face.

"Can't a guy visit the museum when he's in need of a little culture?"

"Did you turn in your report?" he asked curtly.

"Not yet."

"Why, I have a good mind to report you to the Fine Arts Insurance Board myself for disregarding your duties."

"I can assure you, Mauricio, I'm not negligent in my duties. As a matter of fact, I have some news to share with you. I was hoping to share it with both you and Daniela. Is she here?"

"No, I figured she had gone off with you somewhere. She hasn't called in two days."

"What? She hasn't been to work for two days?"

"Is there an echo in here? Now, what grand news did you want to share with me?"

"The news, yes. I've uncovered a clue which I believe is tied to the disappearance of the art—in a warehouse, right here in Bogota."

I watched Mauricio as I spoke. Perspiration beads formed along the line of black hair on his forehead; his gold-rimmed glasses fogging slightly before taking them off and rubbing the brow of his head with his hand. "What sort of clue did you find, Arlan?"

"Oh, those are mere details. The good news is, I think I'm getting closer to understanding what happened to the artifacts from your museum. That's what's most important, right Mauricio?"

He cleared his throat twice. "Of course, it is. I assume you have shared this information with the police?"

"On my way now."

Chapter 41

The Wiretap

Kathy turned in her chair. "I'm forwarding the article from Brisbane to you."

"Got it...yes...yes, I think this is very similar," Gerry stated.

Kathy saw a call coming in. "It's Cougar."

"Kathy."

"Cougar, what did you find out?"

"Daniela's not here. Mauricio says she hasn't called in two days. I need you two to monitor Mauricio's wiretap, he may make a call any minute. By the way, how's the research coming?"

"We've found a few similarities between art robberies in a couple locations."

"Good work. Let me know the minute you have something from Mauricio's office. I'm on my way to the police station."

"Kathy's pulling it up now," Gerry said. Cougar clicked off. "Kathy, let me know if you hear anything. I'm going to hack into the museum's security system. Maybe there's a clue as to what happened to Daniela."

"I have a hunch their videos get deleted faster than love messages on a government server."

Chapter 42

Famous Piece of Work

Mauricio marched down the hall and into Daniela's office, shutting the door behind him. He pulled open the desk drawers and rifled through her paperwork, making a mess of the drawers. The papers held no clues. A file rack to the left held several manila folders. He pulled them out, reading the headings on each one. Nothing caught his attention as being unusual. He returned the folders back into the chrome wire rack. As he did, a picture floated onto the desk. He picked up the trimmed picture and stared at it. It had been copied from one of the books in the historical archives. He flipped the page around. Daniela had written a note on the back.

He stood swiftly, his legs sending the chair backwards into a credenza. He marched back into his office. His arms and hands shook as he grabbed his phone. "Donny, get down here immediately…the museum, that's where!" Mauricio—agitated, pushed the end button on his cell. He looked for something to throw, instead he grabbed his cell again and placed another call. When Gustano answered, Mauricio unleashed his rage. "Can't you and your men do anything right?"

"I'm growing tired of your dribbling accusations! We have the girl. So, if I may be so bold as to ask, Mauricio…what's your problem?"

"My problem? Our problem. The girl? She's the least of our problems, it's that insurance investigator you guys failed to kill—again!"

"Arlan Jensen? Impossible! My guys shot him, and he drowned."

"Then I just saw his ghost, you nitwit! He was just in my office thirty minutes ago—playing dumb. If he gets to the bottom of this, we're all going down, and I will ensure you fall the farthest. Now find him and kill him, or do I need to take care of this myself?"

Gustano nearly threw his phone again. He would have but was tired of waiting for replacement phones to show up. *Mauricio taking care of it himself, I'd like to see him try, that pompous jerk.* "I'll get to the bottom of this and take care of it personally."

"You better, that's why I'm paying you." Mauricio clicked off and proceeded to the human resources office. Selma waved him in.

"Hi, Mr. Lopez, what can I help you with?"

"Daniela, have you heard from her?"

"No, we haven't, do you want us to send a wellness check to her home?"

"Yes, hopefully she's okay," said Mauricio, "and if she is, and doesn't want to show up for work, there are plenty of other educators that would love to work at this museum."

"Yes, sir. I'll get right on that."

"Thank you, Selma."

Mauricio seized the late morning air. The cement steps of the museum were warming. A steady trickle of patrons marched by, grabbing at their purses and wallets.

There was a time when Mauricio thoroughly enjoyed art. Afterall, that's why he chose becoming a museum curator in the first place. The history of countries so intricately displayed through art fascinated him, just as it still did for Daniela Perez. Somewhere along the line he became dissatisfied with the miniscule salary given to curators, and the constant demands from directors and boards of trustees. Soon afterwards, he became dissatisfied with history, artifacts, and stupid people pulling at their wallets and spending their money to view boring ancient and inanimate relics. That's when he contacted Donny, his pal from college. Mauricio devised a sophisticated art heist scheme, with Donny playing a leading role. Donny would hire on with the insurance company that underwrote for that specific, targeted museum. With Donny's experience, he quickly moved into the insurance agent position for that museum. Once there, the plan was set in motion.

Donny saw Mauricio standing next to an outside column. "Mauricio, what's wrong?" he asked.

Mauricio reached into his back pocket, pulled out and unfolded the picture and handed it to him. "Do you recognize this?"

Donny's thick red mustache bowed. "It's a picture of the painting I have—it's in books, you know, it's a famous piece of work."

"A famous piece of work that you took for yourself when I told you it was too risky to keep around. And where do you have it? In your house, up on the wall."

"I'm not sure why you're so upset. Nobody's going to see that picture in my place. So, I have a priceless piece of art. You could keep anything you want. Keep that golden goblet you couldn't stop ogling over in Australia, I don't care." It felt good standing up to Mauricio. Donny was getting tired of playing second fiddle in their grand scheme.

Mauricio turned the page over. Donny read the notes. He shifted his 6'2" stocky frame. His red bushy hair matted at his sideburns. Donny asked, "Gustano has the girl, so what's the problem?"

"Arlan Jensen."

"He's dead."

"He was in my office less than an hour ago."

Donny's smugness drained from his eyes. "How's that possible?"

"Gustano and his band of neophytes failed again."

"That's very unfortunate. Have you talked to Gustano?"

"He says he will take care of it personally."

"How much do you think Captain Moreno knows?"

"Not sure."

Chapter 43

No Tricks this Time

“Wake up, sweet angel of mine.” Fabio said, sliding the door shut behind him. Amelia winked at Daniela.

“Where’s Brigitte this morning?” Amelia asked.

“Her and the boss are sleeping. That means I’m all yours this morning.”

“We have to use the bathroom, please!”

“I’ll let your friend use it first.” Fabio cut the zip-ties from Daniela and led her to the bathroom.

Fabio pushed open the door slightly. “Please shut the door,” Daniela demanded.

“Got to make sure you’re not up to something crazy,” Fabio said with a snicker. “I’m not looking anyway, you’re not my angel.” Fabio turned, gawking at Amelia tied to the chair. Her long white hair, ratted and filled with knots, hung over the back of the chair. Below the backrest, her slim figure unmistakable inside her tattered flight suit. “Come on out of there—now!”

Fabio zip-tied Daniela back in her chair. “Your turn now.” Fabio’s face lit up like a kid finding a dollar bill on the ground.

As Fabio ushered her to the bathroom, Amelia whispered in his ear. “I thought about you last night.”

“Really?” Fabio’s heart pounded. “Wait, you’re just saying that.”

"No, I really did." Amelia squeezed his hand before closing the bathroom door behind her.

Fabio cracked open the door, "Do you want me to come in?"

"No, I have a better plan. Close the door and I will tell you about it when I come out."

Fabio closed the door. This could be the best day of his life. Using his hands, he stroked his hair back. The door opened and Amelia wore a brightened look. She whispered again in his ear.

Fabio replied, "No tricks this time."

Amelia rubbed his arm. They walked hand in hand past Daniela, out the door to the C-47. "It's going to be a little cold in there," Fabio exclaimed.

"Are you afraid of a little cold?" Amelia asked, batting her eyes at him, and brushing her hair back using her hand.

"Me—no. I'm pretty tough."

"Of course, you are, just look at those muscles." Fabio tightened his bicep and opened the C-47's door. Amelia looked up the aisle. Some of the seats had been removed, but it was her dad's plane for sure. Her heart raced.

Fabio grabbed a packing blanket that was on the floor and spread it out. "I'm going to get ready up here, don't peek, okay? I'm a little self-conscious."

"You don't need to be, Angel; Fabio likes you the way you are." Amelia walked to the cockpit and slid the curtain closed. Fabio unbuckled his belt and kicked off his boots. Amelia flipped on the transponder and tuned it to 7700. "What's taking you so long?"

"One more minute, honey," she replied.

Fabio pulled back the curtain. "What in the blazes are you doing? Turn off the power!"

Amelia didn't move. Fabio swung his arm, the back of his hand struck her forehead, snapping her head back. "You said no tricks."

"No, you said no tricks." Amelia's left eye instantly teared up.

"What did you do?" Fabio yelled.

"I'm just fantasizing about flying this big thing."

"Come on!" Fabio pulled Amelia out of the seat, she fell on the floor, scraping the other side of her face. Fabio dragged her down the aisle and out of the door. Brigitte was standing next to the airplane as Amelia fell out.

"Did you get your jollies, Fabio?"

Fabio stepped out and fastened his belt. "Yes, I did, come on Angel." He tied her back to the chair. Brigitte followed with a tray of food.

"I hope you've had your shots, ladies; eat up." Brigitte set the trays of food on their laps and left.

We got Something

"Thank you, Kathy. Is Gerry on?"

"Right here, Cougar."

"Gerry, were you able to determine what he was looking for in Daniela's office?"

"No, but whatever he was searching for, it sounded like he found it."

"Did he say the name of who he was talking to on the phone?"

"My guess is Gustano, but he didn't actually say his name."

I thought for a minute, if it were Gustano, where would he have taken her?

"Cougar?"

"I'm here, just thinking to myself. Kathy, will you check in with Riley and see how the satellite mapping is going? Also, try once more to locate Gustano's residence. Gerry, those airplane tracks we saw at the warehouse?"

"Yes?"

"It's a long shot, but let's see if any satellites picked up a flight path out of there."

"You're right, that's a long shot."

"Thank you both."

"Did you get any new information at the police station?" Kathy asked.

"Very little. I told them about the painting Donny had hanging in his house, and how it had been stolen five years earlier. Detective Dias was marginally pleasant this time—at least in the beginning. When I got there, Captain Moreno was busy with someone in his office. Once he finished, he called Detective Dias and I into his office and proceeded with his characteristic unpleasantness, with Andrea quickly mirroring his disposition."

"Are they going to take any action?"

"I wouldn't hold my breath." I clicked off and leaned back in the taxi.

Gerry greeted me at the door into Kathy's room. Kathy was seated at her computer, all four monitor screens were showing something different, as she spoke with Riley.

Kathy glanced over her computer. "Cougar, I am glad you're back, we got something."

"Cougar." Riley's voice boomed from the computer speaker. "We have a location. We can't be positive this is Gustano's place; but we were able to track a flight from the warehouse to a location out in this area." I watched the screen as a circle was drawn around an area of about forty square miles.

David spoke up. "The satellite lost the flight about here. Rebecca has been combing through satellite images all night." David changed the image on the screen and zoomed in. "Earlier today, and for only three minutes, an emergency transponder code went off…here." A light appeared on the image. As David zoomed in, a C-47 shaped aircraft appeared next to a few other airplanes and building structures. "We think someone may have been trying to send a signal. We've detected some movement there, but no sign of Gustano or Daniela"

Riley broke in. "It's a long shot, Cougar, but it's the best lead we have for you."

"Any signs of a T-6?"

David clear his throat. "None, sorry."

"Thanks for checking." Gerry and I glanced at each other.

Chapter 45

Interrogation

Gustano opened the door of the barracks building, with Brigitte and Javier a step behind him. Gustano circled the two women zip-tied to their chairs. "What happened to your hair?" Brigitte looked the other direction when Gustano's eyes rested on her. Gustano shook his head. "Well, no matter, no one's going to see you here, and you two aren't going anywhere. So," Gustano turned to Amelia, "have you decided to talk yet?"

"I told you, I was just searching for my dad."

"Who's your dad?" Javier asked.

"He's a pilot." Before she could stop herself, she blurted out. "He's the pilot of the C-47 you have outside." Amelia trembled, weeping.

Gustano glanced at Javier with a malicious grin on his face. Miguel, sliding the door open further, entered the building. "We needed your daddy's airplane," Gustano replied. "And may I share how much I appreciate the meticulous way in which he cared for it...why it looks practically new and hasn't given us a lick of trouble."

Amelia tugged at her wrists. Rage filled in where her heartache had been seconds ago. "What did you do with my father?"

Gustano turned to Miguel. "Miguel can give you those gruesome details if that's what you really want to hear."

Daniela yelled, "Leave her alone!"

"No," Amelia cried, "I want to know."

"Of course." Gustano nodded to Miguel.

"I take it the old man was your father. The younger man, John?" Miguel winked at Gustano. "Well things didn't quite go his way this time. He got scared and ran. Good runner too; fast. Not as fast as a bullet, mind you. We shot him and threw him off a cliff. The old man, he tried being a hero, but that didn't work out very well for him either. After a brief moment of courage trying to save his co-pilot, he jumped off the cliff. Of course, that was after we shot him. I guess he didn't want us to throw his body off—some people, huh?" Miguel, Gustano, and Brigitte laughed uproariously.

"Where?" Amelia demanded, her green eyes dark and piercing.

"Little girl, haven't you heard enough? Now as for you Miss Educator. Have you figured out why you're here?"

Daniela twisted in her chair. "You're going to kill me, right?"

"See," Brigitte said, "this one's smart." Brigitte fidgeted with her hair.

"Of course, that's our job." Gustano remarked, wearing the same wicked turned up lip.

"I know you're working with my boss. You guys stole Colombia's history, didn't you?"

"Stole Colombia's history?" Brigitte, Miguel and Gustano broke out again in laughter. Gustano stepped closer, putting his hand on Daniela's shoulder. Brigitte wrinkled her brow. "Miss Perez, your boss has officially terminated your employment." Brigitte's brow relaxed.

"Please let us go," Amelia demanded.

Gustano rubbed at his chiseled face. Daniela's stomach turned. Perspiration formed on her nose. "My pilot, Javier and Brigitte, your dutiful cook, and myself have a…consultation we must attend. We will be gone for a couple days. When we get back, your time will be up." Gustano slid his arm off Daniela and onto Amelia's white hair. "Enjoy your stay. Fabio and Miguel will take real good care of you while we are gone."

Gustano exited the barracks with his clan following close behind him. The door slid shut with a loud bang. Three seconds later, the padlock fell against metal.

"Nobody's coming for us, are they?" Daniela asked.

Amelia shook her head slowly. Visualizing Fabio filled her throat with repugnance. She gagged, nearly throwing up.

"If only two of them are left behind, do you think we can trick them like you did Fabio earlier? Maybe we can escape," Daniela said.

"Or get shot. They both carry pistols."

"Wouldn't that be better?" Daniela observed her skirt and her legs. She had wanted so desperately to be married and have children and be the curator for a famous museum like Bogota's.

Amelia asked, "Tell me about your museum. What's it like?"

"Do you really want to know?"

"Yes, please tell me, and don't leave anything out."

Daniela's cheeks lifted as she shared about Colombia's ancient treasures and the museum patrons, and the children with wide eyes as they walked through the galleries.

Mitu, Colombia

Kathy, Gerry, and I chartered a flight to Mitu, Colombia. We were able to fit all our gear into the Kodiak single turbine engine aircraft: Kathy, her computing equipment, Gerry, his SAMs or drones, an inflatable boat, specialized equipment, courtesy of a Trinity Hot-Flight, and with the remaining space, my gear. Soon Bogota fell behind us. The ground turned dark and menacing. Beneath us were ragged mountains and valleys filled with vicious creatures, only we couldn't see them in the early morning darkness. After going over some final details, I shut my eyes and tried to sleep.

A pitch change from the engine woke me up sometime later. I raised the window shade—blackness. We started our descent into Mitu. A sliver of light broke the horizon. As we descended further, the sliver disappeared, and we were back in darkness. Available forecasts for the area proved unreliable. A warm front was expected later in the day and, along with it, a sizeable amount of rain. The pilot aimed for a dark patch between a dimly lit area on the ground. As the plane descended, the dimly lit area turned into a small town. The pilot dropped the Kodiak between two dark hills, lining up with a narrow-paved runway. Five minutes later, chipping from the tires eased Kathy's anxiety.

The runway sat at the edge of town. As the turbine engine spooled down, silence filled the air. A small van with a lit dome light over the driver's seat moved slowly toward us.

When we finished unloading the airplane into the van, daylight broke over the thick green hills. I thanked and complimented the pilot on his flying skills.

The hotel room fit Kathy's needs perfectly. Gerry fidgeted with wires, satellite positioners, repeaters, and other communication equipment. He asked with his nose buried behind a CPU, "Kathy, did you check on their cuisine here?"

She chuckled. "No, but I'll be fine. Your cuisine will be those piranhas Cougar talked about earlier."

"Funny," Gerry quipped, "I picture wild boar roasting over an open pit with fresh fruit on the side and native vegetables cooked in heavy seasoning. Then some homemade cobbler for dessert."

"Gerry, there are no Hilton hotels where we're going," I jested. "You'll be lucky to eat grub before it eats you." After setting up Kathy's equipment, we gabbed a quick bite to eat at the only place open, then back to Kathy's hotel room to ensure the communication equipment ran flawlessly, performing checks both to Gerry's and my personal mics and inner ear speakers, and then to headquarters known as the mothership. After that, we said our goodbyes.

The rubber inflatable snapped tight as Gerry turned off the switch on the attached cannister. I mounted a small outboard to the stern while Gerry strapped bags of gear carefully to the synthetic rigid segmented floor. The gentleman with the van returned with petrol to fill our two small external fuel tanks.

Without delay, we unceremoniously pushed off from the shore, heading west along the Rio Vaupes River toward a dot on our GPS. Gerry steered the small inflatable boat as I inventoried the equipment. Gerry brought a swath of his best gear with him. I methodically filled the pockets of my mission suit and my backpack with some of the items. My fingers pulled at my M&P pistol holstered underneath my suit. I loaded the magazine and stashed two additional magazines in my suit.

Small explosives were prudently wedged in my backpack along with a unique shooting taser and binoculars. Gerry's bags also contained an automatic rifle, a compact rocket weapon, and surveillance gear. "Did you bring enough gear, Gerry?"

"The gadget you need is the one you forget to bring," he recited.

"Philosopher and poet, a double threat!" I teased.

"I don't have a good feeling about this mission, Cougar. Something isn't gelling."

"What do you mean?"

"I can't put my finger on it. Call it intuition from a tinkering technology specialist. This whole mission has me perplexed. Maybe it's straight forward, like the Colombian government is telling us, but maybe not. Have you ever considered maybe the Colombian government is behind this?"

"Like a conspiracy?"

"Yeah, like that."

"I don't believe they are. What does have me perplexed is why the Bogota's police have not uncovered any tangible information. Some of the clues we uncovered were not that well-hidden. Even a junior detective should have found some. If this art is that important, doesn't that strike you as odd? Slow down a little Gerry, I see white water ahead."

"The river map showed several challenging areas. This must be the first one, hold on!"

I tightened the straps on the equipment bags and grabbed the oars and pulled hard. We bumped and made it up several green slimy rocks. Gerry had the outboard pulled up. I orchestrated the rubber raft up another five feet of clustered rock before it slid sideways. A torrent of water formed quickly in front of the boat. Suddenly, the boat heaved, sliding rapidly down the rocks. Gerry twisted, losing his balance, and toppling against the motor. I stuck the oar down deep, catching a rock. The boat swung around violently but held momentarily in place. Gerry, unable to catch his balance again, plunged into the water. The gear flung hard against the straps and the onslaught of water tried summersaulting the boat onto itself.

"Gerry! Grab the rope!" Gerry's head went under. The boat spun another 180-degrees, dropping off the last rock, back to where we had started. There were no signs of Gerry anywhere. The water wasn't deep, but it was very turbulent. "Gerry? Gerry?" I looked into the water. "Gerry?" Nothing. Something bumped under the boat. Rock? It bumped again. I stuck my head down as far as I could but couldn't see anything. Quickly, I tied the rope to my waist and jumped in. Cloth material floated to the side of the boat. I reached under, connected with Gerry's arm, and pulled him from under the boat, heaving him up against the rubber raft. I slapped at his back. Gerry took a partial breath, then choked, spraying the inside of the boat with river water from his mouth. I pulled myself up into the boat, grabbed Gerry, and pulled him the rest of the way in.

"Cou—"

"Keep coughing—Keep coughing." Gerry was bleeding from his head. He also had several leaches on him. I quickly pulled at them before they could get through his skin.

"I…didn't mean to do…that!"

"Let me see your head."

Gerry rubbed at it and brought his bloody fingers down to his eyes. "I hit my head on a rock. Lucky, it was softened with moss or something green and gooey. Got a little disoriented down there."

"You think?" Cougar said.

"I repeated to myself, *hold your breath Gerry—just hold your breath.*"

"Well, the cut's not very deep, but you may have a slight concussion."

"I'm feeling better. Thanks for fishing me out." Gerry coughed, then spit over the side.

"Are you ready to try this again?"

"Did we lose anything?"

"Just you. Let's try over there."

Gerry twisted the throttle and motored the boat over. After several less-exciting minutes, and with the help of the outboard's propeller halfway in the water, we made it to the top of the small cascades and into calmer running water. Gerry checked the strange looking five-bladed composite propeller. There were no chips or cracks detected.

"You made that one virtually bulletproof, Gerry."

"Thank you, I did bring an extra just in case." Gerry took off his shirt and searched for more freeloaders. "Cougar, you got one on your left sleeve."

I flicked it into the water.

"Pretty humid out here." Gerry squeezed his shirt, letting water trickle back into the river.

"Are you sure you're okay?"

"Yep. It's just my head…and this arm." Watery blood from his elbow beaded up before running down his forearm. Gerry wiped it off with his rolled-up shirt. "I was going to grab the side before falling out, but I didn't want to capsize the boat and lose our gear."

"Really? That's the story you're going with?" Gerry and I grinned at each other before busting up. The GPS on my watch showed we had four miles to go before letting Gerry off at his location.

"I'm going to try Kathy." I twisted the face of my watch. A small LED lit. I heard scratching through my earpiece. "Must have water in my ears, the humidity is unreal. Did you notice the heat ramping up once we broke over that first cascade of water?"

"I'm sorry, I was a little distracted, you said something about being wet behind the ears?"

"Funny…Kathy, this is Cougar. Can you hear me? Over." More hissing and scratching.

"Cougar!" Gerry pointed to the riverbank. Several men were tracking our position from the shore. "Are they friend or foe?" Gerry mused out loud while he squinted and looked in their direction.

"They appear native, they're tracking through the overgrowth pretty good."

"They have spears, Cougar."

"As long as they're not throwing them in our direction, we're good." Gerry reached in one of the equipment bags, carefully pulling out a rifle and setting it on top. He lifted his binoculars.

"I count four of them," Gerry said. Suddenly a spear splashed in front of the boat. We both spun our heads around. Two men were on the opposite shore, one having just thrown the spear.

"So much for wishful thinking." I twisted the throttle until it hit the stop. "Wave the flag." I pointed to a piece of material visible through the unzipped bag. We were given a flag to wave if we encountered issues on our route and were told it would safeguard our journey through the various native groups living alongside the river. Gerry waved the flag high. Another spear splashed just off the left side of the boat. "So much for that."

Gerry lowered his binoculars. "They're just boys."

"Malicious ones."

"Look out, Cougar!"

I ducked. The spear hit the left side of the boat, sinking deep into the air chamber. The inflatable began collapsing. The boat slowed in the water.

Gerry picked up the rifle and held it high, then brought it down, aiming it at those carrying spears. Within seconds, the boys from both sides of the river vanished into the thick jungle. The boat had four air chambers. Only one was punctured. Gerry dug through a bag pulling out a repair kit. The spear penetrated through the top layer of the tube only. I handed Gerry the spear. "Pretty simplistic."

"Effective though."

The repair didn't take long, and soon we were underway. "An hour to go. You think those boys are from the village?"

"If they are, I'll have a talk with their parents," Gerry said, waving a finger at me.

A large branch hung low over the river. Moss draped off smaller branches like fingers, touching the water. The banks narrowed slightly as we pushed on. I tried Kathy again, but still only heard hissing.

"Gerry, didn't Kathy say she found five of the last twelve museum heists had occurred during traveling art shows, like the Bogota art?"

"I'm pretty sure those were the numbers, why?"

"What if those five heists occurred in the same way we're thinking the Bogota theft did?"

Gerry scanned the shore and answered. "So, you think in all five robberies that the art never really traveled, that the robberies occurred before hand?"

The leaves on the shore rustled. Nothing. "I'm just saying, if the art is supposed to be at the destination museum, it sure makes stealing the art from the originating museum that much easier. Maybe when the art is shipped out is when it's stolen. I mean, who's going to really notice, the museum is sending the art out anyway. Somehow, they're able to validate the art is at the receiving museum, only it's really not—Ghost Assets!"

"Hmm?" Gerry nodded slowly. "It also makes the curator position ideal for organizing the loaning of art to other museums."

"Once you get your communications set up, will you have Kathy run another check on just those 5 traveling art shows? See if Donny or Mauricio were anywhere near the lending or receiving museums."

"Sure, but I think she's already run that scenario several times and there were only two matches for Mauricio. She didn't find Donny at either of those locations—only the one here in Colombia."

I slowed the boat down, the location for Gerry's stop illuminated on my GPS. "We'll find the truth soon enough. Have her rerun the search anyway. I have a feeling we're still missing something." I pushed the tiller of the motor away from me, turning the boat towards shore and an awaiting man in tan pants, tan shirt, and a straw hat.

Knight in Shining Armor

Gerry stood at the shore with his thumb in the air. I waved, twisted the throttle on the outboard and headed upriver.

Vegetation encroached on both sides over the water, darkening the sky, leaving only a narrow path the further upstream I traveled. I swatted at large flying insects. Their attacks were calculated and relentless—more Deet spray. After a short time, my earpiece clicked twice, hissed, then came to life.

"Cougar, this is Gerry, can you hear me?"

"Like you're still in the boat. Is Kathy on?"

"I'm here, Cougar. Gerry gave me your message and I'm re-running the information now. We know the museums where Mauricio and Donny worked together, those are the five I shared earlier. And we have a pretty good idea of the thefts related to traveling art, those are the five out of the last twelve. From our earlier search, Donny and Mauricio only have connections to three of those; but I will confirm that shortly."

"Thank you, Kathy."

"How's the river?"

"Except the noise from the outboard and swarms of insects, strangely quiet."

"Gerry," Kathy asked. "Is Jorge taking good care of you?"

"So far. The group has been very accommodating. I learned that it's just three large families living here. They already brought me some bread and dried fruit."

"Any sign of those boys who threw the spears at us?" I asked.

"You mean the ones sitting in the middle of the meeting place being shamed? From what little I understood of their story, it seemed they thought we were drug runners. Evidently, that occurs frequently along the river."

"Or just boys being boys. I would think throwing spears at drug runners just might be the stupidest thing one could do, and quite possibly their last stupid thing. At any rate, it sounds like the community Kathy found is working out as planned."

"Don't give me too much credit, Cougar, Riley actually gave me the name of this group. They've helped the US in the past. I'm just happy they're still on our side."

"Guys, I hate to be rude, I'm entering the yellow zone now. Kathy, if you find out any more information, please pass it along."

"Good luck, Cougar," Gerry replied.

"Be careful and find Daniela."

"I'll do my best."

"Roger that."

My thumb pressed the kill button, silencing the outboard. Various birds sang out, affirming my location. Heat assaulted me like a Japanese steam bath. The oars dug in, slowly pulling the rubber boat closer to the red zone.

A ripple formed next to the boat, but not from my oars. A green snake, easily the length of the raft, worked its way to the shore. I watched the ripples. This place is not for the faint of heart. Maybe it was just curious and needed to check me out. Hostility in the jungle can come in many forms, and not just men with guns and teenagers with spears.

"Cougar, I have a visual on you. The SAM is high above you." I tapped my watch. The image from the SAM appeared on my screen. I turned to the left and oared to shore. The area had a natural built-in hiding spot for the boat under a canopy of a tree. After covering the boat with branches, I stashed the remaining items from the duffle bag into my pockets, grabbed my backpack and headed for the mark.

"Gerry, anything?" I whispered.

"Negative. I'm going to launch the WEAP to your location and fly the COMM to the mark so Kathy can monitor any activity and report back."

"Roger that." Gerry designed and built both drones himself. A genius in the field of specialized aerial machines or SAMs, they are built from composite material and house several high-powered cameras and communication repeaters allowing our team to stay in contact during missions. The WEAP or the weapons SAM has infinitely more functionality than the COMM, the communications SAM and is propelled using innovative ultra-quiet thrusters, giving it incredible power and speed. It houses cameras, too, as well as miscellaneous micro weapons. Even though it's one of Trinity's smaller weapon drones, it still contains an articulating arm.

I brought the blade of the machete down on tall grass and bushes. Birds lifted into the air, squawking loudly. I crouched down and waited. Hearing nothing, I continued. My GPS showed just over a mile to the target. Something caught my eye, a glittering through the foliage. I pulled out my binoculars but couldn't see much through the heavy growth.

With effort I made my way to where the reflection originated. After ducking under heavy wet foliage, I lifted myself and froze. My mouth dropped open. In front of me lay a crashed airplane—a yellow T-6, like the one Amelia flew. I breathed in deeply. It was covered in foliage, but the broken windshield glared through the gaps. Gray clouds were moving in from the west. Thirty minutes more and there would be no reflection. I stepped onto the wing, there were no bodies. I scanned the rest of the airplane. Someone had deliberately covered it with branches. That someone didn't want the plane to found.

My heart pulsed up into my throat when an impossible realization hit me. Could Amelia have gotten tangled up with the same group that took Daniela? Could the satellite image of a DC-3 David showed us be Amelia's father's C-47? If so, I have a pretty good idea what they're using it for.

"Kathy, Gerry," I whispered.

"Go ahead, Cougar," Kathy replied.

"I found Amelia's T-6 airplane. It's crashed about a mile short of our mark location."

"Oh my gosh," Kathy erupted. "Is she—?"

"I don't know. Her body's not here. The crash scene looks survivable but not without injuries. There's blood stains in the cockpit."

I tapped on my watch, then quickly crouched down. A branch moved near the tip of the wing. A large dark bird took to the air.

I finished looking through the airplane, then retraced my steps into a clearing. Swiping a few times, I brought the image up on my watch from the SAM. I could see the DC-3 or C-47, another airplane, and what looked like an aircraft hangar, house, and several other smaller structures. There were no people or signs of activity. A building of that size could hold an awful lot of stolen art.

I walked down an overgrown path, carefully watching for signs of movement. The path appeared to have been traveled recently. There were broken branches, some flattened by vehicle tires. The jungle camouflage ended. At the edge of the foliage, straight ahead, sat a large clearing. A turf runway sat off to my left. To my right, and plainly in sight now stood a C-47. If it was Amelia's father's C-47, it had been repainted.

A dog barked gutturally. It stopped me in my tracks. I quickly backed into the shrubs, crouching down. The barking continued. A man exited a house to the right of the hangar and walked over to a kennel. Seconds later the dog zigzagged back and forth before running full speed my direction. I pulled out the shooting taser and waited. As the dog, a large rottweiler, came within five feet of my hiding spot, it launched itself into the air just as I shot the taser. It froze in midair, then hit the ground. I quickly grabbed it, dragging it the rest of the way into the bushes.

The man who freed the dog was now at a full sprint, coming my direction. His extended arm wobbled as he held a pistol in front of him. I side-stepped through the underbrush until I could go no further, then slid on my stomach back to the edge of the clearing and watched as the man approached where the dog went in. At the same moment he found the stunned dog, I raised up behind him and knocked the pistol from his hand. He swung at me clumsily, almost in disbelief. I blocked his punch, grabbed his throat, and squeezed until his eyes rolled back into his head. I lowered his body next to the dog, zip-tying his arms and legs and taping his mouth shut.

"Kathy, anyone else?"

"Negative," she replied.

Staying close to the edge of the trees and vegetation, I worked myself around to the side of the house. "Gerry, you got my six?" The WEAP drew in closer.

"Affirmative."

I crept up to the side of the house, inching my way over to a window. Paint fell from the seal as I reached up and grabbed it. Two legs rested on a green ottoman. The ottoman belonged to a chair facing the opposite direction. A western played on the TV screen. I quietly made my way to the rear of the house. Through the window, a kitchen lay vacant and cluttered. I dropped back down and walked between the house and what looked more like an old barracks building than a hangar. The only windows in the barracks building had been painted over.

An airplane droned in the distance. I ducked down, hiding behind some rusted barrels stacked up against the barrack's wall and waited as a twin-engine Piper Seneca taxied in. The engines shut down not far from the C-47, opposite where I was crouched.

Two men and a woman exited the plane. That makes five all together, including the man inside the house and the one tied up. I tapped a question into my watch. *Was Gustano one of the two men that exited the plane?* Kathy responded with a yes.

The three walked past and into the house. I left the protection of the barrels and ran to the back of the barracks. The only door was bolted shut.

Gerry's SAM followed, remaining high above me. Trash and rusted metal blocked my path. A damaged airplane cowling leaned against a matching damaged empennage. A much smaller building sat just beyond the cluster of garbage. More barrels with less rust were stacked against the smaller structure. A fuel pump was inserted into one of them.

"Cougar, three men just exited the house."

I inched back, taking refuge behind the junk as I made my way to the other side of the smaller building. They entered the barracks. Two of them ran back out, searching and yelling the name *Fabio*.

Gustano pointed to a Jeep not far from me. The man next to him ran in my direction and jumped in. Tires kicked dirt and rocks against a metal shed as it headed in the direction of the dirt road. Gustano eyed the empty dog kennel. The third man exited the barracks. I heard Gustano yell. "Why didn't you keep an eye on that fool?"

The Jeep disappeared from sight.

"He got up to check on Sting. After he got him to quit barking, I figured he went into the barracks to have a little fun." Gustano said something back to him, but I couldn't understand what he said. The men split up, one walked over to the C-47, opened the door, and poked his head in. Gustano went back to the house. A minute later, he threw the other man a rifle.

"Find Fabio, now!" he demanded. Both men walked off, one toward the bushes on the side of the house and the other toward the runway. I stayed hidden behind objects and worked my way to the front of the barracks. When the men were far enough away, I ran to the barracks. A large sliding door was cracked open with a padlock laying on the ground next to it.

As quietly as I could, I rolled the door open and wedged myself in. Two women sat in chairs. It took a few seconds to recognize them. They both raised their heads slowly.

"Arlan!"

"Cougar!"

Instantly, they faced each other, then faced me. Their eyes were sunk deep into their sockets; their hair, ratted and dirty. Daniela had mascara stains on her face. Amelia's flight suit was marred in dried blood and food. A stench of urine filled the air.

"How did you find me?" Daniela breathed. Amelia looked her direction.

"Can you get us out of here?" Amelia asked.

"I'm going to try. Is that your dad's plane?"

"Yes, these men killed him."

The Jeep's engine resonated. "Stay strong." I ran to the back of the barracks, hiding behind several large wooden crates. A stencil caught my eye, 'Fragile'. I moved to another crate with the top propped open. I jumped up onto the first crate and gazed down into an open one. It was dark, but something was resting in a nest of straw.

"They're coming in," Kathy said.

The door rolled open, light streamed in, and there was yelling. I heard the dog's vicious bark. It ran through the open door, stopped for a second in front of the girls, then heading straight at me. Before I could take care of the dog, Gustano walked in. I slid my backpack off and dropped it in the open crate. The first man called the dog off and held its collar as it lurched several times at me, snarling and splattering the ground with spit. Two other men walked in; one was the man I choked earlier.

"Get down from there," Gustano demanded. "Come on." Gustano's voice was firm and measured, like finding intruders was an everyday event. Sweat dripped from my armpits. "Arlan, I thought it might be you." Gustano held a blank expression. His eyebrows twitched as he walked over to me. Then he slowly turned, facing a woman that just entered through the sliding door. When he turned back, he swung his right hand hard into my face. I staggered as the lights went out, then back on; blood tasted in my mouth.

"You should have sent the memo when you had the chance."

"So, you're Mauricio's hired hands?"

"I run my own enterprise." A woman in her late twenties or early thirties stepped forward. She wore a hard expression. Her brown hair was held up by a metal barrette. She wore tight cutoff jean shorts and a low-cut tank top.

"So, this is Arlan," she said, circling me. "This is the one you two couldn't kill?"

Two of the men held perplexing expressions. "I can understand Fabio screwing up, but you, Miguel. That's unlike you."

Gustano grabbed her by the arm, pulling her back. "Let the girls use the bathroom. Miguel, tie him up—away from them." He glowered. "The Fine Arts Insurance Board, huh?" Gustano shook his head.

"An investigator from the Fine Arts Insurance Board."

"And a major setback to our plan!" Gustano's face reddened as he raised his hand. He stopped midair, letting the blood drain from his face, then laughed almost uncontrollably. The other men laughed along with him. The woman, ignoring Gustano's request, turned to walk out the door. "Brigitte, make these girls presentable for Mauricio tomorrow." Gustano winked at Daniela and Amelia. "I think tomorrow could be your lucky day." The woman stopped, looked back, then disappeared through the door.

Two men zip-tied me to a chair after first searching me. Miguel, a dark-skinned stocky fellow with short curly hair, confiscated my gun. He looked at my watch but left it on. From the outside, it resembled a cheap tacky timepiece. A few minutes later the stream of light narrowed, and the rolling door slammed tight. A clank from a padlock on the outside brought silence. Amelia and Daniela were about twenty feet off to my left. They began discussing something.

I spoke quietly into my lapel. "Kathy, Gerry?"

"We hear you."

"Did you catch what Gustano said?"

"Affirmative."

"There are large crates in here, I think it might be the Bogota art. Unfortunately, I only caught a glimpse inside one before the interruption."

"Are you okay?" Kathy asked.

"Affirmative. I'll give you a sitrep in an hour."

"Roger that," Gerry stated.

"Over."

Amelia and Daniela were in an impassioned discussion. Rain began pinging off the tin roof. "Amelia, Daniela, are you two all right?" They turned. I saw through the dim light their uncomfortable expressions.

"Yes," Daniela said smartly. "What are we supposed to do now? Isn't this what you do? Save people?" Amelia and Daniela bantered again about something.

"Amelia, are you okay?"

"Yes, Cougar. Is this your 'other mission' that was so much more important than mine?" Despite the barracks being only dimly lit by cracks and holes, I could plainly see both ladies now, glaring at me with piercing eyes. I spent the next hour sharing details of the mission, opening up about Trinity, and about Gerry and Kathy.

A squealing interrupted our conversation. The open door exposed a darkening wet night. Brigitte, the woman earlier with the hardened face, walked in carrying a box in her hand. She set the box down. "Anyone hungry?" Her voice was sarcastic. She pulled two small trays of food from the box and set them on Daniela's and Amelia's laps. "Dig in, ladies. And for you handsome, I fixed a special meal." Brigitte sauntered over to me—circling me. "You don't look like an Arlan." She ran her hand down my arm. "For a paper pusher, you sure have nice arms. What do you say we have a little fun before dinner?"

I felt Amelia and Daniela's stare. Brigitte pulled the barrette from her brown hair, letting it tumble across her shoulders. Behind the hardened face and tough presentation, there was an attractive woman. Her hand rubbed through my short blond hair. She held my head between her hands, gazing into my eyes. "I like you," She said. "Do you like me?"

"What's wrong?" I asked. "Is your boss, Gustano, not giving you enough attention?"

She released her hands and stood erect. "I get all the attention I need." She bent over again, "from a-n-y-o-n-e I want." She held her pose, wanting me to observe her exposed cleavage. I turned, facing the other ladies. "Aww, are you shy, Arlan?" She bent down slowly, pulling the last tray out of the box. Daniela called her a name which brought her upright with a snap. Brigitte swore, covering her mouth. "The knight has come to rescue his fair maiden."

Daniela visibly blushed.

Amelia's expression turned somber.

Brigitte swore again. "Get out of here," she said, observing Amelia. "You have a crush on him too?" Amelia didn't answer. "Well, ladies, if this is your knight in shining armor, he needed a little better plan if he was going to rescue you from Gustano. Enjoy your last night." Brigitte shoved the tray into my lap. She turned and stomped to the door. The door slid closed with a loud clank that echoed the tin barracks.

Chapter 48

Playing for the Wrong Team

Brigitte was in the kitchen beating eggs as Fabio walked in. "Is that for me?" he asked, pulling out a chair and sitting down.

"In one day, you and Miguel managed to dirty almost every dish in the cupboard, and then you left them dirty and scattered on the counter. I'm not your maid, Fabio," Brigitte asserted.

"So, is that for me?" Fabio asked again, ignoring her insinuation. He casually glanced at the now clean counter "We had to feed the girls, ya know—while you were gone."

"Well, ya know," mimicking him, "you need to do some chores, too." She poured the scrambled egg mixture into a pan and stirred. "Put some toast down, will ya? You can manage that much, can't you?"

"What's got you all in a bunch this morning? Had to sleep by your-self again?" Brigitte turned and wiped her son's face.

"You can be done. Go play in the other room for mommy, will you?" The boy slid off the chair and waddled into the adjoining room. "Don't be talking like that around him. He understands what you're saying."

"Well? What's got you all upset? Is it because Gustano left you here again? You know, you got it pretty good around here."

"What are you talking about? Everybody takes care of you. I haven't seen you earn your keep since the first month you got here. The only reason you're not dead is because of your brother's talent. You're just a two-bit thug—an easy hire. Gustano can find fifty men like you in less than an hour.”

“My talents, dear Brigitte are these.” Fabio pulled his sleeve back and flexed his arm.

“You should have given your brain some of the nutrients and not just your biceps.” Brigitte scraped eggs onto a plate in front of Fabio, then scraped the remaining eggs onto three smaller trays. “When you’re done with the toast, put a piece on each of these and go feed our prisoners. They will need to pee, too. If you can’t handle it, just let me know and I’ll take care of them.”

Fabio pulled at his shirt, exposing the handle of his pistol. “I think I have it under control, although this may slip out of its holster and smack the guy in the lips after what he did to me yesterday.”

“You mean after he embarrassed you?”

Fabio buttered the last of the toast. “Yeah.”

“I don’t think it was Mr. Loverboy that humiliated you. I think it was you humiliating yourself, as usual.”

“What do you mean, ‘lover boy’?”

“Those two girls are infatuated with him.”

“How do you know that?”

“Oh, please, the same way I know you wish you had a girl like either one of them. The best you’re going to get is Sting. And that’s only if you sweet talk him while dishing up his food.”

“Real funny, at least I don’t beg the boss for attention. ‘*Oh Gustano, you’re so brave, you’re so rich, you’re so...whatever.*’ You’re just as pathetic.”

“I’m done here. I’ve killed enough brain cells talking to you for one day. Don’t forget to feed them. Gustano wants them to look presentable.”

“I don’t know why,” Fabio mumbled to himself as Brigitte left the kitchen.

Mauricio leaned against the warehouse wall. He viewed his watch for the third time. A brief rain squall passed through; water rushed into the gutters. Downspouts reverberated, draining off the onslaught of water.

Mauricio inventoried the stolen art at regular intervals. He didn't trust anyone. Gustano took without asking, and if questioned, was quick with a reason as to why he needed the extra cash. When cornered, he became aggressive. Donny had taken a few pieces, too. But Donny took out of childish impulse, like a kid in a candy store. Mauricio played the game according to the rules. Rules he had created mostly himself.

The sun and warmth returned, evaporating the moisture from the grassy field. The sound of a twin-engine plane hummed in the distance. The dot grew larger until tires hydroplaned along the turf, then slowed down and made a 180-degree turn, taxiing back to the warehouse. As the engines came to a stop, birds rousted from the trees made their way back to their perches. The door of the Piper Seneca opened. Gustano stepped out waving his hand. Mauricio stepped over the low fence and made his way to the airplane. He turned his wrist. "A bit late, don't you think?" Mauricio stated sharply.

Gustano strained at his tongue. He was tired of Mauricio's insolent and despotic remarks. "Bit of a headwind." He finally replied.

"Well, let's get on with it. So, what's this new proposition you've dreamed up for the two girls?" Mauricio seated himself while Gustano closed the door. Moments later the engines came to life; raw fuel spilt from warm exhaust pipes, creating a momentary flame out the back of one of the engines. The airplane back-taxied along the turf runway, turned 180-degrees and lined up for takeoff. Javier, sitting in the captain's seat, glanced over at Gustano sitting next to him. "Ready?"

Miguel slid the barrack's door open. "You each get a one-minute potty break." Miguel was as tough as they came. He was built well, like Fabio, only Miguel had brains to accompany his strength. "Women first, how about you darling?" He cut Daniela loose, shuffling her to the bathroom. He did the same for Amelia. "Okay, Arlan…your turn, and don't try to be a hero. I devour paper pushers like you every day." Cougar followed Miguel's orders. While in the bathroom, he inspected the only window, noticing it was nailed shut at the base.

The morning sun lit up the pinholes in the roof like stars. There was enough light so Daniela, Amelia, and Cougar could see clearly. Miguel left; the door squealed shut. Cougar thought to himself. Gustano wanted Daniela and Amelia presentable to Mauricio, but why? Yesterday, Gustano had asked Brigitte to clean up the ladies, but she hadn't been in yet. Cougar calculated how long the flight should take from their location to Bogota and back. He added that to the time he heard the twin Piper depart and reckoned he had approximately two hours before they were back.

His arms and legs were zip-tied; his legs, to one of the chair's metal legs, and his arms, behind his back. He slid his legs up as high as they would go. Grabbing at his mission suit pant leg, through the opening in the back of the chair, he zipped open a hidden pocket. In it was a small flexible saw blade, made precisely for the purpose of removing zip-ties.

The ladies watched as Cougar freed himself. "Cougar!" Daniela called out.

Cougar stopped in front of the ladies. "It's not time yet, please trust me. I will get you out of here."

"Promise?" Amelia asked.

Cougar ruminated on the situation. Two beautiful women that had been left to eat like animals and urinate in their chairs. Their once beautiful hair now ratted and chopped. And worse, they were both tremendously frightened. "I promise," Cougar replied.

Cougar pulled his backpack from the crate and carried it into the bathroom where a garbage can with a swinging lid sat. Unzipping one of the pockets, he removed two special zip-ties and a small backup pistol. He slid the pistol into his chest holster and placed the backpack in the trashcan under some dirty paper towels.

The door rolled open just as Cougar cinched the second zip-tie to his wrists. Brigitte carried in a box. "Lunch time, and your last meal, lover-boy." She placed a tray on Cougar's lap with a meat sandwich. "Good luck eating that one," She remarked.

She set the box down. "You two can eat after you've cleaned yourselves up. I'll give each of you five minutes to clean up and put on some clean clothes." Brigitte pulled out two sets of clean clothes. "You are to leave the bathroom door open, so I can keep an eye on you." They both gazed up at Brigitte. "One at a time, ladies. You, fly-girl with the witch hair; you're first." Brigitte pointed, prompting Amelia to hurry.

Cougar heard Kathy in his earpiece. "Gerry is flying the WEAP over now. We will be in position and ready soon." Cougar curled his finger and tapped on the watch face.

"Hurry it up in there."

After the ladies were cleaned up, Brigitte set the trays on their lap. "Don't get your clothes dirty; eat like ladies." Brigitte snickered to herself. "I don't know what you see in them, Arlan." Brigitte exaggerated her hips. "It's too bad you'll be dead soon," she whispered. "I could use a man like you around." Her fingers glided over Cougar's face.

Brigitte's heavy mascara, strong perfume, and cheeks were rosy with blush. The day prior, she hadn't worn any makeup. Her cotton tank-top was soft pink, form fitting, and intentionally cut low down the front. She moved her fingers through Cougar's short hair and down his shoulder.

"Shame the way it has to be." She lifted her head, turning to Daniela. "Does this make you jealous?" Brigitte bent over, pressing her lips against Cougar's. "Oh, come on and kiss me you fool." Cougar turned. Brigitte slapped him hard. Cougar's face reddened. "You can have him; he's probably a dud anyway. I like real men."

"Like Gustano?" Cougar asked. "Is he your real man? Does he treat you like a woman—special? It seems to me you're just another one of his thugs. You even dress like one of the guys, except you expose half your body, hoping he'll notice you're still a woman; but I bet most of the time he doesn't, does he? Did you wear that perfume and make-up for him or me?" Brigitte eyed him crossly with her hands resting on her shifted hips.

"What would you know…some shmuck insurance boy telling me about what I like and who I am? Look at you. You're a nothing. You're pathetic! I AM special. I have a son…and I *am* Gustano's girl. We are going to be obscenely rich…and you? You'll be dead, and all because you butt your nose in where it didn't belong. And you two ladies," Brigitte said, glaring their direction, "you've been playing for the wrong team, but Gustano's going to fix that. You two will fetch a high price in the market, despite being slightly older than the preferred lassies." Daniela, and Amelia instantly understood. "Don't look so sad, that's good news. Gustano has decided not to kill you, although you will have wished he did." Brigitte chuckled.

Cougar understood their plan too, and it made him sick thinking about it.

Sold

Kathy's voice resonated in my ear. "Cougar, a plane is approaching."

"Thank you, Kathy. Gerry, is the WEAP over head?"

"I have it sitting on the ground next to the barracks on the side opposite the house."

"Cougar," Kathy interrupted, "this is a different airplane. It appears to be single engine, high wing."

"Looks like more company." I replied.

"Cougar, the twin Piper is right behind it. They should be landing any minute."

"Affirmative. Let's see who all the players are."

Propellers and engines reverberated off the barrack walls. The noise ended with a quiet hush. A minute later, men were talking. I strained to hear.

"Cougar, I count eight people, including three that came out of the house. Two from the single engine airplane, and three from the twin, Mauricio, Gustano, and the pilot." The door squealed on its rail. Light spilled onto the floor, then more light as someone flipped on a switch. Daniela and Amelia wore worried looks. Miguel held a small machine gun in his hands. Gustano produced a trail of smoke from a freshly lit Export A. He stopped and inhaled deeply. The tip of the cigarette burned bright orange as his lungs filled. At his side was a holstered pistol.

Mauricio only gave me a cursory glance, eyed both women, and continued to the crates. "Gustano, this place is a mess, and it stinks to high heaven. You think with all the money I pay you; you could have at least cleaned up before I arrived."

I observed Gustano's expression. "I've kept these three animals in here, of course it stinks!"

"I only count fifteen crates. Where are the other three?" demanded Mauricio.

"We sold the contents of three crates," replied Gustano, as he glanced at Miguel; both held a bewildered expression. "You told us to, remember?"

"Don't get smart with me. Of course, I know what I said. The revenue you gave me was not the contents of three crates. I told you not to sell unless we got top dollar."

"That was top dollar, Mauricio. Not all this junk is worth as much as you think."

Mauricio grabbed Gustano's shirt and pulled him to his face. "This is not junk!" Mauricio said, pointing to the crates. He waved his free arm. "Your place here? That's junk. You play by my rules, my friend, or you don't play at all." Miguel lifted his gun. Gustano shook his head.

"Your rules?" Gustano chuckled. "Let's get something straight. You're not the boss. You're just a pompous, egotistical, trivial cog in the wheel. Yeah, you hired me, and I have done as you've asked. But I'm getting tired of listening to your crap."

"I'm the brains that spins this wheel…don't forget that! You and your goons would still be ferrying drugs if it weren't for me. Show some respect…you ungrateful hoodlum." Gustano's eyes fill with rage. Miguel raised his gun again, Gustano shook his head again. Miguel lowered the gun.

Two men I hadn't seen before entered the building. Smoke trickled from their nostrils. Both were heavily built and had pistols hanging at their sides. The older one took one last drag of a cigarette before demolishing it into the cement floor with his boot.

"So, these are the girls?" one of the men asked.

"What do you think?" Gustano said. "Both very pretty—and thin, just the way you like 'em." The man's face moved within six inches of Daniela and Amelia's. I wanted to pull my zip-ties apart and destroy them both, but I'd never make it before being gunned down.

"They're older than you led me to believe," the man recoiled.

"That's why you're getting them at a bargain. Buy one, get the second one half off."

"Do you want them or not?" Mauricio demanded. "I'm out of patience today. If you don't want them, they die—right here, right now."

"We'll take 'em," the other man replied, looking at his partner.

"Drug 'em up good," Mauricio said. "I don't ever want to see them around Bogota. Understand?"

"Yeah, we got it. You don't have to worry about that. Our girls never leave." The man handed Gustano a wad of cash. Miguel cut the zip-ties and led them outside. Brigitte entered as the girls were led out. A little boy ran in after her.

"Brigitte, for heaven sakes, get your kid out of here!" yelled Gustano. "We're doing business." Mauricio's cell rang. He answered it, gesturing with his hand for Gustano to finish getting the girls onto the plane and out of here. A few seconds later, Fabio carried a submachine gun into the barracks. Mauricio ended the brief call, stashing his phone in his left jacket pocket.

"Mauricio!" I yelled. He turned.

"Feeling ignored? Don't worry, we have a little surprise for you as well."

"So, tell me," I asked. "How much money do you get for ripping off museums and selling art at auctions."

"Auctions? Oh Arlan, such a pity. You should have just done your job and left. Auctions are…trivial in relation to the black market.

There's a sea of buyers who look forward to getting fine art at bargain prices."

"That's it? You're just a two-bit distributor of fine art to the underground? That's your elaborate wealth producing scheme? And of course, the museums receive compensation from oblivious insurance companies. Everybody wins, is that it?"

Mauricio eyes narrowed. "The insurance companies pay what we tell them the art is worth, and what's on the manifest."

"There was no art in the crates, was there?"

"Some." Mauricio chuckled. "You're not going to believe this, Arlan, but some of the art the insurance companies have compensated us for, is still sitting on museum gallery floors." Mauricio puffed up his chest. "It pays to have an insurance insider like Donny. Most of the art of course, is moved off-site and stored for a more opportune…season."

"And you fill the crates with water, ensuring the freight forwarders are oblivious to your scam?"

"You've almost figured it out, Arlan. I figured you were close, that's why we tried discouraging you. You should have heeded our warnings." He gave Gustano a wink. "We spend a few years at each location establishing residency and trust. In those few years, we're able to reappraise much of the art."

"Let me guess, with your own appraisers?"

Mauricio looked annoyed but continued. "I don't mind spending time in these amazing museums. After all," Mauricio lifted his head, "art is my passion."

"Sounds more like theft and greed are your passions."

Mauricio cheeks lowered. "My system keeps us virtually off everyone's radar, including the director and Board of Trustees, lets us live and work in some of the most extraordinary cities in the world, and have multiple streams of revenue; all from art." Mauricio cheeks lifted. "And," he chuckled some more, "I also get paid a decent salary as a curator."

"All that you learned in college?"

"Now answer me a question. In all my years I've never run across an insurance investigator quite like you. We have gotten scrutinized by the insurance board in the past; but once they see the museum's paperwork is in order, spend a few weeks questioning and working with the local police, the board ends their investigation. Tell me, what was it that tipped you off and how much of this does the FAIB know?" Gustano edged closer.

"I was sent to investigate the disappearance of highly valued artifacts. I'm new to this role and wanted to do a good job."

"That's it? You're the new guy that just wanted to do a good job?"

"Sure, I have integrity and a work ethic." I saw perspiration bead along Mauricio's black hairline. "Oh, and the board knows everything about Donny's and your scheme. They don't, however, know about you, Gustano." Miguel pointed the barrel straight at my chest. The noise from the single engine airplane faded away.

"Well, that's too bad," Mauricio replied. "I wish you hadn't done that." He removed his gold-rimmed glasses and scratched at his temple.

Gustano's face wrinkled in fury. He said, "Mauricio, you have put us all at risk. You seem to think you're smarter than us, but you're nothing but an over-educated con-man." Gustano moved to the door. Mauricio tried to follow until Miguel pointed his gun at Mauricio's stomach.

"What's this?" He questioned, indignantly.

"Think about your errors in judgment, Mauricio, and how insignificant you are," Gustano said. Then he exited the building.

"Cougar, another plane is coming in," Kathy stated.

Minutes later, an engine stopped somewhere outside. A short conversation ensued and then Captain Eduardo Moreno stepped through the door with Gustano following him. "Captain Moreno!" I exclaimed. Boy am I glad to see you." He shot me a glance, then stood by Mauricio.

Mauricio cried, "Boss, it's not my fault, I swear. Him! He's the one who messed everything up!" He pointed in my direction.

A gunshot echoed through the barracks. Blood erupted on Mauricio's back before he dropped to the ground. Captain Moreno holstered his gun. Shaking his head, and with a turned-up lip, said, "Arlan, you have cost me a lot of money." He swung his fist. My ear exploded in pain. Miguel adjusted his aim at me. "Why can't people just—obey—orders?"

A crescendo of noise, like a crashing cymbal, echoed inside my head. I unclenched my jaw and said. "I was, just not yours."

Captain Moreno stiffened and nodded to Gustano. Fabio and Javier drug Mauricio's body out the door, leaving a dark red stripe on the cement, marking the path. The sound of a propeller shuddered through the metal walls.

"Captain Moreno left with his pilot, and the other two men are bagging Mauricio's body and putting it in the back of the twin Piper." I tapped lightly on my watch. Brigitte appeared, strutting to me in her worn jean shorts.

"Too bad you missed your chance for a spectacular night. These boys may not be very bright, but they do know how to fight. Goodbye, Arlan." She pressed her lips hard into mine. "You fool!" She swung her hand at me. I pulled my head back; her hand caught my cheek. "I'm glad you'll be dead by the time we're back."

She left, exaggerating her hips as she did. Moments later, the Piper's engines started. The plane taxied by, blowing dirt and dust through the open doorway. The metal walls pounded synchronously. "Now Gerry!" I whispered.

"What did you say?" Miguel asked.

"I said…it's a shame I have to beat the living tar out of you."

Miguel's mouth widened to a grin. "Really…I like hearing that." Javier and Fabio re-entered the barracks.

"The WEAP is in the corner, tell me when."

All three men looked at me. "Let's see if I got this straight. You are Miguel, Gustano's right-hand man. You have probably been with him the longest. Next, we have Javier, the young daring pilot who probably hasn't had much fighting experience. Then we have Fabio, Javier's muscled-up brother, all muscle, and no brains. Am I close?"

"I get him first," Fabio yelled. "After I pulverize you, I'll let my brother disfigure that disgusting smug face of yours. Then Miguel, our resident Kung Fu teacher will finish you off. Then we're going to feed your body to Sting. That's for tas'n him earlier."

"I'm impressed." I said.

"What do you mean?" Fabio demanded.

"You put together some complete sentences. I got to hand it to you, I didn't think you had it in you." Fabio's face reddened. Fabio was not carrying the gun he had earlier, in fact, Miguel had the only gun visible, but he had lowered it. Fabio lunged at me. "Gerry!" I said loudly. All three glanced at the door. When they didn't see anyone, Fabio kicked me, knocking over my chair with me in it. I snapped apart the special zip-ties and jumped up in a karate stance. All three men wore grins. The SAM's camera rotated.

"Look at that, Fabio," Miguel said, "someone's had a little training. Can you handle him, Fabio, or do you need me to help?"

"Shut up, Miguel!" Fabio yelled. "You're not the only fighter here. Watch this." Fabio grabbed the chair and threw it behind him. "Come on, Arlan, show me what you got." He smiled at Miguel with a smug expression. I leaped in the air, spun, and drove my foot into his head. A thud sounded from the hard melon centered between his broad shoulders. His eyes blinked shut—then snapped open. Miguel and Javier laughed.

Javier bantered. "Come on Fabio, you're tougher than this guy. Do you need me to show you how it's done? He's a paper pusher for heaven's sakes." Fabio waved his arm at his brother while circling me.

Gerry said in my ear, "Cougar, do you want me to shoot them?"

"Not yet; but keep your aim on them." The SAM stayed high and in the corner of the barracks.

"There he goes talking to himself again," said Miguel. "I think he's out of his mind."

"Or just plain scared."

I had enough of this. Amelia and Daniela needed rescued—and fast. Many times, women are never found once they are abducted and put into this appalling service. Fabio jabbed at me using his right fist, then swung his opposite arm around. I caught it, but he head-butted me in the face, right above my nose.

Blood dripped. Pressure stemmed between my eyes. "Come on Fabio…hurry up, it's my turn." Javier clucked.

I dropped to the ground, sweeping my right leg. Fabio tumbled, smashing his head against the concrete. Miguel and Javier applauded. Fabio stood, staring at me with glazed eyes.

"For Amelia," I said.

"Come on, Fabio!" Javier was getting restless.

"Fine, Javier." Fabio backed up, rubbing his head. Javier pumped his fists in the air.

"All right brother, let me show you how real men fight." Javier jumped around like a boxer, toying with me. He had a balanced stride. He didn't possess the muscle power of his brother, but he had a street sense about his movement. He kicked at my head, then swung and caught my leg with his other foot. I struck the side of his head with a knife-hand strike, driving the side of my palm deep into his temple. He staggered back a foot or two, grinned and came at me again. As he swung his fist, I grabbed it, spun around, and drove the flat of my right fist into his face, then jammed my elbow into his gut, spun again, and broke his jaw with an upper cut.

"For Daniela," I said.

Fabio swung at me. I blocked his arm, spun, and took him out with a solid roundhouse kick to his head. Both brothers were now on the ground, knocked out cold.

"I guess amateur hour is over," Miguel said. He widened his stance and drove his feet into the cement like tree trunks, then worked his arms in front of him, Kung Fu style. I circled him. He followed. Two 360-degree turns.

"Where did they take the girls?"

"Where nobody will find them," he said. I stopped circling and headed for the door.

He ran towards me. Gerry flew the WEAP down, hovering it just over my head. Miguel stopped dead in his tracks. He stared at the unusual motionless machine. "Who are you? You're no paper-pusher."

"My name is Cougar, United States special agent. Are you sure you want to go through with this? I'll give you an opportunity to surrender if you tell me where they took the women."

"Surrender? What, are you kidding? I am not afraid of your toy drone." Miguel pulled at the gun strap still attached to the machine gun.

"I wouldn't do that. If you want to fight, I'll fight, but no guns. If I win, you tell me where they took them."

"Look at you, telling me what I can and can't do. I'm in control here…got it? I'm gonna beat you to a pulp…you wacko." Miguel slid the strap off his shoulder, then swiftly raised the gun. Gerry released a laser beam, straight into the guns trigger. Miguel yelled, instantly pulling his hand away. The gun dropped to the ground.

"I said, no guns."

"You punk…okay, let's go." Miguel shook his hand, then lifted it up to fight. Slowly, his gaze shifted to the right where his trigger finger had been, seconds ago. Then it lowered, stopping at his burnt finger laying on the cement, next to the gun. He kicked it away.

We circled again, I relaxed slightly, baiting him. He kicked me twice, once to my leg and then to my thigh. Back and forth, we exchanged body blows. "Cougar," Gerry said.

I caught a blow to the head. Ringing erupted from my other ear. Another kick sent me back to the ground.

"Not so tough, huh?" He stomped his leg down hard. I quickly rolled to the right making his leg miss, then rolled back and trapped his foot underneath me. I chopped at the side of his knee. A crack sounded. His leg buckled, sending him to the ground. We both rose. Miguel had picked up something on the ground next to Javier and threw it towards the SAM. The SAM tilted. Miguel ran at me, sending me back to the ground. His fists pounded at me like a jackhammer. Clasping my hands, I drove them into his chest and then to his face. He leaned up. I drove them again into his chest. He staggered up on his injured leg. I backed up and drove my foot into his chest. More cracking sounds emanated from his chest walls. He hunched over. I kicked. He backed up. I missed. He lunged again. This time I sprung up, driving my foot into the same chest area. He folded to his knees. I swung three times into his cement head. The ground sprayed red as his nose broke.

He laid on the ground, barely conscious. I ran to the bathroom, removed my backpack, and tied all three men up. "Gerry, I'm coming your way, hurry and pack, we're going to need your talent and toys. Kathy, where are the girls?"

"I lost them, sorry Cougar. Fifty miles out the signal dropped."

I grabbed Miguel. "Where did they take the girls!" Miguel eyed me with a bloody grin. "Where?" I shook him. He stared with a sadistic scowl. "I'm not going to ask again." I pressed my gun against his forehead. A look of bewilderment crested over his face when he realized I had a pistol.

"Gerry, I'm coming to get you if I can get this old Cessna 180 started."

"Cougar," said Kathy, "did you find out where the girls are?"

"He gave me a location."

"Do you believe him?"

"It's all we have. Gerry, were you able to get photos of the men who took Amelia and Daniela?"

"Yes."

Kathy interjected. "I should have something in the next few minutes. What do you want to do with the men there and Gustano and Brigette?"

"Let Riley know we have three tied up and more than likely found the Bogota treasure—if not more. Better have them send officials we can trust. We'll deal with Gustano, Brigette, Donny, and Captain Moreno after the girls are recovered."

"Affirmative!" Kathy replied.

The Cessna180 sat next to a shed. The engine had oil. The tanks had some fuel. I turned the ignition to start. The prop didn't budge. I placed a couple boards in front of the tires and hand propped until the engine sputtered to life. Black smoke and raw fuel ejected from the sole exhaust pipe. I pushed the throttle forward until the plane bounced over the small boards, then shut the door. "On my way, Gerry."

"There's a field just in from where you dropped me off. Planes use it to bring in supplies and medical emergencies."

"Affirmative, Gerry." I held the throttle and mixture to the firewall. The tail flew up almost immediately. The plane gently swerved from side to side down the strip, lifting slowly into the air. Within fifteen minutes I found the field, Gerry, and some of his new friends waving their arms.

Chapter 50

The More You Cooperate, the Nicer You're Treated

The car pulled into a long U-shaped drive, stopping in front of a two-story textile factory. Two ladies exited the front door, greeted Daniela and Amelia, and escorted them through the factory and up a flight of stairs. That was the last time Daniela and Amelia saw each other. As Amelia was coerced into one of the rooms, she asked, "Are you making us work in that factory?"

"Oh, no, dear, your work is upstairs here." A man came into the room and dropped two pills into the lady's open hand. "Take these, dear, it will make you feel much better." Amelia resisted. The man stepped over, and with a blank expression, struck Amelia in the face. Then he held her mouth open as the lady forced the two pills down her throat. "It's much better if you cooperate, dear. The more you cooperate, the nicer you're treated; you'll learn that." The lady, in her forties, black hair, thin skin, and wrinkles much too pronounced for her age, studied Amelia's body, face, and hair. "You know darling, men are going to love you. That hair is something else."

Amelia's couldn't focus. She felt her soul departing her body.

"I'll bring you something sexier to wear. What you have on just won't do. There's a bathroom through the curtain there where you can clean yourself up. Do you need help?"

Amelia moved her head sluggishly from side to side. As she did the room began spinning. She heard the door close. She looked through watery eyes. The man and woman were gone. She slumped to the ground and crawled to the door. She tried the knob; it only turned a fraction. She wanted to cry, but she couldn't. *Cougar, is he already dead?* She wished she could have told him how she felt about him. How she liked him and thought they would make the perfect couple, having so much in common. He was handsome, smart, and strong. She had noticed the way he looked at her, too.

Daniela experienced the same treatment as Amelia, only in a different room, down a different hall. In the midst of trying to force the pills down her, Daniela flailed her arms wildly. An elderly lady with gray and straw-colored hair, yelled out. A stocky man in his forties returned, forcing Daniela onto the bed face first. The lady pushed fluid out the tip of a needle. It spouted into the air. Then she forcefully inserted it into Daniela's arm. Daniela felt a tingling sensation before falling into a deep sleep. "We'll clean her up later," the lady said, locking the door behind her. "She's very pretty, huh?"

"If you say so—not my type," the stocky man replied.

"You have a type?" the lady asked.

"Yeah, not some two-bit tramp like her. I'm a family man."

"Oh…you'd make a great family man." The lady goaded.

"Oh, you shud…up!"

Chapter 51

We're Here for the Girls

"This looks like the nearest airport," Cougar said, circling overhead. Gerry studied the satellite image on his handheld GPS. Cougar pulled the cracked plastic yoke aft while retarding the throttle. The tires chirped; the tail settled to the ground. Cougar kicked the rudder to one side, turning the old Cessna toward a small building where several older airplanes sat tethered to the ground.

"Look!" Gerry pointed to a Cessna. "That's the plane that took the girls!"

"Are you sure?"

"Positive."

"Can you get Kathy on?"

"I'll try." Gerry pulled out a satellite phone. "Kathy…yeah, we just landed…here, let me put Cougar on." Cougar yanked the mixture back. The propeller slowed to a stop.

"Cougar, I found a match on one the guys, a Schmil Akerr. He runs a large prostitution business."

"Figured as much. Anything else we need to know about him—and do you get a location?"

"He…go…er…volved…ing."

"Kathy, you're cutting out, repeat."

"I said, he was caught years ago smuggling drugs across the border and has been involved in human trafficking. He has a brothel about thirty minutes from where you're located."

"That confirms what Miguel told me. Did you get a hold of Riley?"

"Affirmative. He gave the information to their government. A team should be storming Gustano's place within twenty-four hours."

"Any signs of Gustano?" asked Gerry.

"No, not yet. I turned the solar switch on the communication SAM, but with the clouds moving in, I'm not sure how long it'll stay airborne."

"We need to go. Keep it there as long as you can," said Cougar.

"Bring Amelia and Daniela back."

"That's the plan," Gerry replied.

Cougar picked up one of Gerry's bags. "I got a guy who will take us into town." They loaded into a tan and rust Datsun station wagon.

"¿De dónde eres?" the driver asked.

"America. Sightseeing—Turismo," I replied.

"Sí, mucho que ver."

"Yes…beautiful here—"

The driver pushed in a tape. An accordion with Spanish singers cracked through dried speakers. He grinned, exposing his few remaining teeth. Cougar turned to the back seat. Gerry shrugged his shoulders.

Gerry unzipped one of the large bags behind him, partially exposing the weapons drone. He removed a battery pack and replaced it with a freshly charged one kept in a small Kevlar pouch. A neon light flickered on the ceiling before he turned the power off. He raised his arm, showing Cougar a thumbs up.

Potholes and large trucks necessitated the driver swerve to the shoulder with regularity. Cougar watched as the desolate countryside changed to a densely populated city. He glanced at his wristwatch; Gerry had programmed in the brothel's location. The two dots were now very close.

"Parada," said Cougar. The driver pulled over to a vacant storefront. Gerry nodded. They removed the large bag from the back, and with two other bags in hand, carried them behind the store. It only took Gerry a few minutes to send up both SAMs. They watched the small screen as the COMM transmitted pictures of an old textile building.

"Must be in there," Gerry said.

Cougar watched as two men walked around the premise. "Guards." A large truck exited the textile driveway turning right. It drove past Gerry and Cougar, grinding gears as it did.

"What do you think?" asked Gerry.

"Let's go."

Kathy monitored Cougar and Gerry's position. They strolled down the U-shaped driveway, wearing big grins on their faces. Two men stepped off the porch and approached them. "We're here for the ladies," said Gerry. The two men looked at each other. One lifted his cheek.

"Esta manera." Inside, a sea of young girls and old ladies worked sewing machines—several, barely ten years of age. The man walked Cougar and Gerry to a set of stairs and twirled his finger, directing them to turn and be searched. Cougar spun a full 360. When he was back eye to eye with the man, he pushed a taser into his belly. The man convulsed three times before dropping into Gerry's arms. Gerry dragged his body behind the stairs.

Cougar whispered. "Have the SAM ready."

"Roger that. Go find the girls." Gerry set up in a small vacant office, pulling a thin flexible control panel from inside his shirt. He tapped on the keyboard, taking over the controls of the WEAP. Three men were outside. He adjusted the camera. Two were patrolling the premise. The SAM followed high above them as they marched almost in military fashion towards the back of the building. Gerry brought the SAM in closer, switching over to whisper mode. It hovered behind them at ten feet in the air. The SAM gave off a soft beep. One man turned, the SAM discharged a shock into his chest, sending him immediately to the ground. His partner turned while grabbing at his gun. Gerry launched another shock into him. He crumpled slowly, falling over the first man. Then he went after the third man on the porch.

Rescued

At the top of the stairs, a lady in her 50s with gray and dirty blonde hair greeted me. Her back hunched, her eyes were dark and drawn, and her long blue skirt was worn and unraveled at the bottom. "Haven't seen the likes of you before," she said. Her breathe smelled of last night's liquor. A bulldog of a man behind a desk flashed his eyes at me.

"First time, ma'am," I said.

"What' d' ya like? We have'em in all shapes and sizes. Wait, I bet I can guess what you like, being a young virile man. You want a princess, don't ya?"

"Now how did you know that?"

"I seen your type before. Come with me, I have just the one." She led me down a dark, musty-smelling hall. The upstairs was similar to a hotel, with doors on either side of a hallway.

"We only take cash," she interjected as she turned the knob. The room was dimly lit. The lady took my cash and closed the door. From behind a curtain, a young girl appeared. Silk fabric covered most of her petite body. She relocated herself to the bed and sat down.

"What's your name?" she whispered. A tear escaped my eye. Her noticeably young and drug-shot eyes were barely open. "Do you like me?" she asked.

"Enough not to do what you're being paid for," I replied. Her head turned; lifeless eyes studied me.

"I don't understand," she said. I grabbed her arm.

"I won't hurt you; I need to ask you a few questions." Her face squinted. "Two girls were brought here earlier today. Do you know where they are?" She shook her head, her shoulder now leaning against mine. I steadied her. "Where did you come from?"

"I'm here to please you." She replied.

"Where did you come from? How did you get here?" She leaned her head on my shoulder. I stood up and laid her head on a pillow, then cracked the door open and peered out. Voices radiated down the hall. I pulled out a miniature stun gun, stepped out, and cracked open the next door. Neither the girl nor the man turned; the girl was too small to be Daniela or Amelia. The next room was empty. Gerry keyed my earpiece.

"Have you found them yet?"

"Negative," I whispered. "They've got to be here."

"We need to hurry; do want me to come up?"

"You're right where I need you." I interrupted a couple in the next room. Another room, a girl had a needle out, shooting up. Two more rooms were empty. I cracked open another door. The room sat empty. I peered behind the curtain. A girl had her head in the toilet, retching. "Daniela! Are you all right?" Her eyes lit up. She tried standing but couldn't. I caught her, moving her over to the sink. I washed her face and head with a cold cloth.

"They dr…dr…drugged me."

I stared at dilated eyes. The luster, fire, and life were missing. "Amelia?" I asked.

"Down the oth-er hall…I think." I set her on the bed, pulled out a pill and dissolved it in water.

"Drink this. I need you to stay here. I'll be back in a minute to get you out of here." She tilted the glass back, then laid back on the bed. I scanned the hall. It was clear. "Gerry, I found Daniela. I'm going after Amelia. Did you find a vehicle?"

"Yes, an old Volkswagen van in the parking lot. I have it ready."

"Not much of a get-away vehicle," I whispered.

"Best I could find. Be creative up there, we'll need a head start with this thing."

I peeked around the wall—two ladies and the bulldog behind the desk. I ran at them, shouting in a panicked voice. "She's not breathing, she's not breathing!" I grasped my chest and opened my mouth, impersonating a person struggling for air. "Please, help!"

All three headed for the room. I turned, searching the rooms down the opposite hall. In two of the rooms, men promptly swore at me for the intrusion. The very next door there she was, lying on the bed, mascara streaks running down her cheeks. A tall man stood between us, his hands on his belt. He was well-groomed, in his late 40s, and wearing half of a tailored suit.

"This is my girl. Get out and close the door," the man demanded. Amelia's eyes were not as listless as Daniela's. I knew instantly she recognized me.

"Actually, this is my girl," I replied. He swung at my head. I avoided his blow by dodging to one side, then landed my fist, hard into his ribs, feeling two of them give way. He buckled over.

"Cougar!" Amelia cried. The man straightened up and pulled out a gun from somewhere. Before he got his shot off, I pulled the trigger on the taser. Electrodes sunk into the man's chest. He convulsed, fired the gun into the ceiling, then hunched over. I landed my foot on the back of his neck, sending him the rest of the way to the floor, then grabbed Amelia.

"We need to go—now!" I said. "Can you walk?"

"I think so." There were footsteps, clamoring down the hall. I held out the stun gun. Midway down the hall, two men rounded the corner.

"Aquí está." One yelled. I pulled the trigger. Nothing happened. A light on the gun glowed red. The man pulled out a pistol. I pulled

Amelia into a room, pulled out my pistol and fired a couple shots down the hall. A bullet splintered the door jamb next to me. I pulled the trigger again, dropping one of the men to the ground. The second man opened up with an automatic weapon. Wood chips and metal showered the doorway. I dove to the ground pulling Amelia with me. Screaming erupted from the hall and inside the room. A frightened girl pressed up against a headboard and covered herself with a blanket.

I rolled a scatter grenade down the hall. Moans erupted followed by a thud. I carried Amelia down the hall. The man with the machine gun had hundreds of tiny metal objects imbedded in his body, with several protruding from his neck. A few hit their mark, pulsating blood from his carotid artery. One of the ladies was also bleeding, but not life threatening.

I carried Amelia over the splintered floor, my boots effortlessly bending the tiny metal projectiles that emanated from the grenade. A man ran up the stairs holding a gun. We sped down the hall into Daniela's room just as the man opened fire, sending a volley of bullets and shrapnel in all directions.

"How many are there?" Daniela asked, her eyes brighter than they were before.

"I'm not sure, I think Gerry and I miscounted."

"Gerry?" Amelia asked.

"I told you about him, he's here."

"Cougar, a car just pulled up with three gunmen. They're headed your direction."

"Gerry, change of plans, I need the WEAP in here now!" I aimed down the hall, sending my own volley of bullets. The man ducked into a room. *Too many gunmen for a brothel.* I poked my head out, then pulled back as bullets ripped through the hall, sending more wood and metal into the air. Loud screaming came from the first floor.

"Cougar, it's mayhem down here. Women and girls are streaming out the doors. I have the SAM inside on stealth mode, where do you want it?" Stealth mode not only made the SAM whisper quiet, it also blended it into the surroundings like a chameleon, making it virtually invisible.

"Hover it next to the stairs." Amelia and Daniela observed me curiously. "Okay, we're going now. Hold onto each other and don't let go. When I grab your hand and pull, run with me, do you understand?" Each of them nodded. Daniela's eyes were glassing over again. "Amelia, Daniela is going to need your help."

"We're ready," Amelia replied. I rolled a tear gas bomb down the hall. Seconds later, I heard coughing and random gunfire.

"Gerry, here we come!" I placed goggles over my eyes and sucked into a tiny oxygen tube. I let the girls each take in a deep breath. "Let's go." I grabbed Daniela's hand. We crept down the hall. A sharp yellow glow emanated from a room. I fired, dropping the man to the ground. Another volley of bullets came from an orange glow that cut through the fog. The shots were high. I dropped him, too, firing into the glow. We ducked into a room and sucked in more oxygen. A blinding light lit up the end of the hall.

"Cougar, I sent one to the grave at the top of the stairs."

"How many more are there?"

"Not sure, we need to hurry before more reinforcements arrive."

Daniela and Amelia and I crept to the top of the stairs. The SAM's laser had burnt through the back of a man holding a machine gun. One of the ladies behind the desk was also dead. Daniela's fingers slipped through mine. She fell to the ground coughing. I tapped Amelia's shoulder, then carried Daniela down the stairs.

Distant sirens. The sewing machines sat idle. We ran through the exit just as a bullet ricocheted off the cement floor behind us. "Got 'em!" Gerry exclaimed. Hysterical women dotted the grass and parking lot. A cop car twisted down the long driveway. I shuffled Amelia and Daniela to the parking lot. Gerry's SAM turned visible above us, leading us to the van.

Gerry threw both SAMs into the back of the van as I helped Daniela and Amelia in. I punched the accelerator as Gerry closed the passenger door. The police were hunkered down behind their car doors, aiming their guns at the porch. A car pulling in whipped around and followed us out the driveway and onto the street. "Could be a couple gunmen," I said. Gerry retrieved a bag sitting on the floor next to the girl's feet.

"I have some deterrents for them," he exclaimed. The rear window shattered.

"Get down!" I yelled. Gerry tossed out a grenade. An explosion sounded. The chasing car made it through unharmed. "Missed." A staccato of bullets hit the car. They rammed us, bucking the van violently. A bullet shattered the rearview mirror. "Stay down," I demanded. I pulled the trigger twice. The car behind us swerved violently, then flipped upside down.

A cop car, traveling the opposite direction, skidded 180-degree, and started chase. I smashed the Volkswagen's pedal into the vinyl flooring. The van sped up another 18 kilometers per hour. Two cars blocked our path. I pulled the wheel to the right, scattering people on the sidewalk. A motorcyclist, skidding to avoid us, came to a stop in the middle of the road. The cop drove right over the motorcycle rider. "Gerry, smoke flare." Gerry held the flare out the window. Billows of smoke swirled behind the van.

The nose of the cop car pierced the smoke from the left side. We collided. The van recoiled uncontrollably for almost twenty-five feet before I was able to bring it back in control. The cop pulled up beside us with a pistol hanging out the window. I swerved into them. Gerry tossed the smoking flare into their car. Metal screeched until the two vehicles freed themselves from each other. I watched the cop car swerve back and forth before it ran off the road, sprang into the air and crashed.

All four of us were quiet for a moment. "Daniela, Amelia, you can get up now."

"Are we safe?" Daniela asked, her voice a little stronger.

"For a few minutes anyway, we still have a long drive before reaching the airport, and this van is no dragster."

When we pulled into the airport entrance, the weathered Cessna sat where we left it. "Wake up, Ladies," I said loudly. Slowly their eyes opened. "Gerry, the Cessna needs fuel, if you'll get them into the airplane, I'll put ten gallons in each tank.

I rousted the line boy, encouraging him with a twenty-dollar bill to pull his fuel truck hastily over to the plane, which he did. He watched as I pumped the fuel. Screeching tires arrived at the airport entrance. A long sedan sped through, heading straight towards us.

"Gerry, close the door, we got to go!" I jumped in and hit the starter. The tip of the prop moved twelve inches, then stopped. "Hold the brakes!" I jumped out, grabbed the prop, and pulled it down hard. The engine coughed, the propeller stopped. The car stopped. Two large men with guns exited from either side, scanning the tarmac. Their gaze rested on me. The second attempt on the prop brought a steady cloud of smoke through the exhaust pipe. I jumped in, closed the door, and jammed the throttle to the firewall. My boot stomped the left rudder pedal down, turning the airplane and swirling dirt towards the approaching men.

Gerry held his gun through the opening, firing at the men, momentarily prompting them to dive for cover. I didn't wait for the runway, I kept the plane moving straight and fast, lifting off from the taxiway. Once airborne, I veered the plane back and forth and up and down "Check the wings," I said.

"This one looks good." Gerry replied.

"The tire's deformed on this side," said Amelia.

"Are you ladies, all right?"

"Just scared," Daniela yelled, speaking over the engine noise.

"I'm okay," Amelia said. "I'm feeling a little nauseous though." I leveled the wings. Gerry searched for a bag to hand back to her. In the distance, clouds dropped near the surface. Light rain dotted the windscreen, each drop racing to the outer edge. The Cessna had very few flight instruments, and zero navigational equipment.

"Gerry, I'll need your GPS screen. I'm going to take the plane back to Gustano's place."

"Why there? I thought we were headed to Mitu?"

"Fuel is questionable, we have a flat tire, oil pressure is in the yellow, and the weather's not going to hold. Besides, I don't want to be in this plane in heavy turbulence and clouds—not over this terrain anyway."

"I see your point."

"I'm not sure what we're going to run into at Gustano's, so we need to be ready just in case."

The arthritic Cessna droned on. The cloud deck crept lower and lower. I descended, staying just below the encroaching clouds. Gerry handed me the GPS. I viewed the six-inch screen. The terrain rose gradually all the way to Gustano's place. "Looks like we're getting pinched. Going to be flying in the clouds after all in this thing."

"Do you want me to find a place to set it down?"

"There is no place. Look outside and on the screen." I handed the GPS to Gerry. "Please load up Gustano's place." A minute later, Gerry handed the GPS back. The right side displayed a GPS map, and the left, key instruments. Gerry pulled out a suction cup and I attached the unit to the window next to me. Daniela screamed.

"It's okay." I heard Amelia say to her. It's just a little turbulence.

"I hope their annual inspection is up to date," I said.

"This plane probably hasn't been inspected since it arrived in Colombia." I watched the oil pressure needle move lower. The scenery below intermittently became obscured. After two miles, we were in solid, nothing but gray out each window. Daniela grew more frantic. The dot on the GPS grew closer to Gustano's place. "Few more minutes," I yelled back.

I turned my wrist, cross-checking our location on the GPS screen with my watch's GPS. The airplane's compass was of no use—it had long dried up; the compass card sat skewed. The airspeed indicator was original, showing 108 in MPH. "Gerry, see if you can reach Kathy. I doubt the drone is still in the air, but let's check."

"Okay, but it's a SAM, just saying…."

"I'm going to start calling you Sam."

"I got her," Gerry responded eagerly. "Kathy, Cougar wants to know if the SAM is still airborne. A…huh. Yes…no that's okay. Any word about Gustano? A…huh, okay…we are landing at Gustano's place now. We can't make it any further in this contraption. Also, we have a flat tire so landing may pose a bit of a challenge…we will." Gerry clipped the SAT phone to his belt. "The SAM crashed. She was bringing it back just as it ran out of juice. Oh, and nothing more on Gustano."

I increased the screen detail. We were right over Gustano's place. "I'm going to drop to five-hundred feet above the surface and see if we break out of these clouds." Rain pelted the windscreen. I retarded the throttle; the plane shuddered. I coaxed it around in a lazy circle until five-hundred feet above the ground. "I am going to try three-hundred Feet." I scanned the GPS while straining at the working flight instruments. At 350 feet, we broke out of the clouds right above the barracks building.

"Not bad." Amelia yelled from the back seat.

"We're not down yet. I need you guys to brace yourselves for an extremely hard landing. I'll get us down safe, but I'll need you to hold on to the seatback in front of you and put you heads down please." Amelia calmed Daniela as I turned, lining up to the turf runway. I placed the good tire over the bordering thick grass. "Gerry, get your gun ready just in case." Gerry held the gun at his side.

The field widened. I pulled the throttle back. Cross controlling the ailerons and rudder, I let the good tire touch first, holding off the flat tire as long as I could. As the tire settled to the turf, I jockeyed the throttle up a little to keep the plane pointing straight. The tail wheel dropped to the turf. The plane aggressively spun around.

Amelia yelled. "They have guns!"

Chapter 53

Little Boy

"Gerry!" shouted Cougar.

"Already ahead of you." Gerry lifted another weapon from the bag and laid it next to the rifle on his lap. Cougar gave one last jab of the rudder pedal, and with the throttle, muscled the plane around, turning it toward the approaching men. He kept the prop spinning. Rain pelted the windshield, making visibility challenging.

"It's Gustano's men!" Gerry barked, squinting through the front window.

"Somehow they managed to free themselves," Cougar replied. "Down!" Bullets peppered the airplane; pinging sounds echoed through the cabin. "Amelia?"

"Yes."

"Can you spin the plane around and taxi as far away from us as you can? Stay low so they can't see you. You'll need full right rudder; the tire's still on, but stuck."

"I can do that."

"Great. On the count of three. Three-two-one!" Gerry and Cougar opened their doors and rolled onto the mud in the pouring rain. Amelia dove for the front, jamming the throttle forward while keeping low. She swung her leg over to the rudder pedal. The plane kicked up water and mud, hiding Cougar and Gerry. Gerry tightened his finger against the trigger. An explosion erupted where they last saw the men. Cougar waited for movement.

A bullet ricocheted next to Gerry. Cougar spotted a third man, Fabio, running for a stationary machine gun next to the barracks. Cougar tracked him through the scope, then shot. Fabio fell to the ground. When the smoke cleared, there was no movement. Gerry slowly lifted himself to his feet. Cougar scanned the area. Rain cascaded down his face, his clothes soaked to the skin. The airplane had moved two hundred feet before getting stuck again, the propeller was still turning.

Javier was fatally wounded. Miguel was bleeding badly from his left leg. Cougar pulled off Javier's belt, tore a piece from his shirt and pressed it against Miguel's leg, then wrapped the belt tightly around it. "You should have stayed tied up," Cougar said.

"Gust…ano…is gonna…kill you," Miguel retorted with great effort.

"Speaking of Gustano, where is he?" asked Cougar.

"He…is cleaning up lo…ose ends, like you."

"I don't think that's going to happen, Miguel. Now let's see if we can get you tied back up before you die on us. Gerry, can you get the ladies out and see if you can move the airplane off the runway?"

Gerry slung the odd-looking gun over his shoulder and jogged off towards the airplane. Cougar drug Miguel by his shirt collar all the way to the barracks and elevated the injured leg. Gerry unstuck the Cessna and powered it well clear of the runway. Gerry, Amelia, and Daniela appeared as Cougar interrogated Miguel; they were all soaking wet. "Well, you have some time to think about what I asked. Meanwhile, we're going to dry off and make something to eat in your kitchen." Miguel strained at his ties. "You won't break those loose. You guys go on ahead and fix yourself something to eat, it will make you feel better," said Cougar.

Gerry guided Daniela toward the house, her skin still pale.

"Gerry?" Cougar shouted. "Let Kathy know we're down safe. I'm sure she's anxious to know if we made it. Tell her she can leave now for Bogota."

"Can I look in the airplane?" Amelia asked.

"Of course." Amelia ran to the C-47 and went inside the cabin.

Cougar ended his call with Riley and poked his head in. Amelia was in the co-pilot seat. Tears streaked her cheeks. "The day before my father left for Mexico, he called me his little co-pilot…he was always my captain." Amelia convulsed and wept loudly. Cougar held her; she dug her head into his chest. The pain over the last few weeks befell her; the weight too heavy to keep inside any further. Minutes passed before she calmed down.

"Do you want to get something to eat?"

She nodded. "Promise me you will still search for my dad's body. I need to know he's not just washed up on some beach—all alone." Amelia's tears persisted.

"I promise," said Cougar. "Now, let's get you dried off and some food in you."

Gerry and Daniela made sandwiches. When Daniela saw Cougar, she set the butter knife down and hugged him. "I'm so grateful to you." She gave Cougar a quick kiss on the lips and then returned to the counter. "I'm making enough for all of us." Amelia washed her face and gave Daniela an unpleasant stare before eyeing the young boy sitting at the table.

"Gustano's son?" asked Cougar.

Amelia and Daniela both nodded. "They must have left him here with the men." said Amelia.

"We found him in a bedroom," Daniela added. They ate sandwiches and drank juice.

"That tells me Gustano and Brigette plan to return sometime soon," said Cougar. "Riley said the team from Colombia won't be here for two days."

"Yeah, that's what Kathy said too," remarked Gerry. "Should we wait for Gustano to show up?"

"Riley said to let the Colombian government deal with Gustano, his girlfriend, and returning the artifacts to the museum. He wants us to get to the bottom of Bogota's police corruption and find out who's all involved, then apprehend Captain Moreno. Daniela, can you identify the contents in the crates? The US government needs to give the Colombian government proof. They are hesitant to believe we found the treasure right under their nose."

"Of course," Daniela replied. "I've wanted desperately to look inside them and see if it's really our treasure. If it is, that would make me incredibly happy."

"I figured it would."

"What about the boy?" asked Gerry.

"He comes with us; we can't leave him here. Had I'd known he was here earlier; I would have brought him to you, Gerry, and asked your newfound friends to watch him. I guess in that sense, I'm glad Miguel was able to break free…or maybe it was the boy who freed him…either way."

"I'll help him pack a bag of clothes and some toys."

"Thank you, Amelia," Cougar replied.

The rain had momentarily stopped. Cougar, Gerry, and Daniela opened the crates, and took pictures. "I can't believe we found our history," Daniela said, her eyes wet with tears. "I'm overwhelmed."

"Hopefully, your government returns all the treasure to your museum undamaged."

"I would like to help them, if that's possible." Daniela held her gaze until Cougar answered.

"I'm sorry, Daniela, not until Gustano is captured."

"Of course, I wouldn't have it any other way."

"All uploaded and sent to the mothership," Gerry said, unhooking his camera from a special transmitter.

"Good, that should ease tension between our two countries." Amelia walked in holding the little boy's hand and a large duffle bag. "All ready?"

"Yes, we are," she said, smiling at the boy affectionately.

Cougar's eyes moved from the little boy to Amelia's. "Can I ask you to be my co-pilot on this hop?"

"In the C-47?" Cougar nodded. Amelia's face glowed. "Absolutely!"

Cougar lifted Miguel into the airplane. Gerry shut the door as Amelia and Cougar started the big radial engines. Black smoke and clamoring filled the air. Amelia's face transformed into an eager child.

"Are you ready?"

"More than you'll ever know," she said. "Thank you." Rain speckled the windshield. Cougar nudged the throttles forward. The big Douglas C-47 lurched from its parking spot. Minutes later it passed the old Cessna off to the side and lifted from the turf, then disappeared into the clouds.

"I feel fortunate with all these instruments to navigate with—a far cry from the Cessna we were just in."

Amelia's mouth parted; the edges lifted. "My dad wanted her to look authentic, but he also wanted the latest in avionics…and some of the newer electrical instruments, too."

"Well, you guys did a great job with both. She flies very solid."

"You must have experience flying these?"

"You'd be amazed how many types of airplanes I've had the privilege of flying—although it's not as gratifying as it sounds. In a few of my missions I've needed to be airborne in minutes. Sitting behind the cockpit of an unfamiliar airplane can make for some pretty white-knuckled moments. Here, you fly it." Cougar leveled the airplane, then released his hands from the controls. "All yours." Amelia overcorrected a few times, then settled in, flying rock steady while Cougar tuned in the GPS.

Get Rich Quick

Two cabs dropped us off at a Bogota hotel Kathy had booked. Once Amelia and Daniela were properly introduced to Kathy, we ordered up food. The first several minutes were quiet. Kathy spoke first. "Amelia, Cougar says you are an aerobatic pilot?"

Amelia lifted her head. "My dad and I have an airplane museum and do air shows on occasion. It's more of a summer thing to bring in customers." She raised the meat and cheese sandwich back to her mouth.

"Well, it sounds exciting. And Daniela, you are the curator's right hand? Cougar says you probably know more about Bogota's history than their own government."

"Thank you, that is very kind of you to say; however," her eyes met Cougar's, "I'm not entirely sure that's true. I love history, and I love our country—and working in the museum. It's been a dream of mine ever since childhood."

"Well it seems you two have a lot in common," Kathy added. "Both of you are extremely passionate about what you have wanted to do ever since you were young. You're both truly fortunate, many never find their passion." Both of them nodded in agreement. "I ordered up a special dessert. I hope everyone one is still hungry."

Daniela and Amelia's plates were bare. Gerry stared as Kathy removed the cover. From inside the cardboard box, she pulled out a strawberry cake, resembling a torte. "I was going to refrain from eating dessert," I said, "but after seeing this, I've changed my mind." Kathy grinned, knowing strawberries were my favorite.

"So, what now?" Daniela asked.

"We find out how deeply Captain Eduardo Moreno and his police force are involved," I replied.

"Do you think Andrea Dias is a part of this? I could never quite figure her out. The few times we talked she seemed angry with me, and for whatever reason I couldn't tell."

"My assumption is no, but I'm not sure. During a few of the conversations in Captain Moreno's office, Eduardo was unpleasantly hard on her. Andrea could be unpleasant as well, but when her boss was not around, she was more polite—almost enjoyable."

"What should I do?" Amelia asked.

"Both of you need to stay here with Kathy until this is resolved. We need to keep you safe. If anyone knows you're here, it could be extremely dangerous."

"What about you?" Daniela asked. "How will you remain safe?" I noticed Amelia's quick glare at Daniela.

"Gerry will look after me." He nodded with confidence, trying not to bust up. "If you will excuse us for a few minutes, we need to make a phone call. Are you two okay here for a minute?"

"Of course."

"Yes."

We shut the door between the adjoining rooms. Gerry flippantly punched me in the stomach. "What are you going to do, Cougar? Both those ladies really like you."

"They might be more dangerous than Captain Moreno," added Kathy.

"Thanks, you guys…way to help." I pulled out my phone and called Riley. There was a long pause, then we heard ringing through the speaker.

"Cougar, you guys get settled in?"

"Yes, sir, we're all here. I have Gerry and Kathy with me. Daniela and Amelia are in the next room."

"Hello, sir." Kathy said.

"Hi, boss." Gerry added.

"Any signs of Donny or Gustano?" I asked.

The sound of David Subbarao's voice grew louder in the speaker. "No Cougar…they haven't shown up on any of our surveillance."

"No one knows about Mauricio's death except you guys and a couple officials in the Colombian government," Riley stated. "We need to catch Captain Moreno with his hands dirty. There's not enough evidence to convince the Colombian government of his involvement. In fact, none of us know how deeply he's involved."

David broke in again. "We did find evidence that Captain Eduardo Moreno and Donny Tallman attended art auctions together in the past."

"Together?" asked Gerry.

"Sorry, not together-together, but they were at the same auctions," David clarified.

"It seems they both have a love of art," Kathy responded.

"Or what art buys," I interjected. "Maybe Donny and Captain Moreno were selling art on the side, without Mauricio Lopez's blessing. Daniela saw Donny and Mauricio in a pretty heated argument on the steps outside the museum."

"We need you to get to the bottom of this and fast," Riley stated. "We're back in good graces with Colombia, now that they have proof of the art at Gustano's place. In fact, they have asked, very respectfully I might add, for our help in determining Captain Moreno's involvement. Captain Eduardo Moreno is a decorated police officer with an impressive military background, and so before they overstep, they want substantial proof."

"Understood."

"What about Gustano? Where did he go if he wasn't after Donny?" asked Gerry.

On the hotel room wall hung a framed city landscape. I hadn't realized I was staring at it until the thought hit me. "Donny's picture."

"Huh?"

"There's got to be another warehouse," I said. The crates at Gustano's place contained mostly just the Bogota artifacts. The picture on Donny's wall? It was from an earlier heist. The information you and David uncovered on similar robberies…there's got to be more art…a lot more."

"You're right," Kathy said. "These guys have been doing this for several years."

"Mauricio said they keep the art hidden until it is forgotten and increases in value. He also stated they only sell a small amount to underground buyers as needed—my paraphrasing."

"Well, very few pieces from those art collections have reappeared," said Kathy.

"I think Captain Moreno, Donny, and Gustano tried convincing Mauricio to sell more of the art, ya know, a get-rich-quick scheme. Mauricio wanted to take the safer more conservative approach. The three of them probably grew tired of his turtle scheme, miniscule insurance fraud spoils, and controlling ways. They had him fly out to inspect the Bogota art as a ruse to dethrone him—kill him."

"I think you're on to something," Riley agreed. "We need to find that warehouse."

"It could be worth millions of dollars."

"That's where he went," I said.

"Who?"

"Gustano. They're going to move the treasure to a different location—possibly to another country."

"What about Gustano's child?" Kathy asked. "They wouldn't just leave him there."

"As far as they know, he's still in good hands with Fabio, Javier, and Miguel. And did you catch what Amelia said? She never heard Gustano say one word to that little boy. I wouldn't be surprised if Brigitte isn't with him when he does return for the Bogota art."

"I hate to think what would have happened to the boy," Kathy said sadly.

Chapter 55

Plastic Badge Detective

"This better be an emergency," Captain Moreno demanded. "Uh huh…I warned you that was a bad idea. Well, you should have listened to me and killed them when I told you to and been done with them. …Oh, I know, you're always looking for an angle…I'm not complaining, when I complain, you'll know it, that you can be sure of…Who? …How? …Are they sure? …Where are your men now? …and they're okay…Good. Well, you better come up with a backup plan just in case he goes back to your place. …Well I wouldn't put anything past that imprudent man. Somehow, he escaped your men, right? …Your little boy? Leave him there, you have work to do, besides, you never cared for him anyway, and if Javier or someone else doesn't show up tonight with that plane, you better not either. …Forget the Bogota treasure for now; too risky. Let's secure what we have. Once that insurance investigator is dead, we'll go back for the rest—and you better hope we find him before he blabs his mouth to the wrong person."

Captain Moreno paced back and forth inside his windowed office. Detective Andrea watched out of the corner of her eye, while tapping out a report on her computer. Captain Moreno continued. "How many men will be there? …Double it! Donny and I will be there around five." Eduardo pressed the end button on his cell. He opened the plate glass door, "Dias! Get in here! Shut the door." Andrea shifted her hips, pulling the door closed.

"Tell me you have new information on the Bogota museum case, I don't need another call from Mauricio Lopez, asking why we haven't completed our investigation."

"I've been looking into the claims Arlan Jensen brought to our attention…and, well, it's taking some time."

"Time? Forget Arlan Jensen. He wears a plastic badge. Is that what you are? A plastic badge detective? Did you get your badge out of a cereal box?"

"No, sir—"

"I didn't think so, but he did! He's a clown, a fake, he's an insurance investigator for heaven sakes." Eduardo's eyes burned into Andrea's. "Close the case."

"But Captain."

"Close it! Let Donald Tallman and Mauricio Lopez know we've found no new evidence or reason for keeping the case open any further. I wish we could have solved this one, I really do, but the trail has grown ice cold. Like it or not, we failed our own government. I'll let our superiors, the museum director, and Arlan Jensen know the case is officially closed. I want the paperwork on my desk by tomorrow morning. Now, do you know where I can find Mr. Jensen?"

"I've left several messages on his cell, but he hasn't returned any of my calls. I know he was staying in a hotel downtown—"

"Find him! You should be able to do that much for heaven's sake, you're a detective! Act like one!" Captain Moreno swung the door open, smacking Andrea's heavy thigh. "Get going—now!" Andrea got to her feet, wincing from the pain.

Captain Moreno punched in a number. After several rings, Donny answered. "This is a surprise. What do I owe the pleasure?"

"Cut the crap," Eduardo said. "Where have you been?" Eduardo pressed the phone tightly to his ear. "And how much did we get? …Well, that brightens my day. Are you on your way over? Gustano needs all the help he can get…yes, but we had a little mishap…I'll tell you later."

Captain Moreno scanned the room of green desks and uniformed officers thumping away on keyboards. Two cops sat on a desk, pastries in hand, chuckling over something one of them said. That was before they noticed Captain Moreno approaching them. "Is it break time? Where's the clock." Captain Moreno looked left then right. "There it is. What does it say? Yep, not break time. Does that look like break time to you?"

"N-No, Captain."

"You?"

"No sir, Captain." Eduardo grabbed the last pastry out of a box, perched on the desk between them. After two steps and one bite, he threw the pastry against the wall.

"What is this, day old? You brought in day old doughnuts for your captain to eat?" Neither man spoke. Captain Moreno hadn't eaten doughnuts with them in months. He barely spoke to them anymore except when barking out orders. "I'm not even worth a fresh doughnut?" All conversations and typing stopped. "Clean up that mess," he said as he turned, stopping in front of Andrea's desk. "What did you find?"

"Captain, I just got back to my desk—" Eduardo swung his arm. Papers, folders, a stapler, and a cup containing pens and pencils tumbled to the ground.

"There you go. Now you have nothing to do but what I asked you to do. Find out where he's staying—now!" The captain raised his head; others quickly dropped theirs. "Back to work, I want to hear progress!"

Cora Liberal

"**D**aniela, are you sure you don't remember hearing anything about another warehouse. Please, this is extremely important. Did Mauricio say anything even remotely close about another storage facility." Daniela stared at the floor, then lifted her eyes.

"I'm sorry, but I don't remember hearing anything. I wish I could help."

Kathy broke in. "Do you remember anything about the museum expansion project?" Kathy thumped her keyboard.

"No, why? Should I?" Daniela asked.

"It says here, that in 1997 the Bogota Museum expanded its facilities, incorporating exhibits from two smaller branch museums."

"Yes…I'm sorry, I do know about that. Cundinamarca had two museums that were going to close down due to funding. If I remember the story correctly, the Bogota museum offered to build special exhibit wings to display their art, mainly paintings and jewelry. In return, the two struggling museums would loan indefinitely their artifacts. This took place way before I came to the museum. In fact, I think I was still in grade school, why do you ask?"

Kathy studied me, then Daniela, "What happened to those two museums?"

"That's a long shot, Kathy, twenty-two years ago? They're probably condominiums by now," asserted Gerry.

"Please continue, Kathy," I countered. "It may lead to nothing, but let's hear more."

"Well." Kathy swiveled her chair around. "The museum locations in Cundinamarca are not that far from here. We could check them out just to be sure."

"How far are they?" She hit print, then pushed the paper into my hands. "Let's see, one of the museum's was named… 'Cora Liberal'."

"What? Did you say Cora Liberal?" asked Daniela.

"Yes—why?" Kathy asked.

"I've seen that name…" Daniela's mouth opened, her eyes—expressionless, staring into space. "A folder—in Mauricio's office!" She finally exclaimed. "I remember it because it was underneath some files he handed me to work. I read through the titles before leaving his office. When I read the name of Cora Liberal out loud, he quickly snatched that file folder from my hand, stating he would work that one personally."

"Do you think you could find that file in his office?" I asked.

"If it's still there. I know where he keeps his files, I also know where his safe is, although I don't know the combination."

The room quieted. I eyed Kathy and Gerry. "Kathy, can you get a satellite image of the old museum? Let's see if it's still there. If so, see if there are any drawings available for the interior. Gerry, we're going to need all your toys up and running. I'm going to take Daniela with me to find that file folder. Let's meet back together in…ninety minutes. And Gerry, if this is it, we'll need to appear as if we have an army."

"I know just the trick." Gerry rubbed his hands together, adding in a giant mischievous grin and a snicker.

"I'll get ready," Daniela said.

"Cougar." Kathy pointed to her screen.

"Okay, we know the museum building is still standing. Daniela, I'll be back in to get you in five. Is that enough time?"

"Yes." Gerry and I made for the door. I felt Amelia's eyes on me.

"Amelia, would you help Kathy while we're gone?"

"Thank you, I would like that. I want to be of some help."

"I could use the help, if you don't mind." Kathy interjected.

Gerry closed the door. "We'll need at least four drones—I mean SAMs in the air. Here's what else I'm thinking." I gave Gerry my thoughts as I changed.

"Two minds that think alike," Gerry replied.

"Is it possible to fly a SAM over to the old museum without being detected?"

"Now?" he asked. "From here you mean?"

"Yes."

Gerry scratched at his head then tapped his tablet and observed the map. "I would normally use a much bigger SAM for that kind of thing."

"But can you with any of the smaller ones you have here?" I repeated.

"That's fifty kilometers..." Gerry scratched his head again. "It might be possible. I can set a default for it to return if communications are interrupted or lost...and to stay undetected, it'll need to stay below one-thousand feet and away from airports."

"Great. Transmit the images back to us as soon as they're available. Also, can you leave it hovering over the museum until we get there tonight? We don't know exactly what we're up against. In fact, as soon as the first images come through, patch them through to my watch."

"You don't ask for much, do you? Cougar...what if this is just another dead end?"

"Think positive, besides, we'll know soon enough. I'll be back shortly...and thank you." I patted Gerry on the back.

At the museum, Mauricio's door was unlocked. Daniela remarked how he always locked his door before leaving for the day. She searched his files as I watched. We shared several glances, both knowing what the other person was thinking—we were searching a dead man's office. She turned over files and countless papers, but no *Cora Liberal* file.

"It must be in the safe, unless someone has it," she said.

"Where's the safe?"

Daniela moved a picture. "Here, but I don't think there's much in there. He only kept pending contracts and small fund-raising deposits. Most of the larger donations and fees are ran through the director's or accounting office." I studied the lock, a straightforward tumbler. I rotated the knurls one revolution.

"Three numbers." I said out loud. I took the clicker off the end of my pen and stuck it next to the lock, the magnet held tight. Then pulled the pocket clip out ninety degrees. The clicker turned red. I tumbled the lock to the right, until the clicker turned green, spun it back to the left waiting for another green light, then back to the right. When the light turned green, the handle moved, and I opened the door.

Daniela gasped. Inside, money filled the cavity to the top. "I'm sure that's not from fundraising," exclaimed Daniela.

"Can you find a bag?"

"I have one in my office, kind of a shopping bag."

"Perfect." A manila folder lay against the side. I slid it out and read the tab, "Cora Liberal". I thumbed through the contents, then dropped it into the bag Daniela held open, along with the money. "This belongs to someone, for now, we will keep it with us."

Gerry, Kathy, and Amelia's eyes grew wide as we emptied the contents on the table. "You didn't tell us you were robbing a bank too," exclaimed Kathy.

"That's not the best part, look." I handed the folder to Kathy. She thumbed through it.

"Well, we know where they're taking the treasure, and why they needed the C-47. They'll have to go back for the C-47, right?"

"My guess is they know I'm alive. One of Gustano's boys probably contacted him after freeing themselves. That means they also know I went after Amelia and Daniela. I'm sure word has gotten back to Gustano about the girls being snatched."

"According to this plan," Kathy stated. "Javier and Miguel are supposed to fly the C-47 to the Cora Liberal museum tonight at midnight."

"Why don't we fly it in?" Gerry asked. "They might not know we went back for the C-47 or about killing Javier, Fabio, and taking Miguel."

"That's a big gamble," I said.

"Why can't you guys just have the police raid the place?" Amelia asked.

"We're not sure who we can trust. If all the treasure is in one spot, we can't risk anything happening to it."

"They must have a backup plan," said Kathy, "but there's nothing here."

"Another plane maybe?" said Gerry.

"Maybe, but I doubt it. Probably some inconspicuous trucks would be my guess. According to their plan, they're taking the art across the border into…Venezuela…"

"What is it?" Kathy asked.

"Mauricio knew of this plan; he had the file in his office."

"Do you think he was against it, and that's why he was killed?" asked Gerry.

"I think he wanted to control the art and the timing of when it resurfaced. I don't think he ever really lost his love for art, but it seems he was losing control over his grand scheme to Captain Moreno and Gustano. Kathy, what is the status on Miguel? I think we'll be needing him tonight."

"What?" Kathy blurted out surprised.

"Please tell me you're joking," said Amelia.

"He will be my co-pilot." I replied. I pointed to the bag holding Miguel's phone. "Maybe we can assure Gustano everything's on plan." I gave Kathy a wink.

"I know he's out of surgery, but he's not well."

"I just need him to sit and not die on me. Okay, we have a lot of planning to do before tonight. Kathy," I glanced to the bag of phones. "Have there been any calls or texts to either of those phones?"

Kathy lifted the phones. "Nothing."

"Good. They must assume the plan's still on. Gerry, the SAM image just came through, look." The image on my watch showed two trucks and several men.

"Contact! We got'em," said Gerry.

Chapter 57

Preparation

It was 4:30pm by the time Gerry and Cougar reached the old museum. Two medium-sized trucks, spotted earlier from the SAM's camera, were parked side by side inside a chain link fence. A car and an old pickup truck were also parked just inside the gate and to the right, about thirty feet from the trucks.

The building had no discernable markings. Several neglected soccer fields lined the fence on the far side of a large parking lot. The museum building and parking lot were also in disrepair. It appeared neither had been used in years if not decades. The nearest building to the museum was boarded up and the one next to it had succumbed to a fire at some point. What was left of the roof had partially caved in. Beyond the desolate industrial block, the adjacent neighborhood showed limited tenants.

"Does that entrance light look like it's on?" Gerry asked.

Cougar squinted. "Barely, but I think it is."

"Looks like electricity to me," Gerry exclaimed. "This place is as good as any." They pulled to a stop. Cougar didn't count more than three windows intact. They unloaded the equipment. Gerry bent down and tried an outlet. "Nothing. I'm going to find the fuse box for this room."

Ten minutes later, glass crunched underfoot. "Gerry?

"It's me."

"Good, I'm glad you're back. I know how particular you are about setting this stuff up," said Cougar.

"Me? Hey, you're the one with issues." Gerry twirled his finger around his ear. They both chuckled.

"Did you find the fuse box, wise guy?"

"Better, this place has breakers. Who' d' a thunk?"

"My turn now. Don't get so involved you forget I'm out there."

"Hang on a sec. Let me make sure the SAMs picking you up." Gerry fiddled with knobs on a unit he just switched on. A couple monitors glowed. He slid headphones over his ears and pulled the mic close to his lips. "Cougar, how do you read?"

"So close, I can read your lips."

The left screen showed the top of the museum. The screen on the right, a slant view of the abandoned apartment building they were in. "All good. Okay, be careful, and remember. You must be invisible. Seeing you could jeopardize tonight's mission."

"Thanks for the reminder, Yoda."

"Hey, stating the obvious is a sign of intelligence."

"If you say so." Cougar rubbed some black grease on his arms, hands, and face. He pulled a ripped wool coat over a dirty tee-shirt, slipped on thread-bare jeans, and topped off the vagrant's outfit with a crushed bowlers' hat.

"If Daniela and Amelia could only see you now," quipped Gerry. "I'm not sure either would be fighting too hard for ya, buddy."

"Thank you kindly, sir." Cougar tilted his hat to Gerry and picked up what looked like an old grocery bag.

Cougar approached the museum fence. "Anything, Gerry?"

"All clear, they must be inside." Cougar stooped down and planted explosives on the gate post. "Hang on—someone's coming from around back." Cougar hobbled down a fractured cement sidewalk. Weeds had forced their way between the cracks. Cougar stopped now and then to pick up rusty cans and trash. The man stopped, eyed Cougar for a minute, then headed to one of the trucks, opened the door and pulled out a lunchbox. The man yelled something to Cougar; but he couldn't make out what was said.

Gerry moved the SAM. "You're clear."

Cougar slid under the fence where water had etched a ditch. He planted a few devices along the side of the museum and then one under each truck. A black bird dove at the SAM, cawing in agitation. "Cougar, two men just exited the front, find a place to hide!" Cougar quickly scanned the surroundings, finding only a small dumpster nearby. He crouched behind it, his back to the wall of the museum. A few splintered pallets helped hide him. The SAM lifted five hundred feet. The black bird quieted.

"They're just having a smoke, Cougar."

"Keep an eye on them." Cougar placed special ordnances around the rear of the museum. Then when the smokers retreated inside, crawled back under the fence. A sharp-looking sedan pulled up to the museum gate. Gerry watched through the SAM's video camera. He saw Donny Tallman enter the building.

"Cougar, that was Donny Tallman."

"It appears their plan's moving forward as scheduled. Time for phase two."

Plane Ride

Daniela and Amelia were arguing over whose hand was higher, a straight flush or four of a kind. I could see Kathy was staying out of the dispute. "Cougar, who won?" Amelia asked, holding up her cards.

"The person who doesn't get pulled into someone else's trivial competition." Both ladies judged me scornfully, then threw their cards at me. "Time to go. Kathy, are they bringing Miguel to the airport?"

"Yes, although we made a few enemies by insisting on using him tonight."

"He's still better off than his friends. Amelia, are you ready? You can still back out if you want, I know this is a lot to ask."

"The sooner we get this done, the sooner I have you all to myself…for helping me locate my father's body." Her cheeks reddened; Daniela scowled.

"Daniela, would you stay with Kathy after she drops us off at the airport? I know she and Gerry could use an extra set of eyes while they control the sector." Daniela strained at a smile. Truth be, I didn't want Daniela left alone at the hotel, and it was obvious she understood that not so subtle point.

The C-47 stood tall and proud next to a row of hangars. It was 10pm. Kathy backed out of the parking space and waved. Suddenly the passenger door flew open. Daniela called my name as she ran up to me.

"Cougar, I just want to tell you to be careful. I'm confused, and with Amelia being here…well, I'm not sure what I should be thinking. I care for you very much. I'm sorry for acting like a jealous adolescent." She kissed me quickly on my lips.

"Daniela, you know I care for you, too."

"I know you do."

"We can talk about all this later. In the meantime, please follow Kathy and Gerry's directions. I want all of us to make it through the night safely. After tonight, hopefully it'll all be over." Daniela hugged me, closing her eyes, and pressing her soft lips more passionately into mine. I held her, responding to her kiss. Amelia watched from the rear door of the C-47. The tires chirped as Kathy sped down the perimeter road.

Amelia stared out the co-pilot window, fidgeting with her fingernail. She raised her head. "Can I ask what the situation is between you and Daniela?" I figured that question was coming, but I didn't know how to answer her. I hadn't even answered it for myself yet. "Well?" she asked.

"Honestly, I'm not sure how to answer."

"You do like her, right? It's obvious she likes you."

"Of course, I like her."

"You know what I mean, Cougar."

"I do, but there's more at stake than that. My line of work tends to make relationships difficult, even if I wanted to pursue one. And truthfully, I haven't had much luck in that department. What about you? Is there a man at home waiting for you?"

Amelia dropped her head. "No…I haven't found the right person. I guess my line of work tends to repel deep relationships, too. Oh, I get plenty of offers; but not from the kind of men I would be interested in…none like you anyway."

"What are you saying?"

"What I'm trying to say is—"

"Sorry, the van just pulled up. We'll have to continue our conversation later." Amelia smiled; I think she was thankful for the interruption, too. A midsize white van parked three spaces in with its engine running. I kept my hand close to my pistol.

"Are you Cougar?" The man in the passenger seat asked.

"That's me."

"We got a present for you, but not a nice one. This guy's something else. You must have friends in high places. We were told to do whatever you asked."

The man, dressed in all white, slid the van door open, "We're happy to see him go, even if it's only for a night." Miguel darted his dark eyes my direction.

"Arlan?"

"It's actually Cougar, remember? Ready for a plane ride?" Miguel's hand was wrapped in white gauze. He had a Velcro bandage around his torso and his arms cuffed behind him. The baggy jeans he wore hid any bandage around his injured leg. "You look much better than when we dropped you off."

"Who are you?" he asked, as I helped him to the plane.

"You don't remember, huh? I'll give you a clue, I'm not an insurance investigator."

"If you're wanting me to help you fly this thing, you're going to have to remove these cuffs." He lifted his arms behind him, showing me the cuffs.

"I don't need your help flying." I pushed him through the C-47 rear door. Amelia led him up near the cockpit and sat him down.

"You have your girlfriend helping you, huh? I thought you two seemed pretty chummy, although I wasn't sure which of the two girls was yours. What do you want? Money? Treasure? Is that what your gig is? Let me go and I'll see to it you're both rich."

I locked his handcuff around the seat frame. "Tonight, you're going to help us. Gustano and Captain Moreno are expecting you, Javier, and his delinquent brother to fly this in at midnight, right?" Miguel appeared confused. "Right?" He nodded slowly.

"How did you find that out?" he asked.

"I ask the questions this time. Operation Cora Liberal—relocating the art you have ripped off over the years into a safe place outside Colombia…say…Venezuela, right?" Again, Miguel stared in disbelief. "Let's see if I got this straight. Mauricio was the mastermind behind the insurance fraud scheme, probably long before you and your boss were brought in on this. Back then it was primarily Mauricio and Donny, selling an occasional artifact through the black market. That was a reasonable plan as long as the art didn't surface for several years, but that wasn't good enough for Donny, was it?

"At some point, Mauricio hired your boss to expand their operation—to do the stealing, moving, and storing for them." I measured Miguel's expression. "By the way, it's much easier to steal art out of a museum when the art is not actually there, isn't it?" Miguel's blank expression remained. "That's why very few artifacts were ever recovered near the crime scenes; the art was never there to begin with. The art, at least the majority of it, was nicked during transit, before the crates ever showed up at the freight forwarders. You shipped water. I've got to hand it to you guys, that part was ingenious. Insurance companies were providing full coverage for crates filled with worthless water and a few artifacts strategically placed under the lids; clever."

"Somewhere along the line the Bogota police got too close. That's when Mauricio and Donny cut Captain Moreno, and whoever else, in on the action. They had to or else Captain Eduardo Moreno was going to blow this whole thing wide open, right? Here's where the story gets good. Captain Moreno, Donny, and your entrepreneurial boss got greedy and wanted the money sooner rather than later—much sooner than Mauricio thought best, after all, Mauricio still held a love of art somewhere in the back of his jaded mind. Am I close?"

Miguel's eyes brightened. "Pretty good, Mr. Cougar."

"Here's where it gets a little fuzzy for me. Somewhere down the line roles switched, and Captain Moreno began calling the shots. Mauricio was reduced to just a puppet leader, thinking he still held control. He was against Cora Liberal, wasn't he? He didn't want the art moved, dismantled, and sold into the market. So, you guys eliminated him, knowing there was enough treasure for all of you to live like kings. Have I left anything out?"

"Yes, Mr. Cougar, you've left off one very important fact."

"And what's that?"

"Gustano will kill both of you tonight. He has more men then you know—a lot more. He hires based on demand, and tonight is a demanding night. I don't know what your plans are, but you better rethink them if you want to live." Miguel's tone was measured.

"You're all cold-blooded killers," Amelia screamed, inches from Miguel's face, "and thieves. This is my father's plane!"

"Was, sweetheart," Miguel retorted.

"You murdered him! –and his friend." Amelia had her hands around Miguel's neck.

Miguel grinned the harder Amelia squeezed. He emitted a gurgling snicker. She dropped her hands.

"That's too bad about you father, I'll admit, but I wouldn't call the other man his friend." Miguel turned his sturdy neck from side to side. She slapped his face. "You know little lady; I could have done much worse to you. You should think good and hard before trying that again."

I glanced at my watch. "Time to leave, we'll have to continue this dialogue after capturing your three bosses."

"Three?" Miguel asked confused.

"Captain Moreno, Gustano, and Donny Tallman."

"Donny? That guy's a pawn, dumb as a box of nails. If you ask me, he could have been Fabio's brother instead of Javier." Miguel's face turned serious. "Javier was a good man."

"Yeah, he was a saint like you."

Amelia and I strapped in and started through the checklist.

"Cowl flaps?"

"Open."

"Mixture?"

"Idle Cut-off" We continued, with Amelia reading down the list.

"Wobble up Fuel Pressure?"

"Affirmative." Soon both engines belched as I nudged the throttles, swinging the tail in alignment to the taxiway.

"El Dorado Tower, Douglas 46-Kilo, ready for take-off."

"Douglas 46-Kilo line up and wait," Amelia responded.

"Douglas 46-Kilo, you are cleared for take-off."

The engines fought to be heard. The propellers searched for synchronization as the plane lifted into the cloudless night.

Chapter 59

Let the Men Finish

Light seeped around windows of the boarded-up room. Kathy and Daniela sat motionless; their eyes darted about several monitor screens. Four cars were parked near the two large trucks. Kathy glanced at the time, 2130. Two men walked the old soccer fields, shining flashlight beams and probing the grounds. Gerry toggled his controller. The SAM shifted and changed to night vision. Both men wore pistols off their hips; one also had a rifle slung over his shoulders.

"One thing for sure," Gerry said, "it's happening tonight—right here."

"I'm worried for Amelia and Cougar," said Daniela.

Kathy placed her hand on Daniela's knee and winked. "They'll be okay. I'm not so sure about the men down there though."

"I hope you're right."

"Cougar should be coming into range soon," said Gerry.

Kathy pointed to her screen. Another truck, slightly larger than the other two pulled into the old museum. Two more men jumped out. "Looks like their backup plan has arrived."

"How many have you counted Gerry?" asked Kathy.

"I think I've lost count. More than we were expecting, that's for sure. Hang on." Gerry flexed his fingers and then brought a third SAM in closer. Two men were standing in front of the building, both smoking. "I bet you the man on the right is smoking an Export A. Looks like the other man is Captain Moreno."

"There's Donny," said Daniela, pointing at the screen. A man exited the same door and stood next to the other two.

"All the king's men," remarked Kathy.

"Huh?" Daniela asked.

"Oh, nothing, just a phrase from a movie."

"Let's try to raise Cougar."

Kathy fiddled with a radio, then pushed a few soft buttons on her computer. "Cougar, can you hear me? Over." Hissing and garbles resonated from the speaker. Kathy slid her headset over her ears, switched frequencies and tried again.

Amelia pressed her transmit button. "This is WW2, over."

"What's your ETA?" asked Kathy.

"We'll hit the mark at five after," replied Cougar. "Are we green?"

"Affirmative," said Gerry. "All accounted for. They look to be waiting for you. Also, their backup trucks have arrived."

"Targets?"

"The SAM has detected ten."

"How many SAMs are airborne?"

"Four, three COMM's and one WEAP."

"Is the second WEAP ready for launch?"

"Negative. It sustained a damaged thruster somewhere during transit. We will have to rely on what's currently airborne…I don't have the parts or the time to fix it, sorry." Gerry turned to Kathy, sweat droplets slid down his temples.

"Ro-ger-that." Cougar responded slowly.

"I knew he wouldn't be happy," Gerry said, wiping his brow on his shirt sleeve.

"He's not unhappy with you, Gerry. Have you ever seen Cougar get mad at us?"

"No." Gerry replied.

"I'm sure he's just feeling the pressure. I don't think he was expecting ten people; including Miguel, I guess that's eleven."

"You guys aren't making me feel any less anxious, you know," said Daniela.

"Sorry, we're just trying to anticipate what Cougar will need once he lands."

The radio hissed. "Gerry, once they're on to me, be ready with the gate explosives. Kathy, keep COMM One's video rolling."

"Roger that," Gerry and Kathy both replied.

"We are now five minutes out. Show time," announced Cougar.

"Cougar, they are lighting lanterns along the soccer field for you or rather for Javier."

"Affirmative. We need to play musical chairs up here. Talk with you shortly." Amelia unbuckled her seat belt and slid under Cougar, taking over the controls. "Keep it pointed to the lit field." Cougar removed one of the locks fastening Miguel to the seat frame and sat him in the co-pilot's seat. "Do exactly as I've told you and I won't send a bullet into your skull. If not, one more to the body count won't ruin my day, got it?" Miguel grunted.

Cougar slid back in the pilot's seat. Amelia grabbed a pistol and walked to the back of the plane where nets and large canvas covers were tied down and hid underneath them. Cougar toggled the landing light switch on and off.

"See," Gustano said, turning to Captain Moreno, almost shouting. "I knew my men would be here. They are the best at what they do."

"Well, I take back what I said, good work." A wave of relief drained from Gustano's fingertips. Anxiousness spread across Brigitte's face as she stepped next to Gustano. Leaving her son had been hard but being Gustano's girl required sacrifices. She put her arm around Gustano's waist. Gustano removed her arm.

"Can't I even put my arm around you?" Donny and Captain Moreno watched inquisitively.

"No. When the plane lands, get your kid and you two stay out of the way. We have enough MEN to load the plane."

"What about all the help I've been today?"

"What about it? You want an atta-boy from me? A *good job Brig-itte*? Come on you guys, let's applaud Brigitte's hard work today." They all clapped. "Now, let the men finish the job!"

Brigitte's mouth relaxed as she raised her hand, spreading her two fingers. Gustano placed a cigarette between them and lit it for her. "Sure thing, darling." she replied as she walked off. Donny elbowed Captain Moreno while chuckling.

"Shut up, ya weasel, or I'll light you up like that cigarette." Captain Moreno chuckled also, patting Gustano on the back.

The C-47's silhouette came into view. The landing gear moved into position. As the big plane neared the turf field, Cougar flipped on the landing lights. The plane touched down; Cougar retarded the throttles. The ground was soft, the tail settled into the turf quickly as the plane slowed. Cougar kicked the left rudder pedal, turning the plane 180-degrees, then taxied up to where the men were standing, ensuring the window, where Miguel sat, faced the museum and the men. "Let's see that hand, Miguel," Cougar ordered. Miguel waved through the window. Cougar cut the fuel to the engines. The propellers wind-milled several revolutions before coming to a stop. He nudged the gun into Miguel's thigh. Miguel slid the side window opened and yelled.

"I'll get the door; you guys start loading."

The men turned from the plane and rolled open the tall steel doors to the museum's shipping docks. Inside were stacks of various sized wooden boxes. There were enough boxes to fill the spacious cabin of the C-47 two times over.

The Final Campaign

"The COMM cameras are getting it all, Cougar," stated Kathy. "We need audio of Moreno's involvement before it gets too loud," I replied.

"Understood."

Men carrying boxes waited for the door of the airplane to open. Miguel slowly unlocked the door and waved them in. Amelia aimed the pistol beneath the canvas covers. I remained in the cockpit with my headset on, writing on a pad. Gustano yelled from the shipping dock.

"Miguel? You and Fabio come help, let Javier finish up in there." Miguel looked over. I held my finger up.

"Cougar, Captain Moreno is coming out to the plane now. He's carrying a small box. Gustano's right behind him." Two men jumped down from the rear door of the plane. I signaled for Miguel to join them. I walked to the tail where Amelia sat crouched and hidden.

"Amelia, shut the door once I'm out, and don't open it for anyone unless it's me; and verify it's really me." I jumped down, sliding my hat down low over my face. The C-47 door closed behind me. I shielded the lights with my hand. Gustano stopped to talk with Miguel. I kept walking. In my hand was a small flight bag.

Brigitte pounded on the C-47 door.

"Javier?"

"Let me set this down," I replied to Gustano.

"We have the evidence now," Kathy stated.

"Phase Three will start in—"

"There he is," Miguel cried. "That's him! Shoot him!"

I dove through the loading dock door, taking cover behind some crates. Captain Moreno pulled out his pistol and fired my direction. Two explosives detonated. He holstered his gun, yelling at two men to go after me.

"Keep an eye on him," I yelled.

"On it…he's moving to the front of the museum."

"If he tries to leave, blow the gate." I darted around the box, aiming my pistol, and sending one man to the ground. Men came around the boxes from both sides with machine guns blasting. "Take'em out, Gerry!" Two brilliant flashes appeared. Both men fell to the ground. Two more started after me, stopped, then aimed their guns frantically in the air.

"Get him!" Gustano yelled. "He's only one man." I detonated another charge by the far door. A man screamed in agony. He gathered his intestines in his arms.

"Get him!"

I fired, dropping two more men.

Brigitte screamed. "Where is he? Where's my son!" She beat on the side of the airplane. Bullets ricocheted off the cement floor.

"Kathy, what's the count?"

"Eight—must have missed a few heat signatures."

"I'm getting low on explosives. Where's Moreno?"

"Haven't seen him." Wood splinters erupted near my head. I dove behind another stack. I pulled a grenade from the bag and tossed it in the direction of the gunman. Agonizing screams spewed as the two bodies crumpled to the ground.

The SAM lit up behind me, frying a gunman. "Thank you, Gerry."

"Don't mention it."

"Gerry, light up the sky." Gerry pressed the high intensity button on his control panel. The sky instantly brightened like morning. A man shot at the WEAP. A split second later he dropped to the ground. Miguel raised his hands.

"Don't shoot me," he cried. Kathy hovered a COMM within ten feet of Miguel's head.

She announced, "Miguel, one move and you're dead." Miguel didn't move. Gustano ran into the museum. Brigitte followed him. "Cougar, Captain Moreno just got into a car and is heading out the gate."

"Blow it," I yelled, sprinting to the front of the museum. A split second later, a newer sedan lurched into the air, the hood buckled, sending flames and black smoke spiraling into the sky. Captain Moreno rolled out of the driver's side door, swatting flames off his pants. He eyed one of the trucks. As soon as he pulled himself up to one, I hit the detonator. The truck exploded, flipping into the air. When it landed, it rolled over Captain Moreno's body.

Donny ran out the front door. A person inside shouted, "Run, you coward!" Bullets chased him as he dove to the ground.

I ran over to him; he was laying on his back looking straight up. "Remember me?" I said. He swung his fist up at me. I blocked his arm, clasped my fingers together and drove my fists into his chest. He gasped. I rolled him over and zip-tied his hands and feet together, then guardedly entered the museum through the front door. "Gerry, any sign of movement?"

"Negative on the inside. The heat sensors are unable to detect anything. They must have the heat blasting in there."

"Cougar," Kathy cut in. "Amelia's still in the C-47, Miguel is cooperating, and there's one more man moving around by the loading dock."

"Gustano and Brigitte are in the museum, I'm going after them. If the man tries entering the museum, kill him."

The building lights were barely on, in many places, only wires hung down where fixtures used to be. Perspiration soaked my undershirt. A grand staircase arched up to a second floor. I quietly climbed the stairs. Two steps from the top, the stair creaked. I paused, hearing Gustano and Brigitte's voices. I stepped to the top, hurling myself behind a curtain, just past the staircase landing. My breathing resonated. Behind the curtain was a small theater with worn out wooden chairs stacked up into several neat columns. Steps sounded off the wood floor to my right. I inched myself to a wall. The person clambered down the stairs.

"You're right," Brigitte screamed as she descended. "He's not your kid. I just didn't have the heart to tell you." She stomped the rest of the way down the stairs, then all was quiet.

"Cougar, Brigitte just came into view. She's at the back of the museum and has a machine gun in her hands, walking towards the C-47 rear door."

"Tell Miguel to stop her. If that doesn't work, take her out, Gerry." I turned my attention back to Gustano. I crept out of the theater. The aisle was empty. Large exhibit rooms were to my right, with smaller rooms and offices to my left. I approached the first exhibit room holding my pistol out in front of me. The room was about fifty by forty feet deep, and open to a large aisle. Opposite the exhibit rooms and the aisle, a resplendent railing snaked to the far wall of the museum, with the main exhibit hall twenty feet below it. Dingy white sheets were stacked on top of exhibit tables. I approached the next gallery. There were no signs of Gustano.

"Cougar, situation under control in back," Kathy stated.

I tapped my watch while working my way to a walled room with a door. I swiped at my brow and situated myself against the wall. I breathed in deep and kicked the door open. Bullets sprayed the doorpost and railing behind me. I fired into the room. Bullets traced over my head. I fired again. Pain exploded in my calf. I looked down. Blood soaked my pant leg. I limped back to the large room and barricaded myself behind a sturdy wooden table.

"Come on out, Gustano," I said. "There's no way for you to escape." I pulled up my pant leg, ripped a piece of a tablecloth off, and wrapped it around my calf.

"Who are you?"

"The wrong person to mess with," I replied.

"Where's my son?"

"And you're worried about him because…?"

"I'm not," he yelled from the other room. "Brigitte is…she's a good mother."

"I would say you're both model parents…he's fine. Drop your weapon and come out. All this can be over."

"My life is over."

"It doesn't have to be. There's more life if you surrender."

"I have done too many awful things. I would never be released. What kind of dad wants that for their son…a relationship by prison visitations?

"Better a relationship in prison then at a cemetery."

"He would be better off with a new father—someone more like you."

"You can't think like that. It's never too late to change. Come on out."

"Okay, I'm coming." Steps echoed from the aisle. He turned into the gallery. I stayed behind the table.

"Drop the machine gun and slide it over to me." Gustano did as he was told. "Open your shirt. Slide the pistol over to me as well." Gustano removed his pistol and held it in his hand. "Don't do it," I said. He slowly laid it down and kicked it over to me. I came out from behind the table and grabbed his arm. He swung at my face, catching my chin on the right side. My pistol fell to the ground. I advanced at him. He pulled out a long knife.

"Arlan-Arlan, or whoever you are." Gustano circled me, wielding his knife in the air. "I always have a backup plan. Prisons are for dopes like Donny." Gustano managed to pull out a cigarette. "I'll take that beautiful airplane down there and fill it with enough treasure to sustain the lifestyle I've grown accustom to." He lit the Export A and inhaled slowly.

"And Brigitte?"

Smoke streamed from his nostrils. "She's a little sore with me, but that never lasts long. She's also become accustomed to what I can provide."

"So, you three just fly off into the sunset?"

"Something like that."

"You planned on killing Captain Moreno and Donny tonight, didn't you?"

"They served me well—all of them, but I fly better solo. I actually liked Captain Moreno, but not as a partner. As for you? You will die here in this pathetic museum of horror. This place always gave me the creeps. They should have turned it into a wax museum of torment." Gustano jabbed at me. I blocked his advance. He stuck the knife out again, jabbing. He grinned, holding the cigarette in his lips. The top of his head glistened with perspiration. I kicked the blade from his hands and dove at him. We rolled back and forth exchanging punches. I stood then brought my knee down hard on his chest. Gustano struggled to get to his feet.

"You've had a little training, have you?" He bent over and coughed.

"US government, if you must know. The finest training available," I replied.

"We'll see about that," he said. He swung his leg to my head. I blocked most of the blow. I chopped at his ear. Blood erupted. He wiped his head, pulling back his bloody hand, staring at it.

"Are you sure you don't want to reconsider my offer?" I asked, catching my breath.

"You are weak like your country." He jumped, then pushed his leg into my chest, sending me to the floor. He crouched, reaching behind himself for a pistol on the ground. When he stood, he had the gun in his hand. As he raised it, I ran straight at him, sending us both over the railing and down to the first floor. We landed on a table covered in white sheets. Gustano's body cushioned my fall. The table legs smashed underneath us, dropping us the rest of the way to the ground. The sheets turned red. Glass shards stuck through Gustano's neck, thighs, and arms. I slid off him. His body lay grotesquely halfway off the table. His spine was severed and bent too far in the wrong direction. Cigarette smoke escaped from his open mouth.

I caught my breath, and at the same time checked to see how much of the blood was mine. "Cougar, are you okay?" Kathy asked.

"Not sure, give me a second." Blood soaked my shirt and pants. Several cuts on my arm would need stitches. I removed the wrap on my leg. The blood was dark, but the flow had stopped. My head felt heavy, something about my neck didn't feel right either. "How are we outside?"

"Still secure," said Kathy.

"Get ahold of Riley. Let him know we're secure here—mission accomplished. They can send in Colombia's secret police to mop up. Tell them we'll leave Donny, Miguel, Brigitte, and…you said there was one more still living right?"

"Yes."

"Tell him we will leave them tied up inside the museum."

"Roger that."

"Gerry?"

"Yes, Cougar."

"I need a hand over here. Kathy, once we're secure, start dismantling the gear, we need to be out of here before they show up. It's any wonder they haven't already, considering the gunfire and explosions."

"On my way, Cougar."

Miguel, Brigitte, and another man I didn't recognize were lined up in a row, their knees to the grass, with SAMs hovering overhead. I zip-tied all three. I knocked on the C-47 door and called out, "Amelia, it's Cougar." The door opened slowly. Amelia held a shaking pistol in her right hand. I took it from her and held her. She jumped into my arms, weeping intensely. "Is it over?"

"Yes."

"You're hurt."

"A little." Gerry and I moved the three from the back and Donny into the museum.

Brigitte asked, "When can I see my son?"

"Soon. You made the right choice listening to Miguel." Miguel eyed me respectfully. "I'm impressed. For what it's worth, you really are a good man, Cougar. As for me? I deserve what's coming."

Donny shook his head. "I knew the moment I met you something was up. The FAIB doesn't investigate like you did. I should have caught on sooner."

"How could you? You saw everything through your own greed colored glasses. From the day you left college, you and Mauricio plotted and schemed your way through life, not caring about who got hurt along the way. Don't worry, you'll have plenty of time to develop your new scheme in prison. I hope this time it's more virtuous."

I removed the two undetonated charges around the museum boundary. Gerry gathered up the SAMs and loaded them in the C-47. When he returned, Kathy and Daniela were with him. Kathy and Gerry loaded in the rest of the gear. Daniela clutched me tightly, pressing her lips to mine. We kissed. Our lips parted slowly. "I have never seen anything like that in my life—not even in movies. I was so scared," she said.

"Ouch!"

She released her grip. "Are you hurt badly?"

"I'll be a little sore for a while."

Amelia yelled from the airplane door. "Come on, we better get out of here." Daniela and I jumped in the airplane. Sirens wailed in the distance.

"Start the engines, Amelia!" I ran to the front. "You sit in the captain's seat," I said.

"I can't. I'm too jittery…can you fly?" Her eyebrows lifted; her mouth tightened.

"Okay, let's get this beauty in the air."

As the police cars and firetrucks rounded the corner, we were already airborne, heading into a canvas sky, brightened by an ancient gray moon.

Chapter 61

Beyond Tired

T he sky brightened behind the hills. Daniela and Amelia sat down on one bed, with Gerry dropping onto the second one, leaning back and groaning like a bear emerging from hibernation.

"Before you get too comfortable, Riley wants us to call in," said Kathy. Cougar heated up water. Kathy hooked up her computer and patched Riley in.

"I'm sure you're all tired, so I won't keep you long," Riley stated.

"Beyond tired," Gerry replied.

"Cougar, did you get patched up?"

"Yes, sir. Quick and painless, sir."

"Well, I have some good news. Not only has the Colombian government apologized, they have rolled out the red carpet for us."

"We're glad to hear that."

"Also, the Colombian government will be thoroughly checking into the Bogota police department. I let them know your thoughts, Cougar, that Captain Moreno acted alone. Amelia?"

"Yes, sir?"

"While you were helping Cougar with our mission, I had our team here do a little research into your father's disappearance. It wasn't easy, but we were able to recreate the most likely route Gustano's men took after seizing control of your father's airplane in Mexico. We matched that with tides and weather at the time, and the location of where the co-pilot's body was found. We now have a fairly good idea where your father and his co-pilot were killed."

"Thank you, sir. I appreciate that very much."

"It's the least we could do. I'm deeply sorry about your father and the unfortunate circumstance we were in, having to pull Cougar off your case."

"I understand it now," replied Amelia.

"Oh, one other thing," Riley added. "They located your T-6 and will dismantle it and ship it back to Texas for you. Of course, it will take some time for that to occur."

"Thank you," Amelia replied again.

"Thank you, sir," said Cougar. "After we get a little rest, I plan to help Amelia complete her investigation. Then I will return to the States."

"Gerry and I plan to leave after our naps," said Kathy.

"Daniela?"

"Yes, sir."

"The Museum director is anxious to have you back. The Board of Trustees, director, and the city officials have all been given the details on the theft ring; and most of the Bogota artifacts will be returned over the next several days."

A smile spread across Daniela's face. "Thank you. I'm very much looking forward to being back at work. I can't wait to see all of Colombia's history back on display."

"I'll leave you with the succinct words General David Bellwether said to me thirty minutes ago after our debrief, 'Another outstanding mission—well done.'"

Gerry and Cougar looked around the room. Tired eyes stared back. Kathy spoke up. "All the ladies can sleep here, boys off to your room."

"Thank you," Daniela replied. Gerry and Cougar exited through the adjoining door. Cougar stopped before closing it.

"If you ladies need anything, just ask."

"Thank you," all three said in unison.

Goodbye

My eyes struggled to focus. The clock read 12…something. I pried my eyes open; 12:27, almost five hours of sleep. Gerry grumbled. His pillows were on the ground and his covers were balled up at the foot of the bed. "Rough sleep, huh?" More grumbling. "What's that, sleeping beauty?"

"Too hot; didn't sleep well. The light seeping around the curtains didn't help either."

"Tea?"

"Coffee…charcoal black, please." He flung one leg to the ground. "How did you sleep?"

"Rather good, I didn't have your snoring to contend with."

"I see how this day's going," Gerry said, sitting on the edge of his bed with his hair twisted in lumps.

"Come on, let's get some breakfast."

Gerry tilted his head and took in a deep lungful of air. "Cougar."

"Yeah?"

"Be careful out there. I feel bad you're not coming home with us."

"I will, and don't feel bad. I'm looking forward to helping Amelia. She needs this search so she can finally get to a place where she can move on with her life."

"I sure hope she finds it—whatever it is. What's the chance of finding his body now?"

"I'm not even sure that's the point anymore, but we need to try; I owe her that much."

"I guess you're right." Gerry flipped on the bathroom light. "Quick shower first."

"I'll see if the ladies are up."

Forty-five minutes later, Kathy, Daniela, and Amelia walked into the hotel restaurant. I waved them over to our table. Daniela wore a pair of jeans and a yellow blouse, Amelia, jeans, and a white tee-shirt, and Kathy, leisure pants with a beige blouse. After our greetings, the table fell silent.

"What time is your flight, Kathy," I asked.

"Six."

Daniela raised her eyes. "I'm actually a little sad it's over. I mean, I am happy it's over, but still sad. Having you guys around has been really nice."

"Things are going to be different for you at work. Are you going to be okay?"

"It's not that," she said, gazing around the table. "I really enjoyed getting to know all of you. I work so much that I haven't had much opportunity to make friends or hang out with people."

"You also went through a pretty traumatic experience. It will take some time for your days to feel normal again."

"I guess you're right, but I'll still miss all of you."

"We can talk whenever you want," Kathy said. The waitress bounded to the table and took our order.

After lunch, as I was packing, Detective Andrea Dias called, asking if we could meet. I explained I had a situation to attend to first and would contact her when finished. My phoned buzzed as soon as the call ended. A text from Daniela, asking if I would meet her down in the hotel lobby.

When the elevator door opened, there she was, standing near the exit, staring out the window. "Daniela." She turned; her eyes were smudged with dried tears.

"Please be careful, Cougar." She examined my eyes. "I'm not sure what we have here—"

"Daniela—"

"Sheesh, don't say anything, please. When you're done helping Amelia, then we will talk." She kissed me, then took a few steps before turning around. A forced a smile spread across her face, then she was out the door to a waiting taxi.

Gerry was in the room packing. In Kathy's room, she and Amelia were sitting on the bed discussing something. Kathy stood up and walked over to me. "Here, there is a little something on your lips." She rubbed off the remnant of red lipstick.

"Thank you," I said. "I'm going to say goodbye to you guys here, Amelia and I need to stop off at a store for supplies before heading to the plane." I spoke loudly so Gerry could hear me in the other room. He stepped through the adjoining door.

"It has been another amazing mission, Cougar. I look forward to the next one when we're together." Gerry gave me a bear hug and patted me firmly on the back.

"You be extra careful; you won't have Gerry and me to bail you out." Kathy wrapped her arms around me.

"I will. Please shoot me a message after you guys land. Oh, and don't forget the barbecue. I'll send a group message when I pin down the date."

"We would never miss a Cougar barbecue," Gerry replied.

Kathy added, "Unless of course, we're on a mission."

"Of course," replied Gerry.

"Barbecue?" asked Amelia.

"I'll share the details with you later."

"This year," said Gerry, "I'm having two steaks, one for me, and one for your crafty dog. The last time his sad eyes compelled me to toss half of my porterhouse to him." We all broke out in a healthy laugh.

Amelia and I sat next to each other inside the airplane. I drew lines on a chart, plotting out our search pattern. There was a rap on the fuselage. Amelia jumped.

"It's just the fuel truck," I said, looking out the front windscreen. While the tanks were being topped off, Amelia and I thoroughly inspected the aircraft.

"Shall we?" I held my hand out for Amelia to grab and re-enter the airplane.

"Wait," she said, stepping back to the tarmac. "I want you to know how much I really appreciate what you're doing for me. This is not to confuse you, only to thank you for being such a wonderful man." She reached her arms around my neck and kissed me firmly on the lips. Her breath was sweet, her hair, clean and soft. A subtle floral fragrance seized me. She released her hands. Our eyes stayed on each other. "Now, don't get any ideas," she said. "That was just for good luck."

I took in a deep breath and relaxed my shoulders. "Hey, are you coming?" Amelia asked, hanging out the door.

"Right behind you. Your…um…kiss kind of caught me by…um…"

"Surprise? Good, now come on, let's shove off, Captain." Amelia strutted her jeans to the front of the airplane where they sat in the co-pilot's seat. I drained a water bottle, then sat next to her.

"Prestart checklist?" I said. Amelia read the items off one by one. She giggled like a young woman a few times, as our eyes met. "Stop it," I said. "This is serious business." Lately, and for whatever reason, being around her made all my senses come alive.

"I know—sorry. I think I'm more anxious than I realized. I haven't really thought about what I would do if we find his body." Amelia stopped reading off the checklist. "It feels good to laugh again. I hope I can always laugh."

"I'm not a philosopher, but I've heard time really does heal. Let's get airborne and I will share something else with you."

Soon the big Douglas C-47 was lumbering down the runway. The tail lifted, then the main gear. The sound of the Pratt & Whitney R-1830 radial engines, with their large propellers throbbing against the metal sides of the fuselage, seemed to restore hope and optimism. We turned away from the city and headed north.

Amelia said, "I looked along the northern border facing the Caribbean Sea and never spotted any sign of my father."

"Were you looking for the plane, wreckage, or his body?"

"All the above," she replied.

"This time we're not looking for an airplane, just anything that doesn't appear in nature, like clothes on a beach or perfect angles. We'll also keep an eye out for rescue signals."

"Rescue signals?" she questioned.

"Sure. He may have been able to create some sort of signal before he was killed."

"Oh, okay. I understand. For a moment I thought you were saying…well my heart skipped a beat."

"We should never let go of hope."

"So, what's the story you were going to tell me?"

"While I was attending college, in central Washington, I received a phone call one day. Both my parents had been killed in a horrific automobile accident."

"Oh, Cougar…I am so sorry. I can't even imagine how you must have felt."

"You're the one person who probably can imagine."

"What did you do? How did you get through it?"

"I learned what trusting God really meant. I also had a close friend who knew my parents. We helped each other through the initial hard times."

Amelia was quiet as the engines droned on. "So how did you become a special agent? I assume that's your actual title."

"That's a story for another time. Let me just say that once my parents died, I fully devoted myself to flying. I started to see the world differently. That caused me to make some decisions that eventually, and by accident, led me to Trinity."

"Kathy and Gerry? They work at Trinity full time?"

"Yes."

"Why did you start a private practice?"

"Okay, last question. I liked what Trinity did for those whose situations rose to the level and interest of our government. Trinity specializes in key asset recovery."

"Like your private practice."

"Exactly, and I wanted to provide that level of expertise to others who needed it—of course minus the team and all the cool equipment."

"That's why your Aero Commander is all gussied up."

"Gussied up?"

"You know, all the top-secret gadgets and stuff you didn't want me to notice. So, you opened up a practice for people like me." Amelia stared out at the approaching sea. "I'm glad you did."

"Me, too."

Chapter 63

The Edge

Cougar and Amelia flew the C-47 in long legs, back and forth along the coastline. Through binoculars, Amelia observed the ground, only taking breaks as nausea crept in. As the day dragged on, their conversation diminished.

"I suggest we turn around and fly back to the center point of the grid Riley gave us," said Cougar. Amelia glanced over and nodded.

"I'm discouraged…and hungry…and I'm feeling irritable." Both Cougar and Amelia shared the same doubt and disappointment in their faces. The plane droned on for several more hours, making its way back to the center of the grid.

"There was a clearing we observed earlier, close to the center of the grid, I think it deserves a closer inspection. We can land, check it out and eat our dinner there. Then we'll need to head back to Cartagena. We can spend the night there and broaden our search tomorrow. We may have to work our way up the coast of Central America."

"That sounds good." Amelia unbuckled her seat belt and returned with two waters. "Tell me the truth, do you honestly think we'll find his body or any signs of where they killed him?"

"I'm not sure, Amelia. A lot of time has passed; but whether we do or we don't, you need to recognize inside yourself that you've done all you can. I know many people who love their parents, but I've never seen love acted out the way I've seen it acted out in you. You are a good person, Amelia. When this is over, you should have no regrets. But I'm not giving up yet, so don't you give up either, okay? I have seen miracles occur in my line of work that would boggle conventional thinking."

"You always make me feel better." Amelia shared a partially contrived smile.

"Trust me on this. There will be more springtime and summers for you. This current winter will pass."

Brightness dimmed as night loomed. The C-47 approached the apex of the grid. The clearing near the edge of the cliff was still visible under the rapidly fading sunlight. As Cougar flew low and slow, Amelia inspected the surface. "It looks flat enough. Wait…I see tire tracks."

"That's promising. I'll swing around to land. Keep your eyes peeled for rocks." Cougar and Amelia readied the large Douglas twin. Cougar called out. "Centerline check—Gear down, fuel, lights, flaps…"

The tires kicked up dirt, as the plane slowed. Cougar spun it around, facing it in the opposite direction. Amelia smirked. "Show off." They grabbed a sandwich and an apple. Cool air greeted them as the door opened.

"I'm going to look around," said Cougar, setting his apple just inside the doorway.

"I'm coming with you." She turned on her heels and followed behind him. "These look like airplane tracks." They both studied the grooves in the dirt.

"See these? They all appear to be made from the same type of tires. These are the ones we just made. These, however, were already here. Do you see how they overlap?"

"Don't most aircraft tires look the same?"

"True, but width and depth of the tread mark can vary greatly with the size and weight of the airplane." Amelia looked closer. "Look at this one. A smaller plane must have made these." Amelia stepped over and stared at the ground.

"So, what am I supposed to learn from all of this, Captain?"

"I believe an airplane the size of this one has landed here before."

"Are you saying this could be the place?"

"I'm saying it's possible. Let's look around some more." Cougar finished the last bite of his sandwich and returned to the airplane. He grabbed his apple and two flashlights. "Here, you're going to need this real soon."

"How long are we staying, shouldn't we leave before it gets too dark?"

The sun had slipped below the horizon. Minute by minute the sea beyond the cliff was losing its luster. A radiant moon edged slowly up behind them. "We'll be okay. Taking off shouldn't pose any issues, assuming our landing lights work."

"Amelia?"

"What is it?" She squinted at where Cougar had the light shining.

"Gun casings."

"Oh, my gosh! This really could be the place."

They both stopped suddenly. "Do you smell that?"

Amelia sniffed the air. "Smells like a fire." They quickly turned toward the airplane.

"I don't smell anything in the airplane. It almost smells like…like a wood fire."

"I smell it too, like a campfire," replied Amelia. They spread out searching for the source of the odor.

"There!" Cougar ran to the edge of the cliff. Heat and translucent smoke rose from a crevice in the rock. He moved closer to the hole. Amelia stopped behind him, peering over his shoulders. "What is it?"

Cougar studied the cavernous opening in the rock structure. "The smoke is coming from inside here. There must be a fire at the bottom of this cliff."

"How do we get down there?"

Cougar yelled down through the hole. "Hello-ello-ello! Is anybody down there-ere-ere? Can you hear me-e-e?" Waves echoed through the hole, but no voices.

"Hello-o-o-," Amelia screamed. "Is anyone there-ere-ere." Her echoes trailed off. Silence penetrated the night air. Then a skinny voice came up through the hole.

"Amelia-ia-ia. I'm here-er-er." Amelia's face turned white as a ghost.

"Daddy-addy-addy. Is that you-ou-ou. I'm here-er-er." Amelia's voice turned into hysterical sobbing.

Cougar grabbed her. "Ted-ed-ed, my name is Cougar-ar-ar. I am coming down to get you-ou-ou. Are you okay-ay-ay?"

Thirty seconds passed. "My leg is broke-oke-oke."

"Okay-ay-ay, anything else-lse-lse?"

"Hungry and thirsty-ty-ty."

"Okay, give us some time-ime-ime." Blood returned to Amelia's white face. Cougar held her tight. "This is not going to be easy, but with your help, and the supplies we brought, I think we can get him out of there."

"Tell me what to do," she said frantically. They ran back to the plane, flipped on a cabin light, and went to work fabricating a harness for Ted using a life jacket and rope. Cougar tied together the ends from three separate coils of climbing rope, making one exceptionally long one. From his backpack he pulled out a rope grab, a stainless-steel figure eight, and a couple of carabiners. "Are you going to climb down the cliff?"

"More like a controlled repel," replied Cougar.

"It sounds dangerous. How will you bring him up? How will *you* get back up?"

"I need to see if I can get to him first, then check on his physical condition."

"How long would it take to get a helicopter out here?"

"We'd be lucky to find one and have it out here in 24 hours." Amelia's cheeks drooped visibly under the cabin light, like air being released from a balloon. "Don't worry, we're not waiting. I don't know what condition he's in down there. If we can't get him up, we'll go for help."

Cougar set the rope down and grabbed Amelia's shoulders. "If he's been down there this whole time, he's dehydrated, starved, and most likely, in a life-threatening condition."

"Okay," she said. "Let's hope this works. I still don't understand how you will pull him up though."

"First things first. I need to get to him." Amelia stuffed two water bottles and some food in a small waterproof pouch that Cougar clipped to his belt. He tied one end of the rope to the right landing gear strut and threw the remaining rope off the cliff, listening for it to uncoil all the way to the bottom. A slight breeze blew in from the water and up over the precipice, lifting fine tan dirt into the air.

"Did it reach far enough?" Amelia asked, wiping her eyes.

"Hard to know for sure. The last step might be a doozy."

"Stop it!" she exclaimed. She socked Cougar in the arm. "I'm already frightened enough." She twisted like a nervous teenager. She shook her head back and forth and wiped at a steady flow of tears running down her cheeks.

"Everything's going to be okay, trust me."

"Okay, but please be safe. I can't take anymore tragedies. Cougar…please bring him up."

Cougar grabbed her with both hands. "I will, now turn your radio on."

"Got it."

"Can you hear me?"

"Yes, barely." Cougar reattached the small mic on his collar further up and pushed in his earpiece.

"How about now?"

"A little better." Cougar grabbed her radio and twisted the squelch dial.

"Now?"

"Much better."

Cougar fashioned a makeshift harness, known as a swiss seat, out of twelve feet of rope. Then he connected the stainless-steel figure eight to the rope and harness with one of the carabiners. Amelia attached Ted's harness to the back of him. Cougar backstepped close to the edge.

"Wait!" cried Amelia. She ran over to him and slipped her arms around him. "This is for good luck."

"Again?"

"Yes." She slid her hands up to his head and pulled his face toward hers, kissing him more passionately on the lips. Cougar felt her wet tears against his cheek, then descended out of sight.

Get Him

Green vegetation anchored itself in the crevices of the cliff. Birds had found ledges in which to nest. As I descended, some scattered; some just squawked their disapproval of my intrusion. My headlamp blinked a couple times, then stayed off. I arrested my decent, darkness saturated in. I hung over nothingness, unable to see my hands. My breath grew loud, resonating inside my head. I unclenched a hand and tapped the light. It flicked on for a second then went off. Carefully hanging on to the rope with my other hand, I pushed on the back where the battery was located. It snapped shut and the light came on and stayed on.

"Cougar, are you okay?"

"I'm fine, the birds down here, not so much." I pushed off, dropping another ten feet, staying close to the rock wall. I continued my way down, glancing occasionally below me, but saw nothing. I pushed off again, then suddenly jerked to a stop.

"Are you okay?"

"Yeah, ouch…oh I see what it is, I'm at the knot already. I need to attach the rope grab. I'm a third of the way down. Need to pull up and run the rope through the—"

"Cougar!"

I dropped twenty feet before the rope-grab halted my decent, jolting my hips.

"Cougar—Cougar!"

"I'm here. I hope my next transition's a little easier." Amelia's breathing was loud in my earpiece. I descended the second length of rope. At the second knot, my transition was better. Waves crashed. As I continued, I strained to see below me. There was no beach, only water and rocks. "I'm at the bottom."

"Do you see my dad?"

Clicking the headlamp to spot mode, I scanned the water's edge. "No sign of him. I need to drop into the water. There's a large outcropping of rocks. He may be over there."

"Be careful." I caught my breath and eased down into the tepid water. I let go of the rope and swam toward the rock wall, touching ground three feet out. The cliff over hung the base of the wall by about twenty feet. I tied the rope off to an exposed root jutting between two rocks, then waded through the water, making my way along the wall to the outcropping of rocks.

"Ted!" Waves crashed against the rocks; saltwater sprayed the air like a geyser. I made it to a small opening. "There's a cave. I'm going in."

"O...k...y."

I pointed my flashlight. Rock and dirt with algae sides lit up. "Ted!"

"In here."

"I'm coming." I unclipped a stronger flood light from my belt and aimed it into the cave.

"Over here," I heard. I stepped over a few sharp rocks and wedged myself through a hole twice the size of my waist. Perched on a giant sand-covered rock and toward the back of the cave was a dark figure. It sat up and waved.

"Boy, am I glad to see you," he said in a shaky voice." Ted looked to be in his 60s. The skin on his face was tight and drawn into his cheek bones, and his silver hair, matted and in knots. "Are you from a rescue team?" His voice was raspy and weak. "I thought I'd be living out my last days here. I kind of broke my leg when I landed." He coughed. I gave him some water.

"How have you survived all this time?"

"You'd be surprised what works its way in here." He coughed again, then scanned over to a smoldering firepit. A few pieces of driftwood lay next to some fish bones and shells. "See that stream there?" He pointed to a mossy green trickle. "Fresh water—I got lucky."

"How bad is your leg?"

"It's messed up pretty good. Fortunately, no bones broke the skin, but I took a bullet here." He pointed to a makeshift bandage. "Should have been shark bait, but I found this cave here."

"And your cancer?"

"How do you know about that?"

"Amelia."

"Oh, my sweet Amelia. She's just like me—tenacious. I was afraid she might try to find me—could have gotten herself killed."

"What about your cancer?"

"That's the good news. The doc said I'll be all right. Of course, I'll need to make some changes in my life, but that should come easy compared to this. How's my angel? Are you a rescuer? Oh, sweet Amelia. I knew she would try to find me—could have gotten herself killed."

"She really loves you. Do you mind if I look you over?"

"Have at it, son." Ted was weak, but there was no indication of blood poisoning or trauma to his head. "Now who are you again?" he said for the third time.

"Let's get you out of here. I'll give you the full rundown once we're on top of the cliff. How painful is your leg? Do you think you can handle me carrying you on my back?"

"I can handle it, son; but how are you going to carry me on your back? I guess I'm a lot lighter than I used to be. Is there a rescue helicopter? I heard noises."

"We plan to pull you up if you're strong enough. All you need to do is guide yourself with your good leg. The rope is hanging away from the side of the cliff, so there shouldn't be much pressure on your body until you get closer to the top. Do you think you can do that?"

"Yee…" His eyes swam to the back of the sockets. I gave him another drink.

"You still with me, Ted?"

"Yes, I can do that. It's better than staying down here another night." Ted had splinted his leg with driftwood and some fabric from his clothes. I took out some Velcro straps, left the wood in place and secured his leg.

"Are you ready?"

"Ready." I hoisted him onto my back, piggyback style. Ted didn't make a sound.

"How are you doing?"

"Okay," he said. Stepping carefully along the slippery rocks, Ted and I squeezed out the small crevice, making our way out of the cave. Waves cashed in our faces. I slid off a rock. Ted slipped down.

"Hang on!" I yelled. I found my footing and hoisted him up again. Saltwater splashed. My eyes stung. I made it past the outcropping, then waded, with Ted on my back, to the base of the cliff.

"Cougar, I can hear you now. Are you okay? Did you find my father?"

"We're both out of the cave and at the bottom of the rope."

"Thank you, God," She exclaimed.

"I'm coming up. This may take some time."

"Okay."

"I'm attaching the walkie-talkie near your dad's collar."

"Angel? Is that you?"

"Daddy…Daddy, I was so worried. I thought I lost you forever." Amelia sobbed.

"I'll be up soon, honey; I'm okay. This nice man is helping me to the top." I fitted the makeshift harness around Amelia's dad, then found a large rock for him to sit on.

I started up the rope, moving very slowly. Ted sat perched below me. I inch-wormed my way up, hoisting and pulling the line though the figure eight, followed by raising my leg and locking the rope grab that was connected to my foot. Ted slowly disappeared beneath me. The light from the flashlight he held was barely visible now.

"How are you doing, Ted?"

"Ted?"

"I'm here." I stopped and slid the microphone back up.

"Sorry, that's on me. Are you okay?

"I guess I'm a little anxious."

"Are you cold?"

"A little, but I'll be just fine. You concentrate on climbing that rope, son." No one had called me son in a very long time. I hooked into the second section of rope and continued upward. The moon was higher now. I could see much better than when I had descended.

"Amelia, everything okay up there…Amelia?"

"Sorry, I'm here. I was drinking water. Everything is perfect. Daddy, are you okay?"

"I am now, sweetheart." My arms burned and my legs shook uncontrollably. I reached the last section of rope near the top. The rock wall jutted outward. My leg dangled free as I pushed with the other leg against the rope-grab. My lifting slowed, then stopped. I couldn't stop my leg from shaking. After a short rest, I pulled with all I had and brought my leg up as high as it would go, straightened, then reached my hands out. The saltwater on my shirt had dried and was replaced with sweat. I struggled to ignore the incessant itching on my stomach and back.

Finally, I dragged myself over the edge. A light beam flashed in my eyes. Then two arms pulled me the rest of the way over the ledge. "You made it! You actually made it!" She rolled me over and kissed my sweating lips.

"What was that for?" I panted.

"For not dying on me."

"Okay, give me a few minutes to recuperate, then we'll pull your father up." I leaned against the airplane's tire. "Ted…how are you doing?"

"Still here. No sharks seem to want me."

"I'm glad you still have a sense of humor."

"I'm feeling a little better. I think the water and whatever this candy is-is helping."

"I figured it might." The stream he'd been drinking from didn't look particularly clean to me. Amelia and I took our positions. Amelia stood next to me, facing the opposite direction, As I pulled on the rope, she would pull in the slack, ensuring two loops were always around the main landing gear strut.

"Okay, here we go. Ready, Ted?"

"Ready." I hauled in several yards, taking in the slack. Ted hollered. "Are you okay?"

"Just a minute, I skipped like a rock. Okay, I'm underneath the rope now." I pulled, then Amelia brought in the slack. I pulled again, followed by Amelia bringing in the slack. We worked side by side, sweating, grunting, hands burning through our gloves. The first knot made its way around the landing gear strut.

"A third of the way there," Amelia yelled, her handheld perched on the ground.

"Not a bad view from here," Ted said. We continued the relentless tugging and pulling. The second knot came through.

"One more to go."

"How are you doing, Ted? —Ted?"

"Dad?"

"He's still on the end of the line, we haven't lost him. Maybe the walkie-talkie fell." We pulled with more intensity until he was close to the top. "Wrap it around the strut three more times. Okay hold it there." I tied it off and walked to the cliff. "Ted, are you there?"

"I'm here…your radio isn't…sorry about that." I grabbed the rope and leaned over until my eyes rested on a silhouette of a man.

"This last part might be the toughest. Are you ready?"

"I'm ready." I backed up, grabbing the rope, and digging my shoes into the tan soil.

"Amelia, stand behind me and when I say pull, pull. Ready? Pull, pull, pull." Ted's arm reached over the edge. "Go get him, Amelia." Amelia ran to the edge and pulled him the rest of the way up while I walked backward with the rope. We all fell to the ground. Amelia dropped on her dad, hugging him, and crying.

When Amelia told him it was his C-47, a look of surprise spread over his face. "How did you? I mean…how?" Ted's mouth gaped open. We gave him water and a little more food. Amelia and I flew him to Bogota, where we checked him in to a hospital. Amelia stayed at the hospital; I found a nearby hotel. As I pulled the covers up, I fell into a deep and perfect sleep.

Chapter 65

Don't Be So Hard on Yourself

ougar's phone rang. His fingers fumbled for the phone. Blurry eyes focused on the screen. It was Riley. "Good morning, sir."

"I hope I didn't wake you."

"You did, but I needed to get up, so I appreciate the call." Cougar observed the face of the alarm clock situated next to him; it read 10:14.

"I called to check in on your search…see how it went yesterday."

"We found Ted."

"You actually found his body?"

"Yes, and his breathing lungs and talking lips. He is alive."

"Ted's alive?"

"Very much so, thanks to you and the team's help in pinpointing a probable location. He was not far from that apex." Cougar briefly thought about that clearing. The first time they had flown over it they saw nothing, so they kept searching. If it hadn't been for the evening fire and smell of smoke, he'd still be down there.

"That is excellent news, Cougar. How is Amelia doing?"

"Overwhelmed with emotion, as one might expect. They're both at the hospital here in Bogota. Ted is severely dehydrated and weak. He took a bullet to his leg while jumping off an extremely high cliff; then broke his leg when landing in the sea. I have no idea how he survived that fall. It must have been a couple hundred feet down. He's a pretty tough guy."

"Most veterans are. The US military produces many outstanding human beings. Well, I can't tell you how happy I am this turned out well. By the way, when are you returning home? Is your plane still in Texas?"

"It is, and it will be nice to get back to it. Next time, I hope I don't have to leave it so far behind. I have a couple things left to do here. Detective Andrea Dias wants to see me before I leave, and then there's Daniela."

"Kathy and Gerry explained your—um…predicament."

"I'm not sure how I get into these—situations."

"It's called life, Cougar. You're not a robot and nobody here is asking you to be one. There's nothing in your job description that says you can't have a wife. Who knows, it might even do you some good. I know you love your dog, but Cougar, seriously, there's room in your life for human companions too. Don't be so hard on yourself."

"Thank you, sir. I know you're right."

"I'm sure you'll figure it out and do the right thing. Gerry tells me you're planning on another barbecue at your place. If I'm invited, I hope my wife and I can make it this time. You know I'd never miss one of your barbecues if it's at all in my control."

"Of course, you're invited sir, and I will send you my report once I'm back in the States. Thank you again for your help with finding Ted and paying some of the expenses for Amelia."

"We have one more surprise for our veteran, although before we talked, we thought it was going to be for Amelia. We will have the C-47 painted back to its original color scheme."

"Thank you, sir. Ted and Amelia will appreciate this gesture very much. Have a good…evening."

"I will, and Cougar?"

"Yes, sir?"

"Another incredibly fine job you and your team did."

"Thank you very much." Riley clicked off. Cougar checked in with Amelia on her father's condition. His leg had to be reset and pinned, but his spirits were high. The bullet wound would heal without permanent damage and his brain fog had largely vanished. He made plans to swing by later and check on them both. He poured himself another cup of cheap hotel tea and called Daniela. After briefly sharing about finding Ted, he made dinner plans with her for later that evening. The last call was to Detective Dias. She was out, so he left a message for her to call him. Ten minutes later, Detective Dias returned his call, and he agreed to meet her at the police station in an hour.

Cougar stepped out of the hotel into a cloudless day. The warmth assaulted him in a perfect way, the way his heart felt at that moment. He found a quaint café, the food, simple and recognizable. As he ate, he thought about what Riley had said to him about a wife. Why did he feel he couldn't marry? Was his last relationship destined to scar him forever—loving so quickly and so deeply and then losing her—like the void he felt after losing his parents? Or was it his passion for his work and his dedication to helping others? He thought about Daniela and Amelia until there was nothing left on his plate. "Factura, por favor," he said to his waitress, as she passed by with a tray of dirty dishes.

As he entered the precinct, he waved to Andrea and she motioned him over.

"Good afternoon, Detective."

"Please, Andrea," she replied.

"Good afternoon, Andrea." Cougar tilted his head to her.

"Let's find an office where we can talk." She lifted herself from her chair and made her way to a vacant glass-walled office. Along the way, several police officers patted Cougar on the back as he followed her.

"What's that all about?" he asked.

She shut the door and scooted into a seat. "They know you helped solve the case. They also know about Captain Moreno. Everyone here appreciates what you did—especially me. It's still so surreal to think he was involved in all of this."

"Involvement is an understatement," replied Cougar. "I'm not sure how much they told you."

"We weren't given many of the details. We know Mauricio Lopez, Donald Tallman and Captain Moreno were all part of a major theft ring, and somehow, Captain Moreno got himself killed."

"I'm sure your officials don't want a lot of this getting out."

"I'm sure you're right, it wouldn't help our public image any. We've been having enough issues with the public's perception of our police force." Andrea adjusted herself in the chair, tried to cross her legs, then decided against it. "I don't know why I wear such tight clothes," she said looking down. "I'll never be able to fit in them anymore. Well, I could, I suppose if I stopped eating so much." She shook her head. "What I wanted to tell you, is that…well, I made things really difficult for you. It wasn't me…well it was, but I was told to be that way by Captain Moreno."

"It's okay—really, Andrea. It took me a while to figure out the dynamics between you two, but once I did, I understood the position you were in. I can also appreciate your mindset about some foreign insurance investigator stepping in the middle of your investigation."

"Well, it does make it difficult sometimes for us when that happens."

"Again, no apologies necessary."

"So, what do you do now? Report it all to the insurance board and they grant Delrow Insurance Agency to pay out what wasn't recovered?"

"Something like that."

"Well, I just want to say again how appreciative we are for your assistance." Andrea glanced around the office, then refocused on Cougar. "I also want to thank you for treating me so respectfully. People can be so rude sometimes. They poke fun at my weight. It doesn't matter that half of the policemen in here are as big if not bigger than I am. I'm the one they make fun of…and it hurts…a lot. But you never looked at me that way. You're a real gentleman. I just wanted to tell you that in person."

"I appreciate that very much, Andrea. This office and Bogota are lucky to have you on the police force. We all have areas we wish were different. Some of us have them outward, and people notice, some of us have them inward, thinking no one will. There's one thing I've learned throughout my life, far above anything else that continually brings me joy."

"What's that, Arlan?"

"For real happiness, one needs only to be loved by two; God and themselves. God loves us unconditionally, so that one's taken care of if we fully recognize and accept that fact; but it took me a while to do the same for myself. Once I did though, my world has never been the same. Be good to yourself Andrea, you are worth loving."

Detective Dias stared at the desktop. Tears welled up in her eyes. "Thank you, Arlan. Please look me up if you're ever back in town—please."

"I absolutely will." They embraced. Cougar walked out of the precinct as several police officers waved from their desks.

Stories

When the elevator reached Ted's floor, it stopped with a clunk. Ted was propped up in bed, watching a western movie. "How are you feeling, Ted?"

Startled out his preoccupation with John Wayne, he replied, "Cougar, I'm fantastic! If I were any better, I'd be doing the foxtrot. Come, have a seat." I walked around and sat next to him. He turned the volume down using a bedside remote. "Amelia went to the cafeteria for a snack. She should be back any minute. So, my angel hired you to find me, huh? A private investigator. Tell me, what's it like being a PI?"

"Most of the time it's very rewarding. Occasionally, it even puts food on the table."

"Never a dull day, huh?"

"Not every day I'm repelling off cliffs." Ted laughed, giving an honest and hearty chuckle from deep inside his chest.

"You sure have made an impression on my little girl."

"Dad!" Amelia said, walking in holding an iced drink and a scone. "Here, I brought this for you." She set the scone down next to Ted. "Good afternoon, Cougar." She leaned over, kissing the side of my face.

"Your dad was just telling me how he can dance the foxtrot."

"Oh, he was, was he? Well, right now he needs to stay in bed for one more day. After that, the doctor says he can return home. They cast him up pretty good. He won't be able to fly for a while on one leg though." She stole a piece of his scone.

"Amelia, I can fly better using one leg and one arm than most can with two." He winked at me and whispered, "provided Amelia is my right hand."

"I have some news for you, Ted."

"Oh?"

"It seems a benevolent uncle has wished to return your airplane back to its original color. So, when you're ready, just let me know and I will ensure the job is done to your satisfaction—and there will be no cost to you."

"Well, who would do such a thing? Uncle, huh? I don't recall knowing any uncle who would pay for this?" This time it was me winking at Amelia. "You're a good lad, Cougar. I'm glad my daughter selected you to find me. By the way," turning to Amelia, "how did you select him. You said he's from Washington State?"

"He is," she said. "I did my research and found he's the best at asset recovery."

"Asset? Am I the asset or the airplane?"

"Both sir, that's what I specialize in."

"Hmm, well you recovered us both, so I guess it's true." Amelia's eyes softened. Her platinum hair folded evenly around her shoulders on both sides.

"I'm glad I found him, too," she said matter-of-factly. She turned quickly to her dad; the hair slid off her shoulders. "Because I got you back safely."

"Is that the only reason?" Ted asked, shaking his head slowly.

"How is your day going? Did you meet with Daniela yet?"

"Not yet, I plan to see her later today. I met with Detective Dias."

"And?"

"It seems they're all very thankful we helped solve the case."

"What case is that?" Ted asked.

"I'll tell you about it later, Dad," Amelia said.

"Sir," I interjected, "Amelia has shared a little of your story flying F-4 Phantoms during the Vietnam war. She also shared about her grandfather, your dad, Conrad Thomson, and his role flying the hump during WW II in the very C-47 you own. I'd love hearing more about both your careers. I find airplanes and war history very fascinating."

"Be careful what you ask for; I just might bore you someday and do that," he replied. "By the way, Amelia tells me you're not a slouch at the controls either. And something tells me I'm not getting the entire picture of your line of work." Amelia gazed at me, offering up an innocent shoulder gesture.

"Flying back to Texas, we can both share some stories. What time are they letting you out of here tomorrow?"

Amelia grabbed a piece of paper laying on the counter and unfolded it. "Nine in the morning."

"I'll swing back later tonight and see how you guys are doing. Would you like me to bring you anything?"

"No thank you," they responded. I shook Ted's hand, hugged Amelia, and left for Daniela's apartment.

Last Kiss

I slipped the phone in my pocket. "Change of plans," I said to the driver, "Bogota museum, por favor." The driver pulled to a stop in front of the museum. The broad steps held shadows from the roof line creating a jagged diagonal all the way up the stairs.

"Come in," Daniela said softly, waving her arms. She held her finger up, signaling she was almost done with her call. I glanced at the walls of her office, reminiscing the first day we met. Daniela, through this whole ordeal had been nothing short of brave and amazing. I admire people, who when thrown into such circumstances, are able to find an inner strength they didn't know they possessed. I focused on a picture I didn't remember seeing before. Near a bookshelf was a smaller framed picture of what looked like Daniela and her parents in front of this museum, only Daniela was very young.

"I'm done," she said. "Sorry."

"No need to apologize."

"Without a curator, my day has been very busy. I'm getting calls from the director about every hour."

"I can't even imagine." I turned pointing back to the picture next to the bookcase. "Is this you and your parents?"

"It is, I was nine years old in that picture. I loved going to museums. Every birthday, I would beg them to take me. In fact, that picture was taken on my ninth birthday."

"Are your parents still living in Bogota?"

"I kind of figured you'd know all about them."

"I hadn't got that far."

"No, they moved west to Cartago. I'm done here if you're ready to go."

"I am, let's go have a nice dinner. I've been looking forward to it."

"Me, too," she said. The taxi weaved through town to a quiet restaurant located on a slight hill with a view of the city. The night was perfect. The temperature allowed for lighter clothing and the gentle breeze only brought more warmth. The sun lowered, giving a reflective brilliance from the windows and metal structure from the city below.

After being seated, Daniela removed a canary blazer, exposing a delicate white silk camisole. Her golden skin appeared fragile and innocent. A terrifying thought flashed into my head, reminding me of the horrors that could have been, had we not rescued them from the hands of those set on destroying pretty young women. But Daniela and Amelia were safe, and I'm here at this very moment with this very beautiful and elegant woman.

"Your eyes tell me you're somewhere far away."

"I was just thinking how fortunate I am that you're safe and here with me now," I replied.

"I am safe, thanks to you and your team. You no longer need to fret. Let's enjoy our night. A night of freedom."

Daniela nibbled at cheese and fruit. We both shared stories about our past. Several times as we talked and ate, we held each other's hand. I could tell Daniela had something on her mind. Probably the same thing I had on mine, the same thing I had been thinking of the day I started having feelings for her. Finally, I asked, "What's on your mind? Now it's your eyes that are somewhere far off."

She twirled pasta around a fork and skewered a prawn, then set her fork down. "Cougar, what are we? I mean, I care for you very much, and I could see a life with you—a very wonderful life."

My heart pounded. My brain commenced its usual skirmish. "I've been struggling with the same question, Daniela. I care deeply for you too." Daniela's face sat motionless. "There doesn't appear to be a simple answer. Your life is here and mine is in the United States. I don't feel right asking you to give up your life here."

"Cougar, I've been wanting to tell you something. This morning, they offered me the curator position."

"The curator position at the Bogota Museum?"

"Yes."

"Daniela…that is wonderful. Being the curator of Bogota's biggest museum has been your dream ever since you were a little girl. Why didn't you tell me earlier?"

Daniela poked at her prawn. "I knew you would want me to stay and take the job. A part of me does, a big part. I can't even imagine a dream like that coming true, but another part of me wants to see what life would be like with you."

"You have to take it, Daniela. It's you dream."

"What if my dream now is to be with you?"

"I want to be with you, too, but we have to look at this realistically. We haven't known each other that long. What if it doesn't work out?"

"Well now it sounds like you're ready to give up before we've given our relationship a real chance."

"That's not what I'm saying."

"What are you saying?" We both sat in silence, poking at our food.

"I don't want to be the one who stands in the way of your dream. I know you wouldn't ask me to give up my dreams: airplanes, my private practice, and working for the government."

"Of course not."

"And I'm not going to ask you to give up your dream."

"Maybe that's not for you to say. I have more than one dream. I dream of someday having a family and raising children and having a home out in the country."

"And the museum and being a curator? Is that not a big dream, too?" Daniela's eyes reddened. Tears worked their way down to her cheekbones, pooled, and dropped onto the tablecloth.

"I don't want to lose you," she cried. Her body shook. I grabbed her hands.

"You won't. We care very much for each other, that much is obvious, but you need to fulfill your childhood dream. Daniela, whenever you talk about the museum, your eyes sparkle. When you observe children looking at art the way you did when you were young, it lifts your world. You love what you do, and you are very good at it. The world needs you." Daniela dried her eyes and breathed deep. "I travel a lot; you haven't lost me. Now, please, tell me more about the curator offer."

"You promise to keep in touch and visit me when you can?"

"Promise." Daniela spent the next twenty minutes excitedly explaining how the museum director wants her to expand their school curriculum. The Board of Trustees likes what she has set up with the area schools and believes the students and country could benefit from an even more comprehensive and far-reaching program. She talked about Colombia and Bogota, and the more she talked, the more excited she became at the prospect of being the curator in her hometown.

We stood in the lobby of her apartment building. "Do you want to come up to my room?"

"I promised Ted and Amelia I would visit them tonight."

"Okay…please tell Amelia hi."

"I will."

"Thank you again—and not just for dinner."

Before exiting the door, I glanced back. She rushed into my arms. We held each other tight. She smelled of a place I never wanted to leave. Her thin waist melted into mine, her muffled voice pleading with me again, "Promise you'll keep in touch." She leaned back. "Please, Cougar, don't let our relationship die. Even if we are just friends. I want to always know you." I leaned my head down. She wrapped her hands behind my head, pulling it closer, kissing me openly and affectionately.

I felt her tears on my cheek. She parted her lips and focused her eyes, giving one last hug before turning.

I watched her yellow skirt sway back and forth to the elevators. She looked back and waved. The elevator door closed.

It was a few minutes before I walked out of the apartment and onto the sidewalk. I walked a block or two before catching a taxi to the hospital. *Maybe I am married to my career*. The entire cab ride I couldn't stop thinking about Daniela and our last kiss.

Chapter 68

We Came on a Little Strong

Cougar knocked quietly and cracked open Ted's hospital room door. When Amelia saw who it was, she rushed over and hugged him. "I'm glad you're here," she said.

"Where's your dad?" Just then the bathroom door opened, and Ted limped out. "Are you supposed to be on that leg?"

"The way they built this cast it wouldn't break if I skydived with it on, and that's even if my parachute didn't open."

"Dad get back in bed," Amelia responded sternly. Ted limped over to the bed, pulling his gown closed at the rear.

"So, Cougar, Amelia tells me you were on a date?"

"I did not say that!" Amelia quickly replied, glaring at her dad.

"It's okay, in a way, it was. I got to know Daniela while working on the mission I was sent down here for. I'm sure Amelia has shared some of the details I left out yesterday."

"So, are you the 007 type that leads women on?"

"Dad!" Amelia protested.

"It's okay, really. I don't mind answering your father's question." Amelia sat back down, staring up at Cougar. "Ted, I'm trained to recover assets, that's what I do, whether it's for the government or clients of my PI practice. I take my role very seriously, but it's always my second priority. My first is being a Christian, a man of God—"

Ted interrupted. "A Christian secret agent? Is that even possible?"

"I can assure you, it is, although not without seemingly endless challenges." Cougar's shoulders relaxed. "I only share this with you, knowing you have a young daughter, and a beautiful one at that. Bottom line, sir, I don't sleep around. I leave that to the Ian Fleming books. I do my best to treat women with the respect they deserve. I also try to not get emotionally involved with clients, it's just easier that way, although to be honest, this is an area where I currently struggle."

Amelia turned away, remembering the kisses she gave Cougar, then turned back, tilting her head. "What about Daniela? You like her, don't you?" she asked.

"Of course, but the mission is over, and I need to return to the States, and she has a museum to run here in Colombia. Now, are there any more questions I can answer for either of you?" Cougar's cheeks raised in a grin.

"Sorry," Ted replied, "I guess we came on a little strong."

"I'm sorry, too," Amelia said. "I'll be back in a minute. Do you guys want anything from the coffee shop?" They both shook their heads. Amelia walked out of the room.

"Cougar," Ted said in a low voice. "You know my daughter is head over heels for you, right?" Cougar's eyes narrowed. "That's why I was quizzing you. I care deeply for her, and I don't want her to get hurt. She told me about the kind of man you are. I thought she was joking, but I can see she was telling me the truth. You really are that *one in a million* she referred to you as. I want you to know I personally respect that. Not many are so open about their convictions."

"Thank you, Ted; but I may not be as virtuous as your daughter has made me out to be. There's a lot I struggle with, especially when it comes to relationships."

"We all do."

"By the way, are you still cleared to leave tomorrow?"

Amelia reentered the room with a china coffee cup in hand. "I just stopped at the nurse's station and asked if she would send the doctor in to let us know that very answer."

"Why do we need the doctor?" Ted said, "I'm good to go now!" Ted turned to Cougar and asked him more questions about his profession and training. The conversation changed and lingered on World War II airplanes until the doctor stepped into the room.

"How are you feeling, Ted?"

"Been out of bed a couple times, limping on it like you requested."

"And?"

"Seems to be fine."

The doctor flipped a page on a clipboard. "I don't see any reason to keep you here. All your vitals are stable, and your leg is properly set. I will release you tomorrow morning. When you get to Texas, have your doctor's office contact us, and we will send over the information they will need. And Ted, change out the dressings twice a day on your wound, and don't forget to use your crutches; don't be a hero." The doctor smiled at me, then at Amelia. His eyes stayed on her until he was almost out of the room.

"That's great, Dad."

"First thing tomorrow, lets head north," Ted replied.

"I'm good with that," responded Cougar. "I'll get the supplies we need, create the flight plan, and have the plane ready when you guys arrive in the morning."

"Do you want me to help you with the supplies tonight?" asked Amelia.

"I appreciate the offer, Amelia, and would like that, however, I think it's best if you stayed here and you and your dad got some rest. It's going to be a long day tomorrow, and I'm going to need your help in the cockpit. We have some long stretches ahead of us. I'd like to stay within gliding distance of land, so it will take us a little longer. I want to ensure we have a place to set down in case we run into problems."

"Smart," Ted replied. "Don't count me out, Cougar. I can still fly with one leg if you need me too."

"We can certainly use your help, Ted, especially navigating us back to Texas."

"You got it."

"I'll have the plane ready by seven. You guys get there when you can; I'll have breakfast waiting." Cougar shook Ted's hand, hugged Amelia, and left to pick up supplies.

Homeward Bound

At 7:42 a taxi pulled up close to the C-47. Ted was already out of the cab by the time I made it over. "So, they really let you out, huh?" Amelia's perfect teeth sparkled. I reached over with one arm and hugged her. "I'm glad to see you both this morning." I helped Ted to the C-47 Skytrain. His eyes lit up brighter than I had seen them before.

"Sit me up front, close to you two," he demanded.

"Already got your spot ready." I lifted him in and helped him up the sloped floor to a seat just behind the pilot and co-pilot bulkhead. Amelia closed the back door, strapped down a few bags, and then fastened her seatbelt.

"I never thought I'd be flying the C-47 home with my dad onboard. Thank you again, Cougar."

"You're very welcome, Amelia. I'm glad this tragedy has a happy ending."

"We aren't home yet, you two," Ted grumbled cheerfully from the back. "Get this Gooney Bird in the air!"

"That sounds good to me, Ted." Amelia and I went through the pre-flight and engine starting checklist. The two engines coughed, belching black smoke as they came to life, rumbling the big C-47 Skytrain. Fifteen minutes later, the wheels lifted off Colombian soil.

As we climbed, Derby popped into my mind. Having to leave him for so long is never easy; he's the only family I have. So, at the end of every mission, he's the one I think about when coming home.

"Cougar—Cougar?"

"Sorry, Amelia, I…never mind."

"I just wanted to make sure you were okay, you seemed to be drifting off somewhere and so is our heading."

"Just thinking about my dog back home." Amelia laughed a pretty and most petite laugh. Our flight routine settled in. Hour by hour we made our way north. Occasionally we had three-way conversations. Then when Ted slept, Amelia and I talked about airplanes, childhood dreams, and future goals. When Texas came into view, Amelia and Ted were emotional. Ted knelt between the pilot and co-pilot seats with his casted leg straight out behind him, gazing through the windscreen as tears wet his cheeks. Amelia hugged him; it was a very touching moment.

The city was aglow in lights, by the time the C-47 made it to the San Angelo airport. The runway end identifier lights guided us in. I pulled the throttles back; the Skytrain slowed, touching down softly.

Thomson's Air Museum

I woke to the noise of a departing jet. Ted and Amelia offered me one of their spare rooms to sleep in, insisting I stay with them as their special guest. The room, located in a hangar up a staircase and to the right, was just up from their maintenance bay. It was a windowless room. Amelia and Ted's rooms were down the hall.

Rain resonated from a downspout outside. I cleaned up and called Mary, my office assistant, to let her know we arrived safely in Texas. She shared we had a potential new client. We glossed over a few other business details, but nothing in the conversation stood out, needing my immediate attention.

I tapped in Sarah's number to check on Derby. Sarah was her usual joyful self. She held the phone to Derby's ear as I talked to him, telling him I'd be home soon.

Grabbing my bag, I descended the stairs and walked through the empty maintenance building. Next to the door, I found an umbrella sticking out of an old oil can. I grabbed it and ran to the Aero Commander. The clouds were dark, heavy, and low. The door opened to a well-appointed cabin—my cabin. I sat at the back of the airplane, flipped the table up and turned on the electronics. A few minutes went by before Riley answered through the communication system. We exchanged pleasantries before getting to the point of updating him on the final aspects of the Trinity mission, the conversation I had with

Detective Dias, and the flight back to Texas. I gave him the date for my upcoming barbecue. He said he would be there, unless something out of his control came up, and unfortunately, something usually did.

A knock rang on the door of the Aero Commander. I turned and saw a tall man standing outside under an umbrella. I ended the call with Riley, opened the door and stepped out, ducking quickly under the high wing.

"Good morning, Cougar. My name is Jeff Fuller. I'm one of the museum helpers here, Ted asked if I would retrieve you for breakfast."

"Thank you, Jeff, breakfast sounds really good about now."

"Cougar, all of us here owe you an enormous thank you for bringing Ted and Amelia back safely. We are all a little overwhelmed as you can imagine. We spent many weeks believing Ted was dead. We're also very sad about John Burrow, although none of us knew him very well. I think Ted probably feels the worst about his death, he was closest to him, mentoring him like a son."

"Well I appreciate the gratitude, Jeff. I'm sure things will get back to normal before too long." Jeff fixated on my eyes as if they held magic. "What's for breakfast?" I asked, breaking his concentration.

"They're cooking up a feast from what I could see and smell." Rain slid down the luminous yellow umbrella he held in his hand. "This way, please?"

I followed Jeff back into the maintenance hangar, up the staircase, and down a hall into a large open concept loft. A kitchen, dining room, and living area all occupied the space. Ted motioned me over to table.

"How did you sleep, son?" he asked.

"I slept very well, thank you, Ted. How did you sleep?"

"Honestly?" he asked, not expecting an answer, "I didn't sleep all that well. I'm very thankful to be home and in my own bed, and to have my daughter home safe; but I keep thinking about John Burrow's last few moments of life. I have decided to hold a memorial service here for him. I'm also thinking of naming one of our exhibit halls after him."

"I think that's a great idea, Dad." Amelia's long platinum white hair floated over her shoulders as she walked in. She leaned over and kissed her father on his forehead, then shifted over, wearing tight expensive jeans and a pastel green camisole to where I stood. Silver hoop earrings dangled from her earlobes, and a floral scent touched me before she did. "Good morning, Cougar, did you sleep well?" She kissed me on the cheek and gave me a quick hug.

"I did, thank you both for letting me stay here."

"Oh, please, Cougar, you will always be welcome here," Ted remarked.

Amelia grabbed my hand and led me to a chair next to her dad. "It took me forever to curl my hair this morning, but I didn't want to look all frumpy before you left—you might not want to come back."

"You're joking," I replied. "There's a lot here that would draw me back, especially you.

Ted cleared his throat. "I don't mean to interrupt, but how about we say a prayer, then we can eat."

"Sounds good to me, Dad," Amelia replied, still gazing in my direction.

When breakfast was over, Amelia and I walked through the museum together, just talking about planes until she grabbed my hand and swung me around.

"I know we have two different lives," she said, speaking quietly. "And I know you are a secret agent who travels all over the world, and me? Well I'm here, helping my dad share aviation with as many as we can, trying to keep some of it's amazing history alive. Well, what I'm trying to say is that…I really like you. And…and I really don't want you to leave today, but I know you have to. I just—"

"Amelia, we've been through an awful lot together over the last several weeks. You have been amazing, and I have grown very close to you too, closer than I've admitted to myself. I don't want to leave either, but as you know I must. You and your father have an amazing operation here, and you have a gift that you need to share with others. I watched you pilot the C-47, and I can see in your eyes your love of flying. You have a rare and special connection to airplanes. I'm sure your dad taught you a lot, but some of what I saw doesn't come from teaching. It comes from instinct." Amelia stared at a distant airplane.

"Thank you, Cougar. I appreciate your kind words. Words of encouragement that I need, actually. I'm sure once the adrenaline triggered over the last several weeks subsides, I'll be okay. I just don't want to ever forget you."

"Let's not let that happen, and besides, you haven't received my final bill yet, so it's not like we won't be talking." Amelia's face lit up and chuckled.

"Oh…you are correct!"

"Besides, you and your dad are coming to my barbecue, right?"

"Wouldn't miss it."

"Then let's not say goodbye. The aviation community is not that big; we all need to stick together." I reached out and held Amelia's hands. "I especially want to stay close to one very talented pilot; and who knows what the future may hold."

"That sounds like a good way to leave it—for now. When are you leaving?"

I turned toward the window and looked out. "As soon as I prepare my IFR flight plan."

"Can I help?"

"I'd like that very much."

Chapter 71

PI Office, Washington State

Mary's fingers shuffled through folders in the top drawer of a filing cabinet. Cougar stepped out of his office. "Any luck?"

"Not yet, you said his name was Tanner?"

"Tanager!"

Mary turned back to the open drawer. "That's probably why I couldn't find it," she said. "Here it is." She pulled out a sizeable folder and handed it to Cougar. Cougar set it on Mary's desk and flipped through its contents. "What are you looking for?" she asked.

"This." Cougar pulled out a picture. "Remember the case a few years back about a missing Cessna Citation Jet? It was stolen during a business trip to Mexico?"

"I do remember that one. It took a while, but you found the jet and returned it to Dick Tanager's company: The Ascent Corporation." Mary held a puzzled look.

"I didn't catch all the thieves that were involved. There was one guy, a middleman who orchestrated the airplane theft for this band of drug dealers, and I was never able to locate and capture him."

"I'm sorry, Cougar, you're going to need to spell it out for me today, my coffee hasn't kicked in yet." Mary stared closely at the photo as Cougar stepped back into his office, returning seconds later with Amelia Thomson's folder. He pulled out a clipping from a Texas news agency on the tragic death of John Burrow. Mary studied the picture for a second. "That's the same person!"

Cougar sat on Mary's desk and ran his fingers through his short blond hair. "I kept telling myself after seeing his picture in the news that I had seen that face before. Then after seeing the picture of John at Ted and Amelia's place, something clicked. I don't think the theft of Ted Thomson's C-47 was by accident. I think John Burrow positioned himself into Ted Thomson's operation, waiting for the opportune moment, airplane, and customer. When Gustano's request came through, the plan for the C-47 was put in motion, very similar to what happened with the Ascent Corporate Jet."

"Oh my gosh," said Mary, covering her mouth. "What are you going to do?"

"Well, I might have done nothing, except now Ted wants to memorialize this guy. He needs to know the truth. I can't prove for sure that John set him up, but I can share what I know. I need to find out from Ted what influence John had on his decision to fly to Mexico in the C-47. Amelia hired us to finish the job, and we're going to finish it."

"I'll call the museum and get Mr. Thomson on the line."

"Thank you, Mary, I'll be in my office." Mary was put on hold for ten minutes before Ted picked up, then she transferred him back to Cougar.

"Ted, Cougar here."

"Nice to hear your voice so soon. How was your flight back to Seattle?"

"Flying the Commander never tires me. Do you mind if I ask you a couple of questions?"

"Of course not, what's this all about?"

"Your original flight to Mexico for cancer treatment."

"Oh?" responded Ted.

"How did the decision to be treated in Mexico and fly your C-47 all come about? I hope you don't think I'm being too personal. I'll share more with you in a minute on why I'm asking."

"Not at all, I'm happy to share with you, Cougar. Amelia and I were looking up alternative methods for fighting cancer. One afternoon while Amelia and I were sitting together in front of her computer, John walked in and saw us looking up cancer treatment centers. John had been working for us a few months by then and I had gotten to know him pretty well. He kind of looked up to me as a mentor.

"Anyway, evidently John had a relative who had cancer and was treated at the same place we flew in to. It was John's suggestion that I go there. His suggestion may have saved my life."

"Why fly the C-47 there? You have faster, more efficient airplanes."

"Well, that was part my idea and part John's. Amelia knew I wanted to commemorate her grandfather, my father, Conrad Thomson, and those men who flew the hump during the second world war. I had just finished the C-47 restoration and I was concerned, because of my cancer, that if I didn't make that commemorative flight soon, I may not be able to. John suggested we fly the C-47 to Mexico and kill two birds with one stone. He eagerly and quite frankly downright begged me to let him be my co-pilot on the flight. I was okay with that even though Amelia wanted to go. I thought it would be better if she stayed and ran the museum while I was gone. So, that's more or less how it all took place, does that help?"

"Unfortunately, it does. I need to share some information with you." Cougar shared the facts he had on John Burrow with Ted, including his real name and past record of equipping men like Gustano with tools to execute their illegal activities.

"I'm not sure I understand," said Ted. "If John was working for them, why would they kill him, or Terry, or whatever his real name was?"

"Middlemen like Terry often think they're invincible or irreplaceable. Gustano wasn't the type to leave loose ends. When you work with criminals long enough, sooner or later you work with the wrong one."

The phone was silent on Ted's end. Puzzle pieces quickly connected. Coincidences were no longer chance happenings but revealed themselves to be well calculated plans. Ted's stomach churned.

Ted spoke up. "Let me be the one to share this with Amelia, please."

"You got it, Ted. Sorry to drop this on you, but I felt you needed to know."

"I appreciate the information, Cougar, I really do." Rustling noises were heard through Cougar's earpiece. "Amelia really did hire the best. We owe you our lives."

"Your presence at my barbecue will be payment enough—on top of my fees for finding you, of course."

"Of course," Ted replied. They both laughed. "Money well spent."

The Barbecue

Derby stretched himself in the tall grass, gazing at the action through his contented brown eyes. Riley phoned yesterday, explaining why he had to cancel at the last minute. In all the years I've known Riley and invited him to my annual barbecue, he has only made it twice.

Derby lifted his head, making eye contact with me. I smiled at him. He laid his head back down. My best friend Jack and his new wife Rebecca were playing lawn darts, an old relic of a game. "Jack," I called. "The grass is that way." Jack sent a dart into the herb garden. Mary sat next to Kathy and her husband on one side of the patio table with Ted, Gerry, and his wife sitting across from them, all playing a board game.

I opened the grill lid; alder-infused smoke rolled out. The salmon edges were pink and sizzling. I squirted lemon across the top and added more dill. Amelia waved to me as she stood up after picking up her horseshoe. Jack walked up to me. "You know, Cougar, it's okay to love again. Not everyone you love dies. I know losing your parents and then losing Kela still have you messed up, but what's the alternative? Living alone with your dog? Don't get me wrong, Derby is wonderful, but Cougar, it's time for you to move on with your life. Look at me, I'm happy now."

"Thank you, Jack. I appreciate that, I really do." He patted me on the back and went back to his game. Frank, Sarah's husband, danced in a circle with his arms stretched out after beating both Sarah and Amelia in a game. "Cougar, please? I need you on my team," begged Amelia.

I turned the grill down and walked over to her. Her hair glistened bright in the afternoon sun. A simple turquoise blouse complimented her white shorts and disciplined body. Our gaze froze until Sarah tapped me on the shoulder.

"Um, Cougar, are you ready to play?"

"Ready to get beat is more like it!" Frank shouted. It was good to see Frank so lively.

Amelia grabbed my hand. "Our team is going to win," she said, squeezing my hand tightly. Her floral perfume mixed with the fragrant alder from the barbecue.

"We do make a great team, don't we?" I responded.

"Yes, we certainly do," she said. "I'll admit, I do love having you all to myself, but I have to say, it sure would've been nice if Daniela could have made it."

"I agree. It sounds like she's very busy in her new role—and very happy. Besides, that's a long way to travel for a barbecue, even if it is the best barbecue this side of the Rockies."

"Really?" Amelia asked, lightheartedly. "Isn't that a bit of an exaggeration? Remember, I'm a Texas girl."

"Okay then, best barbecue—"

"Honestly, I can't wait to try it," she said.

Sarah cleared her throat. "Okay, your turn, Cougar," Jack hollered, losing another game to his wife. Mary brought us over a pitcher of lemonade and refilled our cups.

Sarah asked, "Mary, is there still a bottle of white wine in the cooler?"

"I'm not sure, I'll go check."

"No, let me," Sarah replied. "I think these two might want to play by themselves anyway." Sarah shot me a wink. "Frank, let's give lawn darts a try."

"Careful," I said, "You'll need to sign a waiver if you want to play with those."

Jack yelled, "I am giving instruction in two minutes."

Rebecca, his wife added, "On what not to do."

When the steaks, prawns, and salmon were finished, we sat and blessed the food. I thanked God for amazing friends, good food, good health, and good times. After the prayer, Ted raised his glass.

"I want to thank all of you who had a part in helping me and my daughter. You are all heaven sent. I couldn't ask for better friends." Ted's eyes watered. "Here's to all of you."

"Here-here!" Glasses clanged. I slipped my arm around Amelia. She turned to me, clutching my hand and holding it close. Jack beamed approvingly at me and nodded.

The End

Shane K Twede is an author, commercially licensed pilot, and life coach. The creator of the Trinity Operations Novels and the popular children's book series The Adventures of Derby and Charlie, Shane has a love of storytelling for all ages. He was born in the State of Washington and has spent much of his life working in the business world, from simple start-ups to Fortune 500 companies. Shane is a pilot and aviation enthusiast, and when not writing he can be found active in aviation, health and fitness, and life coaching. For more information visit: https://shanektwede.com/